Reunion of the Heart

Anthology Collection

DeLora Conley-Walls

THREE SKILLET

REUNION OF THE HEART, Conley-Walls, DeLora

First Edition

The Reunion Series, Book 4
The Anthology Collection

 THREE SKILLET

www.ThreeSkilletPublishing.com

Cover by Farley L Dunn

ISBN: 978-1-943189-70-0

This Anthology Collection
contains the three complete Reunion novels,
including:

Trusting Heart Reunion

Timeless Heart Reunion

True Heart Reunion

Trusting Heart Reunion

— 1 —

"JANE WAGGONER, you're a silly old fool."

Jane, nearing sixty, although she looked a decade younger, peered in the mirror, running her fingers through her hair. Still beautiful, with softly retouched tresses and only the barest of crowfeet, she'd kept a trim figure with a regular workout.

Her makeup was the problem.

Her hair had fought her at every turn of the brush, but she'd finally beaten it. Her mascara? Dried out. That was the first tube. The second? Blue instead of black. Then, thank the stars, at the very back, hiding from her, she found the third, black, like she needed.

Her bloodshot eyes? Don't even go there. Her eye drops had barely made any difference.

"Sheesh!" She grabbed her keys and her red clutch and yanked the door open. She'd never make her lunch date now. At least it was only Peggy Lynn Johnson.

She hit the remote to unlock the car door, only to fumble her keys to the ground. She was tired, too tired. That same nightmare. Bill, his accident.

All he'd done was head out for the weekly paper. She'd continued dinner preparations, totally unaware he was dying a block away. Even the sirens hadn't triggered any real alarm.

How would she ever pick up those thirty-three shattered years?

"Well, girl, you can at least pick up these keys," she muttered, leaning down to snatch them with her carefully manicured fingers. If she hadn't figured this out in three years, she guessed she never would. It'd take a miracle from the past to make a difference now, or maybe God's finger on the clock of life, moving the hands back for about thirty-six months.

Yeah, that would do it. Thirty-six months, and she'd talk Bill out of going after that paper.

Jane climbed into her car and sighed, her finger resting on the start button, not yet willing to push it. The truth swept over her with a rush of clarity. It wouldn't have mattered. Talking Bill out of going out that morning wouldn't have made a difference. The heart attack would have happened at home or in the car.

She whispered her pain into the silence, "God, don't you care?"

She glanced up at the sky overhead, the endless blue laced with cotton candy clouds. It was beautiful. Despite her gritty eyes and troublesome mascara, there were good things about her life. The blue sky overhead, a good car to drive, and Peggy.

What would she have done without Peggy?

She pushed the button, smiling at the soft rumble of the engine as it came to life, then the small clicks and purrs as the car worked through its startup diagnostics. This was Bill's last gift to her. He laughed when she said she wanted candy apple red, telling her it was the color of a ridiculous female. She explained to him it was the color of love.

It was six months after he died that she placed her order. She had the dealer wrap it in a giant white bow in the center of the lot. It was his last gift, and he didn't even know.

"Thank you, Bill." She backed out of the drive and turned toward the Community Center. She would enjoy this day. She would be pleasant, even charming, and Peggy would know that she was over Bill's death, ready to move on with the rest of her life. She would. She would.

She didn't even have to wipe tears away on the way to the Community Center. It was three days since she'd last cried. That was an improvement.

Maybe, just maybe she was putting Bill's death behind her.

JANE TAPPED THE WHEEL, debating on whether to leave the car running or kill the engine. She could afford the gas, but Peggy was normally as punctual as a pincushion, and Jane was hungry.

"Your car may be in the shop, Peggy Lynn," she growled, "and I don't mind picking you up, but you do own a cell phone. It wouldn't hurt you to text me, so I know what's going on."

She opened the door as she jabbed the ignition button—harder than she should—to stop the engine. The words of her favorite song died away, but Jane murmured the lyrics in her own variation. "Stop in the name of love, don't you know I'm waiting on you." Then she punched the words, "Peggy Lynn!"

She laughed at how clever she sounded, and she closed the door and pushed the button to lock the car. She looked around before moving toward the building. The Center was pretty. Even with all her moping that morning, she had to admit that. Flowerbeds lined the walks, and the giant oaks created ever-changing patterns of dappled light. Well, it ought to look pretty, she decided. That's why she paid such high taxes on her house, so the city can afford the water bill when the sprinklers turned on.

She took a deep breath and decided it would be cooler

under the shade, not standing in the lot in full sun.

No more had she made it to the front of the car when she saw her friend coming out of the door, trailing a small group of her adult students. It was a pottery class, continuing education, definitely not for college age kids. It was mostly seniors that attended, that and the occasional young mother who needed a break from the joys of motherhood. Jane raised her hand to wave only to see her friend in a deep discussion with one of her students. She let her hand drop to shade her eyes before turning to the car. That was when she heard Peggy call to her.

"Jane, can you believe it, after all this time?" The words quivered with excitement.

"Believe what?" She turned, putting a smile on her face.

"Who would have ever thought he would have turned up here?"

"Who—" Jane started, but a very familiar voice interrupted her question.

"Me. They say a bad penny always turns up now and again. Well, here I am."

The interruption was laced with amusement, but it was the voice, deep and penetrating, that stopped Jane cold. She felt the temperature had jumped ten degrees, and she knew it had nothing to do with standing in the sun. That voice was a tidal wave from the past, an avalanche of explosive memories, and a dark tide threatening to overwhelm her.

The man at Peggy's side was as tall as she remembered, but his hair was now woven with silver. Those eyes, though. There was no mistaking those caramel eyes. Still, the voice had been enough. Even in the darkest night, over the most distant connection, she would know that voice. It belonged to the only man she had ever loved. Yet, it couldn't be him.

Her heart told her differently, though. It beat faster, just like all those years ago, threatening her with discovery, telling the world around her that Bill hadn't been the only man in her life. There had been someone else, and if she'd had the chance, if things had played out differently, then she and Bill might never have been . . .

She caught herself. No longer. At one time he was the only man she'd ever loved. Then, Bill had filled the void left by Tarzan, and her life had eventually come back together. Slowly, but eventually.

What was he doing here?

TARZAN, KNOWN WITHIN his family circles as Tres Juan, was actually Juan Cordello Rivera III. Growing up, all his friends had been mesmerized by Saturday afternoon television. Their favorite show had been Tarzan. Say Tres Juan quickly, and the outcome was inevitable. Tres Juan became Tarzan, and, naturally, being Jane, she was paired with him. Tarzan and Jane, the lords of the jungle.

At first it had put her off, but Cord, as he liked to be called, was very TDH. That was Tall, Dark, and Handsome. Half Hispanic and half Irish, he was dark-haired with lightly bronzed skin, and every teenage girl swooned when he walked by. Eventually, Jane had caught the bug, and they became a couple.

Now, after nearly four decades, they were back together once again.

"JANE, ARE YOU AWAKE?" Peggy had made it to the car by then, and she reached and rapped Jane on the forehead with her knuckles.

"Jane?" This time it was Cord who quizzed her, in that resonant voice, rattling Jane's bones . . . and her heart and lungs and kidneys, too, she supposed. She pulled herself together.

"I'm sorry, Peggy. Of course, I recognize him." She held her hand out. "Welcome, Cord Rivera." She heard her voice. Her words were little more than terse, and she refused to look him in the eyes. Why, oh, why was Cord here now?

"Don't you mean Tarzan?" Peggy laughed, her hair bouncing around her face.

Jane was furious. She wanted to grab Peggy's mahogany mane and yank those curls to get her attention. Cord was the last man her friend should be flirting with after how he'd treated Jane all those years ago.

"Don't be a flirt," Jane hissed, batting at Peggy's arm. "I do *not* want to be around this man." Her words went unheard, as Peggy laughed again, her chortling covering her friend's hissed command.

"Nice to see you, too, Jane." Cord gave her a slow and easy smile.

Good Lord, I hope he didn't hear that. Jane shuddered at the idea of having Cord around again, but she didn't feel the compulsion to be rude, either. Not with her heart going ninety miles an hour just at the sound of his voice. Good heavens! How could she be attracted to a man she hated so much?

It was only then that he took her hand. She'd forgotten she'd offered it. Forty years since they'd last touched, skin to skin, and the electric shock jolted her as hard now as it had then. She was certain he could see the fire she felt in her face. This was Texas, and spring in Texas could be very warm, but it was outright hot. And it wasn't the weather, she was sure.

Well, she wasn't going to let him win at this game. He had abandoned her, not the other way around. It wasn't her fault the world had fallen apart all those years ago, and besides, this was her town. Not his. His family were the rich ones all those years ago, and hers had barely grubbed by, but no longer. She and Bill had done well. They were respected in the community. She could beat Cord at his own game.

"It's good to see you, too, Cord Rivera." Jane gave him her brightest smile. She wouldn't let him see her emotions. They would remain masked. Too many years and memories had gone by to let a meeting like this reveal any-thing. "Good-bye, Cord Rivera. I expect you have things to do, and maybe we'll meet up again. However, Peggy and I have plans, and we have to run."

She shook her hand free, only then realizing she was shaking inside. She turned without looking him in the face and made it to the car in record time.

"Oh, look at you!" Peggy dropped into the car and put her hand on Jane's arm. "I think I saw sparks of romance out there."

"You did not." Jane barked the words, and she hit the start button and flipped the temperature to its lowest set-ting, closing her eyes as the fan came on high. "Don't even suggest that, Peggy Lynn."

"I invited Tarzan to lunch. Oh, *Cord*, I forgot. I invited *Cord* to lunch."

Jane looked to see a grin on her face. "Sure, said the Wicked Witch of the West." She pulled the lever into re-verse, only to see a black Escalade in her rear-view cam-era. "We're blocked in. Just hang on."

"Jane."

She looked to see Cord standing beside her car. With a groan, she toggled the switch and let the window slide into the door. "Yes?"

"If you ladies don't mind, I'll chauffer you in my ve-hicle. I'm not sure where we're going."

"Do something, Peggy," Jane hissed, glaring at her friend.

"Sure!" Peggy leaned over the console and waved. "Isn't that so sweet of him, Jane? This will be the best lunch, ever."

Jane hit the switch and let the window close off her tormentor. Then she decided she'd just trapped herself with another one. Cord? Peggy? She guessed it didn't mat-ter much any longer. The day was beyond redemption, so she might as well make the best of it.

"Okay, evil woman. You get your way. We'll have

lunch with that man, but there'll be paybacks later. You can count on it." She reached for the door handle and flipped the lever.

Before she could push the door open, Peggy grabbed her arm and quipped, "Sure. Paybacks. Anytime." Then she pushed the button on the dash and opened her own door. She grinned. "Just don't forget the keys, honey."

And she was gone.

BY THE TIME JANE reached Cord's truck, Peggy had already claimed shotgun, leaving Jane to climb in on the driver's side, taking a seat next to him.

"Thanks again, Peggy Lynn," she fired off as she pushed up the armrest to make room. She brushed her friend's offer of gum away, only to feel Cord leaning over her. Frowning, she already had a sharp retort ready when she saw the seatbelt in his hand.

"Just to be safe. Right, ladies?" He leaned into her as he snapped the latch.

"Hey, thanks for the reminder." Peggy held hers out, unlatched, and began searching for the connecting end. "Safe is as safe does!" She was smiling like the Cheshire cat, as if she'd planned it all.

Jane knew better. She was never safe around Cord Rivera. Not forty years ago, not now, and not in a hundred years. And especially not in this truck with his leg pressed against hers and nowhere else to go.

Oh, she hated this.

"Where to?" Cord's rich, honey voice broke the silence.

"How about Grubstake Barbeque?" Peggy was *so* cheerful and buoyant. "It's out off the highway."

"Sure. I know that place. The one that was under construction two years ago, right? I saw it yesterday coming in."

And you don't know where we're going? I bet. Jane fumed. Yet, she had to admit one thing. Cord was at least being sociable. He'd always been the strong, silent type. Incommunicado, her father had once suggested. Cord had told her that he had trouble sharing his feelings. She wondered what made her think of that. What would he say if he decided to actually talk to her? I screwed up? I abandoned you? I left you in the lurch, and I'm a dog for doing it?

Well, at least I can make you wish you'd treated me better, Cord Rivera. Look at my hair. It's as thick and beautiful as it was in high school. Even if it needed a little color every month to stay that way, something she rarely admitted even to herself. And her dress, fitted, deep lapis cotton. Peggy had adored it at the shop, telling her it matched her vivid sapphire eyes. She was glad she'd dressed up a bit more than she usually did for a lunch date. She hadn't let herself go, and this man would see what he'd missed all these years.

Let him suffer.

Suffer? She was the one suffering, sitting next to him. She felt herself grow hot again. Five weeks after graduation, and he had dumped her, just disappearing. Then he'd married someone else only weeks later. How could he have done that to her? It was a betrayal that could never be forgiven.

That's why she'd stayed away from this town so long. Cord Rivera and his betrayal had hurt too much anytime she returned to see her parents. She'd only given in when Bill retired. Her parents were gone by then, and the oil had come in on the family farm. Then there was Peggy, her dear friend Peggy, Wicked Witch of the West.

And now here she was sitting next to Cord.

Time will not heal this wound, Cord Rivera. I know what you're up to, and you, too, Peggy Lynn. Tarzan and Jane are long gone, and I'm not climbing that tree again. You can count on it!

Out of the corner of her eye, she could just see Cord's face. He had a grin on his lips, and that made her fume even more.

I hate you, Cord Rivera. I hate you, I hate you, I hate you.

Her heart told the story differently, as did her leg pressed against his. And she couldn't even reach to wipe the impending tears away, because then he would know. He mustn't know what he was doing to her.

He must never, never know.

— 2 —

CORD TOOK IN THE broad expanses of the nearly new restaurant. The paint still smelled new. The dining area was surrounded with green-tinted glass, and just at the edge of his hearing, the clatter of glass dinnerware sparkled in the background.

The aroma of barbeque was like a velvet glove, drawing him in.

Even so, he could barely focus on the restaurant, the views from its windows, or the tantalizing odor of slow-stewed, spicy meat. It was Jane that had him preoccupied, well, perhaps not *Jane*, but what he needed to say to Jane, and that meant Jane was the center of his preoccupation.

Time. It was said that it healed all wounds. Not his wounds. Not the scars that crisscrossed his heart, leaving him sweating in bed at night, wishing he could go back forty years and rewrite what could never be rewritten.

He had seen Jane's eyes, the way she refused to look at him. Her words, spoken to Peggy, hadn't been so muted that he couldn't hear every cruel word. Even after all these years, he felt the shame of what had happened brush his ears with fire.

He had taken the only alternative open to him, and it hadn't been Jane.

Dear God, that week had ripped his heart from him. He would have cast his family aside, thrown his own reputation to the winds, just to have Jane at his side for the rest of his life.

However, it was Jane's reputation, too. Him? He'd take the heartache just to be near her. For Jane? For Jane, he'd give up anything, even his happiness.

That was exactly what he'd done: broken up with her, disappeared, and married a woman he hadn't loved.

All for Jane.

Now was his chance to undo all that, and Jane didn't want him here.

"Cord?" It was Peggy. "Everything okay?" She placed her hand on his arm.

"You know me." He laughed. "I'm always okay. Why do you ask? Oh, and I see the greeter is on his way. Are you ready to be seated? Jane?"

"No, you don't." Peggy pushed Jane the way of the greeter. "You go on, honey. Tarzan and I will be right there."

"Peg—" Jane began.

"No questions, sweetie. I said we'll be right there." She pushed on Jane's shoulder with a light laugh. "Go, now. Don't keep the nice boy waiting."

"Said the Wicked Witch." Jane's eyes flashed, but she turned and walked away, her hips swaying in an in-your-face manner.

"Whew, but she's a bobcat, just like always." Cord chuckled, but he felt it fade away. "She's not happy to see me. Are you sure I should have come?"

"Now, Cord Rivera, since when do you let others' opinions of you dictate what you do? You tell me that, 'cause I've never heard of such a thing. You're going in there and have lunch with that woman, because you two need each other. You waffle now, and I'll pinch your ears so hard you'll beg for mercy." Her face told the truth of what she said with narrowed eyes and a tight mouth. "I'm not funning about this, either."

"Funning?" He could finally grin, and it was real.

"Oh, you!" She slapped him on the shoulder. "Git, you hound dog!" She pointed the way Jane and the greeter had gone.

"Okay, trail boss. Your arm, though. I need fortification." He held his out, waiting until she slipped hers inside before moving forward.

"So, what will Jane think?"

"About what?"

"You and me as a couple."

Cord laughed out loud. "She'll ring the wedding bells, glad to get rid of me for good."

"No, not Jane. We need Tarzan and Jane back together again, just like old times."

"Are you blind, woman?"

"Blind? I see what I see, Cord, and I see you two back together."

"And I see a woman who couldn't bear to look at me. That's what a seeing person sees."

"Well, it's just lunch, and we can do this, can't we? Just talk to her. She needs to know where you've been all these years. You can do it." She patted his arm, before releasing him to walk at her side.

"So, there's the happy couple!" Jane was in a booth, and she patted the seat next to her. "Peggy, I saved you a seat, unless you want to sit next to your boyfriend." She didn't sound nice at all.

"Hm." Peggy paused with her hand on her chin, as if in doubt about whether to take up Jane's offer. "I don't think so, Jane. Those long legs of Cord's, he really needs the side with the most room, and that's next to you. So sorry." With a grin, she plopped in the seat across from Jane, sliding over, and placing her black shoulder strap bag so that the rest of the seat was taken.

"So, I'm—" Cord stood at the end, letting his voice drop off. His gut was sour. Age was what he blamed it on, not taking his acid reducer that morning, and he pushed aside his disappointment that Jane was so antagonistic. This was to have been a reunion, not an emotional wrestling match.

"There." Peggy pointed without hesitation. "Jane saved that spot for you."

"Well, you're here, just like Peggy wanted." Jane glared at her before turning to Cord. "So, if we must visit, you might as well tell me what's been going on for *forty* years. Wouldn't that be nice, Peggy, to know what's kept Cord Rivera away for *forty* years? Make it good, Cord, because I'm all ears."

"Hum-ho, you're as feisty as ever, I see. And good morning to you, too, Jane." He chuckled, willing himself to get over his trepidations. For forty years he'd wanted to sit next to this woman, to have the chance to talk to her again. Well, it was here, and it wasn't coming back to him if he didn't jump on the bronc and ride it till the bell. "Well, I got married—"

"He got married! How about that, Peggy? Cord Rivera got married during his forty-year hiatus. What do you think of that?" Jane pressed her mouth tight, her irritation flashing from her eyes. "Was that it? Forty years and only a marriage to show for it? I thought you'd do something with your life. Marriage! Pshaw! That's nothing. I've even done that."

"Jane, honey." Peggy grabbed her hand. It had been waving in the air, and she pulled it down to the tabletop. "Where are your Sunday manners? Let him say just two words. After all, I'm here, too, and he was my friend in high school, also. I wasn't exactly Cheetah. Well, maybe I was." She grinned. "But I was his friend, too. Now be quiet and listen."

"You're right. I'll try." Jane reached to wipe under one

eye. "That was very rude of me. I apologize. I thought I had all this behind me."

It was their waiter that saved the moment. Before Jane could say anything more, he stepped up and passed out menus, one to Peggy and two to Cord. "Good morning. My name is Holden, and I'll be taking your order, today. Would you like to choose from our new weekday brunch menu? It's been such a success on the weekends, we're offering it daily."

"Brunch? Absolutely." Peggy rubbed her hands together in anticipation.

"The brunch menu is on the back. Coffee for everyone?"

"For everyone." Jane's voice still had an edge, and Peggy frowned at her.

"Decaf for me," Cord murmured, fighting a smile.

"Decaf, sir?"

"Yes. With milk." He'd always consumed it black in high school, but times had changed.

"Mine, too!" Peggy closed her menu. "Jane wants hers black, like her mood. Waffles, anyone?"

"Let me give you a bit. I'll get your coffee while you decide." Holden smiled and made as if to walk away. "Five minutes?"

"Not necessary. We're ready," Cord announced. "I'll have the brisket, and wings and waffles for everyone. Mine with blueberries, the sweet lady at my side wants bananas on hers, and you, Peggy, strawberries, still?"

"Strawberries? Absolutely!"

"Anything else?"

"Extra sugar. We need to sweeten someone up." That was Peggy, and she nodded knowingly toward Jane.

"No sugar. Just the coffee, barbeque, and waffles." Cord glanced at Jane. Fire and ice, just like always. Well, she had been more fire at the end, and he couldn't believe he'd lived without her for four decades. Now, here she was again, just like all those years ago, if only he could fix things.

"So, your family. Tell me everything. I have to know." Peggy had her elbows on the table, staring at Cord, as if mesmerized by his sudden waltz back onto the local scene. She winked. "Speak up, Tarzan."

"Drop the Tarzan, Peggy. Please."

"But why? That's who you are. To the two of us, anyway. Right, friend Jane? Me Cheetah, you Jane, and you Tarzan. Now, swing for us, Tarzan. Tell all." Her eyes twinkled.

"I married, like I said." At Jane's narrowed eyes, he held up a hand for her to be patient. "But I'm not married now."

"You dumped her, too?" Jane's comment was muttered, but it was very clear.

"No, not dumped, Jane. I'm a widower."

"Oh, Cord, you poor thing. How sad. Jane knows just how you feel, don't you, Jane. Jane's husband died, and she's been so down, *for three years*. Haven't you, Jane?"

"You can shut up, now, Peggy."

Cord was beginning to be amused. He laughed. "Let me handle this, Peg, please."

"Peg?" Jane spit the question.

"She's my friend, too, if you remember. You weren't the only friend I had in high school."

"Obviously. After all, you did get married. Go on."

"Coffee's here! Everyone smile!" Peggy moved the placards on the table aside to make room.

"Here you go. Black, decaf with milk, and decaf with milk. I'll have your barbeque and waffles out in a jiffy."

"You're so sweet, Holden. Don't forget the sugar. Despite what my friend here says, we do need it. Don't we, Jane, sweetheart? Oh, did I say sweetheart? Holden, did you know these two were sweethearts forty years ago? High school sweethearts. Think of that. How old are you, dear?"

"Seventeen, ma'am."

"Oh, that's so sweet! Do you have a squeeze, Holden?"

"A squeeze, ma'am?"

"A girlfriend," Cord growled, glaring at Peggy.

The boy beamed. "Sure. Autumn Dumas. She's on the track team."

"Well, don't ever dump her, Holden. That just causes hot water for everyone." Peggy nodded sagely.

"No, ma'am, I won't. Oh, your food's here. Let me get you set up."

Once he was gone, Peggy laughed. "I like that boy. He reminds me of you back in the day, Cord. Polite, mannered, and one to stick by his girl. Now for the rest of the story. I'm all ears."

And all mouth, Cord thought, but he let that go. At least he could keep his mouth stuffed with food for a bit. He needed a break. The barbeque and waffles had arrived just in time.

"ONE DAUGHTER." CORD pushed his empty plate away. "Veronica. She's married, in Lubbock, with two children. Closer would be nice, but what can I do? They had to go where the jobs were, and they weren't here."

"One daughter. You sure about that?"

Jane had spoken into her cup of coffee, and Cord looked at her, with one eyebrow raised. He chuckled and let it go as nothing more than Jane's irritation with him, questioning everything he said.

"She and Don met at Tech, married the year after graduate school."

"Your wife, though. What happened with her?" Peggy reached her hand to his, although she didn't quite touch him.

"Shelly? Cancer."

"Oh! Breast?"

"Lung. Cigarettes. She couldn't let them go, even at the end. But that was five years ago."

"You haven't been around here, though." Jane plunged in with her comment, her voice surprisingly civil. "Bill and I, that's my husband, moved back five years ago, and I haven't seen you around."

"We were in Sweetwater for twenty-five years. We were on the ranch helping Mom and Dad, but after they were gone, the place held too many memories." *Me. You. Why I left. Driving by your parent's place, knowing I'd never see you again.* He left those unsaid, though. That was old water, tossed out long ago.

"So, Sweetwater." Jane looked as if she was interested. She smiled. "Just for interest's sake, you understand. I've been to Sweetwater a few times with my church group, and I had no idea you lived there."

"Well, I don't anymore. Sold the place about six months ago. Now I'm back at the ranch. Still working for Pipeline Fitters, Inc, just like in the old days. Some things never change."

"You never sold the ranch? Good for you." Jane sounded almost enthusiastic. "My family never did, either."

"You next, Jane." Peggy reached across the table and pushed on her friend's arm. "Cord's bled his past. Now's your turn."

"Now, I never said—"

"Please, Jane Lane. Forty years I don't see you, and I deserve just the bare bones."

"Forty years in the next town."

"Not anymore. Just talk to me. Please?"

"I liked you in high school, Cord Rivera. I really did. But this isn't high school, anymore. Forty years under any bridge changes people. I'm not the silly girl I used to be. I'm not naïve any longer. Don't you think I am."

"Please?" *For me? For old times' sake?* If he could only break the ice just for this one meal, then he would at least have something to take with him, a memory he could cherish, one that would hopefully replace the hurt he'd heard in her voice all those years ago. What a fool he'd been to not even go to see her. Who breaks up with the best girl in the world over the phone? Only a stupid, idiotic fool!

"Oh, sheesh!" Jane made a sour face, then let it smooth. "Sure. Masters in interior design at UNT. Bill, my husband, was an industrial engineer. One stepson, Billy, still married, and two grandchildren. They lived in Plano until Bill died. Now they've moved closer. Ages? I haven't kept track, but all teens, and you know teens. Enough?"

"That's so dry, I could mop the floor with it. You can do better, Jane." Peggy winked. "Did you notice he called you Lane?" She snickered.

"Yes, I noticed," Jane retorted, "and he's heard enough."

"No, I haven't. Billy, what does he do for a living?" Just the sound of Jane's voice was enough for the moment. Anything to keep her talking.

"If I must. Architect. I bet you want to know where Bill and I lived before moving back to the ranch."

"Oh? You were somewhere else?" *I kept away for no reason. How sad.*

"Garland. That's Dallas, if you haven't heard of it."

"I know Garland." He looked away and smiled.

"Everyone's heard of Garland. Be real, Jane. Cord's not stupid."

I was forty years ago, he thought. Anyone would be stupid to let Jane Lane get away for forty years.

"Remember all those parties at the ranch? Three hundred years in one family, and the best ones were when you were there."

Jane laughed, her expression nicer, almost pleasant. "Sunday lunches. Your family really seemed to like me. They invited me every week."

"They did like you. Very much."

"Just not you, not at the end?"

"Ouch. I deserve that, I guess."

"Enough of that. How long are you staying, Cord?" Peggy's voice was bright and engaging.

"It all depends."

"On all your new oil wells?"

"Oil wells?" Jane looked hard at him. "Since when are you drilling oil wells on your land?"

"Well, I couldn't let your family take all the black gold."

"We needed the money, Cord. Your family has cash to spare. You'll destroy the ranch."

Was there concern there? Her tone gave him hope. However, before he could engage her on the topic, they were interrupted by a familiar voice.

"Well, hello, Peggy and Jane. How's lunch?"

Jane nodded and smiled.

Peggy answered, "We're fine, Calvin. And do you remember Tar . . . I mean, Cord Rivera?"

Calvin Harris smiled and extended his hand. "Why, of course, I do. I see your name on paperwork at the bank all the time, and I've even faxed a few documents to you lately. I was beginning to wonder if I'd ever get reacquainted with you. I'm glad you finally decided to do some business in person. As your banker, I'm happy to assist you on any transactions that need to be made. We like keeping everything local and family oriented at the bank here. The Rivera name is a highly respected one. We've always appreciated your family's business."

Cord stumbled to his feet, annoyed at the interruption. This was to have been all about reconnecting with Jane. However, he smiled as he shook Calvin's hand and said, "That's what I'm here to do all right, take care of business in person."

His eyes were on Jane, though. She was the business he hoped to take care of in person. She might think everything between them ended forty years ago, but he hoped not. If only she would reopen negotiations, they might be able to do business once again.

She had at least broken down and spoken to him. That was progress, of a sort. And for that, he let himself hope.

— 3 —

AT LEAST LUNCH was over, but Jane wasn't amused. She was back in the center of the truck, and Cord wasn't keeping his distance.

Peggy seemed oblivious.

"So, you'll be at the Round 'Em Up Inn, I guess." She had her monstrous black purse in her lap, and she smiled. "Round 'em up, cowboys! Yee-haw!" She giggled.

Jane ignored her. However, as much as she tried to put space between them, Cord took it up with those long legs of his. And Peggy! Did she really need half the seat? Good heavens!

It was Cord's mellow, throaty rumble that got her attention.

"Is there another hotel?" He laughed, as he pulled up to the Center, parking next to Jane's red Lexus.

"If you get bored, give me a call. Jane might be conveniently too busy—" Peggy jabbed Jane in the ribs with her elbow "—but I have lots of time on my hands. I'd love to go out to dinner with a tall, dark, and handsome man." She giggled again, ribbing Jane once more. "Did you hear that, Jane? TDH, just like you like 'em."

"Yes, Cord. Peggy's divorced, now. She has plenty of time to go out with you, unlike me, who still holds down a job." Jane could hear her bitterness in her words, and she tried to contain it, but it was useless sitting next to this man. He did a number on her, and she hated that she let him. She took it out on Peggy. "She doesn't have to worry about her kids bothering you. They live in Colorado and North Carolina. I don't think they could get any farther away, could they, *Peg*?" She never called her Peg, but she couldn't resist.

"And I love it that way. It makes it so much more exciting when they come to visit, because they miss me so much. And," she reached across Jane and put her hand on Cord's arm, "they can't just drop off the grandkids like Jane's stepson does." She nudged Jane again.

"Oh, get out, Peggy. I need to get home." Jane was finally fed up. She could see Peggy's agenda, and she was having none of it. "Thank you, Cord, for the ride, but I have dinner to prepare. I have company coming tonight." She would now, if she hadn't before. She'd beg Billy to bring the grandkids over, even if she had to keep them all night. He and Jasmine would love that, to have a night free from the little tornadoes.

"Oh, Jane is a fabulous cook. Cord, we've got to get you out there before you get away. You cannot miss her fajitas. They're to die for!"

Cord laughed. "To die for, huh? I don't think I can afford to miss that. But I'm going to be busy the next few weeks getting the old home place livable again."

"See, Peggy? Cord doesn't need my cooking. Now, will you get out?" Jane felt her patience growing thin, although she was perceptive enough to know it was more than that. It was her need to get out of this man's truck. He had hurt her too badly to want to be this close to him for this long. Especially with what he was doing to her. She wouldn't fall in love with this man a second time, not after

— 23 —

what he did the first.

He wasn't to be trusted.

"Not so fast, sweetie." Peggy patted Jane's knee. "Did I hear you right, Cord? You're remodeling your parents' place? Why, it's been empty for a quarter century. You must need the whole place reworked."

"It's not that bad. Dated, maybe, but no water damage, and the plumbing still works. Paint, carpet, and a bit of furniture. It's the hardwoods that need the most work. Refinishing's a mess, and I've put it off as long as I can. I can't move in until that's done."

"Well," and Peggy leaned back in her seat to open her purse. "I happen to have one of Jane's business cards with me. She does exactly what you need. It's only part time now, because she cooks all the time, but she worked for the biggest design firm in Dallas. The Ratcliff Company. Everyone's heard of them. Here." She held out the card.

"Jane, do you want me to take it?" Cord looked at Jane, then at the card Peggy held. "I could use the help. You have the contacts. I have to call every number in the book, just hoping to get someone responsible."

"I'm not designing your house, Cord." Jane took a deep breath. She wanted to get away, and Peggy was determined to smash them together. She wanted to grind her teeth, but her dentist would give her an earful, if she did. "Numbers, only. I'll give you those, but I won't be responsible for who you call or what they do."

"She's teasing you, Cord. Playing hard to get. She designs interiors for Billy all the time. She adores it, and the results are fabulous. She even did her stepson's office. Hubba, hubba! It's that amazing!"

"Jane?" Cord still hadn't taken the card. "Do I dare? Or would you rather me make my own decisions. Purple and green are my colors of the moment. And I'm considering an orange ceiling. Sort of that citricy, summer thing that's so popular now."

Peggy giggled.

"Orange is not popular and has never been." Jane narrowed her eyes, daring him to tell her otherwise.

"Not since 1972." Peggy hooted. "I remember your bedroom carpet back in high school, Jane. Shag. Orange shag."

"That needed replaced, and my parents didn't have the money."

"So, do I get orange shag, or will you help?" Cord held his hand towards the card, but not close enough to take it.

"Yeah, Jane. Will you help?" Peggy moved the card closer.

"Oh, do it! Take the card!" Jane couldn't stand any more. She felt her eyes burn, and if she didn't get out of this truck, she knew she might not be able to keep her tears under control much longer. "Now, can I get out?"

"Almost, sweetie. Now, about an appointment. Cord, what's a good time for Jane to meet with you?"

"Meet?" Jane could hear the ragged edge in her voice. "I said I'd give him numbers."

"Numbers? They might paint his ceiling orange, and your name would be all over it. Is that the reputation you want? No, way, Jose. Now, I happen to know that Jane is free tomorrow, Cord."

"I am not! We have breakfast plans. We're heading to the Galleria tomorrow, and it will take all day." There. Dodged that bullet. Jane was relieved.

"No, girl." Peggy smiled wickedly. "That's how I know you're free. I've cancelled our day in favor of Cord's ceiling. It simply cannot be orange. Even you have to admit that." She chuckled.

"Not orange, and is tomorrow alright? For the sake of my ceiling, if not for me?" Cord seemed amused, but he also seemed to be at least trying to control his laughter. "I'll pay, whatever you charge, plus travel, lunch, anything. Whatever it takes for you to say yes."

Peggy was making no such effort at self-control.

"Take it while you can get it. An offer like this comes along only once every forty years."

"Sure." Jane had no doubt her sour answer sounded perfectly horrendous. However, whatever it took to get out of this truck. "You don't know my prices, though. I don't work cheap."

"She's not cheap, Cord." Peggy had her hand over her mouth, but it wasn't to hide her words, clearly.

"No, I'm not!" Jane had reached the end of her patience. Really, this time. "I do good work, and I charge a fair price. If you want a painter, they're a dime a dozen at 1-800-PAINTER—"

"I don't want a painter, Jane."

"Good. Who do you already have working on this?" It was her professionalism kicking in, she knew, and she didn't want this job, but good lands! She had loved that old house when she was there all those years ago. She could not let it be painted orange and purple. She would not!

"Well, no one, really. I had a cleaning crew in . . ."

"Good. I'm redoing that house. Top to bottom. I trust you have a lot of money, Tarzan Rivera. You may need those oil wells by the time I'm finished. Now, out, Peggy!" She groaned as she realized she'd called him Tarzan, and was equally relieved to see her friend reach to the door and release the catch.

"Eight? At the house?" Cord sounded hopeful, as if he couldn't believe she had actually agreed to this. "Should I pick you up at your place?"

"I can drive, Cord Rivera. Unless you've let the drive go to ruts and rocks, and if you have, I'm redoing that, too. For a fee, of course." She pushed on Peggy's shoulder. "Out!"

The two women didn't say another word until Cord's Escalade was gone, then Peggy ventured, "Mad at me?"

"I don't know, yet. Maybe." Jane hit the remote, the car beeped, and she pulled her door open. "I ought to be."

"Saving the old house from a seventies' vibe. That's worth something, isn't it?"

"Something. This? I haven't decided." Jane was pleased that Peggy at least seemed contrite. She slipped into the car and watched as Peggy placed her purse in the back seat before climbing in beside her.

"I really am your friend, Jane. Can you trust me?"

"Can you leave my love life alone?"

"You're not a pretty widow. You need a man," said very softly, as if she wasn't sure how Jane would take it.

"But I am a widow. Can't you see that? You divorced Roger, and you've always thought, 'Good riddance.' I didn't divorce Bill. He died. Can you see the difference?" Jane felt her eyes welling up. She hated that Peggy had brought her to this, and after those awful nightmares last night.

"I can see the difference, but three years is long enough for any widow. You're too sweet, kind, and beautiful to turn old on me now."

"Oh, you're so kind." She thought the tears really would come, and she fought them. "No, I'm not mad at you. I just don't need Cord back in my life. You don't know what he did all those years ago. You don't know at all."

"I would if you'd tell me. I am your best friend, after all."

Jane started the car. She waited for a moment, as all the electronics cycled on. Brushing her fingers under her eyes, she let out a deeply held breath, then she began to laugh.

"What's that about?" Peggy adjusted her air vent and reached to the radio, but didn't power it up.

"Oh, nothing. It's that man. You think we belong together, and I know we belong as far away from each other as we can get. At least I'll get something out of him this time. Lots and lots of money. He owes me big time, and I'll see that he pays."

She was surprised that Peggy didn't reply. Instead, she pushed the power button on the radio, and she began to bee-bop with the music. Jane was pleased to hear her favorite oldie still playing. *Stop in the Name of Love*. Then she remembered and laughed to herself. It was on the car's hard drive. Of course, it was still on. Why wouldn't it be? Just because the song had been turned off didn't mean it had disappeared. It was there waiting on her the whole time she was gone, ready to start right back up where it left off.

Like love, but she dared not think of that. No, love was very different. Love didn't wait around for a repeat performance. When it was gone, it was gone, and it could never be replayed again.

She did hum along, though, singing the words softly when they came up, "Stop, in the name of love . . ."

— 4 —

"STOP, IN THE NAME of love . . ."

Jane turned her head to look at the face of her alarm clock. Six-thirty. At least her night had been dreamless. She turned her face into the pillow and let the song play itself out. It was her favorite, even if it meant nothing. Two men had abandoned her, one by running away, and the other by dying. She guessed it was all the same, though. They were gone.

"Oh, drat it." She sat up. "Eight is too early for an old widow like me. I should have told Cord nine, or ten, or maybe next year. Then I could sleep in."

She wouldn't, though, and never had. It was track day at the local high school, and she had to be there and gone before the teenage groupies showed. She did smile at that. They weren't groupies, not like she'd been as a teenager, attending concerts with Peggy and their other on-and-off friends. Then, they hadn't been groupies, either. Just teenagers laughing and singing along with their favorite songs, like, "Stop, in the name of love . . ." She belted it out with the radio before laughing to herself. She'd never been able to carry a tune, not like The Supremes. Then, no one sang like The Supremes, not then, not now, and probably not ever.

Especially not Jane Waggoner. Jane Lane. Especially not Jane Lane.

She hadn't been called that in more decades than most people had been alive. She'd forgotten how it rhymed. "Jane Lane." She whispered the words to herself. She had loved to hear it called out in the high school hallways. *Jane Lane. Wait up!* Or on the practice field over the speaker system. *Jane Lane, first up, in the 100-yard dash.* She'd never make the hundred-yard dash now. They'd be carrying her away on a stretcher. She'd do good to get in her two-mile jog before the high school girls began to lap her on the track.

And she wouldn't get that done if she didn't get out of bed.

Yet, there was her daily devotional on the bedside table, and she picked it up. She didn't look at it last night. Shame on her. It was Cord. He'd caught her off guard with those long legs, and Peggy was right. She did like TDH, and that was Cord to a T. And a D and an H. She giggled, then felt silly, like a school girl.

"Well, I'm no school girl. They don't have to get their honey blonde tresses from a bottle. That's for sure."

She opened the devotional. It just fell open, and before she could turn it to the correct day, her eyes caught the words.

"Be kind to one another, tenderhearted, forgiving one another, as God in Christ forgave you."

Oh, Jesus. Not that scripture. Jane closed her eyes, her heart pounding. *I don't want to forgive Cord. I don't, Jesus, and for good reasons. You know why, too.*

She glanced back at the book, blinking away the moisture in her eyes. This couldn't be King James. It was "as God for Christ's sake" in the Bible she preferred.

There, Ephesians 4:32 from the ESV. No wonder. The

English Standard never got it right. She put the slim book down, knowing full well what she was doing. She was attempting, with every excuse in the book, to discount God's hand in bringing that verse to her mind. *Kind . . . tender-hearted . . . forgiving . . . as God forgave you.* She wasn't any of those to Cord yesterday, and he hadn't snapped back even once, and he sure had the right. She would have deserved it, too.

Oh, well. Today was another chance to earn her wings. She would try. Hard. As God *for Christ's sake* forgave me. After all, she'd played half the fiddle all those years ago. Her nightmare wouldn't have happened, if she hadn't provided half the devil's ammunition.

She had her running shorts, tee, and track shoes on by then, and she looked in the mirror. No one looks good at six-forty in the morning, she tried to convince herself. Still, she grabbed her brush and gave her tresses a quick swipe before tackling her sunglasses. She'd need them by the time she got to the track, and they'd hide her bloodshot eyes. Twenty minutes on the track, and she'd look a mess, anyway. But then, who was there to care?

Keys and water bottle, and she was out the door. It was only five minutes, but the track was filling up by the time she arrived. Too many old people trying to hang on to their youth, and she was one of them. She laughed at herself. Better than being in a wheelchair. That was certain.

A few minutes stretching, and she put the crunch of the track underneath her soles. She enjoyed the repeated crunch, crunch, as she made her way around the giant oval. Eight trips around, then home and a shower. *Might be tight to get to the ranch. Might be tight to get to the ranch. See Cord. See Cord. Silly Cord. Silly Cord. Tar—.*

Jane shook her head. That was not a mental running pattern she wanted to keep up.

Jane Lane. Jane Lane. Jane Lane.

Nope, not that either.

"Good morning, Jane."

She almost tripped over her own feet. She stopped, panting, and watched a very familiar man jog past her. She barely got out a "Morning" before he was too far away to hear her.

Cord, on the high school track before seven? She did this almost every day, and he'd never been here before.

"Well, it's my track, too. I pay taxes, and I can run if I want to." She tightened her mouth, waving at several people who looked at her funny, and started up again. *Avoid Cord. Avoid Cord. Avoid Cord,* she chanted over and over. That was all she had to do, avoid him, and things would be fine. After all, the track had dozens of people on it. What was one more? Who cared if Cord ran, too? It was just a high school track.

By her eighth lap, she was expecting each person who came up behind her to be Cord, and that kept her running at her top speed. He never did, and as she came to a stop, stepping to her bag for her water bottle, she looked for him. Over by the field houses, yellow buses were offloading long-limbed boys and girls, the slender ones that went out for spring training on the track. A few were already coming out of the field houses in their bright purple shorts and shirts with the team mascot on it. The giant bear with the extended claws was as familiar to her as her own hairbrush, but there was no Cord to be seen. She must have frightened him off, after yesterday's escapade.

She laughed and finished off her water. He'd called her a wildcat. Even her church hadn't erased all her fire, although she controlled it better now. She'd be good when she met him at the ranch, show him how a good Southern Christian woman forgave and forgot.

Well, maybe not *forgot,* but you couldn't have everything. She sure hadn't had everything in her life. Cord didn't deserve everything, either. Not her, anyway, as if he really wanted her again. He'd been done with her forty years before, and now he just wanted his ranch done over on the cheap.

Ha! She laughed to herself as she climbed in her car. Good work is never cheap, Cord Rivera. Not from Jane Lane.

In the shower, she got hold of herself. How could she react so strongly to a man she hadn't seen in decades? She and Bill had been happy. Even the happiest of couples had dry spells, and maybe hers and Bill's had lasted longer than some, but they had loved each other, hadn't they?

She let the warm water wash the tears away. She and Cord wouldn't have had any dry spells, she was certain. She wouldn't have allowed it. She wouldn't have allowed him to leave her, either, if he'd tried to break up in person.

Where did your Christian go, Jane Lane?

That was when she caught herself, and she was able to laugh. Jane Lane. She'd been Waggoner for four decades, and here she was thinking of herself as seventeen again. Fool. You never get seventeen again, and she had a house to remodel.

A dry towel, oatmeal, orange juice and coffee, and she was ready to face that man, she thought. If not ready, then braced with caffeine. Besides, she had her favorite oldies on the radio, and she'd belt them out all the way over, on key or not.

As she drove up, she glanced around. She didn't see anyone. It was when she opened the door that she heard her name.

"Jane, don't go to the front. I was being generous yesterday when I said it was in pretty good shape. The front door's out of whack. Sorry! Go around back."

She looked up to find him on the roof, pulling a broken terra cotta tile out. There were several new ones lying off to the side. Cord was shirtless and covered with sweat.

"I thought that run this morning would have done you in." She waved.

"Just a warm up, I'm afraid. I told you I couldn't get good workers. I've been doing most of it myself. You are indeed a sight for sore eyes, you and your remodeling contacts." He grinned as he waved back.

Walking around the house, she shook her head. How did a man his age stay so fit? He looked as good at nearly sixty as he had at seventeen. She wasn't here for that, though. Cord was a love 'em and leave 'em type of guy, as her own experience had taught her, and she was just here to earn a few dollars to pad her retirement account.

Indeed, her thoughts were already clicking. Winding sidewalk, large patio. She could already envision a beautiful water feature with wrought iron tables, chairs, and an outdoor kitchen off the main patio next to the family-size pool. It was there in her head like it was already finished.

She hoped Cord wanted to keep the original integrity of the Spanish architecture. That was what was coming together for her, with pictures of a hacienda-style revision that remained faithful to the heritage of the original structure.

It was when she stepped inside that she almost stumbled for the second time that morning. The dining room. Memories. Cord's family, the laughter, some of the happiest moments of her life.

Her family? She snorted. Her father, closet alcoholic. Mom? Beat down until she was a wounded cur. This place was the only family she knew that was real, that had cared about each other, that had made her want to really have a family of her own.

When she learned that Cord was married, that was the day she packed her bags and drove to Denton. UNT was her home from that point on, a dorm for two years, then that little apartment with Peggy. Peggy, her family after leaving her own family that had been little better than no family at all.

"Well, is it worth saving, or should I level it and start over?" Cord came through the door behind her, pulling a tee shirt over his head.

"Oh, no! Don't even think about tearing down this house. It has so much character!"

"That's what I was hoping you'd say."

Cord stepped past her, closer than she would have liked, close enough that she could smell his morning run and his time on the roof all over him. Her heart turned inside out. It was the same as before. High school, football, the smell of him when he threw his arms around her to celebrate a win. It was Cord, just how he was, and how could she have forgotten his smell?

"Strip it all out—"

"No, you don't, not with me as your designer."

"Whoa, Nellie." He laughed. "I should have prefaced that with, 'The last designer wanted to . . .' Sorry. My apologies. However, that tells me I picked the right person for the job."

"Picked?" He *picked* her? "I seem to recall it was by chance, and I volunteered, if you'll remember." She laughed. She did like Cord. That had never changed. If the unthinkable hadn't happened, they would have married forty years ago, and there would have been no Bill or Billy, or the two grandkids. And she would have a child of her own, all grown now. But that wasn't real, life had gone on, and they were where they were. And it wasn't together, and that's the way it was.

"Okay." He smiled at her, and he picked up a short piece of trim. "You volunteered, and I'm glad you did. This, though. I tried to pick out some trimwork at the local big box, but I don't think this is it."

"It certainly isn't." She took it from him. "Maybe this would look good in a fifties' ranch, but not in this place. Your grandfather built this, didn't he?" She let her eyes rove to the coffered ceiling with its boxed beam structure. The insides were done with painted tin panels, and she'd try to save what she could.

"After the tornado of thirty-two. That's nineteen—"

"Well, it certainly wasn't eighteen thirty-two." She cut him off, laughing and placing her hand on his forearm. She felt the fire leap from his skin directly to hers, and she immediately got quiet.

"Are you sure you want to do that?" Cord looked at her hand, then into her face. "Yesterday you couldn't even look at me. Today you're holding my hand?" His eyes twinkled.

"I'm not holding your hand!" She yanked it away.

"You could have left it there. I didn't mind."

"Well, I minded." She took a deep breath, certain the temperature had gone up ten degrees. "Texas weather. Not even eight-thirty, and it's already hot in here."

"Not to me," Cord mumbled. "Must be something else heating you up."

"Don't start." Jane raised herself as erect as she could. "We have to get off on a professional footing if we're going to get you into this house. What do you envision for yourself?"

"Four bedrooms are useless. Knock them all out and give me a big master and one guest suite. Then outside, lots of living space, shaded of course, and maybe a hot tub."

"A spa, you mean." She had her tablet out by then, and she was tapping away at it.

"Hot tub." He said it like he wanted to get a rise out of her. "For two."

She looked up to see him wink, and she laughed to show him she wasn't taking the bait. "I brought a tape measure, and I'll be busy a while. Why don't you go off and do some roof-type stuff."

"Roof-type stuff?" He reached up and ran his fingers through his gray-speckled hair.

"You know what I mean. Anything not where I am. Out, cowboy."

It was close to noon and a tablet full of measurements and notations later that Jane's concentration was interrupted.

"Are you about ready for some lunch?"

Jane jumped at the sudden intrusion. "It's just you,

Cord. I was focused on my work." She let out a little laugh, but she was certain her face was pale. That had startled her.

"Oh, I'm sorry. I didn't mean to frighten you. I just saw you standing there and thought you might be ready for a break."

"You're quite right. I do need a break. I'll tell you what, I'm heading into town for a bit, and I'll be back later this afternoon. Will the house still be available? I'll need back inside."

"My house is always open to you, Jane. You must know that."

"Grow up, Cord. I mean, will someone be here. I don't have a key, and you've already said you're not living here. Obviously. It's a wreck, and there's no real furniture, not even a bed. But that's what I expected. If you'll be here, I'll see you at one. If not, leave a door open, and I'll lock up when I leave." She took a deep breath, and headed to the front door, leaving Cord looking at her wistfully.

She pretended not to notice. She didn't need wistfully. She needed cash, and lots of it.

— 5 —

JANE BREATHED A DEEP sigh of relief as the garage door went down. While her garage might not exactly be *town,* it was certainly *in town.* It had been years since she'd lived on the old home place and considered it country. It was more like the town had come to her, but certainly not like Cord's place, out among the sticks.

Of course, it was the drive to get there more than how far away it was.

She was placating her guilt, she knew, like putting a bandage on a broken arm. Or better, like trying to fix a broken heart with a happy face sticker.

Still. At least her garage door was closed, and she was safe. Now for some lunch, even if it was the leftover tuna from day before yesterday. It couldn't stink any more than what Peggy had dragged her into.

Cord! Like they said, men. Can't live with them and can't live without them. But, after forty years, she had a pretty good head start.

She barely had her things on the counter before the doorbell intruded.

"Not Cord! How'd he find me here?"

Jane felt a moment of panic—she refused to admit to hope—before she realized how he'd found her. Of course! That Escalade had a GPS navigation system! She yanked open the door, prepared to snap, only to find someone much more familiar.

"Peggy! Why didn't you call and tell me you were coming over? I might not have been here. I might have been working at Cord's place."

"Well, are you?" Peggy still had her finger on the buzzer, and she pushed it one more time. "I like the sound of a door bell, sort of like an old friend come to visit, from forty *years* ago. Thanks, sweetie, for inviting me in." She flounced past, leaving Jane holding the door.

"I was, I'll have you know."

"You was what?" Peggy turned and grinned.

"Not was. I were what. No, that's not correct, but you know better English than that, Peggy Lynn. Use it." Jane heard exasperation buzzing at the edge of her voice.

"I know, but you said was, so I said was, and you never answered my question. You was what?"

"Oh, you!" Jane threw up her hands. "I was at Cord's for the morning. I'm headed back at one."

"Oh!" Peggy dropped onto the sofa. "You were there all morning, and you're heading back. Here, girl. Tell me all about it." She patted the seat next to her, a wide-eyed look on her face.

"There's no tell about it. I was measuring rooms the entire time. Cord and I hardly talked."

"But, you said you're heading back. Was he here for lunch?" She peered toward the kitchen, as if she might see him there.

"What's with you?" Jane disappeared into the kitchen, calling back, "I've got to go, or I'll be late. What did you need?"

"Need? Everything!" Peggy followed her. "Have you even checked the mail this morning?"

"You do it for me. I'm headed to Cord's."

"To Cord's, or to Cord?"

"Stop it, Peggy. If there's a romantic side to this, it's between the two of you. After all, he already calls you Peg. No telling what you call him. Boyfriend?" Jane laughed sharply. "He won't even be there this afternoon, and he was on the roof all morning. This is a business deal, and I have a proposal to prepare."

"Then I'll just tell you what I got in the mail. It's our fortieth."

"Fortieth what?" Jane grabbed her keys and flipped open the door to the alarm system. "I'm headed out. Are you in or out? Stay if you want, but turn the alarm off if you need to open a door."

"Jane!" Peggy pulled her arm away. "You're doing this to irk me, and I'm starting to get it. Irked, that is. Reunion. It's been ten years."

"That's right! The twins, wasn't it? Skiing accident?" Their thirty-fifth reunion had collapsed out from under them at the last minute. There were lots of complaints, but no one had volunteered to step in and flesh out the details. Poof! Opportunity gone!

"Don't start. Speedboat, except they were fishing and got in the way. Kenny still has that limp. I feel sorry for him every time I see him."

"And Raymond still drinks too much. That's why I don't feel much sympathy. Bill said their boat was full of beer cans."

"Well, anyway, no one felt like hosting number thirty-five that year. So, we have to go this year."

"Says who?"

"Oh, Jane. Why do you have to be so grouchy today, of all days? What happened to my Christian friend who's polite to everyone?"

"Yesterday happened," Jane snapped back. "Oh, I should be sweeter. But I can't, not just now. My nerves. You know. They're not what they used to be."

"They're working pretty well today." Peggy pulled out a chair and made herself at home at the kitchen table, pulling a mini chocolate bar from a bowl piled full and unwrapping it. "I mean, I came here with good news, and all for you, and you cut me off like mold on a brick of cheese."

"You came here like Agnes and Francis came to church that Sunday, requesting prayer for their husbands, when they wouldn't have needed to had they been in church."

"I understand. This is about the Cord thing yesterday. You're mad, aren't you?"

"A little irritated."

"Too irritated to go to the reunion?" Peggy smiled sweetly.

"Did you notice yesterday, but you finagled me into a remodel job out at Cord's place, and I still haven't prepared my proposal? I'm pretty busy for the next few weeks."

"Surely you'll be through in six. You think?"

"Let me get out my crystal ball. Hm. Nope, can't tell. Sorry."

"Ooh! I hope you don't bring this snappy attitude to church on Sunday. We might need to pray you to the altar and back again." Peggy licked her fingers and smiled. "Really!"

"I absolutely need to go." Jane checked her watch, pausing for a minute. No one would be there to check her time, and besides, she wasn't getting paid just yet. What did it matter? She sighed and gave in. "Cord's not there this afternoon, so I guess you can requisition my time for a few. What's so important about six weeks? There are only about thirty of us left. You tell me when and where, and I'm sure I can make the time. I won't plan it, but I'll make a point to be there. Grubstake again this year? Everyone loves barbeque."

"Not Grubstake." Peggy had a bit of a coquettish look

in her eyes. "Better, but you want to sit down for this one."
She reached to her side and pulled out the chair next to
her.

"Okay." Jane lowered herself into it, setting her clutch
and keys on the table. "But not here. I'm not having thirty
people in my house. No way. It's not happening."

"Better. Guess." Peggy grinned expectantly.

"Better, you tell." Jane glanced at her watch again and
stood up. She wasn't playing this game any longer. She
had to stop and pick up something to eat, now that Peggy
had stolen her tuna time from her. She was surprised when
her friend pulled her back down again.

"Rancho de—" She motioned with her hand. "Rancho
de— Say it, Jane."

"Rancho de. I don't get it, and I've really got to go.
Eat all the chocolate, Peggy, because I'm not. That's from
Halloween."

"Yech!" She pushed the bowl away. "I guess I'll have
to tell you, because it's only fair that you know. Rivera."
She nodded smugly.

"Rivera? Is that all? Rivera what?"

"Oh, good heavens!" Peggy stood and put her wrist on
Jane's forehead. "I knew it! A fever! Come on, Jane! Rancho de Rivera. I thought you should know, since you never
check your mail anymore."

"Rancho de Rivera? Cord's place? It's a wreck!"

"It won't be in six weeks, will it? Well, I've told you
my news, and I'm off now. You can get back to your little
rendezvous with Mr. Cord de Rivera." She said his name
with a romantic lilt and a grin.

"I—" Jane sat down again. "I'm supposed to get that
place ready for a class reunion in six weeks? Have you
been out there?"

"Once or twice. Here. I brought you my invitation, just
in case you didn't have yours handy." Peggy pulled it out
and laid it on the table. Opening it, she pointed, and right
there was a map to Cord's ranch.

"He planned this? Without asking me?" Jane was irritated now, and she felt duped. Tricked. Again, like forty years ago. "I think I might have a thing or two to say about this."

"Jane, honey." Peggy drummed her fingers on the table to get her attention. "Didn't you say he was on the roof?"

"Yes." Roof? Who cared about the roof?

"I think he thought he could do it all himself. You know, throw up some paint, put in a few flowers. You know men, all git 'er done and no sense—"

"The no sense part, anyway."

"Yesterday was a lucky break for him, you showing up. Don't be mad at Cord. He didn't want to ask you. I had to beg him."

"You begged him?" Now this was a horse of a different color. "What does that mean?"

"Oh, look at the time. I do have to go. I have a class in fifteen minutes, and it'll take me ten to get to the Center. Can you take me, sweet Jane? My car won't be ready until later today." She smiled sweetly.

"Here." Jane pulled a set of keys from the drawer. "You take Bill's old jeep. There's no air in it, but it'll get you there. I am not going to be late. The Center's on the opposite side of town, and I can't do both." She stopped dead. "Six weeks, you say?"

"Read and weep." Peggy swept up the invitation and held it out to her.

"Oh, but I do have to hurry. There's no electricity out there, and I must get all the measurements tonight. I can't do this in six weeks. How could Cord do this to me?" She flew out the door.

"Want me to lock up?" Peggy called after her.

Her answer was the squeal of the Lexus' tires on the drive as it tore away into the midday sun.

PEGGY PULLED OUT HER phone and dialed in a number. When it picked up, she laughed.

"Cord, you may have a wildcat on your hands. She's on her way out, and I can't tell if she's mad, glad, or sad. You know how hard she is to read. I showed her the invitation, so at least she knows what she's up against."

She reached back into the candy bowl, as she listened for a minute, smiling one moment and pursing her lips the next. Then she laughed.

"I know you don't deserve her, walking away all those years ago, but you paid your dues. Shelly was a jealous screamer, and I don't know how you stuck by her all these years. This is your second chance. Don't mess it up."

There were a few more minutes of conversation, then Peggy nodded and said, "Good luck, Cord," and hung up. It was the last thing she heard over the line that pleased her most. She didn't know how fast Jane had driven, but there was a screech of tires, and she'd heard Jane call out, "Thank goodness you're here, Cord. I talked with Peggy, and we have a lot less time than I realized."

It was the word "we" that impressed her most. Jane was thinking of her and Cord as a team. If they could be a team for six weeks, who knew but what they might be a team for a lifetime, even if it took manipulating Jane into accepting what was best for her.

Anything for Tarzan and Jane.

And Cheetah, too, of course. Tarzan and Jane had to have a Cheetah, and Peggy would enjoy playing the part again, even if the last time she donned that suit was forty years ago.

— 6 —

"TOMORROW. WE START tomorrow and no later, no matter how many strings I have to pull."

Jane said the words aloud into the emptiness of the old home. She had the house to herself. Cord had needed to run some errands.

The timeline would be tight, especially as the sun was fading fast, and she had more work to do. There was no electricity in the old place, and the interior was growing too dim to be safe.

Still, all wasn't lost. She had her plans roughed in. She could come up with the details as the initial stages progressed. It was the rough work that needed to happen tomorrow, walls ripped out, electrical and plumbing started. Oh, this was going to be a mess, even if she already felt the adrenalin surge of the upcoming challenge as a tidal wave sweeping her forward with it. A good remodel was always this way with her. The challenge was the taste of life.

Heading out the back door, she encountered a more immediate problem. Her shoe caught in the doorway's half-rotted sill. As she went down, her first thought was for her tablet and all the information she'd loaded during the day. It couldn't be lost! She reached for it, and two strong arms got in her way.

"Jane, are you okay? I'm sorry I didn't get back from town sooner. It's too dark for you to be walking in the house alone!"

"Oh, it's you, Cord!" She was startled, and on several levels. She had been alone all afternoon. She hadn't expected anyone to be around for the rest of the day. Then, that someone was Cord. The real culprit, she pushed aside, was his arms around her. How had she forgotten this, how good they felt? "I, I think I'm okay now."

"Are you sure?"

"I said so." She *would* say that, even if she wasn't. "You can let me go anytime."

"You're right, I could. But what would be the fun in that?" He chuckled, and the deep sound rumbled in the darkness, complementing the night voices just starting to build outside. "Here's your tablet, although I think it might be too much for you to carry in your condition. I might have to transport you to your car. Better yet, to my truck. I think there's the distinct possibility that you might need to go to the emergency room, perhaps with home care afterwards. I'm very good at home care."

"I'm sure you are, but this has gone far enough. I think everything is in working order," she said, embarrassed by his attentions. "In fact, if you'll let me stand, I can assure you that everything's fine. And thank you for helping me rescue my tablet. I want to go over these plans for the house so we can get started on them tomorrow. Do you want to come by later this evening or look at them in the morning?"

"What's best for you?" He still hadn't released her.

"Turn me loose, Cord Rivera." She pulled away and fought to a standing position. "I'm not infirm. Remember, this is a professional endeavor. You lost any hold you had on me four decades ago. No touching. Back to business. Tonight or tomorrow? I also have to get a contract signed."

"Jane! How can you think that? You don't need a contract with me." He looked hurt.

"Oh, yes, I do. S.O.P. Every time." *Especially with you*, she thought. *If I'd gotten a contract forty years ago, you wouldn't have run off and left me. It would have been called a marriage contract, and I would have held you to it, buster.*

"S.O.P?"

"Standard operating procedure. Get a contract or get stiffed. Are you planning on stiffing me?" *Again?* "And I need to put in orders now for everything, and I mean everything. You don't know, Cord. Six weeks is an impossible schedule for a total renovation like this."

"But you can do it, right? It will get done?"

"Are you paying me forty grand?" She let that sink in. She hadn't really discussed money with him yet, but her commission would be at least that, if her figures today held true.

"Forty *thousand?*" He looked pleased. "To redo the entire house?"

"Grow up, Cord." She reached her stylus to tap him on the chest, only belatedly remembering how she used to do that in high school when they met between classes. "That's just my commission. Twenty percent plus reimbursable expenses. Like my gas out here twice today. And lunch, since this is a working day. It could easily hit another ten on top of the forty. I'm good, and I'm going to do it right. You do want it done right, correct?"

"Ouch. I had no idea. Forty thousand is twenty percent." He looked like he was doing some quick numbers in his head. "Yeah, I can put that together in six weeks. Sure. You got it. Where's the dotted line?"

She laughed. "You haven't even seen my proposal yet."

"You just told me, and I accept." He nodded at her, as

if that settled it.

"Plans, colors, designs? Don't you want to see what shade of orange I'm painting the ceiling?"

He laughed. "Any color is fine, as long as you're the one doing the painting."

"Okay, then we need some clarification. I, personally, don't paint anything. My crews will do that. All I do is set them up and tell them the colors. And you're willing to accept anything I come up with?"

"Absolutely. Anything. I trust you implicitly."

"Okay. Done. I'll be on the phone tonight bribing all my crews to get them here on the double, tomorrow, if possible. However, I still need you to sign." She pulled out her tablet and clicked it on.

"You have a printer in that little toy?"

"I don't have to print. We live in an electronic world, Cord. Welcome to the twenty-first century. All I need is your signature on my tablet."

"Oh. Interesting."

She held it out. "Be sure to click the exclusion box, telling that you decline the right to consultation. That gives me the freedom to make any and all choices in the design process. This is a real boon to me. It cuts off days and days of haggling over minor details."

"Days and days, huh? What if I want to haggle?"

"Then don't click it, and don't expect this to be finished on time. I'm sure the reunion will go ahead just fine at Grubstake, and you can host the reunion for our forty-fifth." She smiled charmingly, daring him to push her even further.

"Okay, wildcat. You've got a pen?"

"I've got my stylus, or you can just use your finger. The tablet will resize your name to fit in the blank. Right there." She pointed, then took the tablet back when he was finished.

"We can still meet tonight, though?" He sounded hopeful.

"Whatever for?" She had the tablet back in her bag, and she looked outside. She would need a flashlight to her car, if she waited much longer. She was also aware her ankle had begun to ache. She hoped that didn't get any worse.

"I do want to see what you plan. You can do whatever. I don't mind, but I am interested."

"Well, I guess that would be okay. Time?" She looked at her watch.

"I have to meet with someone. Let me see." He thought for a moment. "Can I call you after I leave Peggy's?"

"Peggy's?" Now why did Peggy not share that with her?

"Oh, sorry. Peggy invited me to dinner. She said she makes great spaghetti and meatballs. I can call when we're about finished." He smiled. "She probably wouldn't mind if you came along."

"Sure. But I don't think so. I've had Peggy's meatballs. You'll enjoy them more." That irritated her, although she wasn't sure exactly why. After all, Cord wasn't hers, and he'd only been back in her life for two days. Six more weeks, and he'd be out again. C'est la vie.

"Then I'll just call?" He made it sound like a question. A hopeful question.

"I'll be at home. You have navigation in that truck, I'm sure, and Peggy knows the address."

That gave her a good reason to exit without further ado. She did favor her ankle as she walked over the uneven terrain. In the car, she realized that her last five minutes at the ranch had almost been her undoing. Feeling Cord holding her had made emotions surface that she thought were long gone. How could she feel that way, when her mind knew how he'd treated her? He was the reason she'd been forced to live with the horrible decisions she'd made. Now, here he was like nothing had ever happened. She needed to be away from him. The farther the better.

In the shower, she let the hot water run down her leg and over her ankle. It was nothing that she couldn't handle. Still. The warmth felt good.

In the kitchen, she pulled a large salad out of the fridge and transferred a small amount to a manageable bowl. With a glass of lemonade, her tablet, and her salad, she made her way to the living room to organize her notes.

It was only when she put her feet up on the ottoman and rolled up her pant leg that she noticed the purple band around her ankle. And the size! No wonder her shoe had begun to hurt!

She hobbled to the kitchen—it was really hurting by then—and filled an icepack. On the way back, the doorbell rang. Pit stop, she thought, diverting to the door. She peered through, surprised at her visitor.

"Yes, Cord? I thought you planned to call." She opened the door wider, as she *had* promised to meet with him.

"Icepack, Jane?" His eyes fell to the pack in her hand. He leaned forward, his forehead crinkled with concern, and holding one hand on the doorframe, as though he would just step inside at the least welcome.

"Icepack. You're very perceptive. You didn't call." She shifted the icepack in her hand, in pain and now irritated.

"I did. You didn't answer." He made a face, a mix between a grimace and a smile. "I tried."

"But my phone . . ." She didn't know where her phone was.

"In your car, maybe?"

"I don't think so." She thought but couldn't remember using it at all since out at the ranch.

"Or maybe in my pocket." He pulled it out and held it to her. "It was on the porch after you left. I guess you dropped it. I would have missed it, too, except Peggy called to ask you to join us for spaghetti. Well, you couldn't exactly answer it, so I did. I told her you weren't answering your phone."

"Oh, you did, did you?" She looked back at her chair. Her foot had *really* started to pain her.

"What's wrong?"

"It's my ankle. I hurt it worse than I realized." She turned and limped toward her chair.

"Let's get you seated and your foot propped up." Cord helped himself inside, taking her by the arm, as she limped along.

Actually, it felt pretty good to have his helping arm at her side. Bill had been rather distant most of the time, letting her manage her own aches and pains. She'd learned not to mention them at all. This? This was a welcome break.

"Does this hurt?" Cord gently touched the discolored skin around her ankle. "Here, and here?" He moved it slightly, causing her to wince.

"Only when you press on it." She laughed, but it wasn't funny. It really hurt.

"Point me to the kitchen. I need supplies." He stood, heading in the direction she pointed. After he disappeared, Jane heard him call, "Baggies?"

"In the cabinet next to the fridge, Tarzan." She winced, vowing never to use that name again.

"Found them," he yelled back to her. "Getting some ice." The refrigerator kicked on, the mechanism dispensing the ice loud even from across the house.

"I have an ice bag, Cord," she called to him.

"You need two." He stepped into the room. He looked around at the furnishings filling the space. "Pretty room, but you need to be in bed, and you don't need to be walking on that. Let me carry you." He put his bag of ice on the ottoman and bent to pick her up.

"No, you don't. I can stand." She did take his hand, and once she got on her feet, she proved she was right, but she knew that was as much as she could do. "Okay, I can't walk. Help me hop that way."

"I'll carry you that way." With no time for a response, he swept her up in his arms.

"Stop, Cord! You can't carry me! I'm too heavy. Put me down, now!"

"You're not any heavier than the sacks of feed I carry down for the cows on my place. What do you weigh now, a hundred and ten pounds?"

"Hundred and ten?" She laughed at his numbers. "I weigh more than that."

She had no choice but to point him in the direction of her bedroom, clinging to him as he carried her down the hall. She was surprised by the close guess, though. She only weighed about twenty pounds more.

Cord gently placed her on the bed and began to rearrange the pillows and pull the duvet and blankets back for her. She glanced around the room trying to judge the distance to her dresser where she had her nightgowns.

"What do you need?"

"Well, I normally do not sleep in jeans and a tee shirt. I usually wear a nightgown. I'll be okay, though."

"No, you won't, and I'm here to help. Tell me where they are, and I'll get one for you. There's no need for you to get up and put weight on that ankle. You can change while I go out to the truck and get my calculator. I still want to go over what I'm spending all my money on."

"If you insist. I'll need my things from the living room." She thought of her food. Well, wasn't this a mess? "I left my supper, too, a salad and a glass. Those too, please?" She smiled.

He nodded. "Gotcha covered, girl."

His remark was made in such an off-hand manner that Jane felt much easier immediately. She told Cord where her gowns were, directing him with her hand. He opened the drawer and pulled out a gown from the bottom layer. He then tossed it to her and headed out the bedroom door.

"I'll be back!" He called out, dropping his voice in a

deep tone imitating Arnold Schwarzenegger, causing her to laugh and smile.

— 7 —

"OH, MY!" JANE SAT up and frowned at the lavender gown Cord had tossed her way. "This is entirely inappropriate."

It was one of her flimsier, short, see-through ones. Oh, well. She also had a sheet and duvet on her bed. She would be as protected from his eyes as she would be at a pool or in a sheer summer blouse.

Standing on one leg, with an eye on the door, she shimmied out of her jeans and tee. As quickly as she could muster on one leg, she pulled the gown over her head and threw the bedding back. There was no way she was having that man in her bedroom, with her wearing something like this. Gads! That was when her devotional from that morning caught her eye. *13 Weeks with Jesus.* How many weeks had she attended First Congregational in the last forty years? And what had she learned from all those sermons? She sat on the edge of the bed and picked the slim volume up, remembering her verse from earlier. *Forgive. Forget.* How could she do that? She felt her eyes burn, and she refused to be red-eyed and emotional when Cord returned. He might think her an easy target—again!

She laughed at herself as she wiped at her eyes. This was a business meeting, for heaven's sakes. Cord wanted to show off his place at the reunion, and she had the skills to get it done in six weeks, if barely. It was no more than that, and she was a fool to think it was. She had about convinced herself that he'd returned after forty years, after a long and happy—she presumed—marriage, just to court her. And she wanted to hurt him like he'd hurt her. It was all so pointless. She was no more than a fool.

She flipped open the slim volume, praying, *Okay, God. Give me another word from you. Make it a good one.* She read:

"Be not hasty in thy spirit to be angry: for anger resteth in the bosom of fools."

Well, Ecclesiastes. What did I expect? At least it's good old KJV. But, no thanks, God. I don't like that one.

That verse hit entirely too close to home. She *had* been angry, and she *did* feel like a fool. But this couldn't be the random word God had for her. She flipped it to another page, certain that God would be kinder this time.

"There is no fear in love; but perfect love casteth out fear: because fear hath torment. He that feareth is not made perfect in love."

She slapped the book closed. She knew that verse without even looking. 1 John 4:18. Her Sunday school class had studied it just three weeks before.

I don't love him, God. Maybe once, but not after forty years. Do you remember what he did to me?

Do you remember what Mankind did to me?

Jane took a deep breath. She hadn't thought that, had she? What Mankind did to God? Yeah, she knew. And all about the forgiveness and all that. But this was her and Cord, and that had been a knife in her heart. She'd forced it under the rug, then Cord had returned, making the pain real again, just as hurtful as ever.

Just like when you are angry without listening to my

word.

What word? She didn't want to know.

You're holding it.

She looked down at the book. *13 Weeks with Jesus.* What had she read today? *Forgive. Forget. Don't be angry. Love.*

What do you want from me, God? She felt the tears rising again. She wiped at her eyes, setting the book on the table. She looked up at the ceiling. *What, God? Please talk to me.*

I did. You didn't listen.

Okay. She calmed herself, taking a deep breath. *Once more and I'll pay attention this time.*

Forgive. Forget. Don't be angry. Love.

Oh.

She heard the front door, and she crawled under the covers, pulling the bedding to cover herself appropriately. *Sure, God,* she thought. *Well, here's your chance to prove yourself. I'll try to do my part, but I need you to do your part.*

And that is?

I don't know. Just do it, God. Please.

"Jane, are you decent?"

"Not for the past two days, but I am now." Cord wouldn't understand, but God would. "It's you I'm worried about, coming into a strange woman's bedroom." She laughed, making sure he could hear it.

"I see you still have your sense of humor. That's what first attracted me to you all those years ago. Jane Lane. Remember what people called you? Instead of June Bug, they teased you with Jane Bug."

"I'd forgotten all about that. Oh, what memories that brings up." She leaned her head back and closed her eyes. At least that could hide the redness. And she really had forgotten. Jane Bug. She had hated it then, but it was funny now.

"Your food. You said you had food in the living

room, and I forgot. Where can I put this?" He held up his calculator. "And this?" He held up her bag with her tablet inside. "I recognized it from today. You said you needed your things, and I figured this was it."

"Thank you, Cord. On the bed will be fine. You'll need a chair. Get the one from the make-up table in the bathroom."

"Right Bach!" It was his Arnold voice again, and he was gone.

"Better, God? I am trying."

The door bumped, and Cord walked in with both hands full. "Talking with someone?" He grinned as he set her glass on the bedside table.

"Just myself. You know, conversation with God, that sort of thing." She laughed and waved her hand at him to make it light.

"Had a few of those, myself. Let me get that chair, and we can get started."

She pulled out her tablet and tapped it on, entering her passcode to get inside. She tapped her way to the Rivera file, opening her Bridge program to allow her access to the banks of files she could use for inspiration. Rows of small icons opened, all ready for her to touch and drag into the Rivera file as key examples of the different features she imagined in each room. She began tapping them, dragging them to Cord's file. She knew them by heart, and this was the easy part. Tap and shift. Tap and shift.

"Whoa, there, Jane. Are you typing a letter?"

She looked up. "What do you mean?"

"Your fingers, ninety to nothing on that little glass thingy. What are you doing?"

"No. I'm sorry. This has all my idea sparkers. See?" She turned the tablet to him, and she touched the small icons one at a time. As she touched each one, a larger image exactly the same appeared at one side of the screen.

"Whoa. Hold that one." Cord grabbed her hand, forcing her finger back to one particular icon. The picture that pulled up showed a bank of French doors, all open, with billowing sheer fabric wafting into the room. "I like that. Can we do that?"

"I thought this was my project. You did sign that wavier."

"Oh. Sorry. Yeah, I did."

"But, yes, we can." She touched it again and sent it to his folder. "Now you have French doors and diaphanous fabric panels that will blow in the wind. How about that?" She sat back, smiling, strangely pleased with how the first five minutes had gone.

"Show me some more." He pulled the small chair from the bathroom up beside her bed. "This is fantastic. You click, and I have a house."

"Not exactly. There's still a lot of in between stages, like knocking out walls, and jackhammering floors, but, yes, I click, and you get a new house." She reached for a sip of her lemonade then pulled the bowl of salad to set it on the bed beside her. "Excuse me while I take a bite. I haven't eaten since lunch."

"That reminds me. Your ankle. How is it?"

"Hurting, but otherwise fine." She'd forgotten it for a minute, distracted by Cord's company. "I never did put my ice pack on it."

"We can resolve that." Cord reached to the foot of the bed and grabbed the bedding.

"What are you doing?" She wasn't dressed for him to take off the duvet.

"Get a grip, Jane. It's just the foot of the bed. I'm not going to ravish you or anything."

Absolutely right you're not! But before she could get those words out, she caught her devotional out of the corner of her eye.

Forgive. Forget.

"Don't be angry. Love. You forgot those," she muttered.

Cord glanced at her, a puzzled look on his face. "What

did you say?"

Jane let out a deep breath. "Nothing. That's the end of that God conversation from earlier. Just ignore it." She chuckled. "*I'm* trying to, but God won't let me."

"It's just that I heard the word love, and I wasn't sure what you meant."

"I'm not sure, either. Now, about my foot, pull back the bedding. I'm in your capable hands." He looked at her strangely once more, but she just waved his look away. "To it, Dr. Rivera. Make the cripple whole. Wait, I think that was Jesus' job. Your job is to apply the ice pack in just the right spot."

"That, I can do."

It did seem to Jane that he held her calf in his hand a rather long time, much longer than it took to apply an ice pack, but then, she'd never sprained an ankle, and she'd never had a man apply an ice pack to one of her legs. Maybe that's the way it was supposed to happen, hold the leg while the ice pack does its work. Anyway, it felt very good, and she didn't mind him holding her leg. Not one bit.

— 8 —

"WELL, ENOUGH OF THAT." Cord sat back. He could feel the heat in his face. And on his torso and the back of his neck. "Let me get a towel to put under your leg so the bed stays dry." He stood and headed into the bathroom. He didn't care about the towel. He needed some space.

"Get the big one from under the sink," Jane called to him from the bedroom. "I never use them. Bath sheets, I think they're called."

He opened the cabinet. "Red?" They came in a rainbow of colors.

"No. ecru. The red might stain the sheets."

"Okay, missy," he muttered, pulling out the beige one. "I hope this is ecru."

He stood, pausing and refusing to look into the mirror that spanned one whole wall. He knew what he was feeling, and it wasn't something he should be feeling in a bedroom with a woman who wasn't his wife. He should also go. That was the part he was struggling with. He should really go. If he looked in the mirror, he'd see it reflected back at him. But how, after forty years, could he just walk away? He was here. Now. In her house.

"God!" He didn't know if it was a prayer or despair. A little of both, probably.

"Cord? Did you find it?"

"I found it. Be right there." He did glance up, and he didn't see himself in the mirror. Instead, he could see Jane in her bedroom, sitting up in her bed. She had the bedding pulled away, and she was fanning herself. Maybe it wasn't just him that was hot. That was a relief.

Then he realized what she was fanning with. It was the bottom of her nightgown.

"Oh, Jesus, keep me strong."

"What is that Cord?"

"I've got the towel. I'm coming in." He kept his eyes from the mirror. "Ready, Jane?"

"Of course. Why wouldn't I be?"

She was covered demurely when he reentered the room. That was an onion shaved in a paper-thin slice!

"We can do this tomorrow." He stood beside the bed holding the towel.

"The bed will be already wet. Put it under my foot. Don't be silly." She pointed, pulling the mounded bedding out of the way.

"Oh. Sure. That. You're right." He grinned sheepishly.

"What were *you* talking about?"

"The house. It's late, and you're injured—"

"And better taken care of than I would be alone. Now, about that dining room ceiling—"

"No, really. I need to go. Anything. You do anything, and it's gravy. I'll love anything you do. Are you comfortable here for the night?"

"Cord? Why the change of plans? I thought you were interested."

"Ho, ho. You don't know." He chuckled, running one hand through his hair and turning away. "I'm interested, all right, and that's why I'm leaving. Surprise me. You always have, and I want this to be no exception."

"Sure, but I don't understand. Thanks for all your help." She set her tablet aside, waving to him as he stepped to the door. As he disappeared into the hallway, she called, "My phone. Cord, can you bring me my phone?"

He closed his eyes. *Give me strength, Jesus, If I go back in there, I may not make it back out.*

"Oh, never mind, Cord. It's here on my bed."

Thank you, Jesus. Cord knew he'd be okay if he could make it to the front door. The phone had made it convenient to just show up at Jane's door, but it had almost sunk his self-control. As he started his truck, he shivered at how close he'd come to making the same mistake he'd made all those years ago. All it took was being alone with Jane, and he was seventeen again.

Seventeen never comes back. Never.

He felt his hands shake as he pulled on the highway. He didn't blame it on his need for Jane. It was probably too much coffee or sleepless nights. Not Jane. Not Jane.

He must have said that to himself a hundred times before he pulled in the motel parking lot.

— 9 —

"JANE, HERE."

It was dark in the room, and the phone was cold to her touch. However, she was up.

Awake, anyway, even if not completely dressed.

Nightmares, or sweet dreams, depending on how she looked at them, had haunted her through the dark hours of the night. Years before she had dreamed of Cord, that he would return to rescue her, telling her that his phone call had been a mistake, and that he loved her as much as ever.

Then Bill had come along, and now she regularly dreamed of Bill's untimely death in the arms of that tree.

Last night, Bill hadn't come to her. Cord had returned to her dreams, but not the seventeen-year-old she remembered from high school. He had strolled into her night standing tall, with silver streaked hair, and, of all things, on her roof!

Now, where had that come from?

"Hey, girl! How's your ankle?" The words, bright and cheerful, so early in the morning, could only be Peggy.

"Better." Cord was still with her in her half-awake

state, and she didn't have any banter to toss over the line.

"Well, that's a real conversation starter. What am I supposed to get from that? Like, is it still swollen, or, can you walk, or maybe, do you need to go to the emergency room? That would help me out."

"I'm sorry, Peggy. Did Cord talk to you? I don't mean to pry, but he must have. By the time he left, I was exhausted, and I fell asleep in my clothes." Well, that was the truth, part of it, anyway. She was in her clothes, even if it was her nightgown. And exhausted? That came from mulling over just why Cord exited so abruptly. After all, it had been his idea to come over in the first place.

"I get it. You don't want to ask for my help, and that's okay. I'll be right there. Tarzan made it sound like you needed an ambulance and an operation. I thought you'd be in a cast by now." She giggled. "He was so upset when he called me last night after he left you, that I could tell he felt bad about what happened. He feels like it's his fault. He sounded really guilty on the phone."

"That's ridiculous. I told him last night not to worry about it, that it was my fault."

"Sure, sure. Well, I'm bringing eggs and bacon, and you don't need to tell me about cholesterol and all that. Just for once, an egg won't kill your blood veins. So, get ready to eat up. And call Cord. He's worried about you."

"Sure. Kill me with kindness, if you must." Jane was sitting by then, and she stepped gingerly to the foot of the bed, tossing the damp, ecru towel through the bathroom door. "I'll be dressed and ready to kill."

"You do that, pumpkin." The line clicked and was dead.

"Well," Jane snorted, holding out the phone and looking at it. "Who claims to be the good Christian, now? Peggy, be careful, or you'll be taking first prize."

She did appreciate her friend's concern and phone call. And breakfast would be welcome. Her foot was part of the reason for her nightmares, she was sure, because it had throbbed, waking her up repeatedly during the night. It was only well after midnight that she had dozed off and remained asleep for any length of time.

By the time she had loose slacks and a cotton blouse on, one in complementary grays, the doorbell went crazy.

"Come on in, Peggy." To get there was too much effort on her shattered leg.

"I can't, sweetie! My arms are full. Can I get a hand, here?"

"Oh, why do I bother with friends at all?" Jane groused as she stepped gingerly to the door. She swung it wide to see Peggy with a sack looped over each wrist.

"Surprise! Egg and bacon muffins on one arm, and nursing supplies on the other. One way or the other, you are going to feel better by the time I leave."

"I expected real eggs and bacon. Like the ones in a shell." Jane could smell it as Peggy walked by.

"It is. I didn't say I was going to cook. Gads! You do want to live to see another day, don't you?" She strode right into the kitchen, leaving Jane to follow. "Now, I want to see that foot, so don't wander too far off."

"Too far off? I can barely hobble."

"Jane the Hobblet?" Peggy stuck her head through the door and pointed, laughing. "About ready. You coming, or am I bringing it to you?"

"Here, please?" Jane found the ottoman and lowered herself. "I didn't realize walking would start the swelling again. I'll do better to keep off it as much as I can."

"That's what I told Cord." Peggy reappeared with a tray, orange juice in crystal goblets, and two red tapers burning merrily away. "Breakfast is served, and not too bad, if I do say so myself. You move to the chair, cause you're sitting on my table." She slid the tray onto the ottoman as Jane moved aside. "Oh, the rose. I forgot. Hang tight!" She flounced into the kitchen and returned with a long-stemmed red rosebud in a footed vase.

"Beautiful!" Jane reached for it and lifted it to her

nose, drawing in the fragrance. "Where did you find this?"

"Um, that might be a sticky question. Because the answer is in your garden."

"What?" Jane frowned then let out a laugh. "Oh, you dropped the receipt. The name of the florist doesn't matter, because it's beautiful."

"No, no. I got the rose from your garden. You know that bush by the mailbox? It had that really tall bloom, and I just couldn't let it go to waste. I knew it would cheer you up, and that was so much better than wasting it out there."

"It wasn't exactly wasted. I enjoyed it every time I went to get the mail."

"Well, as I recall, you don't go get your mail, and so it was wasted. Now it's not. Besides, if you want to start checking your mail again, you've got another one about to open, so you won't even miss this one." Peggy reached for Jane's muffin and unwrapped it for her, placing it on her plate.

"I can unwrap my own muffin. It's my leg that hurts, not my hand."

"Okay, Miss Prissy. Then I'll take yours." Peggy swapped plates, reaching and taking a bite. "So good. I should have these for breakfast every day."

"And die an early death of clogged arteries."

"And die an early death, but a happy one. One day closer to Jesus." Peggy grinned.

"You're impossible." However, Jane had hers unwrapped by then, and she took a bite. "This is good. Very good."

"Told you." Peggy winked knowingly. "Did you call Cord?"

"I was getting dressed. Now I'm eating breakfast. Give me time."

"Well, he needs to hear from you. He's taking you getting hurt really hard."

"That's a laugh, him feeling bad that I got hurt." Jane rolled her eyes. "First, he came over, then disappeared as if

I'd said something awkward to him. Second, it wasn't his fault." By then, she was irritated that Peggy kept insisting she call. Cord coming over was starting to feel a little self-serving, and that made her want to snipe at him. She murmured, "And third, Cord couldn't even begin to imagine how badly he hurt me."

"See? You're hurt, and you can't even own up to it."

"I'm not talking about last night."

"I get it now. You can't let loose of the past. Well, maybe it's because he knows he hurt you once and never wants to do it again. Have you thought about that?" Peggy bit into her muffin as if she'd something innocent like, hello, how are you?

Jane looked at her hard, thinking about Peggy and her pushy conversation. She compared Cord to the man she remembered from four decades earlier and the one who'd shown her such empathy last night. It seemed that he was two people. One was friendly and charming, and she loved that one. The other was careless of others' feelings, and that one had run over her with a steam roller.

Jane couldn't get past the steam roller. She bit off her words like snapping peas, and she spit them out one after another.

"He'd have to care to feel guilty, and since he doesn't seem to have feelings, I don't think he's capable of those emotions." Jane set her sandwich down and closed her eyes, leaning her head back. She didn't want to cry this morning, not after her dreams of Cord during the night. He'd been caring and concerned there. Not like in the real world.

"Now what?" Peggy tapped the side of Jane's glass with her fork. "The food's not good?"

"Whose side are you on, anyway?" Maybe if she had more sleep, or if her ankle stopped pounding, but that wasn't getting resolved this morning. Not with Peggy here.

"Quit it! You know I'm your best friend. All I'm saying is people do change over time. Maybe Cord has grown up some over the past forty years and is trying to let you know he's not the same person who left you back then." Peggy finished with a frustrated sigh. "Why are you making things so difficult?"

"Maybe if you knew the truth—"

Ding! Dong! The doorbell interrupted Jane's crushed response.

"Oh, they're here!" Peggy jumped up and headed to the door.

"What?" Just when she was about to bare her soul. Maybe it was for the best.

"Oh, thank you. Flowers, Jane!" Peggy turned around with a huge basket of star lilies and roses with baby's breath and greenery throughout. There was a card attached.

"From?" They were beautiful, making her rose look forlorn by comparison. It had paraded so wonderfully before, standing alone and proud. Now it simply looked lonely. "Did you give the driver a tip?"

"Oh, honey, he said he was tipped on the other end." Peggy pulled out a card. "Here, who's it from?"

Jane took the card, looking at Peggy suspiciously. She expected it to say *Peggy* on the card. Either that or *Cord* in Peggy's handwriting.

Instead, it was a handwriting she remembered from back when life had been fun and easy, at least when she was at the Rivera ranch. *Cord Rivera,* with that little flourish at the end of his name that she always remembered. Now tears really came to her eyes.

"They're beautiful. They've already filled your house with love, er, I mean fragrance."

"Say anything you want, Peggy. Why didn't he think about how I felt all those years ago? I've grown up since that happened. Back then I felt so betrayed and alone. He didn't even have the decency to talk to me face to face. I never got to see his expression or let him see mine. He never saw my pain. Twisting my ankle is nothing compared to the heartbreak I suffered."

"Sweetie, sometimes you just have to forgive and forget, and start over from scratch. That is if you want to find love." Peggy patted her arm.

13 Weeks with Jesus. Forgive. Forget. Don't be angry. Love. Is that you talking, God?

"And unless you think I'm just blowing smoke, that's directly from God. Ephesians. I heard that on the radio on the way over." Peggy picked up her glass and tossed the rest of her orange juice back. "Now, let me look at that leg. I don't see how you walked in here, but it's not as bad as Cord said. I think you might even live."

"You think so?" Jane closed her eyes as Peggy began to feel of her leg. It was nice to be taken care of again, but it wasn't quite Cord. Not like last night. Had that been God talking to her again, or just Peggy? If Peggy, then God was getting desperate. She chuckled at the thought of Peggy with wings.

"What's so funny?"

"I was imagining you with wings. An angel, and I can't quite do it."

"Well, fancy that. I was just thinking the same thing about you. Daresay Cord doesn't have that problem."

"I bet he doesn't. Who's his angel? You?"

"Oh, girl!" She slapped the side of Jane's leg. "Grow up and step out of those Pampers. I'm talking about you."

"Ow, ow, ow!"

"What?"

"That was my sore leg!"

"Oh, honey, I'm so sorry!"

But as the tears rolled, Jane peeked, and from the look on Peggy's face, she didn't think so. And, oh, great goodness, she didn't know her leg could hurt so much.

She released her inhibitions, and she let the tears fall like rain.

— 10 —

JANE WIPED AT the tears.

Love. What's love? What she and Bill had? She had loved Bill, but she'd never been in love with him, not that butterflies in your stomach, can't wait for his next call kind of love, the one that makes a woman stay up all night, and the next day she's still not sleepy, because-her-heart-is-so-full-of-him kind of love.

She'd been in that sort of love once. Cord.

Somewhere along the line, about forty years ago, she'd broken his trust. Why else would he have left her, jilted and compromised, standing alone in her fog of grief?

Was she angry with him? Or was she angry at herself? She didn't know, anymore. She knew one thing. Her foot and Peggy's inept ministrations were bringing up muck that should have remained buried for all time.

"Peggy, can't you at least pretend to be gentle?"

"I am, honey. Well, as gentle as you need me to be. What do you think I am, the Easter bunny?" She snickered. "I do like pink, though. You know, they make pink elastic bandages. I wonder if they carry them at—"

"No, you don't, and I will not wear pink wrapped around my leg." Jane took a deep breath, feeling stronger, and she pushed the old desire for Cord into the dusty and dark corners of her memories. "I'm stronger than you think, little Miss Easter Bunny."

"What does that mean?" Peggy adjusted Jane's leg on the ottoman, and she stood, her hands on her hips.

"You know what I mean." Jane toyed with the rest of her muffin, debating taking a bite. Then she thought of all the miles she wouldn't be able to run, and she pushed it back.

"That you won't eat my breakfast gift, even if you're hungry?" Peggy picked it up and broke off the corner, popping it into her mouth. "Hm, yours is better than mine. I wonder how that is?"

"Justice?" Jane did take a drink. At least the juice was healthy for her.

"Now, I know you don't mean that." Peggy sat down, taking another bite, talking around the food as she was eating. "Tell me what's really got your goat, and I know it's not that foot. That foot hurts, but the pain's coming from here." She pointed with the last bite of the muffin to Jane's heart. "Don't you try to tell me otherwise, either."

"Got a coat hanger?" Peggy was determined to pull this from her, and besides, with her leg, Jane's endurance was wearing thin. She was about to fall through the ice, and giving in was her lifeline to sanity.

"You need a coat hanger, with everything else we're talking about?"

"You're about to hang me out to dry. I prefer to do it in private. I want in the drip-dry closet, not out on the clothes line for the entire world to see."

"So, you're ready to dish?" Peggy glowed in anticipation. "Give me the nutshell first, then we can go back and rehash all the details. I've been waiting forty years for this. Make it good, too."

"I don't have to make it anything. It's not like baking a

cake, you know." Jane snorted in derision.

"Cakes are good." Peggy set her elbow on her knee and leaned in. "Icing on the outside, and all the tender tidbits inside. I'm giddy with anticipation."

"And anything forty years old is more fruitcake than devils' food. Trust me. I wish you'd left this dead. It's one of those things that only hurts when you poke it. You and Cord have poked it a lot the past few days."

"Whatever. Just tell me the story. Remember, bare bones the first time. I want it short and sweet." Peggy smiled encouragingly.

"Well, for better or worse, here goes . . ."

Despite the knot in Jane's stomach, it did feel good to bleed the misery and despair from that awful year to someone else's ears. She'd endured the torment of rejection, the pain of being alone, and the ridicule of her parents; and all with no one's shoulder to cry on. It had been truly a year she had wished gone from her life and memory, except that it never was.

Nothing, not time or marriage or a fulfilling job had been able to take away the worst thing that had ever taken place in her life.

"WELL." PEGGY SAT BACK, her eyes wide. "I knew there must be . . . I mean, I guess I suspected there was something deeper, just hiding under the surface. I never knew it was this big."

"I'm not the Loch Ness monster. Neither is my news."

"Pretty close, all hidden under the water, with just a tiny little bit sticking out." She looked at Jane. "Girl, I tell you what. You don't want to do the ranch house, I'll tell Cord myself. Buzz off, Buster!"

"That's not a solution, and you know it."

"I know something else. You're a stronger person than I ever knew. I cannot imagine what I'd do if a man ever did that to me."

"Divorce him." Jane smiled.

"That's right. I've been there and done that. Still, at eighteen? You were fighting this battle all alone while I was still hoping for my first real kiss, and no, those prom pecks on the cheek don't count."

"I was in love. Truly. I would have given Cord anything. For a long time after, I would have forgiven him, if he'd just let me know there was a reason for what he'd done."

"Truly? Oh, you *are* being generous. Like forgiving a rattler that's just bitten you."

"When you truly love someone, you don't care. I just couldn't maintain that forever." Jane took a deep breath as she looked away. "I had to move on. Bill offered me his life and his son, and I took him up on the offer. I'm not sorry, either, even if what we had was less than what I wanted."

"Been there, remember." Peggy patted Jane's shoulder. "Haven't wanted to go there again. Not just yet, anyway."

The jangling of the phone burst into the moment, and both women laughed.

"Yes, Jane Waggoner speaking." She looked at Peggy with a frown. "I have a what?" She covered the mouthpiece, whispering to Peggy. "Do you know anything about an appointment?"

"Hair or nail?" Peggy glanced at her fingers. "I have one that's peeling, so make one for me while you're at it." She put it to her mouth to chew the edge.

"It'll be brain surgery, then. It's Dr. Widdener," Jane teased. "The surgeon's office finally found you."

"Oh, so it's not hair or nail. He only does ordinary stuff. Tell him I don't need anything."

"It's for me, not you." Jane spoke into the phone, "What's this for, if I may ask?"

Peggy stood, whispering, "I would expect a broken heart. Confirm it, Jane, then we'll get you back in hot pursuit for a new man." Peggy laughed, reaching for the plates. "You take care of your conversation, and I'll get things cleaned up."

Jane waved her hand at her, talking into the phone. "I don't have an appointment." She listened a minute more, then said, "10:40, it is. I'll be there. Thank you." That gave her less than an hour.

"So, what does *your* brain surgeon need?" Peggy called from the kitchen, and there was laughter in her voice.

"He was looking for you, remember?"

"But, and I will continue, even though you interrupted me, so why would he be calling you?"

"How come you can hear every word every single person whispers in Sunday school, but you can't hear the sarcasm in my voice? It's Dr. *Widdener*." Jane handed Peggy her glass. "Take this, too, since you're playing house maid."

"For all I know, Dr. Widdener could be a brain surgeon. Maybe there are two Dr. Widdeners in this town." But Peggy had a smile on her lips as she said it.

"It's my foot. Someone scheduled an X-ray."

"Good. You need one. Did I hear 10:40?"

"So you do listen." Jane smirked.

"Of course. I just choose what I want to forget. Who scheduled it?"

"They didn't say. I thought you."

"Guess again, and oh, look at the time." Peggy picked up Jane's keys from the table. "Are we taking your car? I'd look good driving your red Lexus."

"Right. Look at the time, and you have a class at ten. I drove home last night. I'm sure I can make it to the hospital."

Actually, she wasn't. If Peggy didn't schedule the appointment, it had to have been Cord. He was the only other one who knew, and she wasn't calling that man for a ride. She'd rather skip the appointment, even if it took another week to get in or she had to wait in the emergency room for twelve hours, before she asked Cord over here again.

"If you don't mind waiting afterwards, I can juggle you in." Peggy sat on the edge of the ottoman and placed her hands in her lap contritely, holding her keys in her hand, as she studied Jane's face.

"Juggle me in?" Juggling was the last thing she needed with her sore ankle.

"I'd just have to pick you up after class. Do you want to wait that long? If not, I can call Cord."

"No, you cannot call Cord. You head on. I can manage fine by myself."

"Suit your own manikin. When you're crippled for life, just tell the doctor that a very good friend offered you a ride, and you refused." Peggy stood with emphasis and opened the door. "Not too late to take me up on my offer."

"Out!"

It was after her awkward and actually quite difficult shower that the phone rang again. The hospital, surely, telling her the appointment had been a mistake. She hopped to answer it. "Hello?"

"It's me. Thought you might need a ride." Nothing else.

Cord! Here to be her knight in shining armor. Her eyes narrowed, but the tingle in her stomach told her she didn't mind. The pain in her ankle screamed a little louder. It cried, Thank you!

"Did you set this up?" It had to have been him.

"Set up what? I'm just the taxi service." His amusement bled through with his words.

"Doesn't matter. I'm glad you're here. Give me ten minutes."

He clicked off without replying, and Jane set the phone down. Now, she was under pressure. Ten minutes to be beautiful. She didn't know if she could do it.

A hint of makeup, quick mascara and too-heavy lipstick, and she headed for the closet. Black crops and slinky lavender fit the bill. Cord would be wowed. Then, one squirt of her favorite perfume, and she stood back to admire the damage as well as she could with one hobbled ankle and a time frame shorter than a high-speed raindrop filmed as it fell, splattering all over a windshield.

She felt about to splatter over a windshield. But two people now knew the truth, and she had someone at her back she could call for an emergency survival rescue. At least she hoped Peggy was now on her side.

When she opened the door, there was Cord, not sitting in his truck, but waiting on the step. He held out his arm to take hers, and she was relieved. She might have had to ask for it, and she didn't want to make out that she needed him. She preferred for him to think she was just being polite by accepting.

It was better that way.

"I thought I knew beautiful, then you walked out the door." He said it looking straight ahead.

"Ha," she replied. "Let's get down and get your eyes checked." Secretly, his comment pleased her immensely. He sounded sincere, and while he hadn't exactly said she was beautiful, it was very close. She hadn't heard that from someone who meant it in a long time.

"I'm an eagle, and I sighted the best thing in the landscape."

She yanked his arm. "What does that mean?" But she laughed, too. Just like always, he drew her in with his charm. Away from him, she was safe. In his presence? No one was safe in the presence of Tres Juan.

"If only you could see through my eyes, my little senorita, you would know the most beautiful thing in the world is at my side."

"I know a charmer when I hear one. I'm coated with lead. You're not getting through that easily."

Yet, despite her words, she knew he'd made a big dent. She refused to check her plating too closely. He might have pierced it, and she didn't want to admit to that.

She did notice Cord smiling, and in that moment, she

suspected he'd gotten just what he wanted. And she couldn't even hate him for it, because, as much as she hated to admit it, the tiniest part of her wanted it, too.

— 11 —

"WELL, THAT'S ENOUGH of waiting." Cord stood abruptly, stepping across the waiting room to lean against the counter. "Ma'am, when do you think the results will come in?"

"It will be a moment, sir. We'll call you when the X-rays are ready." The receptionist smiled, but she held her pen poised, a signal that she had clearly been interrupted.

It hadn't information that Cord needed. It was space from Jane. To sit next to her was to be a rocket attached to a jet airplane, buffeted constantly by unseen winds and the forces of nature.

"Thank you. Should I just wait over there?" He nodded his head towards the seat he'd just left.

"Probably. There's free coffee down the hall in the cafeteria. Donuts, too, if there are any left. By this time, no promises." She smiled pleasantly, but it was clear he was being dismissed.

"Thank you." He turned away, catching Jane flipping disinterestedly through a magazine. She was beautiful, just as much so as he'd thought her in high school. What a fool he was! Still, water under the bridge and so on. What had been done couldn't be undone. He could only go on from here.

"Coffee?" He walked as close as he dared.

"Only if you make it black. No sugar needed." She didn't look up.

"Ouch." He remembered Peggy's remark in the restaurant. With sugar, to sweeten Jane's black mood.

"Why ouch?" Jane looked up, with just the hint of a smile on her lips. She set the magazine aside.

"Nothing. It's just that, yesterday . . ." He ran his fingers through his hair, leaving one spot mussed, the ends sticking out awkwardly. Then he hit it again, the hair lying flat the second time. "Well, black? Really?"

He wasn't sure he wanted to get into yesterday. Not and mess up what they had right then. After all, Jane was here, and he was here, and they were in the same room, even if it was the hospital for an injury she had received at his ranch.

Still. Here. Them. Together.

"Black, really. Sometimes we need to get rid of the sugar coating and deal with the real issues, don't you think?"

Oh, my, he thought. "Sugar coating?" He really should go for the coffee and let this fade away into, perhaps, next year.

"Jane Waggoner?"

"Here." Jane held out her hand. "That's for us. Help me stand."

"Guess the coffee'll have to wait. After, maybe." Cord reached for her hand. It was warm and a little moist. Nervousness about the results of the X-ray, he figured.

"Maybe." She walked gingerly. "It's called follow-through."

"Follow-through?" A nurse was just in front of them, waiting. "What does that mean?"

"Keeping promises. Do you promise coffee, or only if

it's convenient?"

"What?" He had no idea what that meant. It had been just coffee, and just to fill the time. Or, at least, to give him space to think clearly.

"Think, Cord, think." Jane stopped and tapped him on the forehead with her knuckles. "What have our lives been about? Yours and mine?"

He did notice her eyes were red, but then the nurse was there, and they were invited into a small consulting room.

"A bad sprain, Mrs. um, Rivera?" The unfamiliar doctor looked at a chart. "Ah, Mr. Rivera. I'm Dr. Perkins."

Jane laughed and coughed, covering her mouth with her hand. "Not Mrs. Rivera."

"No? My apologies. The notation is that Mr. Rivera made the appointment and is paying the bill." The doctor shrugged.

"Mrs. Waggoner is working for me. She was injured on the job." Cord felt himself warm. He held out his hand. "Cord Rivera. This is Jane Waggoner. It's nice to meet you, Dr. Perkins."

"Ah, I see. Waggoner." He marked on the chart, scratching something out and writing a note. "Let me pull up your X-rays on the screen." The doctor turned to a computer on a side table.

"So, I'm an employee? Do all your employees get coffee and an X-ray?" Jane whispered the words to Cord.

"Do you still want the coffee?" Cord sank lower in his chair. Employee? Why couldn't he have said friend? "With just a little sugar?"

"Now, what does that mean?"

The doctor interrupted. "Ah, now, here we see the damage." He went on to explain that it was no more than a bad sprain, but a bone density test might be advisable to guard against the possibilities of early-onset osteoporosis. "Elevation. That's the key. Keep the leg elevated and put heat and ice on it for a few days. It should heal just fine."

On the way out, Jane paused on the steps, and she touched Cord's arm.

"Yes?" He had his key in his hand and was just slipping his sunglasses on his face.

"My coffee?"

"Oh, I forgot." She was right. He wasn't dependable. Still, he could fix that. "There's Grubstake. I can get you a coffee there."

She laughed. "Not Grubstake. Let's try IHOP. It's easier to get in and out." She offered her arm again. "Oh, and thank you in there."

"For?" Just the feel of her arm energized him. "I didn't do anything except forget your coffee."

"You met the doctor with me. I appreciate that."

"Thank you, but what else would I have done? Sat and read a magazine?"

"Some people would." She brushed her hair from her face, only to have the wind catch it and blow it back over her chin.

"Fools. Only a fool would do that."

"Bill did." She looked away.

Cord didn't think she'd meant for him to hear, but he had. He wondered if that was a positive comparison or not. He glanced at his watch. "11:55. Do you think IHOP can serve lunch with that coffee?"

"Um . . ." She looked frightened; wary, as if lunch might be a dangerous assignation.

"No lunch?" Was that indecision he heard? He watched her face, seeing emotions flickering across its surface. "What is it, Jane?"

She brightened. "Why, thank you, Tarzan. I think that would be lovely. What restaurant did you have in mind?" She ended with her voice almost in a whisper, as if she'd made the effort to be bright and cheerful, but it had been difficult.

If only he could tell her everything had been a mistake with Shelly, and if only she would believe him. More importantly, he could tell her about Veronica, his daughter. He wanted to set the record straight.

However, the way he felt at this moment, he just wanted Jane. The ache had never gone away, no matter what he'd done over the past forty years.

He knew that's why he'd been so successful in his job. The ache had driven him to fill up his life with something, and the oil fields had allowed him to do that. The work was hard, the hours long, and he hadn't had to think much of the time. It was easier to fall into bed exhausted and numb than to think about how he wished life had been.

Nevertheless, it was his fault, and he had owned up to that. Now, he had a chance to make things right with Jane. That was what he wanted most. He wanted her to trust him again, and then maybe, just maybe she would love him again, too.

He was determined to find a way, and get through to her, he would.

— 12 —

"DAIRY QUEEN! I THOUGHT I said IHOP." Jane laughed. She hadn't been here in twenty years, and it hadn't changed in forty, except perhaps the fresh paint and the newer, brighter marquee. "Cord, I had no idea this place was still in business."

"And how long did you say you've been back?" He chuckled as he turned into the lot. "Don't mind me. I'm not surprised you didn't know. It just reopened last month."

"No. It was closed? Why?" She knew she'd been in a fog since Bill's death, but to not know this? True, she didn't do the fast food thing much, not watching her waist-line, but to have missed this entirely?

"It's a new building. See that empty lot across the street? That's where it used to be."

"Oh, get out of here." Jane found she was enjoying Cord's company, and she felt good for a change, like life was coming up before her, a brilliant sunrise in her soul. "This is the place I remember, except for that high-tech sign running the length of the building. Look at that! They still have banana splits, and they're on sale today. What I wouldn't give to be seventeen again!"

"That empty lot is what you remember. Peggy filled me in. There was an uproar about the place being a local landmark, but the new highway in the works preempted that, so they assuaged the naysayers with this retro building. It's all new and modern inside, with flush toilets and everything."

"I guess I should get out more." She felt an unwelcome tug on her heart, a reconnection with all those happy moments when she and Cord were really in love, she supposed. "Too bad all this got away from us."

"Did it?" The truck was still running, and Cord reached to the dash to cut the engine. "It's here. We're here. We can do this over again."

"That's a nice dream." A very nice dream, but one that had evaporated in fog and mist, burned away by the brutal sun of reality. This was just lunch. Coffee and perhaps a bite to eat. No more. It didn't have to be fog and mist, a reconstructed dream. It only had to be lunch. It might even be fun. "It's crowded."

"You'll be surprised. It's bigger on the inside than it looks from here." He reached for the door. "Ready?"

She looked at him. Was that anticipation in his voice? His inflection was so familiar, a thing he'd done all those years ago when they went somewhere. Like he was excited to show her off, like he was proud of her, and he wanted the world to know. She missed that. She'd enjoyed it then, she'd lost it with Bill, and it felt good.

It was the abandonment that hadn't been so wonderful, and she couldn't risk that again. Not even for this. However, she could enjoy it for this one day. Then, she could climb back in her shell and be morose and grumpy about life mistreating her with Bill's death and, she grudgingly admitted, losing Cord all those years ago.

"What?" Cord still had his hand on the door.

She realized she'd been looking at him but hadn't answered. "Nothing. Just . . ." It was, too, something, but that was old water, and she wasn't sure the bridge was even still there.

"Look at that." He pointed. "That cannot be . . . but it is. That's Eddy Burns." He laughed. "And he's coming this way. He's still got those big teeth. Remember, Jane? Rodeo team? We nicknamed him after that horse from TV."

"Horse? What TV?" She searched for the memory. "From when we were kids?"

"You know. That show with the talking horse."

Jane remembered, and she felt the giggles well up in her. "Oh, *that* TV show. Mr. Ed, the talking horse TV show."

"I think he's coming to talk to us." Cord grinned, reaching and placing a hand conspiratorially on hers. "Should I roll down the window or speed away, spinning my tires?"

"You cannot speed away, not if he's coming to see us." She didn't even notice the hand. It was as natural as being here with Cord in this truck. Instead, a picture of Eddy from school flashed into her head. He'd been skinny, and when he smiled, his teeth were the only thing you noticed. It would be hard not to call him Mr. Ed. It had been mean, but everyone had done it behind his back.

Cord put his finger on the window control. "No funny business, now." He looked at her and grinned.

"We can't laugh at him, Cord."

"That might not be feasible." Cord's eyes twinkled. "Here goes." He hit the window control, and it slipped soundlessly into the door. "Eddy." He reached his hand through the window.

"I thought that was you, here in this fancy truck. And there, Jane? Jane Waggoner? Fancy seeing you two together, and here." He glanced at the restaurant. "Just like old times, huh? Tarzan and Jane-bug. Y'all coming in?"

Jane tried to cover her mouth, but Eddy's teeth were

all she could see. He carried more weight now, and walking over, he'd looked fine. As soon as he started to talk, it was high school all over, and she couldn't control herself. Laughter poured from her.

Cord looked at her, and he began to laugh, covering his eyes with his hand.

"What's so funny, Jane? You and Tarzan have some inside joke you want to share with me?"

"Nothing, nothing at all. We were just thinking about the good old days, that's all." Jane tried to speak without her voice bursting into a fit of giggles, but it was hard, and she knew she wasn't being successful. That brought on another set of giggles.

"Well, Tarzan, I haven't seen you around here in a while. Where you been keeping yourself?" Eddy's teeth continued to flash, causing a new round of laughter from inside the truck.

"Been busy, but now that retirement's looming, I thought I might move back to the hacienda. I'm having some renovation done, and Jane's helping me with the design work."

"That's right." Eddy's teeth flashed, his grin exposing white against his tanned skin. "The reunion. It's out there, isn't it? I'd wondered about that, you being gone and the place empty so many years. I noticed some big trucks out your way. You thinking of drilling?"

Jane watched the men talking, but it was the scar on Cord's cheek that had her attention. It was her fault, and the memory came back sharp and clear. Barbed wire. It was because of that fence he'd been repairing. She'd been at the ranch for the day, and his mother had asked her to carry the hands' lunch to them in the ranch's old Jeep. When he saw it was her getting out, he raised his hand to wave, the wire cutters held high, and a coil filled with razor sharp barbs had leaped to his face, leaving a bloody cut six inches long.

It was still visible after all these years, just barely,

when he smiled, a part of her life that he carried with him every day. She wondered if he remembered that day, and when he saw it in the mirror, if it reminded him of her. She shook her head, taking a deep breath.

"Eddy?" She had to get out of this truck. She was sinking way too far into old memories that were entirely too, too, *something*. Enticing, if no other word fit.

"Yes?" He smiled at her, those big teeth coming through loud and clear.

"Cord and I were headed inside. What about you?"

"Yeah, Eddy. You had lunch? Jane and I, we were—"

"I couldn't intrude. You, too, now that you're back together—"

"No, Eddy. We're not back together." Jane interrupted, grabbing her door. "This is a working relationship, only." She released the latch, and she pushed the door wide. "Cord, I need help getting down, please. The doctor said not to put any pressure on this, and this truck is very tall."

She looked back just in time to see Eddy wink.

"Sure. Professional. Whatever you say, Jane-bug. If y'all are heading inside, I might sit with you, though, if you don't mind, since this is just a *professional* relationship." He grinned, as if he didn't believe it.

Cord's phone went off, and he pulled it from his pocket. "Excuse me, Eddy. I need to take this. Just one minute, Jane." He pushed the door open and stepped to the back of the truck.

"How long you guys been back together?" Eddy had one arm on the door of the truck, and he leaned inside. "You and Tarzan back there." He continued to grin.

"Two days ago, Eddy. I sprained my ankle, and Cord drove me to the hospital, that's all. But we'll catch up inside. I want to know everything that you've been up to since your rodeo team days."

"You remember that?" He laughed and slapped his leg. "Doesn't anyone remember that I was also on the Calculus Team? We went to state, but no one remembers that. Funny." He turned as Cord walked up to him.

"That was Veronica."

"Veronica?" Eddy looked puzzled.

"My daughter. She thinks the hacienda should be finished, all because I've been working on it for a couple of weeks. She doesn't know my skill level at carpentry. I didn't know my skill level." He laughed. "Nonexistent. However, the grandkids are begging to come out. They've never seen the ranch.

"I told her it would be at least another two, possibly three weeks before I would even want them anywhere near. Too dangerous with exposed wires and nails everywhere. We are going to have exposed wires and nails everywhere, right Jane?" He looked at her with a grin.

"If you'll help me out of this truck and into that shiny new DQ that I didn't know existed. Maybe I'll get to it, if I can ever get my coffee. You did ask them to wait?"

She didn't need his daughter around, not with the state she was in. It was that grin. It was melting her heart once again, and she didn't want it to. Not and leave her in the cold like before.

"Veronica understands, but since they're out of school for a few days, she was looking for something to do. She had her hopes up, but I suggested she rein in the team for another couple weeks."

"Coffee's sounding pretty good. Hey, guys, with seeing you again, I'm paying. Lunch is on me. Come on in. Cord, Jane?" Eddy waved them his direction and headed inside.

"Be right there." Cord leaned into the truck. "She really wants me to babysit. Veronica and Josh would probably enjoy the quiet without the boys. I told her as soon as the house is habitable, I'll have them down for a week. I think you'd like them, Jane. They're good boys, even if they are a little high spirited."

"I've got a couple just like that. Now, if you want to

help someone out, that might be me, and to do that, I need you on this side of the truck. Come on, Tarzan. Help Jane out."

She laughed, using Eddy's monikers, but the memories those names brought back were bright, warm, and entirely too real. It was Eddy, she guessed, bridging the connection to all those years ago. It wasn't going to work, though. Cord wasn't going to use his daughter and his grandchildren to woo her back into his life. Old memories were fun, but it was the reality of life that counted. Six weeks, Cord. Six weeks, and she was gone, just as he'd been gone from her life all those years ago. She'd be gone, and she'd never look back. He'd see what it was like.

She wouldn't be let down by Juan Cordello Rivera III ever again.

— 13 —

JANE PULLED INTO THE drive winding up to Cord's home, pleased that at least the three days she'd been stranded at home hadn't been wasted. It felt good to be back on the job. With a six-week timetable to get the remodel completed, not even three days could be allowed to slip by without whip and megaphone driving the progress forward.

Three days of barbeque and DQ breakfast sandwiches hadn't helped, either, not her waistline, anyway. And she hadn't been able to convince Cord that a boiled egg and toast would feed her just fine.

Still, it was better than Bill. When she'd broken her arm at the skating rink, he'd hired a maid service, rather than lift a finger to help her out. The maid? Appreciated. She'd rather have had Bill's help, though.

With Cord? While the attention was nice, the feelings that ratcheted up anytime he came over left her jittery and unable to calm down afterward. Not exactly appropriate feelings for a recent widow.

Even Peggy's visits hadn't helped. She kept prodding

her to be nicer to Cord. Goodness! If she were any nicer, she'd have to invite him to move in!

Billy had been her lifesaver. He'd called the second night while Cord was there, unaware of her injury, and he'd demanded to know all about the new job and the extent of her injury. His voice had set her straight. It had reminded her of Bill, and that had cleared the emotional overtones from the room.

Thank God for Billy.

"Jerry!" She rolled her window down and yelled to her foreman, Jerry Vanagas. "Good morning!" She pulled her Lexus next to where he stood with a set of plans unrolled on the hood of his truck and pushed the door open.

"Good morning, Mrs. Waggoner. We have made good progress, even without you here driving us forward." He spoke formally, with each word carefully enunciated, although the two knew each other well. It was his early background steeped in Mexican culture that was the cause, but his words were said with a smile.

"That's why you're my best." She pulled herself out of the car, using the door to balance. "I see the plans came through. When did you get them?"

"Two days ago. The walls, they were already torn out, and I had begun to worry. Then, this showed up, and there was no more problem. All will be beautiful." He smiled, his teeth white against his brown complexion. "And you, you are walking, but not well."

"Oh, I'm walking pretty well, Jerry. Just not fast. You don't worry about me. You worry about putting all those walls back right where those plans say." The plans weren't detailed, and they would be useless for anyone who wasn't Jerry. But they'd worked together on too many projects, and when she said bathroom, he knew where she would want plugs, drains, and lights, and she never had to worry.

Choosing the correct tiles and colors? There she had to worry, but that's why she got the big bucks, because she took big risks in pleasing her high-profile clients.

The house was a beehive of activity. The damaged roof tiles Cord had been working on were on the ground, and new, undamaged ones were in their place. A team was still working on one corner, applying a new layer of stucco. In a few days, it would be ready for paint, something rich and sandy to complement the dark wood trim.

"Ah, Jane!"

A voice called to her, and at first her heart raced, as she turned looking for Cord. She was disappointed. No, she told herself, *surprised* to see it was Lester Fortinbras, her trim man. The entire interior needed done, and several places outside had early rot. But that's why she had him on board, to get that ripped out and rebuilt.

"Les! Give me a minute. I'm a slow, old woman today. You heard about my ankle."

"I can see it." He nodded. It was wrapped nearly to her knee. "Several years back, my wife did the same thing. She was out of commission for a month. Surprising, you being out here today." He chuckled. "Tells me that Margie maybe could have been back to cooking long before she did."

"Don't start that, Les. You leave Margie alone. This still hurts, and a lot, too. How'd the porch columns come along? And the door? Did we have to replace the whole thing?"

"The columns," he started, slapping the closest one. They were mammoth-size twisted wood columns imported a century before from Mexico. "Three were pretty good, with only a little rot at the bottom. That one?" He pointed to the last of the four. "Eaten up with critters. Had to rip it out." He paused grinning.

"And?" It looked the same as the others. There was no way he could have gotten one shipped in this quickly, not and get it installed, too. It even had weathering that matched the ones that were original. "What did you do, Les? Steal one from a house in Westover?" She referred to the priciest, old money residential subdivision in the city of Fort Worth.

"You know the guesthouse." His eyes twinkled.

"I know the guesthouse. Just tell me, Les. Five and a half weeks, and this must be finished. What about the guesthouse?"

"Those two half-relief columns? Remember those?" He grinned.

"You . . ." She stepped onto the porch and walked slowly that way, wishing she could go faster. If he did what she thought he did, it was brilliant. But what did that leave her on the guesthouse? "Don't tell me you patched this together from those."

"Okay, I won't, but where else was I to get one of these? They don't even make artisans that can carve these, at least not in Texas. Can you find the seam?" He was clearly very proud of his handiwork.

"You think that these might have once been . . ." She reached and traced the graining. "Here. This is the seam, right?" She turned to him and saw him nod, smiling broadly. "No. We couldn't be that lucky. You mean these were originally one column, and it was cut in half for the guesthouse? We couldn't be that lucky."

"Not lucky. You always say it, and you've about got me convinced. God watched over us—"

As Les said those words, she caught movement across the yard, and she glanced up to see Cord. He was carrying lumber, the boards balanced on his shoulder, clearly unaware she was there. His tee shirt was dirty and stained with sweat, but he was laughing at something the men with him had said. She wished she believed God had been watching over her forty years ago. Right now she wasn't so sure.

"—because there I was, out back moaning about how disappointed you'd be, and there these were. I knew, I don't know how, that these had to be a match, and being under the portico, they were pristine. We pulled them down, and mated together, the graining told the tale. Brother and sister reunited—"

Brother and sister reunited. It was the reunited part that caught Jane's attention, seeing Cord, and thinking about the times they'd had here on the ranch. She was heartsick, because he was there, and she was here, and that's all it was. That's all it could ever be. The past never came back, no matter how many times one called to it.

"Inside, Les." She turned from the column, needing an immediate diversion. "What's been done in there?"

"Oh, right. Lots, but only in some of the rooms. We're working on the dining room right now. That tin? We've only lost two panels, so far, and I think I've got someone lined up who can replicate them exactly. What do you think of that?"

She started to say he was wonderful, but another voice interrupted her.

"Well, what do you think? I suppose you *can* teach an old dog a new trick." Cord beamed, clearly proud of the massive efforts that had been made on the old hacienda.

That threw her off kilter. She thought he was still on the other side of the yard. Yet, here he was, stained and laughing and obviously excited about being back at the old place.

She didn't dare think it might have anything to do with talking to her.

She spoke more firmly than she might have otherwise, keeping a firm grip on the tremor she heard in her voice. "It's beginning to really take shape on the outside. Now, you've got to concentrate on the inside and getting the guesthouse rebuilt. You seem to be missing some trim."

He laughed. "You mean the columns. Yeah. I saw those, and I told Les to rip them off. I'd always thought they came from one piece. He didn't believe me, but I insisted, and I was right. Pretty amazing, huh?" He grinned.

"Les?" She turned. "You knew, and you didn't know how?"

He dropped his head and grinned. "I didn't say *how* I knew."

"Oh, did I say something I shouldn't? My apologies, Les." Cord didn't look repentant at all. "Oh, Jane, I think I'm mistaken. I remember how it happened, now. Why, there were Les and me, chewing the fat out back—only after a hard day's work, of course—and he said to me, I am in need of a replacement column, and I think these might do the trick. From there, it was the hand of God directing Les' every motion, from pulling those suckers down to gluing them back together again."

Les was laughing by then. "Not exactly, but I'll take it."

Jane felt herself caught up in Cord's charming rendition, laughing at his hokey phraseology, and enjoying the camaraderie between the two men, and before she caught herself, she thought, *I really should marry you, Cord Rivera. I would love to spend the rest of my life with you.*

She turned away, feeling sudden heat fill her face. The laughter was gone, and she felt tears threatening to overwhelm her. No. This was too much. She didn't want to marry Cord. He'd betrayed her, and another man had come along to rescue her from the detritus of her abandonment.

Then she turned back to Cord, his story still on, bantering with Les about the details involved. She pretended she was crying with laughter, but it was guilt. She felt she was betraying the man she was married to for nearly forty years. The questions of what if, would I, and should I hunkered on her shoulders, weighing her down. She pressed them back, but they only surged into her consciousness once more.

Did I really marry Bill only so that little Billy would have a real family? Would I have married him if he hadn't had that poor, wide-eyed little boy, so cute, so darling, and so much like the child she could no longer hold?

Had she been that empty? That little boy had loved her unconditionally, and in her loss, she had needed that. His father? At least he had given her free reign with his son, even if he hadn't been the father he could have been.

The husband, either, but he was dead now, and she wouldn't think of him that way. It was dishonest and mean, dirty, even, to think ill of the dead.

It was hard not to make the comparison, though, with Cord standing feet from her, roughed up and dirty, charming one of her workmen, and, she had to admit, charming her.

Oh! This was so much easier when she didn't have to spend time with him. Her grudges were so much easier to carry around when he wasn't nearby to work his way into her heart.

Then, unbidden, as if she needed to be reminded, the cover of *13 Weeks with Jesus* popped into her head. It showed a grand piano in front of a stained-glass window. There was an Oriental rug on the floor. It was beautiful. It was the words that went along with the image that yanked at her heart.

Forgive. Forget. Don't be angry. Love.

"I can't, Jesus," she whispered, so softly she was sure no one heard. "I can't do all that, not after forty years." She looked at Cord, laughing, and she wanted to. God help her, in that moment, she wanted to. Yet, she had lost too much, given up something very precious all those years ago, and how could she ever get that back? She couldn't forgive, could she? Not this.

The ache made her burn inside with indecision.

Forgive. Forget. Don't be angry. Love.

The words wouldn't go away, and Jane didn't know how she could do five and a half more weeks. She couldn't do it. Not at all.

— 14 —

"JANE? ARE YOU BUSY?" The words filtered through the dusty air.

Jane lifted the short board from the plans in front of her, letting the sheaf of papers snap into a tightly rolled tube. She glanced around, relieved at having a break in the day. The house was coming along, with floors torn up and patched, and new plaster on many of the interior walls.

The countertops had been the only sticking point. Cord had left everything else up to her judgment except that. She had argued with him that a lighter color would contrast better with the dark wood in the rest of the room, and she'd had to bring in multiple samples before he'd conceded her expertise on the topic.

She was about to decide she'd read something more into his intentions than she should. Maybe she'd wanted something more. However, he'd been nothing if not proper and well-mannered, even preoccupied at times. He'd kept out of her hair, mostly, although the emails, texts, and phone calls sometimes ate up minutes a day—minutes she didn't have if she was to finish in only three weeks.

"In here, Cord." She turned, remembering the misstep she had made here all those weeks ago, and how it'd left her ankle sore for two weeks. That weak spot in the threshold was the first thing she'd had repaired.

"In here, you little varmints." Cord leaned into the room, smiling. "I brought you a little company." He disappeared again, but the sound of running feet and laughter echoed in the empty rooms.

"Company?" Jane took a deep breath. *Little* company she didn't need. Billy provided her plenty of that when she kept the babies, although she knew they weren't babies any longer. They just acted like it.

A woman Jane didn't recognize appeared in the doorway, and she smiled, reaching out to catch a small boy by the hand just as he darted by. She had strawberry blonde hair, and a spattering of freckles tickled her nose. The boy was equally light.

Then Cord stepped into view, holding another boy about the same as the first under his arm. The boy squirmed, but he was laughing at the same time.

"I told you they were restless little critters." Cord grinned. "This one's J-4, and that's one's Gabe."

"I'm Gabe," the one under his arm squealed.

"Oh, you are?" Cord laughed. "I know what Gabe sounds like. Let's see if you sound like him." He dug his fingers into the boy's side, grinning at Jane when he squirmed and howled in mock pain.

"Ow, ow! I'm Gabe! Promise, Granddaddy!"

"I guess you are." Cord dropped him unceremoniously. "Promise, Jane, I can't tell the difference unless they howl. Gabe howls louder."

"Daddy, stop it. Introduce me to your designer." The woman turned to Jane. "This is amazing, you know. I remember the place, but it's been twenty-five or thirty years. I don't remember it like this."

"I've changed it a bit." Jane looked from father to daughter, finding no resemblance at all. "You're, um, Veronica, right?"

"Daddy! What do you two talk about? I at least thought you would have shown her my picture." Just then, J-4 tore lose, chasing after his brother. "I'm sorry. I'll be right back. They'll break something if I don't keep them corralled." She disappeared the direction of the boys.

"Told you." Cord grinned.

"That's Veronica?"

"None other. And my grandbabies. Chip off somebody's block, tell you that. I never was so wild as a kid. At least I tell people that." He'd walked up beside her, and he unrolled the papers she'd had out. "Kitchen? Is that granite here, yet? I want to see a big slice."

"All in. Do you want to wait on your daughter?"

"Veronica?" He yelled her name. "We're headed into the kitchen."

"That's how you do it?" Jane laughed. "You just yell?"

He winked. "Works. With those kids, no telling where I'd find her. Come on. Let's get out of here while we have the chance. The little tornados might be back any time."

Despite herself, Jane felt lighter, as if she wanted to run into the kitchen with Cord and hide. She had to put the brakes on that impulse, but it somehow *felt* right, even if she knew it was no good.

She and Cord were no good. That'd proven itself forty years ago. However, for the moment, caught up in his escape, she followed him to the kitchen.

"Hey, look at this." The granite, honey gold, stretched for what seemed acres. "I like this." He ran a hand over the surface, lifting it to see his palm coated with dust.

"Everything's dusty in here and will be until we're finished. It's coming along, though."

"So, what's with the kitchen plans? This looks about done to me." He reached up and grabbed a dangling light fixture, one designed to be recessed into the ceiling. " 'Cept this, of course." He smiled.

"I'm reworking the cabinets under the sink. I decided to upgrade to a tankless water heater, and the model I've chosen doesn't want to fit. It will, though." She leaned against the cabinet, crossing her arms across her chest and her legs at the ankles. "I'm good at this. I might even get it finished by the reunion."

"You might, huh?"

Several men lumbered in through the door, carrying a large wood beam. They were speaking rapidly in Spanish and kicking things out of the way.

"Pedro! Sammy! The boss is here!" Jane waved at them.

"Ah, Mr. Rivera." The men set their beam down on two sawhorses, and wiping their hands on their pants, they stepped forward to shake. "Our hands, they are not freshly washed, but please shake with us. We are pleased to meet the owner of such a fine establishment. This will make you and Mrs. Waggoner a good home."

Only one of the men spoke, but the second murmured, "Si, senor. Verdaderamente excelente!"

Jane felt her face go hot. "No, no, Sammy. Not ours. It belongs only to Mr. Rivera."

"Ah! Only yours?" He pointed to Cord. "Such a big home for one man. So very sad. Perhaps someday?" He motioned between them with his hand. "Algún día?" He had a hopeful look on his face.

Jane knew enough Spanish to understand his question. "No, not algún día." She couldn't even look at Cord. She did hear Sammy turn to Pedro and speak in rapid-fire Spanish. She only caught a few of the words, but it was clear he was explaining that the happy marriage was not to take place after all.

"Happy marriage?"

She looked at Cord to see him smiling broadly. Oh, God, what was this going to turn into? She'd forgotten he was fluent in Spanish. He must think she'd been telling the workers they were getting married. All she'd said was that

Mr. Rivera *might* get married someday, and the house had to have at least a bit of a woman's touch.

This was going to go downhill quickly!

"I never said that, Cord." She turned to glare at Pedro and Sammie, but Pedro had such a sad look on his face that she almost wanted to give him a hug and tell him it would be all right.

Instead, Pedro turned around and walked back out the door, muttering, "Muy triste."

"Pedro is sad. Very sad." Sammy held his hands up, palms out, as if in apology. "We will go be busy. You have much to say to one another, I am sure." But he winked as he backed away.

"Jane?" Cord turned to her. "What was that about?"

"I have no idea. None. Trust me." She laughed, and couldn't believe she did. A nervous reaction, she figured. "I'm glad your daughter wasn't in here to hear that. My goodness, what would she think?"

"About what?" Veronica came struggling through the door, pulling one boy by the arm, and with the second hiked up on her waist. "Here, Dad, this one's yours." She leaned the one on her hip to Cord, letting go as soon as her dad had his hands on him. "Now, you, buster, you've kicked me the last time. Do you want me to lock you in the car?"

"She wouldn't really," Cord mouthed at Jane. "It works, though." Indeed the boy quieted, although he had a bit of a sulk on his face.

"So, which one are you?" Jane stepped to the boy, glad to have something to do besides discuss her workmen's social gaffes. "Is it Gabe, or are you," and she looked up at Veronica, "C-4?"

"I'm J-4," the boy said, then he buried his head against his mother."

"So, I've got Gabe again." Cord looked at the boy in his arms. "I might need to test the siren and make sure."

"No, Granddaddy," the boy yelled, throwing his arms

around Cord's neck. "Don't, please!"

"Just a little?" He touched the boy's side with one finger.

"It's really me," Gabe squealed, thrashing his legs.

"Okay. Now that I'm sure. Although, if I make the other one squeal, then I'll know for certain."

The boy at Veronica's side grabbed his mother, hiding behind her. "No, Granddaddy. Please, Mommy?"

"Granddaddy, don't tease like that." Veronica patted J-4's head. "They're just kids."

"Nitro-glycerin on two legs, but you're right, as usual. I'll back off."

"Thank you, Daddy." She reached up and gave him a kiss on the cheek, then she turned to Jane. "Daddy's told me all about you, despite the fact he hasn't said a thing about me. Some daddy, huh?" But she laughed. "I feel I know you already."

"He did talk about you some, but I expected . . . well, maybe a bit more of your father's looks. You must take after your mother." It had been forty years, but Jane couldn't seem to recall Shelly with strawberry blonde hair. Oh, well. Shelly hadn't been one of her close friends, and who knew where the genes were hiding for that fair skin. Not with Cord, unless through his mother. She was Irish, after all.

"Jane, are you there?"

She looked at Cord. "I'm sorry. I was thinking of your mother. Didn't she have red hair?"

"Don't worry about it." He winked. "You'll never figure it out. Now, though, I want to show Veronica the house. Want to tag along?"

"Three weeks is all he's given me to finish." Jane reached to touch Veronica gently on the arm. She laughed. "If I get off track even one minute, it'll never get done, and your father will never forgive me."

"Oh, he'll forgive you, all right. You're the best thing that's happened to Daddy since I can remember. You're all he talks about. Thank you."

That took Jane aback. It sounded like Veronica expected her and Cord to be more than just business partners. Surely not! However, it was what Veronica said as she and her father stepped into the other room that really got Jane's goat.

"Do you think she suspects anything?"

"Shush! I haven't said a word."

"What word, Granddaddy?"

That was J-4, and Cord reached down and wrapped him in his free arm, tossing him over his shoulder.

"My word, you little wildebeest. And I say you're all shook up!" As they disappeared, Cord rocked him back and forth, leaving the boy howling with laughter.

Suspects what? Jane frowned. Oh, well, she had a house to finish, and she hadn't been teasing with Veronica. She didn't have an hour to spare. She turned to her rolled paper and frowned at the space under the sink that didn't quite want to accommodate the tankless water heater that Jane was determined to fit there.

And it would go, if she had to take a Sawzall to it herself.

— 15 —

JANE PULLED UP TO the jobsite, her engine running, and the lights cutting across the new concrete drive. There were bushes and shrubs carefully organized off to the side. She knew it was carefully, because she'd been the one to stand there and point out where the nursery was to place them, the first to go in on the outside; the last to be installed at the back.

All those bushes presented a problem, too. They blocked the drive, or at least the part that took her directly to the guesthouse. She would be forced to divert through the main residence.

She clicked her cheek when she saw a light go on in the main house. She watched the window—there were no curtains or blinds in yet—to see who it was. Cord, possibly, or his daughter or grandchildren, at an outside chance. She shook her head. He wanted this completed in a week, then had decided to move in and slow everything down. If she'd known that, she'd have focused more energy on the guesthouse, rather than leaving it for last. He wouldn't have been in anyone's way there.

Still, the house was Cord's, and he did pull the strings, financial as well as otherwise. The ones on her heart? She didn't dare answer that question. Not after five weeks of working at his side. She might make another mistake, and she couldn't afford another four decades of living with the consequences.

Now he wanted her in the guesthouse. *You'll get so much more work done.* Right. Yet, there were her things in the back seat, her swatches and paint samples, as well as a small suitcase and an overnight bag.

Was she a fool, or was she a fool? Toss the coin up, and either way it fell, the odds were the same.

Well, the guesthouse didn't have to be complete for her. The windows were in, and mid-May, the air systems didn't matter much. That was on tap for this week, and she had a fan until then.

She didn't need a kitchen. Cord had offered his, sort of a test run to see if everything was in working order. It had made sense, in an off-kilter sort of way. She wasn't sure her back would appreciate the air bed in the trunk, but she'd last, she thought. A week? Who couldn't manage that?

The hard thing? She was growing very attached to this old house. She usually enjoyed her projects, even wondered if they were places she would enjoy living, but this? She had wanted this life all those years ago, and now here she was remaking it into whatever she wanted it to be. Even those feminine touches she'd wanted, the small things like the shell soap holders in the half bath. Her own special touches, ones that would hopefully be appreciated by the future woman of the house.

Whoever married Cord.

"Not me." She cleared her throat. "Cord Rivera, you keep to your side of the breezeway, and I'll keep to mine. Kitchen's neutral ground, and don't you forget it." She wouldn't have done this for any other person, and she was quite aware, she shouldn't be doing it for this one.

She killed the car, opening the door and pulling her things from the back. By the time she got to the house, she knew her ankle wasn't as well as she tried to convince herself. By the time she fumbled the front door open, Cord, stocking feet and pajamas, was there to greet her.

"Hey, moving in, I see." He grinned. "I've got coffee and toast in the kitchen."

"Not moving in," She growled. It sounded so salacious that way. She didn't need salacious. "The drive to the guesthouse is blocked with plantings. I've got to cut through. Here, take these." She handed him the cases. "I've got my bed in the car." She turned to head back outside.

"You can sleep in the guesthouse. That's why I offered it to you." Amusement filled the words.

"I intend to." She didn't turn, the connotations in his words working her emotions. "What else did you have in mind?"

"Your bed . . . in the car. I didn't mean, um, it was just a joke." He coughed, as if with embarrassment, or perhaps an off-hand apology. She couldn't tell which.

"Thank you at six-thirty in the morning. I like my jokes at ten. I'll be right back." She stepped outside, pulling the door tightly to. Her words had been sharp, but it was to cover her heart. It was swelled inside her, choking her mind, and keeping her from thinking straight.

And why had that man still been in his pajamas? He knew she was coming over about sunup, and the sun would be up in another half hour. What was she supposed to do, sit at home and wait for him to call? Oh, wait, she'd done that at eighteen. Only he never had, and then he had married someone else, never coming to see her or contact her in all those years.

Like he'd been too happy to care.

She was digging in her trunk, blinking the tears away, when she heard a voice at her side.

"Anything I can carry?"

Gracious, Cord, here I am sniveling into my trunk, and I don't even have a tissue. How could this morning go even further down the tube?

"This." She handed him the box containing the airbed without turning. "I have to set that up."

"This?" He held it under the trunk light. "You can't sleep on this. I'll—"

"You'll what?" She turned to him, drawing her sleeve across her face as if wiping away sweat. It was for her tears, though. "You invited me. You going to swing a hammock between two trees? That'd be a sight, me sleeping in the out-of-doors in my p.j.s. I do wear p.j.s, you know."

Cord laughed. "Whoa, missy. I don't even have a hammock, that is unless you ordered one in and it got delivered without me knowing it. I was thinking, I could take the guesthouse, and you could have my room. Just for the week. It'd all be honest and aboveboard." He leaned against the car, holding the bed in his arms like a baby.

"Don't you think you're doing that to me, Cord Rivera." She chuckled, but it wasn't in amusement. "I'm here to help you get done on time, but nothing else. Is that plain?"

"Jane." He set the box back in the trunk. "What have I done that you don't trust me? What? Have I kissed you or in any way compromised you, or even suggested it?"

"Now or then?" He had. Not this spring, but on a long-ago spring, very much so.

"Ouch. Again."

"Why again?" She felt her heart strings, and he was yanking them. Maybe this wasn't such a good idea.

"Five weeks ago, you said something similar. It hit home then, and it hits home now." He stopped, looking away.

"Okay, Cord Rivera. I have no idea what I said five weeks ago. You remember. What made it so important that something I said stuck with you?" She crossed her arms and leaned against the car, really wanting to hear this.

"Jane, you think you're not important to me, but you are. Forty years ago, our world fell apart, and I know who was to blame. I've beat myself up for decades. I can't do that anymore, and when you remind me, it's like a knife, hot, serrated, and buttered, slipping inside and taking my heart out all over again."

Jane couldn't talk, and she was glad the sun wasn't quite up. How could that man peel back forty years so easily, as if it were a blanket, and all those years were lying underneath, just waiting to come to life again? Her heart in her throat, she reached for the bed.

"Can't leave this. I'll need it tonight." She felt the huskiness in her voice, and she didn't want to be betrayed. She turned away and marched toward the house. "Shut the trunk. I'm finished in there."

He'd almost given her an apology. That's all she'd wanted, just for Cord to acknowledge the pain he'd put her through. She could almost love him for that.

Almost, but not yet. That water under the bridge hadn't quite made it back to her heart, yet.

"BILLY! IT'S NOT EVEN seven. How did you know I'd be up?" Jane looked out the window to see Cord heading toward the house.

"Mom! When are you not up before seven? Besides, Aunt Peggy said you were headed to work early, and you'd be out at the old Rivera place all week. The kids want to come out and see you. Jasmine, too. She knows she'll never get to see the infamous house, if she doesn't get an invite before you wrap things up. When it comes out in *D* magazine, she wants to tell people she was there in person with the designer." He chuckled.

"I'll ask, honey. Maybe the day of the reunion. How about then?" She turned at the sound of the door.

"What are you asking me?" Cord winked at her.

She covered the mouthpiece. "Who said I was asking

you anything?"

"You said you'd ask honey. That's me, right?" Cord grinned.

"Oh, shush!" She smiled, waving him away. "This is Billy, my son."

"Hey, Billy!" Cord called loudly enough to carry over the phone.

"Mom? Who's that?"

"The homeowner, son. He's out here with me."

"At seven in the morning?" He chuckled.

"Not all of us can get up at nine. Sorry. And we must start early if we're finishing by the weekend. I'll get with you later today. Bye, sweetie." She palmed the phone off as she slid it into her bag.

"So, what are you asking?" Cord still stood in the same place.

"My daughter-in-law, Jasmine, wants to see the house before I turn it over to you. Do you mind?"

"It's not finished, yet. Does she have a brilliant imagination?" He fought a smile. "Then, if she's pretty as you, she can stay the entire week, and she'll get to see it in its final form. You might even persuade her to help. Does she paint?"

"You fool." Jane laughed. "She's twenty-three years younger than me. Of course, she's prettier. Besides, she can't hold a brush, not unless it has makeup on it. At that? She's quite skilled." She pushed the bed's box aside with her foot. "Billy was saying this weekend. Maybe before the reunion. They'll have the kids, I'm afraid, but they can come early and be gone before it starts."

"They can come anytime. My grandkids will be here. Throw yours in, and it'll be like a bunch of little Cheetahs in here." Cord laughed, and his eyes lit up.

That made Jane giggle. "Little Cheetahs? Well, Tarzan, I don't think we're done here, yet. There are still a lot of loose ends to finish up. You'll have to wait a little while longer before you can swing through the trees with Cheetah."

"Thank you, Jane." Cord had a wide smile on his face.

"For what?" She was still trying to get her smile wiped away.

"For laughing with me. It was almost like old times. My house" —he motioned all around him— "is beautiful, but without you in it . . ." He stopped and looked at the ceiling, his eyes red.

"What, Cord?" She watched him expectantly.

He laughed, wiping his hands across his face, the tracks of his hands glistening. "I'd rather swing through the trees with Jane any day than with a silly monkey." He laughed again. "Well, that shows what a fool I am."

"Typical male, always ready to hang out with the girls when there's work to be done." Stupid comeback, but his words certainly caught her off guard. Unable to deal with any more, she grabbed her box and walked away, calling back to him over her shoulder, "I'll be in the laundry room and office if you need me."

Swing through the trees with Jane! However, his comment pleased her more than she intended to let on.

— 16 —

"ARRGH!" JANE RAN HER fingers through her hair. "May! In Texas!"

It was the humidity. It had rained three times in two days, and her hair had become a wild mess, uncontrollable and in her way. And she didn't have time to roll it and set it. Not and get this job finished.

Even that wouldn't bother her if everything wasn't going wrong. The air installer had brought the wrong compressor for the guesthouse, none of her hand-drawn sketches were matching deliveries, and oh! In the distance, more rain threatened, with black clouds hovering against the horizon. Of all days! The landscapers were due that afternoon to plant hundreds of shrubs. They had to go in by Saturday. It was the day of the reunion.

She looked up at the sun, then at the shimmering pool. At least that was working, even though she couldn't take time for a dip. It was tempting, though. Very tempting. If she had a suit . . .

"Jane! Come take a break."

She looked at the main house to see Cord hanging out

of the new French doors she'd had installed. *Sure, Cord. And it doesn't matter if the house is done or not.* Still, she waved and smiled. "Working! Sorry!"

"Hold on!" He disappeared. Through the glass, she could see him doing something in the kitchen. In moments, he stepped through the door holding two glasses.

"What's that?" *Duh! Obvious.*

"Your break. You won't come to it. It comes to you." He smiled that disarming, charming smile that got her in the stomach every time.

"It *is* hot. I'll give you that. Thanks." She reached for one of the glasses.

"No. Over here." He motioned with his head to the new chaise lounges that had come in that morning. "We have to try these out before it's too late to send them back. Sit with me." He placed the glasses on a small table centered between the chairs and adjusted the cushion on Jane's. He motioned and waited for her to sit before he fell back on his.

"This is good." She took a deep draw from one of the glasses. "The tree overhead is better." She laughed, and when she looked Cord's direction, he was smiling. "However, if I'm sitting here, I'm working."

"Jane. It's five minutes." He leaned his head back and closed his eyes. "Like this. You can do it."

"And not be finished on Saturday. We've got rain coming, or haven't you noticed?"

"I noticed, and I don't care. I've got what I want."

She looked at him sharply. There was a lot not done. He couldn't be so unobservant as that. "Tell me, then, if what I've accomplished pleases you so much, what do you like best about it?"

"You being here." His eyes were still closed, but he smiled when he said it.

"I should have expected that." It also felt good to hear him say it, but it wasn't what she wanted to hear. "About the remodel." She chuckled. Men, so single minded.

"These chairs." He shifted position. "Yes, definitely. These chairs."

"Not the granite? Or, how about that tankless water heater. I spent hours figuring that out."

"Soap holders."

"Soap holders? You're spending hundreds of thousands here, and the soap holders are what you like best?" She laughed out loud. "Describe them for me." She had to hear this.

"That big." He held up his hands, making a circle, his eyes still closed. "Scalloped, like a shell, and very feminine."

"So you *were* paying attention."

"Oh, trust me, Jane. I've been paying attention." He chuckled.

"Oh, I bet you have. Back to the house. What's not finished?" Had he even noticed? Well, her air in the guesthouse, but he had working air in the main house. He wouldn't know about hers.

"Us." He lifted his glass and took a sip of tea.

"Cord, get on track. I'm talking business. What have I not yet finished with the house?" He was actually being pretty funny. She let herself lean back into the chase's cushion. This was nice, the pool, the tree, the shade, and talking to someone she enjoyed being around. She did like Cord. It was her trust that had been frayed beyond repair. Well, beyond simple and easy repair. Anything could be repaired, if people worked at it enough.

"Landscaping. Even a blind skunk could see that."

"Blind skunk?"

"I was, you know." His eyes were still closed.

"A blind skunk?"

"Me. All those years ago. I was a blind skunk. Stinking stupid. Except I got Veronica. I'd do it all differently, except for Veronica."

"And J-4 and Gabe?" She felt her heart pounding. This wasn't business, not by a country mile.

"The tornadoes?" He grinned. "They're up for debate."

"What do you mean you would do it differently?" She took a deep breath to calm herself. She cringed as she heard him start to answer.

"C'mon, Jane. You know what I mean." He looked at her. "You and me. Can you tell me you wouldn't do our lives differently if you had the choice?"

She bit her bottom lip, afraid to speak. No, not afraid. Unable to speak. Would she, if it meant no Billy? She loved him, her only child, the one she'd treasured to replace the one she'd lost. Losing Cord had been the devastation of her life, but Billy had been her salvation.

"Jane? This is my last chance. I don't want you to leave this week without us at least talking. I mean really talking. The stuff that's important to us, that we should have said four decades ago, and we were, no, I was too immature to know I needed to say." He dropped his feet over the side of the chase, sitting up and facing her.

"I—" She looked at her tea. "I—" She couldn't get the words out.

"I know this is bold of me. I'm the one who abandoned you. I know that, and God knows how much I've kicked myself around for it. I can't change what I did, although God knows I wish I could. But one day. One real, honest day. Can you give me that?"

Can I? Can I give Cord one honest day? Does he really know what he's asking for? She swallowed, setting the glass aside. This chair, the shade, the pool, even, didn't look so inviting, anymore.

"Too much, huh?" Cord started to run his hand through his hair, and he stopped with his fingers buried. "Me. Bull in china shop. God, I'm stupid!" He slammed his hand down on the chaise, the noise softened by the cushion. "I have you here, even if it's just for six weeks, and I have to spoil it by bringing up the past. I'm sorry, Jane. After forty years, I still haven't learned anything."

"Grubstake. Six o'clock." She stood abruptly, her self-control almost slipping. "You drive, you pay, and you can have one evening. Not a whole day, but one evening. Then we'll see." She walked away, her eyes burning, and afraid to stand near him any longer.

She knew what he wanted. She wanted it, too, or she had years ago. She wanted to trust him, but there was something missing from the equation, something she had given up, and something she could never get back again. There would always be an empty space between Cord and her, and he would never know why.

If only she could back up forty years. Cord wasn't the only one that had made a mistake. She'd made one even bigger, and she couldn't tell anyone.

Not even Cord.

THE SHOWER HAD HELPED, standing under the cold water that wasn't really all that cold. No one could have told the difference between the tears and the water from the nozzle, and that was the way Jane wanted it. It also meant she could let the tears go, pretending they hadn't been cried at all.

Standing in front of the mirror, she patted her face dry, surprised at the person who stood on the other side. She didn't realize she'd been working so hard, but the person staring back at her was much trimmer than she had been since high school.

"Nerves!" She laughed. "Not the best diet in the world." She pulled her hair into a knot at the back of her neck, tying it up before opening her bag to scatter her makeup over the counter, glad she'd given in to Cord's offer to use the hacienda's guest bath. The refrigerated air was refreshing. Thinking of what Cord wanted to discuss wasn't.

Better wow him, she thought, lifting the dress she'd brought in. It was a soft blue with darker lines of peach infused with deeper hues of blue. She selected the matching make-up, intending to trowel it on a little heavier than usual. Night required that, didn't it, and it would be night before they returned.

"Ooh, Jane, quit being bitter. You had a life, and all that was two lifetimes ago, seen from the vantage point of a college kid. Get over it, and just enjoy the fact that Cord's paying, and you're getting a free meal."

The woman in the mirror didn't answer back. She stood mute, as if in reproof.

"I wouldn't talk to me, either. Sorry." She felt ashamed. She remembered what God had directed her to in her devotions. *Forgive. Forget. Don't be angry. Love.* She wanted to do the first. She could never do the second. The third always came back to haunt her, and the fourth? That was the one she had the most trouble with. She was already there, and she was determined not to give in to it.

Then, the woman in the mirror put on a bright face, applied the makeup a little heavier than she should, and sidled into a dress that would have been a size too small six weeks ago. Tonight it fit perfectly. She would be bright, cheerful, listen to whatever Cord had to say, and she would forgive, not be angry, and try to love the entire evening.

It was the forgetting that she refused to discuss. How could she forget what she had given away?

The dress did look good, though, and in her heavy-duty makeup, perhaps even Jasmine would get a run for her money. She slipped on her shoes and flung the door wide, determined to make the most of a very difficult evening.

"Jane!" Cord's word was a murmur, as if he couldn't believe the truth standing before him.

"What?" She checked to see if she had toilet tissue stuck to the sole of her shoe.

"You don't know, do you?" His smile grew wider. "You make Tarzan want to grab the biggest vine in the jungle and take Jane with him." He said it with a little laugh, releasing some of the tension.

"Oh, you're not getting off that easy, mister. You said you were buying my dinner," she shot back at him, forcing a smile. She felt some of the tension go out of her body. This was just Cord, and they were only having dinner.

Yes, that was it. They were only having dinner, and she would be the best date he'd ever had. That's what she would do, if it took every ounce of effort she possessed.

— 17 —

HUNGER. THAT'S ALL it'd been. Hunger.

Jane told herself that. She'd ordered grilled chicken chef salad, extra croutons, and unsweetened tea, and now Cord was plying her with cherry pie. She hadn't succumbed yet, but that hadn't stopped him from teasing her with mouthful after mouthful.

Now she was enjoying his company, rather than feeling sorry for herself. Hunger could do that, couldn't it?

"Jane, just a bite." Cord held a cherry on the end of a fork, his hand under it to catch any drips. "I haven't forgotten how you loved my mother's cherry pie." He pushed it at her encouragingly.

"No, don't." Jane held her hand in front of her face, laughing. "And don't you drip that on me, either. This is the first time I've worn this dress, and nothing on it is cherry red."

"But it would look good in cherry red. Cherry pie red." He turned the fork around and pulled the cherry off with his teeth. "Anyway, too late now, unless you want it the fun way." He showed her the cherry held between his teeth.

She turned her head, looking at the other diners to see if they were watching. She hissed between bouts of giggling, "Are you still in high school? Stop that and act like a grown-up. We're in public."

"So, if I order pie to go, I can do this back at the hacienda? As long as it's in private?" His eyes twinkled, and he fought a smile.

"Not with me in the same room."

"Then one bite, and I'll stop." He speared another cherry, this time with some crust attached. "Just one." He held it out to her.

"No. You men might be able to handle desserts, but us women? All it does is go to fat. I don't intend to be fat."

"That I can tell. Anyway, it's your loss." He ate the second bite. "It's really good."

About that time the check appeared, and the waitress said, "Pay at the front counter. Thank y'all, and y'all have a really good night. Just be careful of the rain. I think it's about to come a gusher." She nodded towards the windows.

"Cord, we'd better be going." Jane turned to the waitress. "Thank you for the warning. I might save my hair after all."

"Glad to help, ma'am. You're pretty, and pretty women deserve to be made special by their husbands. Lucky you." She winked at Jane and tilted her head Cord's way.

"But, we're—" Jane wanted no misunderstanding.

Cord grabbed her hand and interrupted. "Thank you, Miss. That's worth an extra tip for sure." He winked at Jane. "I'll take good care of her, because she's special."

Jane chuckled, letting the girl's misunderstanding slide. She felt good tonight. Much better than earlier in the afternoon, and that was a relief. Cord was already standing, and she grabbed her clutch, pausing at the window and looking out as he paid. It looked like water drops on the sidewalk, but coming down? That she couldn't tell.

It was obvious when they stepped outside. A gust of wind tore past them, then large drops scattered across the pavement. She laughed, and Cord grabbed her arm and started to run. The Escalade beeped and flashed its lights just as they got to the door, and Jane scrambled in, just as the really big drops started. Cord ran to the other side, jumping in barely in time to miss the torrent that began to pound the vehicle.

"At least it's not hot any longer." Jane reached to Cord's shirt sleeve to touch the water spatters. "Not dry, either. Sorry."

"Oh, it's nothing. I'll dry, and this'll be good for the soil. Loosen it up for planting, although most people planning new gardens should have already done so." He pressed the starter on the dash, and the truck came to life, the engine almost silent against the sound of the rain.

"I'm glad you're driving." She pressed one hand to the window at her side. "I never did like getting out in rough weather." She looked at Cord. "How 'bout you?"

"Ever drive a Caddy?" He rapped the dash with his knuckles. "Magnetic Ride Control and—" he paused expectantly "—Stabilitrak traction control. Every driver's dream." He grinned. "Makes rough weather driving worries a thing of the past."

She smiled. "Then radio up, please. And home."

"Yes, ma'am." He touched several buttons on his steering wheel, and the sounds of a sixties' tune gently pulsed through the cabin.

"Nice." Jane worked her way into a comfortable position in the big, overstuffed, leather seat. "I remember this song."

"From?" Cord was pulling out onto the highway, with the wipers going full on.

"Us, remember?" She'd still been a junior, and she and Cord had been at the old DQ in line to order. The song had come on, and she'd sung it for the first time. How had she ever forgotten that?

"In my old truck?"

"At the DQ." She laughed. "You don't remember, do you?"

Instead of answering, he hummed along for a minute, then he reached for her hand. "I remember you. That's better."

"I bet." She pulled her hand away. "Focus on your driving."

"If I must." His voice was husky, though.

"You must." What was she doing? She should be on the far side of the truck, slapping his hand away. She couldn't, though. With the rain, and the song, it felt too right, and she didn't want it to end just yet.

It was ten minutes before they pulled off the road onto the new concrete drive leading up to the hacienda. Cord swung the big truck into the garage, and everything became quiet.

"We're here."

"And dry." Jane laughed.

"Barely. Come in for a minute?"

Jane looked outside at the rain pouring down. "Might be tough getting to the guesthouse in this."

"Even under the breezeway?" His words were soft, almost as if he needed to remind her of something.

"It's early, yet, and that rain is sideways. I'd get soaked, even under a roof. Sorry. You've got to put up with me for a while." It even seemed okay, her last chance to be in the big house as a guest. After all, come the weekend, and she'd be out of Cord's hair forever, and he'd be out of hers, even if it didn't seem quite so appealing as it had that afternoon.

"Let me put on a dry shirt, and we'll have a toast to a great evening. How does that sound, my novia?"

"I'm game." She shot him a "thumbs-up" sign of approval. It wasn't until she was climbing out of the truck that she paused, wondering if she'd been mistaken. Had he actually said *novia* at the end of his question? That was what he used to call her in high school, sweetheart in Spanish.

If so, it was very bittersweet.

Lightning crashed, and they dashed into the house, letting the garage door close off the storm outside. A second crash, and the lights flickered, but they stayed on.

"Candles, Cord?"

He raised his hands in a defensive gesture. "I just write the checks. All this is yours. You tell me."

"That's a man for you." Jane began going through the kitchen cabinets. "Surely you've moved *something* in here. If not, it's going to get awfully dark if we lose electricity."

"Okay. Wait a minute." He stepped down a hallway and returned with a plastic crate. "Veronica brought this in yesterday. Just maybe . . ." He began to dig.

Another crash of thunder, and the lights flickered again, then died.

"Cord? Candles?" Jane could see him in snatches, when lightning gave her brief glances.

"Hang on." He continued to dig.

"It's dark. I don't like the dark much."

"A-ha!" A flame erupted, and then there was another and another.

"They're awfully small." But they were light, and for that, Jane was glad.

"Birthday candles. My grandsons' is coming up, and these are the party decorations."

"You're burning their birthday candles?"

He laughed. "I can get more. Besides, we need them now." He had already moved to the kitchen and was pulling long-stemmed glasses from a cabinet.

"Can I transfer them to the living room?"

"Sure. I'm just looking for the bottle opener."

"I need a plate."

He pulled out one and handed it to her as he dug through a drawer. As soon as she took it, he yelled, "Jackpot!" He turned with an opener in his hand. "What's the plate for?"

"I'm not holding those candles, and if you've never noticed, those little things burn out in about ten minutes. If the power stays off, we'll be using a lot of them."

"Gotcha. There's an extra box in the crate. Get 'em if you think we need 'em. I'll get the toast ready." He pulled a bottle from the fridge.

"Ow, ow!" One of the candles sputtered out. "We lost one." She was laughing, though.

"Here." He reached in the crate and tossed her the fresh box. "Gotta keep the supply up."

"Like camping out." She grinned.

"A first. We never did that, did we?"

"What do you mean?"

"As kids. We were always so busy. Never enough time to do all the things we wanted to do."

"What about the junior weenie roast? That big bonfire, and everyone stayed over half the night." She giggled. "My dad was so mad he could spit. It was only two, and he thought we'd been out all night."

"Doesn't count. This'll be our first, camping out with candles for our campfire." He grinned, setting two glasses on the coffee table.

"Makes a pretty wimpy campfire." She laughed. It was pretty, though, the house lighted with little candles.

"I appreciate this, Jane." Cord picked up his glass, and he swirled the liquid inside. "You, me, here."

"Thank you." She picked up hers. "Toast?"

"Not yet. What I meant was that I appreciate you spending the evening with me. Just us. I've wanted to do this for a long time."

"Cord, be careful. I've had fun, and I don't want it spoiled." With his tone, she hadn't much hope, though.

"We have to talk, Jane." When she made to interrupt him, he held up his hand. "No, listen. I want to tell you the truth. It's time you heard it from me." He took a deep breath and downed the liquid in his glass. "Oh, right, that was for our toast. Sorry." He grinned sheepishly.

"Cord—" she began, not wanting to hear what he had to say. *Four days and we're done. Don't spoil it now, Cord. Don't you do it.*

"I never cheated on you back then."

His face looked like he'd said something he'd wanted to say for a very long time. Relief? Jane couldn't tell, but she did know what she thought about his words. She felt her reaction boil up inside of her, and her emotions exploded with violence.

"What do you mean you never cheated on me? Of course you cheated on me—with Shelly. She was easy, and you just couldn't keep your hands off her. You had to have a piece of her like every other guy in town." Jane spit the words at him like they were venom. This whole perfect evening, and he had to ruin it with this. She had *known* he would do this. She had *known* it! How could she have been such a fool!

And, how could he look at her with that shocked expression after he lied like that? She turned from him, her glass still in her hand, the liquid inside quivering with her rage. If he only had the decency to tell her the truth, she could live with that. Not this. He thought he could lie, and it would all go away. No. He had broken her heart once, and that was enough.

She felt relief flood over her. She'd almost let it happen again. Now she knew, and everything was in the open where it should be. Then the anger boiled up again.

"Oh!" she cried, turning to him, pointing with her glass, shaking it with fury. "How could you, you, you, you *man,* you!"

Then she burst into tears, unable to contain the pain of Cord's betrayal any longer.

— 18 —

"JANE, PLEASE. HEAR ME out before you get your de-fenses up." Cord had hoped, really hoped that their even-ing together, their very pleasant evening together, would ameliorate the moment of his declaration.

What he got was more what he'd expected. Before he could put together more than his lame—even he had to admit that—rebuttal, Jane fired off a volley of anger to implode his hastily constructed redoubt.

"What do you mean before I get my defenses up? They're always up because of you. I've never been able to completely trust another man, thanks to you. I loved you, and you knew it. I gave you all the love I had, and how did you respond? By breaking up with me. All because you'd been with Shelly and, and—" Her voice broke. "Well, Ve-ronica says it all, doesn't she?"

"Jane—" Cord barely got his word out when the can-nons exploded again.

"My parents wouldn't let me stay out graduation night, so you had to find someone else to be with. That really showed how much you cared about me. One night was too much for you to wait. I'm sure Shelly was more than happy to take care of your needs." The glass in Jane's hand was shaking again, and as she used it to emphasize her points, the level of the liquid sank lower and lower, the wood under her feet glistening in the flickering candlelight.

"Then, you didn't even tell me about it until weeks later when you broke up with me. That was the part that hurt most." Her voice was crushed, as if something had broken inside, and her next words were little more than a quivering whisper. "I trusted you. I could have forgiven you almost anything. But to get a phone call from the one person I loved and trusted, and to be told that it was over? No, I'll never be able to let my defenses down. Not now. Not ever."

She turned away, her cheeks glistening.

"Mi corazón," Cord began, his voice thick with emotion. "You don't understand." He stepped to her, hesitant. He wanted to touch her, to hold her hand. If he could touch her, she'd feel how much he loved her, had always loved her, even though forty years had been stolen from them. And they had been stolen. He hadn't known that then, not at the beginning. But they'd been stolen, and he wanted back what he could get.

Even if it was just for Jane to understand.

"I had to tell you over the phone. I knew I'd never be able to do it face to face. I loved you too much."

"You loved me and couldn't tell me to my face that you were marrying another woman? I don't think so, Cord." Tears continued to stream down her face. "You don't love a person, not the way I loved you, and twist the knife you've thrust into their heart. It just doesn't work that way."

"Oh, mi corazón." He'd known even then what he was doing to her, and his hands had been tied. He'd had no choice, and now he'd brought it all back again. "Jane, mi corazón, I wouldn't have hurt you. I couldn't face you, not and move on. I had no choice."

"I had only—" Her voice broke. "You, Cord. I only loved you, and only that once—"

"That once." He took a deep breath. "I've held that in my thoughts as the most precious memory I own. No matter what I did, the abuse Shelly threw at me, I held to our memory. That night was the only thing that kept me going."

"Then why?" She turned to him, her voice soft, the anger melted, the pleading telling of the pain inside.

"The truth." He couldn't say . . . didn't want to say . . . mustn't sully Veronica's birth. His daughter . . . he loved her, and she was his as much as any child could be. "I want you to believe me more than anything, Jane. I really do. But nothing I say will convince you of the truth. I see that now. You no longer trust me." If he told the truth . . . and yet he bit his words back.

"I want to trust you," she whispered. "I want more than anything to believe everything you say and trust everything you do." She put her hand out as if to rest it on his chest, then, at the last moment, she turned it and wiped the tears from her face. "You hurt me too deeply. Then you sit here and tell me you were never with Shelly. Your daughter tells the truth. You can't deny her."

"That night, Jane, graduation night." He felt the words flooding forth, the dam broken, and he could no longer contain the breach. "I so wanted you there. The guys, first they spiked the punch, and there were bottles everywhere. One went in my hand, and I don't know why I did it. Then there was another, and I stumbled off into the darkness. Dear God, how did I let that happen?" He put his hand to his face, covering his eyes, to regain control.

"Let what happen, Cord?" Her voice was calmer, as if maybe this was what she'd wanted after all.

"I don't know what happened. I guess I passed out, and when I woke, Shelly was lying beside me telling me how much fun she'd had."

"Fun?" There was no sharpness in Jane's question, just pleading for an explanation.

"She was," and he rubbed his hand over his head, "and I cringe when I say this, in her, you know, skivvies. And my shoes were off." He grimaced. "Honestly, Jane, I didn't remember anything. Not a thing."

"But yet she said . . ."

Cord nodded.

"And you . . ."

"There's something else you might want to know. It might make a difference to you." He hadn't wanted to make this part of his plea for clemency, but he was desperate. "Veronica's birthday is—"

Cord didn't get to finish. Just then the lights flickered once, and with the gentle whirring of the refrigerator in the kitchen and the low whoosh of air from the vents, the lights came on and stayed. Somewhere in the background something beeped three times, possibly the smoke detectors or the phones.

Jane's face hardened, and the mood for sharing was over.

— 19 —

"I THINK IT'S TIME I got back to the guesthouse. There are still a lot of things I need to finish up before the reunion party this weekend."

Jane had listened to all she could stand. Cord might not have ruined her life on purpose, but ruined was ruined. And who cared when Veronica's birthday was? Good grief! If only that man knew how badly her life had been devastated. Forgive? She was prepared to do that. Forget? This would always be between them like a heavy curtain, their hearts never quite able to reach each other's.

She needed trust. Love? She had loved Cord, and she could easily do so again. But trust . . . that's what true love was, trust. And that was the one thing she no longer had in Cord. Trust. She couldn't believe in him as much as she needed to allow love into the picture.

But she could finish this house, and that she would do.

"Jane?"

She turned. "You're not finished, yet? Okay, what?" She was out of patience with this tonight.

"Are you sure you wouldn't rather stay in here out of

the weather? You can have my room, and I'll be comfortable right here on the sofa."

"We've already discussed this. Why are you still asking me this?" Her voice was sharper than she intended, but it seemed appropriate. They had discussed it, and she had declined. Did he think something so silly would soften her resolve?

"The rain . . ." He smiled. "It's still coming down in sheets."

"In sheets?" Ten minutes ago, she could have laughed at the double entendre. No longer. "I was having a pleasant time with you, and you took a twenty-two and fired a whole load of buckshot into my balloon. I think the guesthouse is just where I need to be. My little casita for the week will do me just fine for the night. However, I'll be out tomorrow." There was no way she was staying another night. No way.

"No!" Cord's reply was edged with steel.

"No?" She raised her eyebrows.

"I'm a gentleman, no matter what you may think of me. At least I must escort you to your door in this weather." Cord spoke in his rich, honeyed voice, yet there was something else there, a new determination.

Jane was surprised to see him grab an umbrella and head toward the back door. She was even more surprised for him to do it with her under his arm. What surprised her most of all was that she offered no protest to his proffered help.

With one hand on the umbrella and the other tightly holding her waist, he safely delivered her to the guest cabana porch. Jane mumbled a good night as she unlocked the door and hurried through it.

Inside, she leaned against the door and let out a deep breath. She was older than she'd been all those years ago, but was she any wiser? It was the thrumming in her wrists and in her neck that told her the truth. It was her heart upside down, and her thoughts in a muddle that screamed at her, telling her that if she stayed here even tonight, she was a sucker, and she would fall for Cord once again, hook, line, and sinker, just as she had all those years ago.

Moving away from the door, Jane sat on the edge of the bed, reaching to turn on the fan sitting on the bedside table. The storm had cooled the air outside, but it was still muggy in her quarters. With a quick twist, she dropped her hair around her shoulders, shaking it free. She wished it was so easy to unknot this problem with Cord, just shaking him out of her hair as easily as one, two, three.

It was working off her makeup that brought her true feelings home. Rubbing the cream into her skin and wiping it away, she caught her eyes in the mirror. They were red and shimmering with moisture. She knew what from, too.

She loved Cord. She'd never stopped loving him, even when she'd felt the most betrayed. She'd just never understood, and eventually, she'd been forced to put it all behind her.

Well, it wasn't behind her, now. It was right out in front, talking to her, taking her to dinner, and letting her design his home and all the furnishings.

"Ooh!" She growled. "Satan, get thee behind me."

But the words that kept going through her head haunted her. *Forgive. Forget. Don't be angry. Love.*

"Ooh!" She growled again. This time she didn't do more, because she knew who those words were from. And she'd better do what He said. After all, it wasn't like He was giving her a choice.

"Ooh!" She growled again.

— 20 —

IT WAS THE SUN in her face that awakened Jane. She turned her head to bury her face in the pillow, only to find it damp with last night's tears. That was the final straw, and she knew she couldn't remain in her bed one more minute.

Besides, blowup mattresses simply did not do for her back what her down-filled one did at home.

Throwing back the covers and standing, she glanced around the room. It was . . . different. She stood, thinking, very puzzled as the dappled light flickered and shifted around her. Then the room darkened as a cloud covered the sun, and just as quickly, the light scattered across the floor like a handful of diamonds cast carelessly across the wooden surface.

Then it hit her. Trees! The landscapers had managed to get the ornamental trees in before the weather had turned yesterday. She pulled her pajamas around her and stepped to the wall of casement windows fronting the pool area. Hanging baskets filled with flowers of bright pinks, orang-es, and reds hung throughout the patio area, making it look like an old, well-maintained Spanish garden on some king's country estate. She smiled. It was as beautiful as she'd pictured it that first day here with Cord, and even more beautiful than it had been when she had first visited here all those decades ago. Good! The old place had needed this, and she was pleased.

Then something else hit her. Last night. Cord, in the house, and his words to her. His lies to her. She looked back into the room, looking at the things she'd collected here, how in just a few days, it had taken on a feeling of home. It was just a blow-up mattress—even if a very elaborate and expensive one—and a chair from the new dining room furniture. That and an old console, one that she remembered from Cord's parents' days. It had been in the attic, dusty, but in very serviceable condition. She had brought it down and cleaned it one evening after the house had gone dark. She wondered if Cord would want it in the house, or if he would sell it to her. It was good quality, and she would pay whatever he asked.

Pay whatever he asked. Humph! It was just a drop of what she was charging him, no matter how much he asked. Maybe it was too much to ask for the console. Besides, it would remind her of Cord. Just the thought of that brought a knot to her stomach.

Rummaging in her bag, she pulled out some personals, and in the small closet, she found a lightweight blouse, teal with gold threading, and tan slacks. Stepping into the bathroom, she ran a brush through her hair and dressed. She peered into the mirror, deciding on whether makeup was called for. This was to be a working day. Working and packing. She wasn't staying another day. She'd made that very clear to Cord.

She took a deep breath. Last day. Back in the Lexus, which she hadn't driven in almost a week. Bill's last gift to her. God knew she could afford a new one on her own. The business was making money hand over fist, especially on this job. Still, it was Bill's last gift, and it had almost no miles on it.

It was the tears that decided her. Sunglasses and a wide-brimmed hat would do the trick. Makeup would run, and with last night's rain and today's sun, the humidity would be unbearable, she was certain. And this room would become a hothouse. It would be nice to get back to her own place, with its air-conditioned comfort and feather mattress.

Stepping outside, the scent of the crape myrtles assailed her. Along with the palms, bougainvillea, and climbing roses, the yard was perfection. Now all the landscapers had to do was clear the patio areas and edge the new grass plantings.

The rain had been better for the landscape than any irrigation system ever could be. She'd have to make sure the underground piping was disengaged for the day so as not to flood the plantings. Note one, she tagged in her head. But it was time for her to gather her things and go home. Home . . . she felt neither the urge to go back nor homesickness to see it. To be honest, she hadn't missed her home in the time she'd stayed here.

When she turned, she saw the note attached beside the door. *In town. See you when I return.* That's all, and in Cord's handwriting. Good. This was her chance to be gone before he returned. Seeing him? That was a two-edged sword, one that cut with love and betrayal. She didn't need that sword anywhere near her. The quicker she loaded her things, the better her day would be.

AS SHE WAS PREPARING to go back for her sewing machine, Jane heard Cord's vehicle coming up the driveway. He honked and motioned for her to stop.

"What are you doing?" He motioned to her suitcase and make-up bag at the back of her car. "Surely you weren't leaving until I gave my final approval?"

Final approval? She felt her tears rise, and she was glad for the sunglasses. Her escape hadn't been quick enough, and she didn't know if she could survive the thrust of the knife one more time. Not after last night.

"My number hasn't changed. It's on the contract if you need to call." She waved and smiled, good at her public presentation. After all, she was Jane Waggoner, designer, and she did work for very influential and important people. She did know how to grease the bumps out of her day. She had to, to survive.

"You can't meet my favorite girl over the phone." He grinned. "She's the new love of my life. I was in town to pick her up at the bus station, but you know how it is." He opened his door and climbed out, motioning to show there was no one with him.

"No, I don't know how it is. Why don't you tell me?" The love of his life? Suddenly, everything was clear. Jane's face was tight, and she could feel her eyes burn. She didn't want to cry, not today, not in front of this man. *Dear God*, she prayed, *I don't want to cry.*

In contrast, Cord seemed very pleased with himself. "Of course, the bus is running late. By several hours, too. Traffic on 20 was stalled for hours by an overturned semi. The desk said by noon, maybe. They'll give me a call since I have to drive back in. You'll still be here then?" Cord finished with a grin on his face. He seemed truly excited about Jane meeting the new love in his life.

Jane barely heard his words. How could she have been so stupid? Of course, he was doing this for someone else, not just himself. He'd planned this all along. He'd used his charm and their old connection to get her to do the very best designs and decorations for his house, and all for someone else, someone who wanted to live in this grand old place, who would cook at the granite counters, wash her hands using the water heater she'd worked so hard to put in, and probably tear out her shell soap holders in the guest bath simply because she liked ceramic flowers better. Ceramic flowers didn't even match Spanish hacienda style!

"No, I believe I'll pass up the honor." Jane made sure her words were carefully modulated. She wanted none of her pain and disappointment to bleed through. She also wanted nothing to do with meeting this other woman. It might be fine for Cord and Veronica to invite a new woman into the household, but she didn't want anything to do with it. She ignored the disappointment on Cord's face. Instead, she pointed to the door of the guesthouse. "If you don't mind, would you please bring my sewing machine from the guesthouse, and I'll be on my way. We'll wrap up the final details by the weekend."

"But aren't your son and his family coming by before the reunion?" Cord's eyes twinkled.

"Billy?" She had forgotten.

"You have another son, or is it perhaps a daughter you haven't told me about?" He seemed amused.

"No." She temporized. "I was planning to, um, sort out the final paperwork and bring the closing statements by, and Saturday will be fine." She nodded briskly, adjusting the sunglasses on her face. With her hat, she didn't really need the glasses, but with her heart, they were proving indispensable.

"Good. You can meet Vangie then. Well, Evangeline, actually. Veronica liked her the first time she met her. They've become good friends over the past few weeks." He laughed. "Veronica thinks you'll like her, too."

That was the final straw, that Cord's daughter thought Jane and his new wife would want to be friends. No, she could wait a lifetime before letting that happen. She was finished with Juan Cordello Rivera the Third.

It was when he stepped to get her sewing machine that he stopped, transfixed. He turned to her. "It was dark when I left this morning. I didn't see all this. Jane, you're the most remarkably talented woman I've ever known. I consider it both a privilege and an honor for you to have designed and decorated both my home and surrounding yard area. I'm blessed to have you in my life."

That knocked the skids from under her. A new woman in his life, and now he was telling her with tears in his eyes how grateful he was to have her in his life as well? That was more than she could handle.

"Well, thank you, but you may not think I'm so great after seeing my final bill. I really do need to go now, and if I've forgotten something, I'll get it later." With the sewing machine forgotten, Jane turned and climbed into her car, careful not to look at Cord. She was afraid he might see the truth in her face, the truth that he had once again broken her heart.

This time it was for good.

— 21 —

JANE HAD NO SOONER left Cord's driveway than a torrent of tears flooded her face. She'd been wrong all along. She hadn't been reading his signals correctly. Now, here she was again with another broken heart.

But this time she had only herself to blame.

She had thought, perhaps hoped at one point, that she and Cord could repair the damaged tapestry in which their history had entangled them. The trust could be rebuilt; the love could regrow. Even the lie from last night. She'd been furious, but that now paled with the news from this morning.

"Ooh!" She wiped the tears from her face, flinging the sunglasses aside when they got in her way. "God, why? How can you let me be so stupid?"

It was those messages from her devotional. She'd begun to trust them. She'd begun to trust in God that He would work this out, that the past could be mended if she simply trusted in Him.

Apparently, Cord didn't share the same feelings for her. To make matters worse, he had a new love. For a while she had thought, or perhaps hoped that he had wanted her and his daughter to be close. It seemed she was wrong on that account as well. Veronica was keeping company with "Vangie."

Why hadn't she been able to read the signs? Yes, he'd been away from the hacienda a lot lately, but she assumed it was because of his job. It never occurred to her that he might be seeing someone else.

And taking her to dinner last night? What was that about, nothing more than a final evening to wind up a job that was in its closing hours? Was she a pariah, someone to be used and cast aside? Was that the lesson Cord had learned from their relationship so many years ago?

Her tears had slowed to a trickle by the time she got home. She let herself into the house and collapsed on her sofa, exhausted from her emotional roller coaster. Her body felt like lead weights had been added to it, and it refused to move. Even when the phone rang, she didn't have the energy to answer. Right then, she didn't care who was on the other line. She couldn't. Even her "line" to God had turned out to be a misleading series of road signs that she had misinterpreted and gone back to again and again to convince herself that an old relationship could be renewed if only she gave in on all her principles.

She curled her legs on the sofa, laying her head on the arm, and closing her eyes. It wasn't more than a few minutes of lying there before she admitted her bed was a better option, no matter how much effort it took. Brushing her teeth, she thought of Cord, that night she'd hurt her ankle. He'd been so kind, here to see that she was taken care of. Bill had never done that for her, not waited on her hand and foot. She guessed she'd let her need for what Cord had seemed to offer blind her to the truth. In forty years, he'd built a life for himself, and it hadn't included her.

Now she had nothing, not the small hope she'd carried underneath all her hurt and pain that Cord somehow still cared, nor Billy, that small boy that had filled the emptiness that had ripped her world apart. She was totally alone as she crawled into her oversized bed, that great envelope of comfortable luxury made for two that now cradled only her.

Her dreams were of a pleasanter time, of school days, those before college or the heartbreak of the year after Cord left her. She dreamed of an old Ford pickup with running boards on the side, a radio that only got five stations and an 8-track player that skipped every time Cord tore over the railroad tracks without slowing down.

In that world she sat at a table in the Dairy Queen, the real one that was gone now, and she was with her friends admiring a long-legged boy in a tight tee shirt, round-toe boots, and faded jeans. It was the first time he'd looked at her, and she'd glanced away, embarrassed. He was Juan Cordello Rivera, his family was the richest in town, and there was no way he was interested in her. Not like that.

He had been, though. Of all the girls in the school, Tarzan had chased her, and she'd run, but not for long, becoming the Jane to his Tarzan.

In her dream, as dreams will do, the Dairy Queen was deep in the wildest jungle. Outside wandered elephants, tigers, and chimpanzees. One of the chimps kept tapping on the window at Jane's side, distracting her. Finally, she turned to it, irritated, and she said loudly, "What?"

The chimpanzee started making hand signs at her, pointing first to Cord, then to Jane. Jane realized it was sign language, and she frowned as she watched the big, bulky chimp fingers form the words.

It was odd, too, because the chimp formed Tarzan, then Jane, but it was the last word, the name for itself that seemed to give it trouble.

"Cheetah?" Jane called the name helpfully, hoping the poor creature could hear her. Instead, the animal shook its head. It was only after several starts and stops that Jane pronounced the words the finger seemed to spell. "Peg

Tee?" The chimp pounded on the window, hooting, and tried again.

Then, Jane laughed. "Peggy! But she's right here." She turned to her side to see that there was no one next to her. "You?" She pointed to the glass. "You're Peggy?" The chimp slapped itself on the chest in affirmation.

Jane laughed. In her dream, she laughed and laughed. It was the best time of her life, and it was all back again. Then, the phone rang and pulled her into the real world once again.

"Hello, yes, I'm awake now." Jane spoke sharply into the telephone, not really awake at all.

"Oh, well, that was some greeting." It was Peggy on the other end.

"Oh, it's you." Jane fell back onto her pillow. "I was resting. I think you woke me."

"I'm sure. It's about time. I just got back from supper." She sounded very pleased with herself.

"Supper?" Jane pulled the clock from the bedside table. "It's only ten."

"In the evening. Have you been asleep all day? I haven't been able to get through to you, and I've called a lot."

"I had a bad night last night—"

"All that lightning. Me, too. I didn't sleep a wink."

"So, what did you have for supper?" She closed her eyes, allowing Peggy to talk away. She usually did, so this should be an easy conversation. Jane was willing to let Peggy think it was the lightning that had disturbed her sleep, but then maybe it was. The lightning in her heart. The other kind? That didn't bother her much.

"Well, Cord called me, and Vangie's in town. I'm so excited. I couldn't talk about her before, but now that Cord's told you about her, well, that means all holds are off. I mean, she's the sweetest thing, and she really wants to get to know you." Peggy giggled, her enthusiasm bleeding over the phone line.

"Whoa, Peggy. Yes, I got Cord's *news*, if you want to call it that, and while he told me enough, it wasn't all that much. Right now, I don't want to hear any more, thank you." Jane was wide-awake now. How could Peggy do this to her? It was the ultimate betrayal, her best friend meeting and having dinner with the new love in Cord's life. Then she had the nerve to call her and tell her about it. What kind of friend was she? Obviously, a fair-weather one, at best.

"I tried to call you all afternoon to tell you about it, so don't blame me. You never answered your phone. I thought perhaps you were going to be at the hacienda, too. But when I arrived, Cord explained how you seemed distracted when you left, so I didn't call you again. Vangie is so sweet. You're going to love her—"

Jane interrupted Peggy from going on any further. "If you would, kindly remember to whom you are talking. I never want to meet or talk about Vangie. I haven't met her, and I'm already sick of her and her syrupy name."

"But, Jane—"

Peggy barely got the words out before Jane lit into her again. "If you were really my friend, you'd have refused the invitation and would never speak to Cord again. He's hurt me so deeply by throwing this other woman up in my face. He told me he wanted me to meet the new love in his life. I've never been so crushed or devastated ever!" Jane's voice broke over the phone, and she hung up.

Her face hot and her eyes burning, she threw the bedding back and stumbled into the bathroom, flipping the shower on high. She needed to wash everything away. Yesterday, and now Peggy's words, clung to her like old sweat, and she could smell it on herself. What was it about her that Cord didn't seem to care about? What could she do to make Cord ever want her?

Of course, it didn't matter now, because he'd found someone new to love. That was the hardest part, knowing he'd forgotten how much they'd once loved each other.

At least he didn't hate her. If he knew the whole truth, he might feel differently, and that would be even worse. She preferred his indifference to his hate any day.

— 22 —

JANE LOOKED AT THE sign just in front of her. Bladell's Department Store. If Cord liked flashy women, then she would prove a point to him, and Bladell's was just the place. They knew flashy, if anyone did.

She flipped the mirror down and studied herself in the reflection. Extra lipstick? Check. Mascara to make a man cry? Check. Seamless perfection? Check. She smiled as she opened the car, careful not to smile too widely so as not to crack the perfection. She was going for the gold, and that meant taking a risk. Getting the gold meant perfection, and she was up for it, including wearing the slinkiest outfit she owned.

This was her fallback plan. She admitted that. It was only fair to do so. She had loved Bill, but he'd been a stand in for the man she'd lost. At first, at least. God knew she had hated herself for that, but what was done was done. She'd been faithful to Bill, a good wife, and a committed Christian all those years, eventually coming to appreciate his stability and caring, if distant, concern. Nothing was going to change that, either. But Bill had abandoned her three years before, even if not by his choice. Still, abandonment was abandonment. Then Cord had shown up six weeks ago, with all his charm and good looks, and as much as she'd railed against all the memories, she'd been attracted to him. It was high school all over.

Now she felt dumped as cruelly as before, only this time she wasn't taking it on the chin. She was fighting back. Even if Cord had another woman under his wing, there were a couple of widowers and three or four divorced men in her class who might possibly show up at the reunion. Who was to say she might not wow one of them? It was time she got back into the game of life. Peggy was right. She couldn't be the grieving widow forever.

She breezed into the store, exuding confidence and bravado, she hoped. She had to. This was a store for the elite, and anything she bought here would eat up a big chunk of Cord's change.

Of course, it was money she'd earned, but it would come from Cord's pocket, and somehow that seemed very satisfying.

A sales associate helped her select three possible contenders. The first had a plunging neckline and tucked tightly at the waist. The waist was good. The neckline? She didn't know if she wanted to be *that* flashy. The second . . . backless? Surely not, she easily decided. The full skirt—diaphanous—would catch in the slightest breeze. She shivered at that thought. It was the third that caught her eye. Rich blue and yellow sequins on a strapless, satin band over a fitted, soft yellow bodice. The skirt had a short slit up the side. She loved it! A minor adjustment to the hem, which she could do in a heartbeat, and it would be perfect.

Bladell's even carried shoes to match.

She couldn't wait to show it off to Billy and Jasmine when they came in. Not too daring, but certainly different than anyone would expect from her. The men at the reun-

ion—she blocked the thought of Cord from her mind—
would be wowed.

New earrings in blue and yellow would set off her
fresh outfit perfectly, and she was so lucky to have an account at J. Gale's across the street. Today was coming together perfectly.

When she stepped out of the store, she laid her new
outfit in the truck of her car and stepped to the curb to
cross the street. That was when she saw the black truck
parked right in front of J. Gale's.

Cord.

"What's he doing here?" She muttered her comment,
and then it hit her. He was parked at the jewelers.

"Probably buying Vangie a ring. Engagement, unless I
miss my guess."

Suddenly she didn't feel the need to shop for earrings.
Her stomach twisted, and she wanted to be away, back in
the safety of her home, and out of public view. She felt
silly with her heavy makeup—no longer perfect, but a
desperate old woman out on the prowl.

Oh, she hated this.

She whipped around, striding to her car with as much
grace and aplomb as she could muster in her desperation.
Before she could shut her door, she heard a whistle and her
name.

"Hey, Jane! Is that you?"

No! He couldn't see her here! "No, it only looks like
me!" She didn't say that, but heavens knew she thought
about it. Instead, she waved and tried to duck into her car.
She almost made it before a hand caught the door and
pulled it wide.

"Oh, you are beautiful today."

He was panting. He must have run across the street.
Even that irritated her.

"Thank you," *as you buy a ring for your new honey.
How's this like forty years ago? Exactly, that's how.* "You
look nice, too."

He was in dark jeans, with pointed boots, and a tailored black shirt. He looked more than good, but Jane wasn't admitting that to him.

"Is this what you're wearing to the reunion?" He seemed extraordinarily pleased with himself.

"No, Cord. This is just an old thing I threw on. My new dress is in the trunk." She put her hand to her face, feeling the warmth build. What was with her? She was being mean and spiteful, not Christian at all.

"Well, whatever it is, I know you'll look great in it. You have such beautiful taste."

"Um, thank you, I guess." Now she was flustered. Compliments? Was he interested? And, of all things, where was his "Vangie" woman? Ooh, things were not making sense to her. "So, what are you doing in town today?" As if he had to explain to her.

"I had to get a few last-minute details taken care of before tomorrow. Veronica and the kids came down late last evening, and they're with Vangie shopping for the reunion. You'd think they've known each other all their lives." He chuckled, and it was deep and resonant.

Jane had no desire to hear about Vangie and how she fit so neatly into the lives of Cord's family members. "Well, that's great and all, but I need to get home. Peggy and I have some plans of our own."

It was a bald-faced lie, but she couldn't help it. She couldn't let him see how desperately she still cared about him, and how he was torturing her each time he mentioned Vangie's name.

"I understand. She'll be out of her pottery class soon, so I won't keep you. I'll see you tomorrow at the hacienda." With that, Cord bent down and kissed Jane's forehead and shut her door.

Jane watched him walk away, and she was dazed. Now she was more confused than ever. With her eyes burning and her nerves shattered, she pulled her phone from her clutch, punching in Peggy's number.

"Peggy, you will not believe . . ." She poured out the entire morning on her friend's shoulders. She wasn't prepared for Peggy's response.

"You've got to start trusting again, Jane. The world isn't your enemy, and neither is Cord. If you'd just try to trust and believe in him, I know you'd see things differently."

"That's easy for you to say. You weren't hurt by him like I was." She was not going to let Peggy off that easily.

"I know he hurt you back in high school. Everyone in town knows that. We all expected you two to get married. But it didn't end up that way. Now he wants to make amends, and you won't even try to trust him."

"What's the point, now? He's already found someone new. He told me with his own mouth he has a new love. And you even went over and had dinner with them." Jane had called for her friend's support, not to have her knees cut from under her. She knew her words sounded hurt and angry, but she felt hurt and angry. She couldn't pretend any other way, not after what had just happened.

"Yes, and I thought you might have been there, too. I expected to see you. But since you refuse to even meet him halfway, I'm glad he has someone who does love him without huge expectations of what he should and shouldn't be. I'm sorry, Jane. Class just let out, and I must get to my hair appointment. Just think about it, though." Without so much as a by-your-leave, the phone went dead.

Jane held up her phone and looked at it. She couldn't believe Peggy. She wanted her to trust Cord again. And she was glad Cord had Vangie? Ooh!

Well, she had a dress to alter, and she planned to bedazzle all those old men and women at the reunion tomorrow. She would be the glittering belle of the ball, and no one would be able to hold a candle to her.

She even tried to push away the words that hovered in the back of her mind. *Forgive. Forget. Don't be angry. Love.* It was the "don't be angry" part that goaded her today. How could she not be angry? Everything had gone wrong, and now even her best friend had abandoned her.

When she pulled out of the parking lot, she was surprised to see Cord's truck pulling out across from her. He rolled his window down and waved, as if she was a good friend, and there was nothing in the world to drive them apart.

Except Vangie, Jane thought. You have another woman, Cord, and that'll keep us as far apart as the east is from the west.

That phrase reminded her of her Sunday school lesson the week before, and she felt a twinge of guilt. That was how far God threw our sins when we repented, and he never remembered them again. That story reminded her of something else.

Forgive. Forget. Don't be angry. Love.

"Ooh!" she growled for the umpteenth time, even as she knew God was right. She had to do it all, and it was going to be the toughest thing she'd ever done.

— 23 —

"BILLY, COME GIVE me a hug." Jane left the front door ajar and held out her arms. They had just driven up, and her stepson's car door was open.

"Hello, Mom." Jasmine waved from the other side of the car. "The kids are wrapping up their movie. They'll be out in a few minutes."

"It's so nice to see you, Jasmine. How was the drive?"

"Mom? A new diet?" It was Billy that responded. He grinned.

"Oh, don't listen to him," interjected Jasmine. "He wouldn't know a diet if he saw one. You look fabulous. You've let your hair grow out some, and I like this softer style. I thought it was too short before, but it was none of my business. However, it looks so good now, I have to say something."

By that time Jane had her arms around Billy. She glanced in the car to see the kids huddled in front of a portable DVD player. She was just glad for the distraction. Bladell's? That had about done her in.

"New car, Billy?" It was blue, and Jane remembered a

green one.

"Just picked it up last week. American made, a Cadillac. XTS." He stroked one fender. "Jasmine keeps it home for errands."

"It's very pretty. Kids? Coming in?" She leaned in through the front door. "Little Billy? Katherine?"

"Hi, Grandma," they chorused, their eyes never leaving the screen.

"Kids!" Jasmine laughed, leaning over and giving Jane a kiss on the cheek. "Thirteen and fifteen, and they still love a good video. Leave them be. At least they're occupied quietly."

She was right, too. The backseat was evidence of that. Popcorn was everywhere, with books, scattered game pieces, and candy wrappers. Jane knew they'd leave her house in about the same condition, if they got a chance.

"Well, I have dinner ready, and they can eat it cold if they're not hungry. How about you and Billy?" He was at the back of the car unloading suitcases.

"You fix it, and Billy will come." Jasmine put her arm in Jane's, walking toward the door. "Now, tell me about this ranch you've been redoing. I want to hear every detail, from the kitchen sink to the bathroom soap holders."

"Oh, you don't want to hear about the soap holders." Jane remembered her rant about those, and she smiled.

"Oh?"

"I think the owner has plans to tear them out as soon as he pays me for putting them in." She giggled, knowing it was silly. "Not really, but you never know. I learned yesterday the ranch's owner has a new fiancée."

"No!"

"He's been redoing the house for her."

"He told you that?" Billy was right behind them with a suitcase in each hand.

"Not in so many words. Billy, you should let Little Billy get those for you." They were inside, and she watched him maneuver them through the door.

"I'm sure he would, if I didn't care whether they made it in tonight or in the morning. I care." He dropped them by the front door. "Did I hear something about food?" He took a sniff and smiled.

"On the stove just waiting for four hungry mouths."

"Will two do?" He grinned.

"Make it three. I'm hungry, too." Jane led the way, waving her family along after her. The food would have drawn them the direction of the kitchen, anyway. Roast and potatoes could pull anyone in.

THE KIDS HAD JOINED them, their plates piled high, and they were finishing cake and ice cream, when the phone rang.

"I've got it. You go ahead." Jane stood and slipped her cell phone from the counter. "Yes?"

"Who is it, Mom?" Billy had cake on his fork, and he tucked it into his mouth.

"Your Aunt Peggy, I think." She took a deep breath, refusing to let her stepson know how irritated she'd been with her earlier. After a moment she said, "They're here now. Come on over."

Jasmine looked puzzled. "I've never figured out how Peggy is Billy's aunt. Is she a great-aunt, once removed, or . . ." She held out her hand, palm up, as if waiting on an explanation.

"Neither." Billy was scooping another spoonful of ice cream from the bucket. "Right, Mom?"

"Aunt Peggy's not our aunt?" Little Billy asked around his latest bite.

His sister hit him on the arm. "Is, too. Right, Grandma?"

"She might as well be." Jane returned the phone to the counter. Peggy was as close to a sister as she'd ever have. For that reason, she'd better let her irritation go. She smiled. "She's your aunt—" and she pointed her finger at Katherine "—just not by blood."

"She's a love aunt?" Little Billy grinned, jabbing his sister in the side with his elbow.

"Stop that," Jasmine said, rapping the table. "You two want to be rowdy, you go in the back yard. You can be rowdy tunes as much as you want out there."

"Okay." Little Billy leaped up. "Rowdy tunes. You're it." He punched his sister on the shoulder, and leaving his chair out, he ran for the back door.

"No fair, Mom. I didn't know he was playing." Katherine sat with a pained expression on her face.

"You know now." That was Billy. "Go get him."

"Okay." Her face brightened. "Can I take a roll?"

Jane held the plate to her, smiling when the girl took two and ran after her brother.

"Bet you're glad you only had me." Billy grinned.

Jane wasn't, though. She'd always wanted more. A daughter. Her daughter. Just one more would have done her fine. That hadn't been the way it had worked out, though.

The doorbell rang, and Jane called out, "It's open."

Jasmine raised her eyebrows.

Billy coughed, "Mom?"

Jane wrinkled her nose. "It's just Peggy. Don't worry about her. She knows her way in the house." As well as out, but that didn't need said.

"Well, how's Jane's favorite little man?" Peggy flew into the room, giving him a hug.

"Not so little." Jasmine reached and patted his waistline.

"Embarrassed." Billy dropped his head, grinning. "Can't I be just Billy?"

"I've greeted you that way for nearly forty years, and I'm not changing now." She turned to Jane. "And you?" She made a sour face. "You done any thinking?"

"Let it go, Peggy. Talk to your nephew."

"How are you, Aunt Peggy? What's been keeping you busy?"

"You know us old hippies; we still do what we like to do. Pottery. Jewelry. Like always. My design classes are going great. I haven't seen my own children since Christmas, but they call about every two weeks or a month, and we play catch-up."

"Not very maternal, are you?" Jane was quite aware she hadn't managed to let all her irritation slip away.

"Well, I'm here, and they're the ones that decided to move away. I couldn't very well chase them down and lasso them back." She smiled sweetly. "Where are the kids? That little Katherine was so sweet last time you were here. I swear she's the image of her mother."

"Out back, being very much *not* like her mother." Jasmine smiled ruefully. "Her mother is better behaved." Billy shot her a look, and she slapped him on the arm. "Not a word, buster."

Peggy laughed. "Peas in a pod. You just can't tell, Jasmine. Are you bringing them to the reunion tomorrow?"

"We'll see when the time comes. Right now, I think we all need to burn some energy." Billy motioned to the back yard, where the children could be heard involved in a fracas.

"Well, I want to remember them as sweet, so I had better go. I still have a few more things to do before the big day. So until then, have a good evening!" Peggy said her good-byes, blew kisses to everyone, and left.

"Dears," Jane said, standing, "you can leave all this, but I do think I'll lie down for a time. Last night was a long one."

"Mom, you're not still having nightmares about Dad's death are you?" Billy put his fork down and looked at her, really looked for the first time.

"No, sweetie, those stopped some months back, but the new one is just about as bad." Cord, but that wasn't her stepson's problem.

"What's it, now?"

"Your mother said she could handle it. Let her be." Jasmine patted his arm.

"She's right. It's really nothing I can't handle. I'm just glad all my babies are here. I think I sleep better when I know you're close by. And no, that's not a hint for you to move here. I'm thinking about coming up there for a few weeks if you think you can stand me for that long."

Billy looked over at Jasmine, who smiled wide. "You just like her to do all the cooking."

"Shush, you big baby. Of course, I do. Tell her we accept."

"Sure, Mom. That would be great. You know we always love it when you visit. Just tell us when, and we'll have the guest room ready." Billy grinned, glancing at his wife.

"It might be sooner than you think."

"Anytime, Mom. Anytime." Billy gave Jane a little pat on her arm.

"Yes, anytime, Mom." Jasmine echoed her husband's words.

Jane retired to her room, not really expecting to get much rest. Peggy had thrown her for yet another loop. *You done any thinking?* She knew what she meant. However, what good did it do? Cord had Vangie, life had ended forty years ago, and all she had was an incredibly expensive dress in the back of her car.

That stopped her short. The dress was still in the trunk, and the car was in the garage.

Ooh! When would she ever get a grip on life? Like, never?

Ooh!

— 24 —

"HOW DO I LOOK?"

"Mom! Look at you!"

Jane turned around, letting her stepson take in her new dress. "Do you think I got it too short?"

"Absolutely not. You'll wow everyone there this evening." He called, "Jasmine, you've got to come see this."

"Ooh, la, la." Jasmine stepped in, still running a brush through her hair. "I should look so good at thirty-five."

Jane felt her face warm. "Do you really think so? Not too showy?" Her nerves were getting the better of her, and she thought perhaps she had gone a little too far in her attempt to get even with Cord for breaking her heart.

"Are you kidding, Mom? You look fabulous, and I mean it. You'll be the belle of the ball tonight at the reunion. Don't change a thing. I hope I look half as good as you when I reach your age," Jasmine finished her compliments and gave Jane's arm a good squeeze. "Don't worry about Billy. He's just not used to seeing you as anything but his mom," Jasmine whispered in her ear.

Jane stepped to the mirror in the front hall, evaluating

herself. Her hair, full and with soft curls, hung just to her chin. Her new hemline cut at her knees, and the satin band with all its sequins glittered.

"Here, Mom." Jasmine stepped to her and held out her hand. "Try these." Inside were two yellow diamond earrings.

"These are beautiful. Wherever did you get them?"

"Billy." She leaned against him and patted his chest. "For our fifteenth anniversary. But tonight, they're yours. The color . . . when I saw your dress, I knew you had to have these on."

"How could I be so lucky to have such a wonderful daughter-in-law?" Jane felt her eyes fill up, and she grabbed Jasmine by the shoulders and gently brushed her cheek with a kiss. "You, Billy, have exquisite taste." She patted his cheek with her hand.

"For the diamonds?" He grinned.

"For the girl." Jane nodded, slipping her gold studs out to make room for the diamonds.

Jasmine grinned.

"Are the kids ready?" Jane thought not, not with the ruckus from down the hall, but she hoped the question would get the process started.

"They will be." Billy started toward the hall when Jasmine interrupted.

"Kids! We're leaving. You coming with us or walking?"

Jane tried to hide her smile as Billy hesitated, unsure whether to continue or wait on a response.

"Right, kids. Like your mother said." He shrugged and made a face.

Little Billy appeared first. "I can't tie this tie." He was in slacks and a dark shirt, unbuttoned, with a tie in his hand. One shoe was untied, and his fly was unzipped. Clearly there was more than just the tie holding him up.

Kathrine appeared, primped and perfect, with a smirk on her face. "He wanted me to tie it. I could, because I

know how, but he wouldn't make my bed, so I wouldn't."
She flounced self-righteously across the room to stand by
Jane. "You're pretty, Grandma. I'm gonna stay beside you
all evening."

"Pretty doesn't rub off, so give it up, squirt." Little
Billy continued to twist at the tie, making no progress at
all.

"Mom!"

"Be nice, kids. Now, to the car. We're all going in the
XTS." Billy shooed them the direction of the front door.

"Can't we take Grandma's? It's red."

"And not big enough." Jasmine laid her brush on the
entry console, picking up her purse. "Now, out, like your
father said."

"Mom! My belt!" That was Little Billy.

"Here, Son." She pulled one out of her oversized
handbag. "Out, now. No more excuses."

They tumbled out the door, and Jane watched them go
by, three dressed to the nines, and the other barely dressed
at all. However, they were hers, and she'd claim them all.

Before closing the door, she did look back in the mirror. Jasmine's earrings made all the difference in the
world. She looked like a million bucks, which she assumed
was about what Billy had paid for these. Having an architect for a stepson wasn't a bad thing, not in the least little
bit.

"DRIVE ON, BILLY. You can't see the house until you're
almost there." Jane motioned with her hand.

She sat in the front with her stepson, but she'd been
amused by the antics in the back seat. Little Billy was in
the middle, and both his sister and his mother had worked
to get him polished to a shine. Jasmine had found a comb
somewhere, wet it in a cup of water, and was smoothing
his hair into a semblance of order.

"You did the drive, too?" There were flowering shrubs
all the way from the road, and they lined the drive on both

sides. The area underneath was mulched with pine needles and interspersed with beds of flowers.

"So the architect approves?" She sat back and smiled. She liked it. Cord had already given it his thumbs-up. But still, she'd needed to hear it from her family.

"You mean you designed all the outdoor plantings and structures?" Jasmine spoke from the back seat. "What about that cute gazebo we just passed?"

"That, too."

"I told you Grandma's smart." Katherine sounded very smug.

"You never said that," Little Billy snorted. "You said you didn't want to come. You'd rather play with your One Direction dolls."

"They're action figures, and I don't play with them. I take them on tour."

Billy cleared his throat. "Kids?"

Jane could tell it wasn't a question, and she was glad to have him corralling them. It got tiresome when she had to go it alone.

Thank God for parents!

"It doesn't matter, Little Billy. And, thank you, Katherine. I like being told I'm smart."

"See? Grandma loves me." Katherine waggled her shoulders. "Ha, ha."

"She loves to see you go home." Little Billy grabbed her knee and squeezed.

"Enough." Jasmine held out her hand to the pair as a signal to stop. "Be sweet just for an evening. This is an old friend of your grandmother's, and we want to impress him."

"Yeah," Katherine muttered. "Impress him."

"You can impress him," Little Billy muttered back, "by staying in the car."

Jane rolled her eyes, calling brightly, "We're here. Smiles, everyone." She opened her door as the car rolled to a stop.

They were in the drive, although they had passed a mowed area with signs and plastic ribbons showing visitors where to park.

"Mom, should I move the car after I let you out?" Billy glanced at the grassy parking area.

"Later, Son. We have two hours before the crowds arrive. There's time." Besides, she thought, she didn't know if the kids would survive that long. Billy and Jasmine might take them home long before the reunion began.

"Go ahead." Jasmine patted him on the shoulder. "You'll get a better parking spot. You can take the kids with you. The walk will be good for them."

"Thanks!" He rolled his eyes, but he was smiling. "Out, ladies. Stay, children."

"How long did it take you to do all this?" Jasmine glanced around at the lush landscape as the big luxury car pulled away.

"Not long enough. This was a six-month job, and I had to squeeze it into the past six weeks. The final landscaping just went in yesterday. So, you think I did okay?"

"Okay?"

Jane jumped. She recognized that voice, even as she refused to turn around.

"This is the most beautiful, or, should I say hermosa palace I've ever seen."

"Have we met?" Jasmine was the first to greet Cord.

"Two beautiful women, here in my own drive, speaking with me. Both of you are speaking with me, right, Jane?"

She turned to face him, to find his eyes glued on her. "What? Did I smear my lipstick?" She wanted to be beautiful. Now, under Cord's appraising eye, she felt nervous.

Jasmine giggled. "I don't think it's your lipstick."

"No, mi corazón, there's nothing wrong with you. You're perfect." Cord's eyes hadn't moved.

Billy was putting his key in his pocket as he appeared, motioning for the children to catch up. He gave Jasmine a hug.

"Who's he, Mom?" Jasmine let out another giggle.

"Excuse my bad manners. Jasmine, this is Juan Cordello Rivera the Third. He owns this ranch. Cord, this is my lovely and precious daughter-in-law, Jasmine." She was grateful to have her words not crack as she spoke them. She continued with the introductions, telling Cord each person with her.

When she finished, and everyone had nodded in all the right spots, Cord began to speak. "You have no idea how much your mother has done to this place. There's nothing left of the old hacienda but the outer structure. She did all the design work on the casita and the patio as well as the hot tub. She even refinished the pool. She knew what I wanted even before I could tell her. She read my mind." Cord finished by putting his arm around Jane and squeezing her close to him. "Without her, this house would be nothing but a tired old part of the past blocking the landscape. But, because of her vision, my family home has come back to life again to be shared by the ones I love." When Cord finished, there were tears forming at the edges of his eyes.

Jane was embarrassed and flustered, and she could feel her hands shaking. For heaven's sake, why was he giving her so much attention? She'd been the director of the project, certainly, but to tell her family that his home wouldn't have existed without her? That was a surprise.

Yet, what amazed her more was that no one thought it odd that this stranger had his arm around her. And even more amazing, she didn't feel the desire to move away. Not quickly, anyway.

She knew she must, though. She felt very old and very uncomfortable feelings, and she knew they would make a complete fool of her.

There was no way she was telling this man she loved him, even though every part of her body screamed at her to do that very thing.

— 25 —

"SHALL WE TOUR the house?" Cord stood at Jane's side. His sudden appearance on the drive wasn't by chance, having been quite contrived. He was standing by the large windows in the front watching for her family's early arrival. He'd promised her son and daughter-in-law a private tour, after all. After yesterday, he'd wondered if she would show.

When she did emerge from the car, he hadn't been able to believe his eyes. She was by far the most captivating woman he'd ever seen, more beautiful than she'd been all those years ago.

"Let's start first by you leading on." Jane cleared her throat as she disentangled herself from his arm.

"If you'll walk by my side." He took her hand and bowed, kissing it. He refused to let her get away so easily. He smiled when he heard Katherine giggle.

"Grandma. You're a princess."

"You are, you know," Cord murmured. "You'll walk with me?"

"If I must."

He turned to the crowd. "You are my captive audience for the next two hours. Well," and he looked at his watch, "the next hour and fifty minutes. You're my first guests, and I wish to show off Jane's creation." He pulled her hand up and kissed it again. "Please pardon the kitchen. The caterers have commandeered that part of the house, so perhaps another day . . ." He looked at Jane, speaking softer. "You will come back another day?"

"Cord," she spoke low and tersely, "I'm finished here. You have your house back for you and your, um, other."

"My other?" He was amused. Clearly, she didn't understand. However, it was exactly how he'd planned today. "Never mind. You tell of your creation, and I'll clap and cheer."

He motioned for the others to gather around, and they headed for the front door. Cord did stop the boy, and he pulled him aside.

"Billy, right?"

The boy beamed. Jane had introduced him as Little Billy, and Cord thought maybe he'd enjoy a more grown-up name.

"Well, Billy, we have a saying out here on the ranch. When the gates are open, the cows like to wander and play."

Billy frowned. "What?"

Cord chuckled. "Your cows are getting out."

"Cows?"

Cord spelled it out. "Your zipper is undone, boy. Zip your pants." He patted him on the shoulder. "You can catch up with us when you're finished."

The boy turned bright red, but that was okay. Cord liked Jane's grandkids, and after spending the weekend with his own, they didn't seem very wild at all.

"THERE ARE GUESTS ARRIVING, and you're the host." The tour was over, and Jane pointed out the window, where two cars could be seen driving towards the house. They pulled off the drive, parking next to Billy's Cadillac.

"Yes, ma'am," Cord intoned wickedly. "Your wish is my command."

Jane laughed. "Stop that. You'd better be glad your Vangie isn't here to see you doing that."

He winked at her. "She would approve, I can assure you."

"I think not, and my grandkids are here. I don't approve."

He laughed and strode away, waving merrily at her family.

"Grandma, are you going to marry him?"

Jane rolled her eyes. "Katherine, you don't marry every man who kisses your hand."

"I would," she announced.

"And that's why you're a dork." Little Billy whispered the words in her ear.

"Mom!"

"Are you ready for us to go?" Billy stepped to his mother's side, while Jasmine corralled the disagreement. "One of us can come back to get you after this is over."

"No." She didn't want them to leave. She needed backup. She might even find the need to use the kids as her crutch. If Katherine did stick to her side, then that would be the witch hazel to ward off Cord's unwelcome advances.

This was turning out to be a complicated evening.

"If you're sure. I know my kids, Mom, better than perhaps even you. They can be toots, no question about it."

"We all have been, at one point or another. Let's give them a chance. I'll talk to them."

Jasmine had them corralled, and both of her grandkids had sour looks on their faces when Jane walked up to them.

"When was the last time you two ate anything?" She looked at them piercingly, and when she didn't get an answer, she spoke their parents. "You two go play. I'm taking these two to the kitchen. I think that's the problem." They were usually better than this in public. And she suspected they were very hungry. She knew she was.

She led them through the house to the back entrance to the kitchen. She tapped a thin man in a white jacket on the shoulder.

"Sir, I have two hungry children here, and I'm afraid they're going to kill each other unless I get some food down them. Do you think you can rustle up something?" How easily the old ranching words came to her. She stifled a grin. She was a Texan, after all. Nothing to be ashamed of there.

"Yes, ma'am. Chicken, barbeque, or enchiladas?" He smiled pleasantly at her.

"You are a sweetheart." She smiled. "Let me check."

They walked away with two covered plates, and Jane carried two glasses of tea. Settling them in the dining room, one on each side of her, she drew in the aroma of the meal, chicken on one side, and barbeque on the other. The enchiladas had sounded more appealing to her, but she wasn't the one choosing. She would snack off the children's plates.

She did need tea, though.

"Children, I'll be right back. Grandma forgot her tea."

The two children nodded at her, more interested in their food than in their grandmother. On the way, she glanced outside to see a dozen more cars had arrived. Out back, people were gathering around the pool. With the evening, it would start to cool, and there couldn't be a better day for a high school reunion.

Then she caught the sounds of a brass instrument, and she knew someone had hired a band. Mariachi, by the sound of the music. She smiled, heading back to her kids.

"Grandma, who is that man, really?" That was from Little Billy, finally asking a real question rather than tormenting his sister.

"An old friend. We dated in high school."

"Before you married Granddad Bill?" That was Katherine.

"Yes. A long time before."

"Why didn't you marry him?" Billy again.

"Oh, sometimes you don't marry the people you think you will. Then someone else comes along, and now I have you two wonderful children." She smiled brightly, giving each one a quick hug. "If I'd married that man, then I wouldn't have you, now would I?"

"Would you have had other kids?" Billy was licking his fingers, but he paused to look at her. "And I could have another sister that's not a *dork!*" That was aimed at his sister, and he leaned around to glare at her.

"Shush, Billy. Your sister isn't a dork." Besides, his comment hit close to home. Another sister . . . well, not exactly a sister, but an aunt. Her daughter, Little Billy's aunt. She felt her eyes water, and she knew she couldn't let that get started. "All finished, here?" She stood. "Up, children. I have a reunion to attend."

"Will you be the prettiest person there? Here, I mean?"

Jane hugged Katherine and kissed her on the forehead. "After you, I think so, dear. I certainly hope so."

"I saw a barn. Can we go explore?" Billy's eye's gleamed.

"A barn, Billy, in your tie and dress shoes?"

He shrugged. "Want to, Dork?"

"If you won't call me dork."

"Okay, Dorklet."

"Grandma!"

"Off, you two. No lights out there, so you have to get there while it's still light. I'll tell your parents." She patted them on the backsides as they scampered away, certain that they would argue, but maybe no one would hear them if they were in the barn.

"THANK YOU FOR THE nickel tour earlier." Jane had a

glass of punch in her hand, and she'd seen Cord by himself during a lull. "What do you think of the mariachi band?"

"Lively. You know mi casa es su casa." He smiled at her.

"Not exactly, but I appreciate the sentiment."

"Ah, we have new guests." He motioned, and sure enough, two new couples strolled in together.

"I'll catch up with them later. I have to wait on name tags."

He whispered to her conspiratorially, "Me, too." He winked and walked off.

"Wow, Mom. You never mentioned him when you talked about the remodel. I don't think I'd have been able to get much done with him around." Jasmine giggled.

"Oh, it's you, Jasmine!" Jane was started by her daughter-in-law's presence, and she felt her breath return. "I didn't know you were here. Are the kids back, yet?"

"Billy has them over at the horseshoes. They'll be okay for a while. I'm on break."

"You probably need it." Jane laughed softly. She's the one that needed a break, but that would happen about midnight when all this wound down. "So, you like my old boyfriend, do you?"

"Old boyfriend?"

"Very old, as in not seen for forty years. Now? He's got a girlfriend."

"Why didn't you snatch him up first? I would have."

"You've got Billy, but I understand what you mean. Bad blood." She laughed. "Just not bad enough to keep me from charging him an arm and a leg for redoing this place."

"Are you sure he has a girlfriend? He seems to have the hots for you, if I'm any reader of body language."

Jane looked at her, aghast. "The hots? Like romantic attraction? Heaven's, no! He told me himself he has a new love in his life, and I saw him coming out of J. Gale's the other day. So, I'm pretty sure I'm not the one for him."

Her sarcastic tone told what she thought of that, she was certain.

"Oh. Sorry."

"Quite alright." The yard flickered, and festive lights erupted across the scene. "How pretty. Let's mingle." Jane smiled at Jasmine. They laughed to see several older teens come running out of the guesthouse and leap into the pool.

"Too bad the kids didn't bring their suits."

"Oh, I bet I could rustle up a few." There was that word again. Jane smiled. "Don't tell them yet, but I'll ask around."

"Hey, Jane! Is that you?"

She turned to see several men coming her way. She shrugged and waved at Jasmine, who smiled and walked away.

"You haven't changed a bit except to be even more gorgeous."

Not sure which one had spoken, Jane just smiled. An exceptionally handsome gentleman with a thickening middle approached her first.

"Oh, I know you." Jane laughed. "Yes, Romeo, it's me," she shot back with a short laugh. She remembered him. His last name was Romero, but he'd always been such a big flirt that the girls called him Romeo, a nickname he'd never liked.

"Give me a break, Jane. I've changed." He flashed a winning smile.

"And you've been divorced twice, or is it three times now?" Jane asked with an innocent smile, knowing good and well it was four.

"None of them were my fault, mi amor. I'm just looking for true love. A woman I can trust. Someone who doesn't gripe all the time if I make a little mistake now and then. A little indiscretion is to be expected by a man."

"You wish!"

"You never gave me a chance in high school; you were so wrapped up in Tarzan. Now, maybe it's our turn."

Romeo blew her a kiss as he waited for her response.

Jane just laughed and patted his arm as she turned away. She saw Cord across the pool, and she waved to him, calling, "Suits? Do you have extras?"

He smiled broadly. "You want to go in?"

"No, fool!" She motioned him over, meeting him halfway. "I have grandkids who might like to. I don't want to get their hopes up, though."

"In the casita. Veronica brought a dozen extra."

"Just for girls?"

He laughed. "Boys, also. Tell your grandkids to make themselves at home."

She did, and they did, soon frolicking in the water, and more importantly, occupied. Now if they didn't drown one another, but as they had a pool at home, and neither one was deceased yet, she was certain they would survive.

It was sitting down to dinner that she got a surprise. Each guest had registered upon arrival, and someone had made out cards for seating. When she found hers, it was right next to Cord's. Just as Jane reached for her seat, a hand came around, and a deep voice spoke.

"Allow me."

"Did you do this?" She didn't even have to look to know it was Cord. Somehow, he'd managed to invade the most intimate part of the evening and sit by her. "I suppose since the party's at your house, you get to call some of the shots."

"Me? I'm innocent."

"I doubt that."

"Do not break my heart, mi corazón. I only wish you to have a good time." He bowed to her slightly.

She doubted that, and she found his behavior very confusing. It didn't help that his proximity to her tonight put her stomach in knots. She'd thought she would be able to enjoy this evening, but she'd been seriously mistaken. Anywhere Cord was, her heart wouldn't leave her alone. Right now, it was pounding against her ribcage like it was about to escape.

"Aren't you going to eat, Jane? The meat's from my herd of prize Angus. I donated the beef for the party. I can't speak for the chicken." He leaned in close, his words whispered in her ear.

As she turned to reply, she happened to notice that she and Cord were wearing identical colors of fabric. The pearl snaps on his shirt were the same as the sequins on her dress. His bolo tie had a huge piece of sapphire surrounded by turquoise. The large stone matched her sequins perfectly. It was as if they had planned their outfits together.

"Is something wrong?"

"It's your shirt and tie. They match my outfit perfectly," Jane mumbled under her breath, not entirely comforted by the observation.

"Well, it's a small world, and even smaller when the choices are limited in this community." He grinned broadly. "What do you think about that?"

She didn't want to think about it at all.

— 26 —

THE EVENING WAS IN full swing. Dusk had overtaken the hills in the distance, the sun winking out like an orange fist that had held the day tightly in its grasp, only releasing its hold as it disappeared from sight. The darkness flooded in, suddenly complete.

Yet, around the hacienda's pool, the mariachi music was lively, and the brightly-colored globes of the party lights glittered like colored diamonds. Dancers twirled or swayed to the music, whatever happened to suit their mood, some very near the swimmers in the pool.

Nothing suited Jane's mood. Neither had the three bites of beef she'd eaten, or the sopapilla she'd choked down. She was irritated at Cord. He'd commandeered her as his seating partner, and now he had disappeared to heaven knew where.

Jane looked around as the music changed, picking up in beat, and strobe lights started to flash. She'd forgotten. The DJ. One had been hired for the final part of the festivities.

"Ma'am, your things? Are you finished?"

A young man in a white apron indicated her empty plate. Her glass was still half full, but she smiled and motioned. "Take it all. I'm finished."

"We'll be clearing away the tables soon. You may want to join the others around the pool. The dance floor will be going here."

"Oh! My! I had no idea we were going all out." She laughed, but it was to charm the boy. She was really concerned that Billy and the rest of the family were nowhere to be seen. She glanced in the pool, but there were no familiar faces, and no bodies on the bottom. She had no idea where everyone had gone.

It was the dance floor that got her attention. A gridwork frame was snapped together on the grass, then a hardwood floor was unrolled in three sections and pinned in place with stakes. Just like that. The first person she saw step out was Romeo. For a minute he was by himself, dancing in the colored strobe lights. Then he saw her and motioned for her to come on out.

She laughed. Why not? She kicked off her shoes and stepped onto the wood surface, taking his hand. The first thing he did was spin her around and drop her in his arms.

"You're entirely too beautiful, mi amor. What does Tarzan have that I don't?" He whispered the words to her.

When he pulled her up, she winked, and with a smile, she said, "It's what you do have."

"What's that?" He looked puzzled.

"Four divorces."

"Uh!" He frowned. "Does everyone know?"

Jane laughed. "Of course. This is a very small town."

"Want to try for number five?" He was all smiles again.

By that time there were several other couples on the floor with them, and Jane asked to be released. She had done her duty, and as she picked up her shoes and put them on, she looked back to the dance floor. There was Cord.

She suddenly felt sick. He was with some woman she didn't recognize. She was entirely too young for Cord, but she had a huge diamond on her finger.

The engagement ring Cord had purchased at J. Gale's. It was on her finger. It must be. No one that young could afford a ring like that! She must be Cord's fiancée, Vangie.

"Oh, Billy, where are you?" She wanted desperately to leave this party. She looked for Peggy and couldn't find her, either. She reached for an arm she recognized. "Roxi?" It was Roxanne Fuller, although Jane knew she'd married and now had a different last name. "Have you seen Peggy?"

"Peggy Johnson?"

"I can't find her anywhere, and she's my ride home." She would be, too, if Billy and Jasmine had already made their exit.

"Jane, honey, I think she was at the little building over there, earlier. That, what did Cord call it, his *Casa di Sita?*" Roxanne grinned. "I don't think that was it, but close, anyway."

"Sure. Thanks, Roxi. I'll check there." What she would do was head to the house. Her handbag was inside—a blue clutch, very tiny—and her phone was in the bag. She'd start calling numbers, and she'd find out where someone was, a taxi, if nothing else.

Inside she located her clutch and pulled out her phone. Scrolling through her numbers, she walked to the French doors facing on the festivities. Cord and his "girl" stepped off the dance floor, laughing. Jane let her phone drop. Surely this wasn't Vangie. Now that she saw her full in the face, she definitely had the Rivera look, especially in her smile. And she couldn't be over thirty-five, although with modern skin care, she could possibly be nearer forty.

She must be one of Cord's nieces. Yes, that was it. Relief flooded over Jane. The girl was one of Cord's nieces, and she'd joined the party because she could. After all, this was her uncle's home.

Even so, Jane had reached her limit. The quiet of the house was nice. Peggy could have her good time for a while longer. Jane would run her down later, if Billy and Jasmine didn't show.

As she walked back toward the living room, she heard one of the French doors open with a whoosh, and a voice called to her.

"Jane! I thought I saw you inside. I have someone I want you to meet." It was Cord, half in and half outside the house.

"Not now, Cord. I'm about partied out." She waved tiredly. "I'm sitting through this one."

"Oh, no, you're not." He grinned. "You want to meet this person."

She drew in a sharp breath, retorting, "Sure, if I must. Let's get this over with."

Cord turned and motioned someone to join him. He pushed the door wider, and the young woman he'd been dancing with stepped in with a smile.

"Hello," she said.

"Pleased to meet you." *And to get a ride home,* but Jane kept that inside. This was one girl she didn't care to meet, niece or fiancée. But, she was here, trapped, and she could be polite.

Cord took a deep breath and said, "Jane, this is Vangie. Her full name is Evangeline Joy Wise. Vangie, this is Katherine Jane Lane."

"Waggoner." Jane corrected the inaccuracy, nodding politely. "Jane Waggoner. Lane is my maiden name."

"This is so exciting." Vangie rubbed her arms, and she giggled. "I have been waiting all my life to meet you."

"All your life?" Jane frowned, caught off guard. "Cord, maybe you should explain to me."

"I'm sorry." Vangie looked at Cord and held up a finger. "You don't know, yet. I don't guess Dad has told you. I forgot that this was a surprise." She giggled again, in a way that seemed very familiar to Jane. Her voice, too. Familiar, and yet not at all.

"I don't know what? Cord?" Dad? Jane felt her head tighten, and she clutched her phone tighter. A lifeline. It was her lifeline to rescue. Peggy, Billy, a taxi. Someone. Anyone.

"Let me." Vangie stepped to Jane and put her arms out. "I want to hug you. Is that okay?"

Jane stood frozen, but she didn't say no.

In the hug, Vangie whispered, "Thank you for loving me enough to give me a chance at life." She backed away, still holding to Jane, as she whispered with a smile and tears, "Mom."

Jane felt the room go silent. She couldn't take it in. Then, she felt her knees give way, and everything went black.

"JANE?"

She looked up to find Cord's face over her, and his hand holding hers. "Did I dream that?"

"Your daughter? No, she's right here beside me." He chuckled. "We didn't mean to scare you to death."

"Are you all right, Mom?" The voice that was so familiar, and yet not familiar at all, enveloped her.

"Could I get some water? My mouth, it's dry." She pulled herself up and into a chair, looking to see Vangie heading off into the next room. "Cord, are you serious?" She nodded Vangie's direction.

"Serious as all get-out." He had an insane grin on his face.

"Where did she come from?"

"Oh, Jane, after all this time, you can't figure that out?" He laughed. "You, girl, have a lot to learn, if you don't know where babies come from."

— Epilogue —

"AND THAT'S HOW IT all happened up to right now."
Vangie finished with a hug and a smile for Jane, having
told of the thirteen years she'd spent with her adopted parents in Brazil, and their death on a supply trip home to the
States when their single engine plane crashed.

Jane patted her face with a tissue. It was really too
much to take in. "Cord, you couldn't tell me about this six
weeks ago?"

"Would you have listened six weeks ago?"

"And you and Shelly?" This part still had Jane puzzled. After all, he did marry the woman.

"Remember, Jane? I tried to tell you. Veronica was
born very premature. Except she was over eight pounds. I
was a kid. I didn't know, so I accepted it."

"How much premature?"

"Two months. Her birthday is in December. It makes
sense, if you think about it."

"And you never figured it out." Jane was still having
trouble taking it all in. Vangie was her daughter, adopted
by a young couple killed while traveling on the mission

field.

"As I said, I was a kid."

"She tricked you." It sounded like Shelly.

"That's as good a way to say it as any. My family had a good name, and hers had threatened to throw her out. That party was her chance. And they didn't have DNA testing back then." He shook his head resignedly. "But that's over and done with."

"And you figured this out how?"

"A hand-written note from Shelly. It was in her desk from years ago. I don't think she remembered writing it, and at the end, she was so sick, she probably didn't care."

"But," Jane hesitated, "that doesn't explain you." She spoke to Vangie. "How did you find us?"

"I didn't." She had pulled up a chair for Cord and for herself by that time. "That was Veronica's doing."

"So, let me get this straight." Jane didn't think she had it straight at all, but she would give it a shot. "Veronica figured out her father and a woman she'd never met had a daughter in South America that had been adopted to a couple on the mission field?" She laughed. "No one's going to believe that. I'm having trouble with it, myself."

"No, it was simpler. Veronica and I have talked it through the past few days. It was the note from her mother." Vangie looked at Cord, suppressing a smile. "When Dad showed her, she was so excited. She'd known they were nothing alike. The note explained something she'd suspected for years. She started researching, and she found her birth father's records. He was a pilot killed in Vietnam less than a year after she was born. The grandparents on that side were gone, also. There was only a third cousin left, or something like that. That was how she confirmed the details. The cousin died shortly after, so that connection is gone forever."

"However," Cord broke in, "that wasn't all she found. Me, on some paperwork with a K. J. Lane. Hm. Wonder who that could be?" He grinned. "And you didn't even tell me."

Now it was Jane's turn to be on the spot. "Self-preservation. I tried to hide it, telling my parents I was in Denton at college. Really, I was in the Esther House for pregnant girls. Your birthday is Valentine's, right?"

Vangie nodded. "Your parents never knew they had a granddaughter?"

"Perhaps." Jane felt guilty about that. "I think they knew something. They treated me as if I should be guilty of something, but we never talked about it. But then, that was my family. We either yelled at each other or swept things under the rug." She felt the tears break through her veneer of self-control. "I hope you had a happy childhood. I truly tried to do what was best for you. I had nothing to offer you with me being so young, and my parents would have been ashamed."

Vangie grabbed her mother and held her close, patting her arm. "Oh, don't worry one bit about me. I had the best life ever. It was all part of God's great plan. He took something that was meant to be for bad and turned it for good. That's the way God is."

"And they were killed on a supply run, you said, in an airplane?" Even for a Christian, that didn't sound so good.

"Yes." Vangie's eyes were red. "But I know where they are. They're with the Heavenly Father."

"But since then, how did you manage?" Jane felt a twinge of guilt that she'd been unable to let go of the simple things God had been dealing with in her devotions. Forgive. Forget. Don't get angry. Love. And this girl had struggled with the premature death of her parents. How sad.

"I was twenty-five when that happened. I stayed there a couple more years until a new missionary family could be trained and placed there.

"I came back to the States and finished my doctoral studies in counseling. Then I worked in various facilities. Last year, I met Jeremiah Cowling, a wonderful doctor at one of the hospitals where I worked. We share the same faith and commitment to God and the hurting world around us. We became engaged and are getting married next month. He tried to come with me to the reunion, but there was an emergency surgery he had to perform just as we were readying to leave.

"We want to start a family of our own as soon as possible, but we also plan on adopting, as well. I'm here this evening hoping my father will give me away, and my mother will be my matron of honor."

"Did you know you were adopted when you were growing up?" That question had haunted Jane for years.

"Of course. My parents always told me that most parents didn't get to choose their children, but they picked me, and I was loved more because I was adopted." She smiled. "I loved it that I was adopted. I felt sorry for kids that weren't."

"You never wanted to look for us?"

"I didn't want to intrude. You did the greatest thing of all by letting me live. I had great parents. Now I believe God wants me to be a part of your lives."

Cord wiped his eyes and asked, "Would you be opposed to a double ceremony?"

"Double ceremony? Who are you marrying?" Jane felt her heart drop.

Cord reached into his pocket and pulled out a velvet ring box from J. Gale's Fine Jewelry Store. He opened it to reveal a five-carat heart-shaped diamond mounted on a platinum band. He carefully took Jane's hands in his. "I've always loved you, and only you, Jane. Will you marry me and make me the most blessed man on the face of the earth?"

"You want to marry me?" Jane had to get her head around this. Her daughter was back, Cord knew what Jane had done, and now he wanted to propose. She could barely speak. "After all this?"

"Yes, and I want an answer now, tonight, before another crazy thing happens. I want to know that you love me and want me to be your husband for the rest of your life." He knelt at her side. "I lost you for forty years. I can't lose you again, mi corazón."

"Yes." She felt her voice tremble, and as she said the word, she knew she meant it with every ounce of her being. "Absolutely yes." She shook as he slipped the ring on her finger.

"It's beautiful." Vangie took her hand.

"Does it fit?" From Cord.

"I think so. How . . ."

"Let me just say Peggy's a really good friend," Cord chuckled. "I had to get it re-sized. I'd just come out of the store with it when I saw you the other day. It was a close call. I thought maybe you knew something was up."

Jane was secretly glad he didn't know she thought he was in there buying an engagement ring for Vangie.

Cord let go of Jane's hands, and he stood up and yelled toward the bedroom, "You can all come out now. She said yes!"

Out of Cord's bedroom poured Veronica and her husband, along with the boys, and then Billy, Jasmine, their children, and finally, Peggy. They all ran up at once and began hugging everyone.

"You mean everyone knew about this but me?"

Billy piped up, "Veronica called me about a month ago with the news. I think it's going to be great to have sisters to share the holidays with."

Jasmine smiled in approval.

Then, Peggy broke in, "I only found out this week because everyone was afraid I'd tell you." She tried to look like she was pouting, but it only produced more laughter and giggles.

Cord spoke up, "When I finally found our daughter a little over a year ago, it was all I could do not to call and tell you right then. But it wasn't the right timing for Vangie. So, I waited."

Vangie laughed and said, "You know what they say: The mother is always the last to know."

Cord finally reminded everyone there was a party going on outside, and he'd better attend to it.

Jane followed him out the door to see what his next step would be. From now on, she planned to be at his side. She was still in a state of elation and shock to know she was finally going to be with the man of her dreams. She had to agree with Vangie that only God could have pulled off something this spectacular.

Cord stepped outside onto the patio and walked over to the DJ booth. He turned off the CD that was playing and asked for the microphone. The surprised DJ quickly obliged.

"Ladies and gentlemen, I have an announcement to make." Cord paused for a moment for the crowd to settle so they could hear his news. Various friends and classmates looked at one another as if trying to figure out what would be so important. "I want you to know that on our fortieth class reunion, Jane has finally said yes to Tarzan. I'll no longer be swinging through the trees alone, but will have at my side our classmate and the love of my life, Jane. Our three children are here to celebrate this wonderful occasion and the uniting of our families."

Friends in the crowd cheered and hooted, while others looked puzzled, trying to figure out the "three children" part. Cord just smiled as he walked off stage and grabbed Jane around the waist, pulling her close to him.

All she said was, "Bring it on, Tarzan."

Timeless Heart Reunion

— 1 —

"WELCOME TO SHADETREE Assisted Living Center."

Beth Taylor covered the phone receiver and called out the words brightly. She was finishing a call, and she sat behind her broad, mahogany Chippendale desk. Her nails were freshly done in glossy gumball pink, and her blonde bob just hit her shoulders. She'd completed high school forty years earlier, but except for a light web of lines around her eyes and lips, she'd been told she was as attractive as the day she'd received her diploma.

As she spoke into the phone, Beth opened her devotional for the day, *Following in the Footprints of Jesus*, and glanced at the morning's words from 1 John 1:9. The book helped her keep her sense of balance when she faced difficult situations, and she made a point to read in it every day. "If we confess our sins, he is faithful and just to forgive us our sins, and to cleanse us from all unrighteousness."

Beth breathed a little easier. *Forgive us our sins.* That was something she could use daily. She'd barely finished her greeting and disconnected when she looked up and caught sight of the well-dressed man coming through the door.

Her heart plummeted.

Beth rubbed her hands together to find her palms were suddenly moist, and her stomach felt like a hundred butterflies had just been released. This was a man she'd never intended to face again, and now he walked her direction. Her high school fortieth reunion was planned in a little over a week, so she should have anticipated him, but he'd never attended a single reunion in the past 39 years, so why should she have expected him now? She had conveniently blocked him out of her mind, like one does old numbers on a cell phone. If blocked long enough, the number seems forgotten. Now, here he was, as tall as she remembered, although the gray at his temples was new. He was still lean, though that lanky, high school trimness was gone. Rugged, with long legs and wide shoulders, he carried the look of a man who knew what he wanted in life, not just a teenager curious about everything. His jeans were pressed and covered the tops of polished alligator boots. A brown leather blazer was open at the waist, revealing a wide turquoise buckle.

She felt her breath quicken as she stood and held out her hand. Her motion was automatic and professional, despite the jelly in her knees. She wouldn't let him see how she felt. She couldn't. She would be poised and efficient, a professional woman in a professional environment.

She took a deep breath as he drew closer. She steeled herself, reminding herself she was more than a professional. She owned Shadetree, a prestigious Type A facility for senior adults, after working here for nearly two decades, then investing her husband's life insurance money to buy out the previous owners. She'd become a competent business woman, and while she maintained the position of director, she was far more than that. Forty years had wiped away any connection between her and this indomitable man, so there was nothing for her to get worked up about.

That didn't stop all rational thoughts from careening from her head and shattering her morning into a thousand bone-jarring pieces, as she was taken aback by his response. His penetrating blue eyes locked on hers, he ignored her hand, and he murmured a softly-spoken question, surely intended just for her.

"Is that how you greet an old friend?"

— *Earlier That Day* —

Beth pulled her car into her officially marked parking space in front of the Center. Director, the sign said. It even reflected her name, Beth Taylor. *Owner*, she thought proudly. Dawn was barely breaking through the trees, and it promised to be a beautiful morning, although the temperatures would soar in the afternoon. It was to be expected on a Texas summer day.

She looked for her young assistant's car. Chloe Owens was wonderful to work with, but some days she was a bit of a panic waiting to happen, and Beth had been out of town for two days. The Department of Aging and Disability Services, known in the industry as DADS, had demanded her attention, and she'd been happy to attend and review the newest policies and procedures for licensing new facilities.

She wondered what Chloe would be panicked over this time. A missing bedside table? An air conditioner on the fritz? At times, it was like the little boy who cried wolf, and Beth the huntress who came to his rescue. She imagined smoothing the feathers of a panicked parakeet who'd never been out of its cage.

She killed the engine and dropped her key fob into her purse before she stepped out of her Cadillac to luxuriate in the heady aroma of the Center's bedding plants in full bloom. They lined the staff parking area, infusing the shade under the massive, lumbering oak trees with cheerful shots of brilliant color. Dew sparkled on the grass, and a spider web glistened in a low boxwood shrub just to her left. Everything was fresh and new, with no hint of the life-altering change that would soon collide with her day. She even looked forward to catching up on all the calls she'd missed.

She walked briskly toward the front door, and with an inward smile, she grasped the door handle, tripping the latch and swinging it wide. She would postpone any changes to the sign at her parking space to another day. Her young secretary had sent her a text that a new resident was arriving this morning, sight unseen; not just coming for a walk-through, but moving in, personal items and all.

That had surprised Beth, but she'd told Chloe she would arrive early to ensure the move went smoothly. Chloe had thanked her profusely in a text ending in a smiley face emoji. The normal procedure was to schedule a meeting, with Beth in attendance when possible, go over the legalities of the contracts, and speak very briefly about payment methods. Then would come the tour of the facilities, of which Beth was extremely proud. Walking prospective residents through the upscale, Type A facility was a favorite activity for her. She would give her facility a superior rating to anyone who asked. It had all the best amenities. She had lovingly decorated the hallways with armoires and bombe chests from local antique shops. Each room had a reading nook with a Queen Anne wingback chair and a Stifle brass lamp. Her favorite feature was the flat-panel television cunningly disguised behind a wall-hanging screen. A touch of a remote, and the television was there in all its gleaming glory. Another touch, and the elegance Beth insisted on in each room reappeared once again.

Beth was fully prepared for her new arrival, and she'd tentatively selected a suite for today's guest. Now to locate her attendant and get things prepared, so there would be no holdups. First would be to ensure the unit was freshened and the bath freshly cleaned.

"Chloe!" Beth breezed into the building, calling her assistant's name, as the soft whoosh of the glass door closing on its pneumatics somehow comforted her. The sound spoke of a facility that was well-oiled, polished, and of the highest caliber. Beth insisted on perfection, and she would allow nothing less. After a moment with no response, she frowned, calling out again, "Chloe, where have you gotten to?"

"Oh, Beth!" Chloe rushed through the grand foyer of the Living Center, dropping several file folders onto a polished mahogany sideboard. Her knee-length linen skirt in pale cream contrasted with her lemon-yellow ruffled blouse underneath her soft green jacket. Her honey-colored hair curled in tendrils and was held by a clip at the nape of her neck. Her nails reflected the color of her blouse, giving her a finished professionalism. It was the pen she pulled from behind one ear and placed soundly on the stack that revealed her chaotic approach to her work.

"About that new arrival. I think Suite 134—" Beth was startled when Chloe cut her off.

"First, let me tell you how my morning's gone. I'm so glad you're here. Why—"

"Slow down!" Beth insisted. Chloe always ran at the speed of a runaway freight train, and Beth hadn't even had her first cup of coffee. "Remember the text you sent me this morning? We should make this decision now. Unit 134 has a private courtyard with that wonderful oak—"

"I agree, but I've got something more important you'll be interested in." Chloe interrupted again, picking up her pen and tapping it on the folders. "See this stack of folders? If you knew what I've gone through for you—"

"Hold that thought, Chloe," Beth interrupted, reaching a slender, elegant hand to place it on the younger woman's wrist. "First, I need an explanation. That new guest coming in today, you said something about my past catching up with me. Before we move any further through this morning, and certainly before our new guest arrives, I want to know this: What do you know about my past? Really, now, what could possibly be catching up with me?"

Widowed for nearly three years, Beth felt positive she had no history worthy of anyone's notice, certainly nothing that could catch up with her. Her husband was gone after a painful but mercifully brief bout of heart trouble, giving him time to sort his affairs and tell his family goodbye, and leaving her with over three decades of fond memories that only brought back warm times. Robert had attended the Methodist church each Sunday, even taught a Sunday school class for two decades, done nothing questionable his entire life, and their marriage, while not that of storybook dreams, had been a series of carefully orchestrated events, tied together like a string of pearls, if not ones that Beth might have chosen. It was what Robert had been good at, organizing life in a way that removed all the rough edges. Her daughters, well, she loved them, but they weren't extraordinary in any manner that could haunt her. The youngest was like Robert, charming, with not a rough edge in sight. Her eldest, Candy, was a spitfire that loved life, and she loved people to enjoy it with her, building long-lasting friendships with people across all walks of life. They had attended church camps each summer, taken a mission trip or two, and were members of their local fellowships. Candy had counseled at Camp Whispering Trees in Florida just out of college. Her grandchildren? She didn't have any of those, meaning there wasn't a trouble maker among them.

She had no past to catch up with her, not from the past forty years, anyway. It was only when Chloe looked her directly in the eyes that she realized her assistant was still talking to her.

"Beth, that's what I'm trying to tell you." Chloe took her boss's hand, bringing her back to the moment, and she blurted, "You know Lily Pearl Cadence, don't you? For years she lived on that big ranch just out of town. Well, her son called while you were gone, and I've got all the information here in these folders. She's ninety-two years old, no longer able to live alone, and she refuses to be a burden to her son. She just up and decided to check herself in. I tried to tell her you'd prefer to schedule an appointment to show her around. She wouldn't hear of it, told me she wouldn't think of waiting. She's bringing out a check for the first month today. When I tried to explain that a check isn't necessary, she said she knows of our guest policy, and she isn't moving in on anyone's dime. She has money, and she can pay her own way. Luckily, she can't make it until ten this morning. I've been running myself ragged since seven trying to clear out a suite in the new wing. I forgot the remodeling was finished in 134." Chloe sighed, the sound filled with the worries of the world. Her expression changed, and she smiled brightly. "She wants to bring her own furniture, and it will fill one of the largest suites we have, so 134 will be perfect. I guess that's why you're the boss. You think of everything."

"Now if we can just get those final rooms filled." Beth smiled with forced brightness at Chloe's compliment. "What did you say the new resident's last name was?"

A slow, sinking feeling had begun to blur Beth's world, and she reached to take the top folder off the stack. She'd heard the name just fine, and she knew what she was doing. She was putting off facing the reality of the moment. She was on a roller coaster beginning its rapid descent, and she had no control. All she wanted to do was scream. She now thought she should have returned Maggie Jackson's garbled voicemail. Her best friend's message had shown up on her phone during the conference, and Beth had been too preoccupied to get back to her. Poorly transcribed by her smart phone, it had suggested something about old times coming round again.

Then to get a similar message that morning from Chloe? She closed the folder without reading what was inside. What she really needed was a moment to adjust to her disbelief. The Cadence name unlocked the storage bins of her mind, dragging out old, well-worn baggage, and allowing thoughts long suppressed to rise to the surface. Candy, oh, poor Candy. She hoped this wasn't about her lovely daughter. The possible consequences of Lily Pearl in this facility didn't bode well for Beth's peace of mind.

Chloe pulled back the cover of the top file, glanced inside, and she paused. Then, her eyes searching, she stopped and spoke very clearly, "Cadence, capital C-a-d-e-n-c-e. That's her son's name, too."

"Cadence." The phone rang, and Beth took a deep breath as she moved toward her office and sat at her mahogany desk. She picked up the handset, and before she answered it, she covered the receiver with her hand, glanced at Chloe, and murmured, "I know how the name's spelled."

She'd also caught the part about the son, and her heart beat faster with dread, or at least that's what she wanted to believe. No other explanation could be possible for the emotions she was experiencing. There could be only one Lily Pearl Cadence. Beth had known her son quite well, although the connection between them was decades in disuse.

Just minutes into her conversation, Chloe stepped back into the room, whispering, "Oh, Beth, wait a minute. I have one more file in my office. Be right back."

Chloe exited, and through the bank of windows separating the two offices, Beth watched her snatch one from the filing cabinet behind her desk. She returned, holding it out.

"Here!"

The bell from the front door dinged, and Beth covered the phone and called out, "Welcome to Shadetree Assisted Living Center." Then she reached for the file, while smiling brightly and trying desperately to cover her troubled feelings. "Do these folders by any chance say who the son is?"

Again, she was putting off what she already knew,

wanting to put as much distance between the past and the present as she could. Despite her efforts, her heart turned over just asking the question.

"Maverick, capital M-a-v-e-r-i-c-k."

A man's deep voice spoke the words, and Beth looked up in dismay. At the sight of the visitor in the foyer, her heart truly turned over, leaving her emotions in a puddle. She gripped the phone in her hand and knew she couldn't maintain a proper conversation to the person on the other end in the light of who had walked in the Center's door.

"Thank you. I'll call back later." Beth spoke the words carefully into the mouthpiece and drew in a deep breath. She dropped the phone into its cradle, slowly and without conscious thought. Cascading ribbons of memories flashed in front of her eyes, few of them welcome. She felt the last forty years of her life evaporate, forty years of perfect children, an equally successful marriage, and a social life that was the envy of half the county. She narrowed her eyes at the tall, silver-headed gentleman in starched blue jeans. A crisp white shirt under a leather blazer complemented his tanned skin. It was the same face she remembered from four decades before. His piercing blue eyes completed her devastation, with the same steely glint he had wowed her with years ago.

She could not have this man here in her life, not now, not ever. There was no room for him under the scar he'd put on her heart. He had run away, and he should have stayed away.

"Maverick?" Beth barely managed her shattered reply. Her voice sounded hollow and shaky to her ears. She felt helpless. Maverick had always done this to her, made her soft and weak, and it was happening again. Unable to respond rationally, she simply stood and reached out one hand.

"Is that how you greet an old friend?" murmured his resonating voice.

"An old friend?" Chloe's eyes danced between the

two.

Before Beth could manage to think through this disastrous moment, she felt Maverick's strong arms pull her off her feet. Her intruding ghost from the past picked her up in a bear-like hug, holding her in an embrace that was a little too long for her to feel comfortable.

"Well, Marilyn, how are you?" Maverick's strong, slow, baritone drawl pulled at her heart. He set her down, and his eyes studied her face, evaluating her. "You look great, and, if you'll allow me to say so without running away to hide, you smell good, too. My word, girl, you're just like I remember from high school."

"High school? What could you possibly remember from all those years ago? I've forgotten so much that I'm surprised I even recognize you."

Beth's lips quivered slightly as she finished the sarcastic words, and she hoped she sounded convincing. She wanted to appreciate his effusive compliments, but a strong undercurrent of irritation in the back of her mind dashed all that like a Texas soaker on a hot summer afternoon. Maverick's comments sent her thoughts reeling through a succession of memories, most pushed aside for more decades than she wished to recount. Her final two years in high school had been the most special of her life, and she had felt beautiful. Then, Maverick had turned her existence into a living nightmare.

She was sure her dismissal of his unnecessary references to a time better forgotten would distance this man from her life. If she claimed she hadn't recognized him, he'd know she'd forgotten all about him. He would see that he was an intrusion into her well-ordered life, and he would wrap up his business with his mother quickly and efficiently, exiting the premises as quickly as possible.

Then Beth's secret and heart would be safe once again.

MAVERICK'S EYES SPARKLED, and his face brightened. He chuckled as he began to speak.

"If you don't recognize me, that must mean I've either gotten better looking or just the opposite. I don't know which I'll claim. You've hardly changed at all. You still have that fabulous blonde hair; it's just not in a shag anymore. I like it down like it is now. It reminds me of your senior picture."

His heart cinched tightly in his chest, as long-forgotten emotions tumbled through his veins. He took a deep breath, aware of the past like a journal that had recorded every event from their relationship, and the pages were peeling themselves away, faster and faster. He hadn't expected this strong of a response. He had been looking forward to staying for the upcoming reunion the following week, but now? He needed to change the subject fast before this woman pushed him to the point of no return.

"MY SENIOR PICTURE?" Beth barely got out the words, but she was determined to control her reaction and not reveal what she truly thought. She couldn't reveal how he'd crushed and bruised her heart all those years ago. Her sweet husband Robert had been her only salvation, rescuing her from the morass this man had strewn across her world. For years, with Robert as her guide, she'd successfully entertained her husband's clients, hosting fabulous parties for the moneyed investment bankers who had been Robert's business associates. Now, alone, she ran this assisted living facility, and very successfully, too. How could she be falling apart in front of this man? She hadn't known this melting feeling inside for four decades, not since the last occasion she'd spent time with him.

She felt her jaw tighten with determination, refusing to reveal any weakness. Her assistant gave a little cough, causing Beth to warm with the thickly layered praise.

"I go by Beth, now, Maverick," Beth whispered, biting her lip. She kicked herself for calling his given name. She knew she must keep this formal, otherwise, who knew where things would wind up? Self-consciously, she adjusted her rose-colored blouse and dark skirt and attempted to make light of the moment.

"I'm glad your looks haven't changed." He winked at her. "A woman as beautiful as you should have the best parking space in the lot, which I see you've taken."

With a flip of her hand in her hair and a bright bravado to her voice, Beth quipped, "It's just that now my blonde gets a little help from a bottle."

She hardly felt as effusive as she hoped she sounded. This morning had fled from her control, and she didn't know how she would get it back.

"A genie from a bottle?" Maverick chuckled.

"I did not say that!" Beth glanced at Chloe, hoping for some help. Instead, her assistant was covering a smile of her own with one hand.

"I'm sorry for laughing, but you'll have to speak up a little, Marilyn. Phnom Penh got some of my hearing." Maverick paused, waiting on Beth.

"No one calls me Marilyn, anymore," Beth repeated louder. She wasn't sure if she felt irritation or relief at having to repeat the words. She knew one thing: Maverick wouldn't be allowed a toehold back into her life.

His next words shook her resolve.

"No? Well, that's a shame with those good looks and all." Humor laced the words, and the big man grinned again as he watched Beth.

Beth felt her face warm as she closed her eyes and stifled a groan. She cleared her throat, determined to ask about his mother. That's why he'd come, and getting back to business was her only hope now. A dozen words from that man's mouth, and her knees felt about to buckle.

Maverick leaned over Chloe's desk and winked at the young assistant standing just behind. "You'd think a woman would enjoy being Marilyn Monroe, wouldn't you? Ours may have been a little thinner, but she certainly looked like a movie star. Well, as far as I can tell, she still does."

"Maverick!" It was hopeless. Beth was convinced her face had turned deep red. She certainly felt the warmth of embarrassment. And to have told such a thing to Chloe! Even so, she remembered those years, and how it had secretly given her a certain amount of pleasure to be compared to the blonde beauty from the heyday of the big screen. She cringed at what Maverick shared next.

"But not this one," he pointed to Beth. "She always said her name was Mary Elizabeth Monroe anytime we tried to tease her about it. Isn't that right, Marilyn?"

"Yes. I wanted to be liked for who I was and not the person someone else wanted me to be."

What Beth wanted to scream was, *Stop talking about all this!* How could she fend off this man if he continued to say things to remind her of how much she had loved him all those years ago . . . no! Not loved! She couldn't have loved him. No, their relationship had been a mistake, and she wouldn't let go of that thought. She had been a youthful, idealistic girl, and he'd abandoned her, shattering her dreams. This man would not charm his way into her affections, um, under her skin ever again.

Only the sound of the carts carrying the midmorning brunch trays shifted Beth's thoughts back to the moment. She tamped down her emotions. These were her surroundings, her office. Maverick was in her place. She put a stern look on her face to make sure there was no question how she felt.

MAVERICK'S WORDS WERE a compliment he'd waited with bated breath to deliver. After all, he'd held on for forty years to make its delivery, and he intended to enjoy this moment to the fullest. He had no trouble reading the nuance of Beth's every expression. He was quite aware this could only be her space. It looked like her. He'd taken in the spacious surroundings, missing nothing, including the small silver-framed photos sitting pristinely on Beth's expansive, hand-carved Chippendale desk. This was an opulent facility, just the sort of environment she'd grown up with. He wasn't surprised by the expensive taste he observed everywhere.

The phone rang, and Chloe picked it up. After a moment, she held it out to Beth, calling, "It's for you, Mrs. Taylor."

Beth picked up the phone and stepped aside for a moment, answering a few questions from the caller. She glanced at Maverick several times, pausing once as if she intended to ask him to come to the phone. By that time, he'd struck up a conservation with Chloe.

"Tell me again Marilyn's last name." He could barely keep the grin from his face. This was a doozy.

"Taylor, but she truly goes by Beth. I've never heard her called Marilyn. She was an actress, right? I've never watched old movies much."

"Taylor, like Elizabeth?"

"Yes, like the movie star. She was in *Lassie*, I think. I watched it some as a girl."

"That and a few others." Maverick began to laugh, thinking that there were about seventy-five more. When Beth hung up, she turned and looked at Maverick with a frown. That caused him to laugh even more.

BETH STARTED TO CALL to him, then the thought hit her, she had pulled up in the best parking space in the lot? How did he know where she parked? Had he been outside all along watching her? It was something he had done all those years ago, telling her he couldn't get of enough of her. She had found it flattering then. Now? She refused to admit his gratuitous words still affected her, even made her knees feel weak.

"Okay, Mr. Cadence. What's so funny?" Beth punched out his name, the snap in her voice bracing her determination. She took a deep breath, steadying herself. She would need to speak carefully to keep this situation under control.

"Your name is now Elizabeth Taylor? So, Marilyn

Monroe wasn't good enough for you?" His eyes crinkled, and he placed one hand on his stomach as he shook with laughter. At his side, Chloe wasn't helping. She was laughing, also.

Beth looked pointedly at her assistant, immediately subduing Chloe's laughter. Then she turned to Maverick. "My late husband was Robert Alexander Taylor. I still go by my married name. I volunteered here when he was still alive, and all my residents have come to know me by that name. I see no reason to change it now."

The words briefly weighed on her. Speaking of Robert made her miss his companionship even three years after his death. She guessed what everyone told her was true. A part of her would probably always miss him.

Then she remembered the phone call.

"That was your mother calling to say she'll be late, but the moving van is on the way. She's made an appointment to get her hair done, and the hairdresser is running behind. She refuses to be seen in her new home without looking her best. She gave me strict instructions to tell Maverick to take the tour in her stead."

"She did, huh?" The laughter was still in his voice, and he turned to Chloe and gave an exaggerated wink. "Sounds as if it's better for her to be here with you two than in her townhouse or out on the ranch with me. She's wearing herself out corralling both her intown and ranch staff. Two houses are far too much for her to manage and maintain her active social calendar."

"Maverick!" For the second time, Beth found reason to call the man on his behavior. That was like old times, too. Maverick never had been one to pay too much attention to rules he thought superfluous.

Just like . . . Candy, but Beth pushed that thought away.

She tried to control her tone by being bright with her next words. "Lily sounds as feisty as ever. I'm sure we'll love having her with us. She'll keep us on our toes."

Beth remembered Maverick's mother from when they were in high school. Maverick had been a couple of years older than Beth, but they'd gone to many of the same functions, even to his house with the sports crowd a time or two after football games. Lily was everyone's mother, having kids over to support the team. She was also one to stick her finger in everyone's pie. Somehow Beth seemed to always get paired up with Maverick at Lily's extracurricular activities.

"Feisty? That and more. After Dad's death three-and-a-half years ago, well, I guess it tripped something in Mom. And now, she's worse." The humor in Maverick's words was gone. His voice sounded dry and empty, bringing a pang of sympathy from deep within Beth. This was clearly a painful topic for him.

"I'm so sorry to hear about that. I remember seeing the news. We'll certain do our best for Lily. Is there anything else we need to know?" Beth could hear the unexpected tiredness in his voice, and tender emotions welled up in her.

"Even when I tell you, you won't believe me. Mom went on a selling spree. You remember how she always collected everything. Toward the end of Dad's life, it almost became hoarding. Suddenly, she attempted to liquidate everything. Well, almost. She still has most of her antique furniture and some of her collectables, but the farm implements and other equipment? Gone. Dad's Model T wasn't even spared. She tried to parcel out the ranch, saying she wanted to live in town for her final years. She'd already sold off twelve hundred acres before I found out, so I told her I'd buy the rest from her. We argued for weeks, but at least she didn't sell the remaining eighteen hundred. I managed to save part of my family heritage and the history that goes with it, but you can't run a whole lot of cattle on that. I don't know what I'll do with it eventually, but that's neither here nor there at this point. For the past three years, she's been living in town. Finally, I've forced her to admit that it's just too much. When I found out some months ago that you were the administrator of this place, it was like an answer to prayer."

That shot Beth's astonishment meter off the charts. She was an answer to prayer for Maverick? Since when did Maverick pray, ever? And for her? Even though her family went faithfully, she didn't remember Maverick ever going to church. This was one more reason to steer clear of this tangled hunk of walking trouble, no matter what her heart told her.

She attempted to steer the conversation onto a more neutral track.

"Everyone says that, Mr. Cadence. The general consensus of our residents and their families is that Shadetree Assisted Living Center is certainly an answer to prayer." Beth caught Chloe's puzzled look, frowning sharply when her assistant mouthed silently, *They say what?* Ignoring Chloe's question, Beth smiled forcefully at Maverick, determined to maintain control of this situation.

"Is there anything I need to do as far as paperwork before Mom moves in? If not, then I want that tour my mom said I should take."

"Paperwork you asked for, and paperwork you shall have, Mr. Cadence. Chloe?" Beth motioned for her assistant to get on the ball. She was feeling his charm, er, his overpowering, um, overbearing assumptions making her nervous. It was Chloe's turn to pick up the slack.

Chloe efficiently handed him a packet. She smiled as she spoke, "This is everything you'll need to fill out before she takes occupancy. Some of the forms will need to be notarized, but we can do that right here. In addition to being Mrs. Taylor's personal assistant, I'm a legally qualified notary."

"Ah! I'm not to be allowed to forget that there are *two* beautiful people in the room." He turned to Chloe and took the packet. He thanked her and kissed her hand, causing the young woman to blush with pleasure. "I'm sure we'll be seeing more of each other."

With those words Beth remembered what she hadn't liked about Maverick all those years ago: his flirting. She could never tell when he was serious, just like now. That was the part that had unnerved her around him then, and it was clear he hadn't changed a bit. Her late husband hadn't been that way at all. He was a considerate man and a stable father to her two daughters. He would sometimes push Beth to do more than she wanted, but that was only due to her natural shyness. He always said it was for her own good, and look how she'd put all that aside, entertaining for her husband over decades, and now running the Center. Thank God for Robert. With him, she had always known where she stood. His consistency had made her feel safe and secure.

Maverick would have never given her safe and secure. He bordered on reckless. Driving too fast, taking too many chances, like signing up for military service, then going off to war. He didn't have to enlist. There was college, the fact that he was an only child, and his parents owned a ranch where he was needed. It had surprised Beth that his father and mother didn't even try to stop him. At least he was one of the lucky ones who came back. Even then he didn't stay long, only a few weeks. As fast as he could get his boots shined, he moved away.

Beth heard he later married and had a son and a daughter. Now here he was, drawn back once more to his old home, checking on his mother.

At least no one could say he wasn't a good son.

"Well, how about it?"

The words interrupted Beth's thoughts, jerking her back to the present.

"What? I'm sorry. I wasn't listening. What did you ask?" She'd tried to rise above Maverick, presenting a very business-like approach in her dealings with him. Now she felt embarrassed. She had no idea he'd been speaking to her.

"Are you going to give me the nickel tour, or do I have to get your pretty little secretary to help me?"

At her assistant's eager expression, Beth brightly called out, "Chloe, can you show Mr. Cadence around?"

"Of course, Mrs. Taylor."

"Chloe can answer most of your questions, I'm sure. Please have a good morning, Mr. Cadence."

With that, Chloe excitedly got up from her desk and put her arm through Maverick's extended one. "Now, this is the main lobby," she began, as she walked him toward the spacious foyer. Pointing to the back of the building, she noted one of the establishment's most elegant amenities. "We even have a Steinway grand, permanently donated to our facility by a resident's family."

The tour disappeared down a hallway toward the new wing. Beth felt like a rag doll long due for a refit. She knew what had done it: meeting Maverick again after four decades. She'd certainly never expected that. If she'd been forced to give him the tour, she wouldn't have survived. Of all things, that man putting his mother here!

It was only a little after ten, and Beth realized she was done for the day. Today Maverick had caught her off guard. She might be forced to deal with him because of his mother, but she would be more prepared in the future. This wouldn't happen again.

She arched her back as she ran her fingers through her thick hair, pushing it away from her face, while trying to ward off an impending headache. Home sounded good. Chloe could corral the residents the rest of the day.

WHAT BETH DIDN'T NOTICE was the silhouette she revealed through her glass office wall. Chloe had forgotten the key to the new wing, and Maverick was waiting in the foyer. He had a very clear view of Beth as she stretched to ease the pain.

"I'm back, Beth," he whispered to no one in particular. "This time I won't run away. I can promise you that."

It was eight days until the reunion, he had already set his trap, and now he had to sit back and wait for it to spring.

— 2 —

THE PHONE JANGLED, shattering the silence of the night, before going quiet. Beth flung her comforter to the side, squinting at the windows stretching across the back wall of her bedroom. She was surprised to see sunlight already peeking in through the plantation shutters. She worked her hands over her face, starting at her eyes, and letting her fingers make their way to her temples.

"I told the decorator my east-facing windows needed light-blocking drapes, not shutters," she moaned. The phone jangled again, and she winced. "My word! Who could be calling me this early in the morning?"

She recalled the sermon last Sunday titled, "Don't Hold Back." The theme had been based on music and how Christians should let the love of Christ be a song in their hearts. She glared at the phone, thinking that if they could just remaster phones to ring in your heart to wake you up gently, that would be fine with her.

When she rolled over and looked at the clock, the time jarred her awake. It was nearly eight. There would be no time for her regular run, nor for her accustomed after-run morning shower. Maggie would have to understand when she skipped breakfast, too. She'd be good to get her face on and out the door by nine. She laid the blame squarely where it belonged, on Maverick. He'd shown back up in her life, and that had her rattled. She tossed and turned until she'd given in and taken a sleeping aid.

Now look where it had gotten her.

When the phone jangled again, she lifted the receiver and placed it to her ear.

"Yes?" She half expected Maverick's gravelly voice, or at least Lily Pearl's. If it was either of those two, she could claim two ruined days in a row.

The response over the line was even worse than she expected.

"Ready, Miss Morning Sunshine?" It was Maggie, and she giggled at her brilliance. "I'm sorry I'm running late, but you know me. How was your jog this morning? I bet you've been five miles, and you're on your exercise bike just waiting on Little Miss Come Lately to show. I had to repair a chipped nail, but I'll be there in ten."

Even though they were the same age, Maggie still had a child-like quality about life. Nothing ruffled her feathers. From cars to shoes, she kept them until they went out of style, or they didn't feel right anymore. The only thing she'd held onto for more than a decade had been her friendship with Beth.

Right then, Beth wasn't so sure *that* was going to survive much longer.

"Maggie, dear, I'm hanging up now. Yesterday was atrocious, and I just can't be friends with you or anyone at this moment. The fact is I overslept, and I need to shower before I go anywhere. Let's make it another day, okay?" Beth felt the memory of Maverick wash over her, and the very thought filled her with looming frustration.

She didn't get a peaceful response, as much as she wanted to wish the world away.

"Absolutely not! You've put me off long enough. Hurry and grab a shower, and I'll meet you at Deep South's for breakfast. I'll have your coffee ready for you. Now, hurry up!" There was a suppressed giggle, and the phone went dead.

What could be so important that Maggie couldn't let her get a few more minutes of sleep, anyway? Beth tiredly sat up in bed. The phone in her hand wasn't in the mood to give her that answer, though, and Beth was in no frame of mind to call Maggie back.

At least it was Friday, and the workweek was almost over.

Knowing it would help force her awake, she hit the button on her bedside table to trigger the shutters. With a gentle whirring noise, the slats rolled around, sending brilliant sunshine arcing into the room. She squinted, but it was working. She would never find sleep again after that wakeup shock.

It was in her closet that she remembered the casual Friday rule she'd let Chloe talk her into several months back. Casual Friday, she considered, touching several of her most easy-going dresses. Then her finger touched one she'd almost forgotten about. Maggie had talked her into it a couple months ago during a trip to the outlet mall, and she had given in because it was on sale.

She hadn't worn it, even once.

There had been no occasion in her leisure time, and it was just a bit more vibrant than she normally wore to work. But Maverick! He had her remembering her high school years—not that it was a good thing—and the soft, raspberry sherbet dress called to her. Besides, it was almost summer, with the temperature predicted to be in the 90s. This along with some casual heels, and she could carry a light jacket for indoors. The dress would be very presentable no matter that it left her shoulders completely exposed, and anyway, the color was perfect.

Her lipstick wasn't.

When she opened the lid, she remembered she'd

meant to stop and pick up some at the mall on her way home yesterday. Then her past had crashed into her day, and exhaustion had careened her into every obstacle that could possibly beset her. The mall had flown from her thoughts, and marshmallow rose was empty.

"Thank you, Candy!" Beth reached for the golden tube she could just see hiding in the back of the drawer. Her elder daughter had bought it for her the previous Christmas, telling her it was to brighten her holiday. It had been bright enough that Beth hadn't touched it since. Despite that, it was quality, and she hadn't been able to bring herself to throw it away. Now she was glad she hadn't, as she couldn't go out without lipstick.

This, though, would have to be dabbed lightly.

It was easier said than done. Trust her daughter to buy only the best. One touch, no matter how gingerly applied, was as good as a fierce stroke of her regular lipstick. Beth made a face, and then she laughed. Her eyes! Where had they gone? Her normal brown mascara was a faded flower against her newly brilliant lips.

She glanced at the clock. There was no time to remove the deep crimson. Knowing just what to do, she reached into her closet and rummaged in a drawer. She had a tube of black mascara from an evening social several weeks before. Pulling the brush free, she nodded, satisfied. This would be the perfect foil for the brilliance she'd inadvertently painted across her lips.

She leaned into the mirror, and with a flick of her fingers and a blink into the brush, she stepped back and tried to see herself in the best light possible.

"Lands! I could see this face if there was no light at all. I'm a walking Christmas tree!"

This was makeup for candle-lit dinners and walks in the dark, not for breakfast in the brilliance of a summer morning. She closed the mascara tube and tossed it carelessly on the counter. It was just Maggie she was meeting. Her friend would laugh at her lipstick, Beth would let her excuses dance around the table, and it would be good for a joke for the next month or so. See? she told herself. You're waking up, after all. Opening those blinds was the perfect way to get that sleeping pill out of your system.

"Breakfast, here I come! Maggie, girl, ready or not, you're in for a shock!"

Giving in to the inevitable, Beth headed out of her bathroom and grabbed her key fob. She hoped the long-wearing 18-hour lipstick would somehow lessen and wear off during breakfast.

It had better. She would be embarrassed to wear it all day.

"WELL, MAGGIE D, I see your Mini, and I see an empty space right next to it. Thank the Lord for that."

Beth was at the signal light, waiting to turn into the parking lot, with her blinker clicking off the seconds. A strip of grass accented by small shrubs bordered the street, and closer to the stone, glass, and metal-roofed building, park benches lined the sidewalk for those who needed a place to wait during the restaurant's busy times. It wasn't unusual to have a twenty-minute line around lunchtime. This morning, the parking lot had plenty of empty spaces, but most of them were in the north forty and nowhere near the shade. With the Texas heat warming up early this spring, a cool spot to park her vehicle was highly coveted. The light glinting on the window of her friend's Mini Cooper suggested a lighthearted playfulness that went right along with its owner, but Beth wasn't in a playful mood.

"Maggie, you'd better have my coffee waiting, because my stomach was growling three lights ago." Beth muttered the words as she swung the long hood of her big Cadillac into the empty space, stopping when her parking sensors screamed at her that enough was enough. One look in the mirror telling her that she was barely inside the line filled her with relief that she'd listened to Maggie when selecting this latest Cadillac. Beth had wanted a new SUV, and Maggie had cautioned her about buying something so large. Now Beth was glad to have a smaller vehicle, even if it was the largest sedan the company made. It barely fit in this space.

Walking up to the glass door, her reflection revealed her care at putting herself together. She smiled as she tucked her hair behind one ear, pleased with how soft it felt. Stepping inside, she was less pleased. The space was bright and open, but the wood floors didn't muffle the kitchen sounds or the chattering voices from the various diners. Something with dim lights and thick carpeting would have been a nice choice, and she began to wish she hadn't listened to her friend when she'd suggested Deep South's. She could do this, though, and she put a bright expression on her face as she looked for Maggie.

Beth's smile froze on her lips. She shook her head as she stared and blinked slowly, making sure her vision was clear. Of all things, Maverick was here, and she didn't see how she would avoid him, as he sat in the same booth with her friend! Her panic rising, she glanced around to see what other options were available. A table, perhaps, or she could request they sit at the counter. Maybe she could by-pass them on her way to the restroom and continue out the back door. She didn't even have to stay for breakfast. Maggie and Maverick had each other for company, and they'd do fine on their own.

Then Maggie waved at her, and Beth knew she wasn't to be allowed out of this. When she stepped up to the booth, Maverick's Stetson and Maggie's oversized purse were next to Maggie, conveniently filling a good portion of the seat. Beth hesitated, wanting to ask if she could move the items, and realizing in the same thought how rude that would sound.

"Hey, there. Good morning, Beth. Hand me your purse, and I'll put it with mine. It'll give you more room on your side of the booth."

Beth had no desire to be rude, and her friend's request left her no choice but to offer to slide in next to Maverick. However, she didn't have to like it.

"Good morning, Mags," Beth mumbled, barely keeping the words coherent. There were three cups of coffee already on the table, one on Maggie's side, and two on the opposite. Beth had yet to look at Maverick. She shot her friend a look of fire before glancing at her seat. She told herself that she had to check to make sure the bench was clear. Some men put their sunglasses or wallet beside them. Good manners. In nice restaurants, one never put keys or other personal items on the dining table.

As she shifted her gaze, her eyes swept over Maverick's bulk, his shoulders hunched over the table, and his hands encircling his cup. In that glance, she knew this morning would come to no good. Good had been the security Robert had provided. Good was a new resident checking into the Center, assuring all the bills were paid and sweet Chloe had a steady paycheck. Good was knowing that the man at your side would promise a relationship and then follow through, rather than running off to a war on the other side of the world. Good was not feeling that the previous four decades had never happened, and that despite all the warning bells in her head, she still fit at this man's side like a hand in a glove.

Beth knew one thing for certain: What had gone on in high school should stay in high school.

No forty-year-dead relationship would be allowed to shake up her life now. She would see to that. A properly phrased rebuttal would set Maverick on his ear. She had promised Maggie she would meet her for breakfast, so she might not be able to turn and walk out the door, without feeling like he had made her leave, but this man would know where she stood before breakfast was over.

As Beth reached for a copy of the menu, her hand shook with emotions she thought long forgotten. She remembered how angry she'd been when Maverick had burned the bridges between them all those decades ago. She'd loved him at one time, but the hurt and anger had long eclipsed that. She refused to admit that her flushed skin and beating heart felt distinctly the same as before Maverick had destroyed every connection they'd ever built between them, and she let her irritation continue to grow. Her carefully phrased retort would have a bite to it when she figured out just what to say.

His next words shattered all that.

"Hmm. You smell good again today. How are you, Marilyn?" He reached to slip the quavering menu from her fingers, and he opened it to the inside, just as he used to do all those years ago. One beefy finger pointed to the section at the bottom of the page. "Just there, Marilyn. Order anything you want. The tab's mine."

Beth glanced at him as he spoke, seeing the old ways his expression danced with his words. He'd been exactly this way at seventeen, taking control smoothly and with no effort at all. She also noticed when he glanced at Maggie, and something passed between them. What, Beth couldn't tell. Not romance, surely! A joke they'd shared before she arrived?

Anyway, it didn't matter. All she needed was time and the opportunity to come up with a sharp retort, and he and Maggie could joke all morning long. For now, she intended to focus on the menu in peace and quiet, without being involved in any bantering conversation. It irritated her Maverick had assumed she wouldn't be able to find the breakfast section on the menu. This wasn't her first time up to bat, or to order from a restaurant menu.

"Beth," Maggie broke the silence, speaking softly and tentatively, "I told you your past was coming back to haunt you, but you didn't call me back to find more."

"Call you back?" Beth looked at her hard, throwing out her words like a brick tossed into a bucket of mouse traps.

"Yes, on the phone. Anyway, we can't undo what's

been done, so, heeere's your past. It's Maaaverick!" She giggled, and it was the same one from the phone that morning. She winked, also, although so slightly it was almost nonexistent.

Beth felt her irritation flare.

The waitress walked up, shutting down the conversation. She topped off Maverick's and Maggie's coffee, and she glanced at Beth. "Honey, you haven't touched a drop in that cup. That coffee's going to get cold pretty soon. I just made a fresh batch. Would you like to start over?"

Beth smiled and wrapped both hands around her cup, and it began to quiver in her fingers. She didn't guess she'd calmed down that much. Taking a sip, she nodded at the waitress.

"It's perfect. I'm fine."

"Okay, honey. You let me know when you want a refresh. Would you like a moment before you order?" She made as if to pull her pad from her apron pocket, hesitating when Beth pursed her lips in thought.

"Thank you. Two minutes, please," Maggie said brightly. "You can wait to bring out our order until then, if you don't mind. We won't starve if my friend can decide. You can decide on a breakfast choice, Beth?" Maggie chuckled, and she winked at Beth.

"Gotcha," the waitress acknowledged. "Be back in two. Gotta get this pot back to the kitchen. Fresh coffee coming up next go round." And she was gone.

Beth didn't bother with the menu. She glared at Maggie. If she'd known Maverick would be here at breakfast, she'd have driven straight to the Center. She could have caught the end of breakfast there, and that would have suited her fine. The center served meals of the highest quality, and she felt honored to dine in the establishment she owned anytime the opportunity provided itself.

With that thought, casual Friday leaped into her mind. Dear jumping jelly beans! This dress! She'd left the jacket in the car. And heaven forbid, she had on Candy's lipstick!

Her heart sank. She pictured her mascara; it was just as bold, and totally inappropriate sitting here next to this man. She'd thought she was a walking Christmas tree. She wasn't just the Christmas tree, she was Macy's on parade, the whole schlemiel down Fifth Avenue. Her arms tensed with distress. Could this morning get any worse?

"Beth?" Maggie tapped Beth's wrist. "I guess you didn't hear me. Your past? Coming back to haunt you? You do remember Maverick, don't you?" Her eyes twinkled as she spoke.

The woman knew she was pushing old buttons that had long been in disuse, and that wasn't sitting well with Beth. She retorted, very drily, "I saw him yesterday, and you could have told me he was coming." *Should have* was what she wanted to say. As in, over the phone this morning. instead of giggling so rudely and waking her up from a sound sleep.

The thought of what she was wearing was ever-present in her mind. There was no way she could hide it. It leaped off her lips and eyes, screaming from her bare shoulders. Look at me! I'm nothing more than a silly junior high schoolgirl, begging to be noticed!

It helped a bit when Maggie complimented Beth on what she wore, telling her she'd known the dress would look this sweet on her, even when it had been hanging on the rack. It didn't help when Maverick interjected his take on her clothing choices.

"You know, yesterday you were in high CEO mode. I knew I was speaking to the same girl I'd known all those years ago, but I was having trouble finding you through all those Mr. Cadences. Now look at you. This is the pretty thing I knew in high school, only better. Whoa!" He gave a soft whistle.

Beth felt her face warm. She was rescued by the waitress, and she eagerly snatched up the menu, focusing on the pictures on the page.

"Honey, you still have a full cup. Let me replace that

in a moment. You don't drink another drop. Coffee cold is nasty as brown water. Now, are you ready to order a bite to eat? A breakfast a day keeps the hunger pangs away." A pop of chewing gum finished the quip.

"Blueberry bagel, please." With Maverick being so close, Beth knew she wouldn't be able to eat. She could nibble, though. That would get her through until lunch, and she could eat at the Center. Veal was on the menu. Veal with baby carrots and apple pie a la mode. Focus, she told herself. Think of lunch. Veal. Baby carrots. Apple pie. A la mode.

"Gotcha, honey. Anyone else? No? Be back with your food right away."

A la mode. Vanilla. Strawberry. Banana nut. Banana shake. Chocolate shake. Pineapple upside down cake. Lunch!

"Is that how you've stayed so skinny all these years, just eating a bagel?" Maverick elbowed her gently.

Beth looked up to see him glance at Maggie and wink. Bagel? This was all about dessert and lunch. Now he was flirting with Maggie? She defended her breakfast choice, and very pointedly. This was her chance to set this man in his place.

"I normally eat a very big breakfast. Veal. Apple pie. A chocolate shake to top it all off. You see, I'm not the girl you used to know. I've changed. I do my own thing now, and I'm very independent. You just mind your manners, Mr. Maverick Cadence." Having burst forth with her un-prepared and totally out-of-character tirade, she sagged inside. Had she really said all that? To Maverick? What if he laughed at her? The morning was only getting worse!

"You don't eat all that." Maverick grinned. "You couldn't, not and keep that waistline. Tell me the truth, Marilyn. What's going on?"

"Yeah, Beth. What's going on?" Maggie rustled her keys. She'd had no problem strewing her personal items across the table, and the banter was growing exciting. She could hardly hold her hands still.

Beth's arrogance fled in the light of her embarrassment. The truth fluttered its age-old butterfly wings against her denial. Maverick was at her side, and without understanding just what had been taken from her all those years ago, she'd missed him for most of her life. Robert had been a stalwart stanchion of security and stability, and her kids had been a bright spot she'd always treasure, but Maverick had been her heart and soul.

With Robert gone and her kids away, she was a tumbleweed on the prairie, blown about by her emotions. She sighed, retreating to something safe and normal.

"I didn't sleep well last night. Maybe I'll want something for lunch, but now, no. Coffee and my bagel will be fine. Besides, I'm not that skinny anymore. I fight the extra pounds every day."

Maverick laughed, and it was the boisterous sound Beth remembered, one that boiled up from deep with his chest. "Don't fight those extra pounds so hard. The ones I see are in all the right places."

"Stop teasing her so much, Maverick. You're making her blush." Maggie dropped two extra sugar cubes in her coffee. Her spoon clinked against the ceramic as she tapped it on the side. "I'm so glad they combined half a decade of graduates in our Fortieth Reunion. That'll make it more interesting. With five classes next weekend at the get-together, it'll be amusing trying to guess who people are and see how much some of them have changed. I can't wait to see Buzz. He was so cute when he was a senior; I wonder what he looks like now."

Maggie rambled on brightly about the reunion, nonstop even as the waitress placed their food before them. That was Maggie, though, ever interested in the latest, newest, and best.

Beth was grateful to have something to do with her hands besides hold a hot coffee cup and try to keep it from sloshing out onto the table. She kept catching whiffs of

Maverick's cologne. It wasn't the same as in high school, but it suited him, with a deep, woodsy scent, not at all like Robert's sports-type fragrances.

In between bites of her toasted bagel, she learned that Maverick was now widowed as well. She didn't pry. She couldn't. She could barely keep her bagel down, although she would have liked to know everything. *Just for old time's sake*, she told herself. He didn't elaborate, and Maggie refused to ask.

Maverick was more effusive about his children. His son was with the government in the Middle East on a peace-keeping mission, apparently burning with the same wild, reckless ambition as his father. His daughter, adopted by Maverick and his wife as a baby, had been killed by a drunk driver a decade before. At the present he had no grandchildren.

"I bet you two are wondering why I'm eating this strange concoction." Maverick had a pile of food before him, and he shifted two of the plates.

Beth had missed his order, and her eyes hadn't left her bagel. She glanced his way to see turkey sausage, an omelet that was clearly egg white only, and a pile of pancakes. His coffee was black like hers.

"You're hungry?" Maggie quipped. She cut a bite of ham and dipped it in maple syrup before placing it on her tongue. "I thought that's why we gathered in this fine dining establishment for breakfast."

Beth cleared her throat. "Turkey sausage?" At the Center they served it all the time. She knew turkey. That meant something. Maverick had heart issues? Concern gripped her, although she put it off as no more than a general feeling of interest in his health. At the Center, it was something she dealt with every day.

"You noticed." He grinned appreciatively, picking up a slice and biting off a chunk. "When Dad was diagnosed with heart trouble about twelve years ago, I changed some of my habits."

"Not you, then." Was that relief Beth heard in her voice? She refused to think so.

"Ticker's sound." Maverick tapped his chest. "Just caution. I'm now smoke free, and I've eliminated as much cholesterol and fat from my daily routine as possible. However, there's one thing I haven't given up. Butter." He grinned as he put a large dollop on his pancakes and covered it with maple syrup.

"Oh, that looks good, Maverick." Maggie held her fork poised in the air. "I just thought ham and syrup was the way to go. I should have ordered pancakes. Strawberries. Can you picture that with sliced strawberries dribbled all over? Talk about dying and going to heaven." She licked her lips appreciatively.

"No strawberries, Maggie." Maverick chuckled. He'd already cut off a big chunk, spearing it with his fork. He handed it to Beth. "Try it. You'll like it." He grinned, imitating an old TV commercial, making Maggie giggle.

Beth glared at her old friend. She didn't want to take Maverick's fork, and especially not the fat-laden, rich pancake. Rudeness was not her forte, and she considered how to demurely refuse.

Maverick repeated his request. "Try it, Marilyn. They really are the best pancakes anywhere. I've lived all over the world, and I'm never satisfied until I come back here. Everything I love is always waiting on me right here in my hometown."

Everything he loves? Pancakes were waiting on him? She couldn't imagine what else he expected to be waiting on him.

"I'm sorry, Maverick, but no." Beth tried to push his hand away.

"But yes." He grinned and refused to back down.

"Just one bite, then, and very small." She took the fork and bit off a portion of the pancake. In that moment, she was reminded of why Deep South's had a reputation for the best pancakes served anywhere in this part of the country. A drop of the syrup ran down her chin, and she lifted her napkin to catch it. Folding the napkin and setting it beside her plate, she handed the fork to Maverick.

"That was good. However, it's office time. Chloe was there an hour ago, and I have things to get in order."

"I thought that's why you hired an assistant." Maggie teased Beth. She also picked up Maverick's fork and cut a slice off his pancakes. She closed her eyes in pleasure when she bit into it. "You're right, Maverick. You should have never left. The sweetest pleasures are always where your heart is. I guess your heart is still here."

"Waiting on me." He reached for his fork, keeping his eyes on Beth the entire time.

"I'm gone, Maggie. Maverick, thank you for breakfast." Beth pressed a clean napkin to the corner of her mouth, trying to remove some of the long-wearing lipstick.

Before she stood, a couple of other classmates, Jimmy Dane and a friend, also local business associates, walked by their table. They paused for a moment as if surprised.

"Good morning, Maggie and Beth. How you doing, today? You look especially nice, Beth. I do believe you get prettier every day."

"Jimmy, you always were a smooth talker." Maggie pointed Maverick's fork Jimmy's direction. "How pretty do I look?"

"Pretty enough for a date. Marry me, Maggie." He winked. It was a running tease between them, and everyone knew it, even Jimmy's wife.

"And look who we have with us." Maggie turned the fork Maverick's direction.

"Well, bless my soul! Maverick! I'll be. How are you? I see you're in good company, as always. You and Beth always did fit together well. No wonder she sparkles like a new penny today."

When Maggie giggled, Beth kicked her underneath the table. "Sparkles like a new penny?" Beth hissed the words under her breath. When Maggie kicked her back, she glanced up.

"Yes, New Penny. You're a lighthouse of beauty this morning," Maggie whispered, as she boldly winked.

Jimmy rambled on, "I haven't seen you in ages, Maverick. Are you here just for the reunion? That's a week away, yet."

Beth felt trapped. Maverick was at her side, and Jimmy stood next to her, boxing her in. Maverick knew she'd intended to leave, but instead of helping her out, he'd put his arm across the seat behind her and kept asking Jimmy questions. Both of them seemed engrossed in answering in lengthy detail, no matter how inane the subject matter.

When Beth thought she couldn't handle the claustrophobia any longer, Jimmy shook Maverick's hand, blew a kiss to Maggie, and assured Beth he'd see her at the Chamber meeting at the first of next month. He laughed, ensuring them they'd have a good time at the reunion the following weekend. His exit was a godsend. Able to breathe once again, Beth slowly and gently set the napkin she'd crushed on the table in front of her.

"They say old-friends-come-again are the best to have around." Maverick dropped several bills on the table. "Wouldn't you say so, Marilyn?"

"Jimmy's never been farther than the next town. I wouldn't know." She did know she needed some space, and she stood. "Thank you once again for breakfast. I must be getting to the Center. Chloe will fall apart if I don't get there and help hold it all together."

That wasn't exactly accurate, but she *had* been gone several days, and there *was* a core of truth in her words.

Once outside, Maverick tossed her plans aside like a bucking bronc with a rider it didn't like.

"I have a special request of you, Marilyn, if you don't mind. I met Maggie at your place of business, and she gave me a ride over, but I don't think I can squeeze into that little tin can a second time. Do you mind?"

"At my place? At the Assisted Living Center?" Beth

seemed flustered for a minute. The Center was her safe haven. Maverick had invaded it the day before, but today she needed its peace and quiet. He'd already been there that morning? Was no place safe from this man?

"If you don't want me to ride with you, I'm sure I can call a cab. Sorry, Maggie. I just can't do tiny again." He nodded her direction.

Maggie just grinned. She didn't seem surprised in the least by his refusal to ride with her.

Beth sighed. "It's not that. It's just, well, it's just that I'm . . . oh, forget it." She reached into her purse for her key, before remembering her new car was keyless.

"I'm with you, then," Maverick confirmed. "Right?"

"Come on. I'm in the champagne pearl Cadillac." Beth motioned the direction of her vehicle.

"I wouldn't expect anything less from you." He blew Maggie a kiss.

"I'm looking forward to next week at the reunion, Maverick." Maggie waved before dropping into her small car and pulling the door shut. She rolled down the window, her hand waving a second time.

"You bet," Maverick called. "I wouldn't miss this one." He opened the car door for Beth. "Nice ride, Marilyn. This car looks like you."

"How is that, Maverick? It's just a car." The Mr. Cadence was gone. A more familiar name was back. Beth hadn't noticed she'd done that. The casual reference from decades before had simply nuanced itself into her thoughts, and it had come out in her conversation.

She shrugged it off. It seemed, well, right, and no one else had called him by his formal last name all morning. Who was she to keep the calves locked in the corral? His answer caught her off guard.

"Tailored and good looking."

"Tailored and good looking?" She laughed, surprised at herself for doing so. "Not beautiful?"

"You don't miss a lick, girl. That's the Marilyn I remember."

The radio came on, and it began playing *Unchained Melody*. Beth reached to the dash to choose something more modern. Maverick stopped her.

"Oh, don't change the music. Leave it. I like this station. Oldies are my favorite. They don't make me feel quite so ancient. Oh, and thanks for giving me a lift, Marilyn."

"Beth. Please stop with the Marilyn thing. I was Beth all those years ago, and I still am today."

"Okay, Marilyn. Whatever you say." Maverick glanced out the window at the old, familiar buildings sliding by.

"You are incorrigible, Maverick Dillinger Cadence." She felt lighthearted in saying the words, a brightness she'd missed from long ago. Robert had been her rock, but then rocks were never really fun. They were steady and dependable. Maverick was incorrigible and had always been. He was *a* Maverick. She smiled at how little he had changed as she turned into the Center's parking lot.

He murmured, "I see you still remember my name."

"Among other things—" Beth abruptly stopped, realizing where her comment might lead. She didn't need or want to go there. She changed the subject. "Well, here we are. I hope your mother really enjoys living—"

Maverick interrupted her, as if his thoughts had been elsewhere. "What do you remember, my sweet Marilyn? Do you remember the night before I shipped out?" He turned his silver head her direction, and his face was serious. This question had meaning to him.

"That was a long time ago. Lots of things have changed since then—"

Maverick again stopped her. He reached and took one of her hands in his, bringing it to his lips. "Yes, lots of things have changed. I wrote you, Marilyn. Hundreds of letters. You never replied. Not once. When I finally came home, you were married with a kid and another on the way. You never even told me. You broke my heart, Marilyn. You truly did." He dropped her hand.

Marilyn felt numb inside. She had no response. His words took her back to a time of her life she thought cleansed from her slate. Now she knew those awful moments weren't really gone.

The reverie was interrupted when Maverick's door opened.

"Again, thanks for the ride."

And he was gone, striding off toward the Center, leaving a dumbfounded Beth reeling in his wake.

— 3 —

OVER THE COURSE of the next week, Beth did her best to avoid Maverick, as Lily Pearl settled in, Chloe ran small errands to keep the elegant woman functioning smoothly, and plans began to ramp up for the upcoming reunion.

Her efforts were less than successful.

Monday afternoon, Lily Pearl made a special request for Beth to visit her in her suite, as she wished to prepare her a special afternoon tea in the courtyard. It was a first, to be invited for a social call to one of her resident's rooms, and normally she would have refused politely and professionally; but there was a connection there, and with the reunion on her mind, she felt she couldn't refuse.

She rang the bell to Unit 134, holding a small spray of fresh flowers in a crystal vase in one hand, and a small box of chocolates in the other. Beth might own the building, but as long as Lily Pearl lived here, she would treat the unit as the resident's personal home, because it was. Even the cleaners and meal service personnel worked around Lily Pearl's schedule, not the other way around.

"Ah, Mrs. Taylor." Lily Pearl opened the door a small

crack, then she pulled it wide. There was nothing frail about the elderly woman. Instead, she was brightly made up, with pristine hair and an immaculate peach suit over a pale-blue blouse. Her orange patent pumps coordinated with the cording on her jacket, giving her a polished appearance.

"Mrs. Cadence. Are you settled?" Beth smiled and stepped inside when Lily Pearl allowed her room.

"Only partially, dear. Mostly the back room's piled high, but this area is well on its way."

The living-dining area was spacious, but it was the high ceilings that kept the tall, antique furniture from crowding the space. A grandfather clock ticked merrily away beside the door, and a wide sideboard held a large vase of flowers. The suite was one of six for guests with their own furniture. Beth looked for a television but didn't see one.

"We can provide you a television, if you'd like, Mrs. Cadence." Beth set the candy and flowers on a side table, and she noted several large paintings that had yet to be hung.

"Lily, dear. No one calls me Mrs. Cadence, unless they're my age, and not many people my age are still around. I don't have time for watching television, not and entertain like I wish. Remember, now, call me Lily."

"Certainly, Lily." Beth smiled. This was the Lily Pearl she remembered.

"Come with me, dear. Things are ready outside."

Beth followed dutifully. Tea with finger sandwiches were spread on an elegant but old-fashioned garden set, served under a glass dome, with small screens covering the glasses.

"You shouldn't have gone to this much trouble, Lily." The china looked to be her best, and crystal was set out for the drinks.

"Oh, I didn't." Lily Pearl chuckled. "I have help in every day for lunch, and she prepared all this ahead. If you'll set out the plates, I have the napkins here."

Beth noted there were three of everything, yet she didn't think anything of it, until she heard the doorbell. Lily Pearl didn't respond, and about the time Beth was going to mention it, she heard Maverick's voice from inside the house.

"Mom, are you outside, already?"

"Yes, Son. Come on through." Lily Pearl was pouring tea, and she glanced up at Beth and smiled. "It looks like my son is joining us this afternoon."

Beth felt her stomach turn over, whether in dread or relief, she couldn't say. She turned to see a look of surprise on Maverick's face, just the same as she was certain showed on hers.

"Well, what have we here at this little rodeo parade?" Maverick looked from his mother to Beth and back to his mother, and he grinned. "I might think this was planned, unless someone tells me otherwise."

"I'm just responding to your mother's invitation." Beth held up her hands to ward off his accusation. "I don't know about Lily's plans, but mine are for tea and some conversation."

"I'm glad I showed up, then. You know, this won't be my first rodeo, and I've ridden a few broncs. Unless you keep them fillies corralled, they can get out of hand pretty quick." Maverick set his Stetson on a wrought iron side table, and he joined Beth and his mother, pulling his chair closer to Beth than she'd prefer. He leaned in and grinned. "Are we out of hand, already?"

"Son, you behave. I invited Mrs. Taylor here, and I want you to treat her respectfully."

"Yes, Mother," he said, giving Beth an amused grin.

With Lily Pearl holding the reins of the conversation, the three adults navigated the pitfalls of forty years apart with an ease that spoke to the elderly woman's social position and Beth's years of entertaining her husband's high-rolling associates. Beth was exhausted by the time it was over, and when Maverick escorted her to the door, she felt relief flood her, as she walked the corridor in silence, and shut herself in her office for a few moments of peace.

BETH WAS FORCED into close contact with Maverick two more times that week, once for lunch on Wednesday, when Chloe found some portions of the contract had been left blank, and Maverick had shown up to take care of matters and insisted to Beth that he had a reservation at a restaurant in town, and if he didn't show, he had to pay a penalty. Surely, she could make this a business lunch, couldn't she? She'd agreed, but only if she could take her car. The meeting had run to nearly two hours, with Maverick musing over the menu, then discussing the merits of tea with sugar and without, as well as the best choice of desserts. They'd brought multiple samples, before Maverik had chosen one. Then he'd requested a coffee to cut the sweet from his tongue.

The second time was Thursday evening, when Maverick caught her as the day was ending and walked with Beth to her car. He asked about the reunion, what Beth knew about it, and how long she'd had her reservations to go. Then he talked about his years in high school. He didn't mention their relationship, and Beth felt drawn into the stories of Maverick on Friday nights, trips to games out of town, and the antics the boys on the bus had gotten up to. There were teachers they'd shared, most of whom Beth hadn't thought of in years, and Maverick mimicked their mannerisms and quirky things they'd said, allowing Beth to be drawn in to the best memories of those happy years. Maverick had taken her hand in his and squeezed it, telling her he'd enjoyed spending time with her, before he'd climbed in his truck and driven away.

Beth had remained in her car, with the engine running and the air conditioner slowly cooling down, for several minutes, wishing she'd had that Maverick forty years earlier, rather than the one that had broken her heart. She forced herself to put him aside. The reunion was coming up, Maverick would soon be out of her life, and she could get on with how things used to be.

As she drove home, that didn't seem as satisfying as she'd imagined, but it was all she had, so it was what she clung to all night long.

— 4 —

BETH PUSHED BACK the drapes and peered out her office window. The clock on her wall showed nearly five, but the Friday afternoon sun still burnished the sidewalks and flowers with a level of brilliance that hurt her eyes.

Quitting time.

For once, she'd be glad to get away from the Center. Fridays were usually a relaxing opportunity to wind down the workweek, to sort out the leftover details for the upcoming weekend, so that she could turn over the Center to her night and weekend staff for safekeeping. Due to harried staff, breakfast has been cold and late. Over the day, Beth had developed an extreme headache. Even her extrastrength aspirin hadn't taken the edge off, and she didn't dare take a muscle relaxer and plan to drive. That solution to her pounding head would have to wait. Now, she wanted to get home, and as soon as possible. Perhaps the more potent medicine and a long, relaxing bubble bath would be just what she needed.

Releasing the drapery fabric, she pulled her keys from her desk drawer and unlocked the top drawer of her filing

cabinet. Pulling the drawer out, she lifted one arm to remove her purse. Behind her, she heard a low whistle. She
looked to find Maverick in the doorway staring at her.

"What are you still doing here?" Beth was startled to
find he'd been watching her, and a bit shocked that he'd
dare whistle. As her heart settled, she realized how her
question sounded, and she smiled.

"I apologize, Maverick. I thought you'd have visited
your mother for a few hours or so and then left. I had no
idea you were still in the building."

"Then you don't remember my mother. You were at
her tea Wednesday. There's nothing she likes better than a
captive audience. Today was her lucky day. She had me all
to herself for hours."

He smiled and backed up when Beth shooed him out
of her office with a wave of her hand. She flipped her
keyring through several keys, found the right one, and
slipped it in the lock. She twisted it and tried the knob to
ensure it was locked.

"Not coming back tonight, I don't guess."

"The staff will forward any important calls to my cell
phone," she explained with a tired voice.

"I heard that." Maverick moved closer and studied
Beth's face.

"Heard what? That I have important phone calls from
time to time?" Beth smiled, glad she could find the humor
even through her headache.

"Besides that. It sounds like you need an entire weekend for recovery purposes. Bad day?"

"It's this headache; I've had it since before lunch and
can't seem to shake it." Beth was unwilling to admit that
the nervous stress of seeing him multiple times during the
week may have been the cause of her throbbing pain. She
reached a hand and rubbed the back of her neck. "I took an
extra-strength aspirin earlier, but it hasn't gone away."

"Here, let me help." Maverick removed her hand and
held it in his own, rubbing deeply into the center of her

palms. "It takes a minute, but this should ease the pressure."

Beth luxuriated in the unexpected attention for a moment, remembering their enjoyable talk the night before, then she caught herself. "I have to admit, that is better. I don't understand how this is helping, but it certainly feels improved."

She watched him press his thumbs into her palm, as the pain in her head slowly melted away. It reminded her of the way she'd felt decades before, anytime she was with Maverick. She might trip on her words when she had to talk with the man, because she never knew where the conversation would go, but his presence had always been reassuring, especially when she was stressed.

"Maverick," Beth started, "where did you learn this? I imagine you out in the oil fields or rounding up cattle, not giving such amazing hand massages. This is something an alternative specialist might do. I don't remember my doctor ever recommending this instead of a prescription." She thought of the pills she seemed to take every day.

"Feels good, right, Marilyn?" He switched hands, and he began to work on the other one. "It's not a permanent solution to a headache, but it certainly helps. Right, baby girl?"

At those words, Beth smiled. She'd been the youngest one to graduate in her class, and everyone had called her baby girl during her senior year.

"You didn't tell me how you know this," Beth pressed him. Maverick was right about it, though. Her head was better, although not cured. As long as he massaged her hand, the pain seemed to sink into the background.

"My doctor signed me up for an experimental study on reflexology. They used this on me, although not quite like this. I have a rubber ball I rub in my palms, and it does the same thing. I wasn't sure this would work for you, but now I can report back with success."

"This is part of your study?" Beth laughed.

"Nah, that was years ago. I can still report back." He grinned as he released her hand. He repeated, "Baby girl."

The words baby girl also brought back unwanted memories. Her senior year was when Maverick had headed off to the military, abandoning her. He was already out of school and attending college, but she had seen him nearly every weekend, even though their fathers had disliked each other.

It had been a frightful year, with only her time with Maverick to ease the stress. Her dad was the president of the local bank, and Maverick's dad a rancher. Her father had positively told her she wasn't permitted to date the Cadence boy, threatening Beth to the point she was afraid of what her father would do if he knew she even liked Maverick.

A soft bell chimed in the background, the five o'clock shift-change signal, bringing Beth back to reality. It wasn't forty years ago, and she was standing in the lobby of the Center with Maverick. She turned to look in his face.

"I wondered when you'd remember you were leaving the building." He put his arm through hers and asked, "Where are you taking me for dinner, or do you want me to cook?"

"Dinner?" She looked at their interlinked arms and back to his face. "I don't have plans for dinner." She faltered as she spoke.

"Home, then? That suits me just fine. Do you want to drive, or would you rather let me?" He smiled widely.

"I'm sorry, Maverick. I haven't seen you in decades, and tonight's not a good time." Beth disengaged from him, and she tried to put aside the touch of his hands on hers. It was a disquieting sensation, all the memories of how he used to make her feel, coupled with the pain she'd endured. It was as real to her in the moment as it had been decades before.

"Just three times this week. I thought we'd broken the ice, Marilyn. Does this mean I don't get to eat? How's that for treating a man like an old used sock?" He seemed disappointed, and he reached for her hand.

"No, I need the evening to rest up for the reunion. Goodbye, Maverick."

Beth felt her heart pound as she let him out the door and made her way to her car. Once inside, she waited until she saw him drive away before she started her car and headed home.

BETH WAS BARELY parked inside the garage and had the house unlocked when the doorbell rang. She left her things in the car and rushed to answer it.

"Maverick? How did you find my house?" She reached her hand to her neck, remembering Maverick's hands massaging her palms, and she sighed. That had been nice, but the headache was blistering. It was now worse, not better.

"It's not a secret, in Wellington Oaks, two streets over from the new country club. Your head's still hurting?"

"It isn't completely cured. How do—" and then she thought of Maggie. *Naturally* Maggie would tell Maverick where she lived. Magpie Maggie had better not have told him much more. Some things Maggie knew about were only between the two of them, and she'd better not forget it. "Thanks, Maggie," Beth muttered in a sarcastic tone, as she stepped aside and invited Maverick in.

"Yes. Thanks, Maggie," Maverick repeated with a chuckle as he stepped past and walked into the house. He called to her, "It's good to be *home*."

She looked at him, wondering what he meant. Then she asked, "Since you're here, I'll let you help me carry my things in from the garage. My purse is in the seat, and there's a few things in the trunk I picked up that go in the kitchen. I'll need to raise the door so you can fit around." She could squeeze past, but Maverick was too large. She walked through the house, pushed the garage door button, and Maverick stepped into the oversized three-car garage.

"This is a nice garage. I've lived in houses smaller than this. Why do you need this much room?" Maverick headed around the car and opened the passenger door, leaning inside and retrieving her purse.

"Robert liked antique cars, and he had one he kept in here. I gave it to Alexandra, my youngest daughter, and her husband, after Robert died." Beth reminded him, "I have more things in the trunk." She pressed a button on her fob, and the trunk released.

"She's a lucky girl to have such generous parents." Maverick gathered the rest of the things and closed the massive trunk lid.

"I'm the generous one." Beth sighed. "I'm sorry. That was less than kind of me. I don't mean to disrespect Robert. Perhaps I don't need as many possessions to be satisfied with life."

"No disrespect read into what you said. Some people need things to validate their self-worth. You, baby girl, never had that issue. You were worth everything to me just being you."

Beth took a deep breath as she felt her heart jump. Those were words she'd needed to hear decades before, and now they seemed too good to be true.

She wasn't sure if he meant them or not.

"Stop it, Maverick. Let's head inside." Beth pushed the house door wide to let him past. She was determined to mask her emotions, although she was pleased with his compliment. She led him through the kitchen, showing him where to place the bags, past the formal dining room, and into the family room, where she dropped her purse and keys into a chair. The walls were adorned with multiple family photographs, reminding Beth that Maverick wasn't in any of them, and she turned to him and smiled.

"Do you mind waiting in the living room? I'll need a small snack to take my medication."

"I do mind." Maverick took her shoulders and pointed her down the hallway. "I'll visit the kitchen. You wait on me in the living room. I'll have you something shortly."

"That's very sweet of you, Maverick. Thank you. You'll find the crackers on the counter and cheese in the fridge. Or dig through any of the bags." She retrieved her purse along the way, opening it as she entered the formal room, and she removed a prescription bottle of muscle relaxers.

She opened the lid and shook two into her palm as she settled into her favorite chair. She slipped her expertly manicured feet from her gold leather sandals and rested them on a matching ottoman.

Maverick returned with a plate of crackers and cheese. "Two?" He set the plate on a chairside table as he hovered at her side, holding a glass of water in his hand. "Do you really feel that awful?"

"I always start with two. Sometimes I need more, but today I hope the headache leaves with these. If you'll have a seat, I'll need that glass of water to take these."

"I apologize. Here."

She took it, and he dropped into a side chair. She took a slice of cheese and two crackers, ate them in four bites, and placed the pills in her mouth. She took a sip of water and tilted her head back to swallow.

"You need a break before dinner, baby girl. You've been on those feet all day. I'll tell you what, let me give you a foot rub."

"A foot rub?" Beth was surprised, but it did sound good. Before she had time to ponder whether she should, Maverick stood, pulled up a companion ottoman, lifted one of her feet into his hands, and resting it on his knee, he began to rub the bottom of her foot with the balls of his thumbs.

Beth closed her eyes. She was tired from not getting enough sleep last night, and she hadn't eaten much today. Now, she had just taken two pills to help her unwind. She wanted to have someone take care of her for a change. Robert had never waited on her. He had expected her to be at his beck and call, not that she had really minded . . . most of the time. This was different, and it felt good. Besides, Maverick was a friend she used to trust, and he had never taken advantage of her.

She relaxed with her perfectly manicured feet in his lap and enjoyed the massage. She found herself getting drowsy, and she struggled stay awake.

Maverick had always made her feel secure. She remembered thinking that, as his hands worked the muscles in her feet. She thought she heard him say something like, "This is the way it was supposed to be." Beth just smiled and wiggled her toes at him.

THAT WAS THE last thing she remembered until she woke up to the smell of bacon frying.

She struggled to come awake, wondering how long she'd been asleep. Her platinum and diamond watch revealed that it was only seven-thirty. *About an hour and a half,* she thought. She looked around. She wasn't on the living room sofa; she was in her bed and in her sleeping nightshirt!

Oh, my word, she thought. *How could I have missed out on getting undressed and into bed?*

Why was she in bed so early in the evening? And where was Maverick? Who was cooking?

Beth wanted some answers; she threw the covers aside, pulled on her robe, and hurried toward the kitchen in search of them.

— 5 —

BETH FOUND MAVERICK in the kitchen frying bacon for BLTs. Her stomach tightened, and her knees felt weak to find him making himself at home in her kitchen so casually, as if he lived here, and nearly forty years of history hadn't come between them.

"Morning, princess," he said to her and handed her a mug of coffee.

"I don't drink coffee at night, it makes me . . . What did you just say?" She felt more confused than ever. Then she glanced out the window to see the sun filtering through the trees. When she looked back, she noticed Maverick's crumpled shirt.

"I said, morning, princess, how did you sleep last night?" He flipped over a slice of bacon with a fork, before turning to her with a grin.

"What do you mean it's morning? How can the sun be up? I just took a nap for a little bit, didn't I?" Beth was aghast that Maverick was also barefoot on her travertine tile floor, and his hair was messier than she remembered.

"Baby girl, this is Saturday. You slept all night and

just woke up. I'm fixing you a BLT since you didn't eat last night. I thought you needed more than a blueberry bagel this morning." Maverick blew her a kiss and winked as he seated her in the breakfast nook. He went back to finish the sandwiches he'd started.

"Didn't eat last night." Beth repeated the words vacantly, still reeling from the shock of losing a whole evening. She replayed the events of the night in her mind, attempting to pinpoint where it had slipped away from her. A pit grew in her stomach as she imagined the talk that would surround her if anyone discovered she had an unrelated man overnight in her home without a third party for a chaperone.

"I'm glad you had something in your fridge. I wasn't wild about the PB+J I had for supper." Maverick sounded cheerful and very conciliatory, as if he wasn't bothered much by his peanut butter and jelly from the previous evening.

What unnerved Beth was that if Maverick spent the night, he must have been the one who prepared her for bed. She felt herself blush just thinking about it.

Maverick handed her a paper plate with her BLT on it. "What's wrong, Marilyn. Are you feeling okay? Your color's a little off."

"I'm . . . I'm okay," she said weakly, as she raised her arm to move her plate, intending set her coffee down. Her robe shifted, and she quickly pulled the front together and glanced up to see if Maverick had noticed. What she saw made her face warm even more. A myriad of thoughts raced through her mind about what a life with Maverick would have been like: intense, breathless, romantic, complete.

Finally, the phone rang, seeming to wake them both out of their trance-like state. Beth tried to get up, and she caught the edge of her robe on the corner of the table. Grabbing the fabric with a yank, she pulled it tight and reached for the phone, knocking it from its cradle.

"Here, baby girl. Let me get that for you," Maverick called, and he rescued the phone from the floor.

Mortified that the phone would pick up his voice, Beth could hardly speak when she reached for the receiver and put it to her ear.

"Beth, here." She heard a giggle and breathed a sigh of relief that it was only Maggie.

"Was that Maverick I heard in the background?" Maggie probed.

"Yes." Beth cringed at her answer, hoping her friend wouldn't ask her to explain.

"Did he spend the night?" Maggie giggled.

"I'm a Christian. You know I don't do that sort of thing."

"Did you like the pajamas, or should I say, lack of pajamas I picked out for you?" More giggling filtered over the phone.

"Was it you who did that? I'm so thankful. I thought it was someone else." Beth stepped away from the kitchen with one hand cupped over the phone, trying not to let Maverick know she was talking about him. Relief washed over her, like warm honey flowing from head to toe. She snugged up her robe again, still self-conscious but feeling better.

Maggie continued to giggle while she explained the evening's events. "Maverick called me about nine last night and asked me for a favor; you know I can't tell a handsome man no. Before Keith and I went out, I stopped at your place with a loaf of fresh bread, as requested by Maverick. He asked if I would help you get dressed for bed, because he said he couldn't be responsible for what would happen if he did the honors. Of course, I knew he was just kidding. You know what a straight arrow he is now that he's a Christian and all."

Beth was surprised, but she tried not to let it show. "Well, thanks. That's a relief. And—"

Before she could finish, Maverick interrupted her,

"Tell Maggie that when I see her tonight, I owe her one."

Maggie called back, "Tell my man, Maverick, I'll be expecting to be paid in full!"

"I'm letting you go, Maggie. You two can finish your conversation tonight." Beth hung up, her worries about the overnight Maverick situation moderated, especially with the news of his apparent faith in God.

"Your sandwich?" Maverick nodded its direction. "Don't want it to get soggy."

"Or cold." She smiled and bit into her BLT. "This is delicious. I haven't had one of these in a while, and I'd forgotten how good they are."

"I thought you might like it."

She looked out the window, resting her eyes on the shrubs and grass filling her yard. The sprinklers had run during the night, and the grass sparkled in the early morning sun. Behind her, Maverick finished making his sandwich, accompanied by the soft clicking sounds of a knife on cutting surfaces and utensils on glass and china. She wondered how her life had gotten so crazy so fast. Here she was in her kitchen, half-dressed, eating with a man who'd spent the night in her house, a man whom she hadn't seen in almost forty years.

"I said, how's the grub? Are you ignoring me, Marilyn?" Maverick's question broke into her thoughts, startling her.

"What? Oh, I'm sorry. It's delicious, really. Either I didn't know I was so hungry, or you're really a good cook." Beth's words came out in a rush, and to distract herself, she took another bite.

Maverick placed his plate on the table and smiled at her as he seated himself. "Maybe it's a little of both. I'm pleased you enjoy my cooking. By the way, how's the headache?"

"It's completely gone. I-I-I can't believe that I slept so soundly for so long. If the smell of the bacon hadn't awakened me, I might have slept until noon." Beth held the last bite of her sandwich in her fingers, watching it longingly, then with determination, she placed it in her mouth and began to chew.

"If you'd stayed in that bed much longer, I'd have gone in and woken you up. Who knows where that would have led?" Maverick glanced at her mischievously, causing her face to warm.

"Now, don't you start, Maverick. I mean it. Not today, please. You know we've got a big day and evening ahead, and I have a lot of errands to run. That and I need to get a bath." Beth stopped in mid-sentence. She'd forgotten who she was talking to, she was so used to being with Maggie.

"I'm here to help." Maverick grinned eagerly.

"See, that's just what I mean. You cannot help me take a bath, and you know it—"

Maverick interrupted her. "I meant the errands, Marilyn."

Beth felt herself flush with embarrassment, "Oh, I'm sorry, it's just that after last night—"

"Nothing happened, baby girl. You must know that I respect you way more than you realize. If I didn't, when I got back from my first tour of Cambodia, the first thing I would have done was punch your . . . but, never mind, let's just leave it at *I respect you*. Last night all I did was sit in a chair and watch you sleep for the first couple of hours. When Maggie arrived, I made myself comfortable in one of the guest rooms. Old habits die hard, so I woke up about six and read my daily devotional." He pointed to his phone and tapped the screen to open the text of a book. "Then I decided to prepare you and me a little something to eat. That's all that happened. I'd never do anything that you didn't want to do first, okay? I thought you knew that already."

Maverick stared at her with those heart-wrenching blue eyes, and all Beth could get out was a weak, "Okay, Maverick." She looked away, and she took a sip of her coffee, wishing this weekend was already over, and Maverick was gone and out of her life forever.

MAVERICK WATCHED BETH, caressing her features
with his eyes, thinking about the past and having no intentions of ever letting Beth get away from him again. Not
when he could feel how attracted he still was to her, and he
could see her being drawn to him, just like back then.

When he was younger, he'd have just grabbed her in
his arms and smothered her with kisses. Now that he'd let
God have control of his life, he had to find a different way.
He knew one thing he hadn't told Beth.

This time he was here to stay. Come hail or high water, he was going to get the girl this time.

— 6 —

MAVERICK HEADED BACK to his hotel room to fresh-
en up. He also offered to pick up Beth's dry cleaning and
go by the florist before he returned. He said to expect him
back around eleven-thirty, and he'd make lunch.

Maverick being away from the house gave Beth plenty
of time to bathe and get dressed without worrying about
him being around. She first pulled out *Footprints,* thinking
this to be a good opportunity to fit in her devotional for the
day, and she opened it to the next marked page. She smiled
at the heading at the top: John 3:16, a verse she could
quote from heart.

"For God so loved the world, that he gave his only be-
gotten Son, that whosoever believeth in him should not
perish, but have everlasting life."

She lit three pillar candles, placing two on the ends of
the tub, and the third beside the sink. She sank into her
whirlpool tub, luxuriating in the gentle massage from the
pulsing jets and thinking about the verse. *Gave his only
son.* How she would have liked that, to have had a son, for
her daughter to have had a brother. Her thoughts turned to

Maverick. She had always felt so secure and safe when he was around, she caught herself thinking.

"Enough of that," Beth scolded herself.

She tried to think about other things, the reunion, the assisted living center, Maggie's and her vacation plans, but Maverick kept coming back into her thoughts. She needed to get out of the tub and get ready for the day. That would keep her thoughts busy.

She had just finished toweling off when the doorbell rang. Grabbing her robe, and with her hair in a towel, she ran to the door, wondering who it could be on a Saturday.

Through the glass door, she saw the white uniform of a delivery service. She opened the door, calling out, "May I help you?"

"Flowers for a Mrs. Marilyn Taylor."

She opened the door to sign and accept the box. Inside were two dozen pink roses and white lilies along with a tiara. The note said, *For Marilyn, Class Sweetheart.* It was signed, *The Class President.*

Beth thought for a minute. Maverick! He was the senior class president her sophomore year.

"If you'll hold for a moment, I'll get you a tip." She held up one finger and glanced back to see if her purse was convenient.

"No, ma'am, that won't be necessary. The gentleman from yesterday already paid extra, plus a generous tip. Thank you, and have a good day." He tipped his hat and backed up several steps.

She thanked the young man and shut the door, admiring the beautiful spray. Maverick had never given her flowers, unless you counted the time she was in eighth grade. He had picked a fistful of bluebonnets and Indian paintbrushes for her when he'd walked her home. That was when her daddy had told her she wasn't to be seen with him.

How did Maverick know she liked pink roses and white lilies? It hit her, and when it did, it was obvious:

Maggie. The two must have communicated more than she realized, especially since her friend had known a couple of weeks ago that he was coming down.

Beth pulled a Steuben crystal vase from the large dining room credenza, filled it with water, and set the spray on display in the center of the table before getting dressed. The vase wasn't her prettiest, but it would do. As she brushed her hair, she remembered she still didn't have her regular lipstick, and what was worse, the one her daughter gave her was that new long-wearing, last-all-day lip color. She took a deep breath, knowing her choices were limited to it or nothing, and she applied the lip color. Then she layered on a heavier coat of mascara and even an extra brush over the cheeks with blush to balance out her lips.

She looked in the mirror, discovering she really did look better. The color brightened her whole appearance.

With a lighter heart, she rifled through her closet and pulled out another one of her new summer dresses. This one was lime green with splashes of oversized plum-and-pale-pink-colored tulips. She put on her new green beaded roman-style sandals. She wriggled her toes, satisfied that her pink toenail polish satisfactorily complemented her sandals and dress. She wanted to look especially nice, though she refused to admit why.

A glance at her watch told her she still had about an hour before Maverick would return, just enough time to do some picture rearranging in the family room. She removed several large, individual photos, and replaced them with smaller, more family-oriented snaps in decorative frames. Locking the excess pictures inside a guest room, she immediately felt better.

Stepping through the dining room, she evaluated the vase with the flowers Maverick had sent. She glanced to the china cabinet, debating on the heavy, Waterford crystal vases stored on top. There were two. They were cumbersome, but they would balance the massive blooms better than the delicate Steuben.

Pulling a chair to the cabinet, she stepped onto the seat and reached for the first vase. Before she could finish, the garage door rumbled, and she looked at her watch. Five minutes early, which wasn't a problem, except she'd need to open the door and reset the alarm.

She grasped the first vase and was just climbing down when she heard the house door open and the buttons chiming on the keypad.

"Maverick?" Not even Maggie knew her alarm number. Had he seen her key it in? She tried to be careful, but she guessed Maverick noticed more than she realized.

"Marilyn, where are you?"

"In here, Cadence," she called. It was a high school thing. Everyone had done it, called him by his last name.

"Oh, baby girl, look at you." Maverick drew in a sharp breath.

"Is . . . is something wrong?" Beth checked to make sure her dress was fastened and nothing was out of place, running her hand over the fabric with a smooth and graceful motion.

"You shouldn't be doing that. You could have waited until I returned. What if you'd fallen and hurt yourself, baby girl?" His voice was husky with emotion. He stepped to her and took the vase from her hand.

"There's a second one. I need it, too." She smiled as he took her hand to help her to the floor.

"That one?" He released her and pointed with the vase he held in his hand. When she nodded, he set the first vase on the table and casually reached up and got the second one down. "Will this do?"

"It's perfect, and thank you for the flowers. I'm trading out vases. These heavier ones will suit the flowers so much better. You know they're my favorites." Beth smiled as she lifted the Steuben vase to carry it into the kitchen.

"A lucky guess," he mumbled, as he followed her to the kitchen. There were several sacks of things he'd brought in, including corsages and a boutonniere, that he slipped into the fridge. He emptied the rest of the sacks and began to put the items away.

"You've been quite the shopper." Beth removed the flowers from their vase and laid them aside, and she snipped the ends of the stems with kitchen shears. She sent Maverick to the dining room for the new vases.

After he set them by the sink, he remarked, "I remembered the dry cleaning. Mine, too, so don't go getting my jeans by mistake, okay?" He grinned.

"Trust me, that mistake won't happen. Yours are thirty-six, and I'm still a twenty-seven length." Beth laughed as she let the water run into the vases. "I'd know the difference. You need to start lunch. I assume you picked up those supplies, too."

"I'm surprised you remembered my pant inseam." He smiled, as he laid a cutting board on the table and slipped a large knife out of a rack.

"Oh, my, the things we remember. Have you forgotten the pants the economics class made for all the senior boys?" She felt her face warm at the admission she remembered such a small detail.

"There's nothing wrong with remembering things about old friends." Maverick had out a brick of sharp cheddar cheese, and he was cutting it into wedges. "I don't suppose you remember my favorite color, my ring size, or my hat size? If not, it's seven and three-quarters." He stopped what he was doing and walked over. He put his hand under her chin, looked into her soft green eyes, and said, "We are that, aren't we, Marilyn? We are friends, right?" He paused, waiting for her answer.

Beth's face burned a little more, and she said, "Of course we are, Cadence. Always have been. Always will be. If you'll pardon me, I need to get my dry cleaning to the bedroom." She wasn't sure her shaky voice sounded very convincing as she headed toward the other end of the house, as far as she could get from Maverick.

RELIEF SWELLED INSIDE Maverick as he continued preparing lunch. At least she'd agreed they were friends. That was a good place to start, or start over. He filled the tea glasses with ice and set them on the table.

Back in the kitchen, he opened a package of pita bread and divided one with his knife, opening it to accept his and Beth's choice of fillings. He had a bag of prechopped lettuce, and the thin-sliced smoked turkey was perfect as it was.

He was finished preparing lunch within ten minutes, and he called, "Baby girl, it's noon. I think it's time you had some lunch."

He waited for another minute. He knew she'd gone to hang up her dry cleaning and, he thought, get her silver glass beaded heels from the closet to set out with her tiara. Perhaps she was in her closet sorting out her clothes and her memories. He chuckled at that. After a few moments more, he headed out in search of his girl.

As he passed through the family room, he noticed it looked different than the night before. He'd carried Beth from the formal living room to her master suite and had passed through the room. When he'd come through later in the night, he'd studied some of the photographs, which were now replaced by others. He shrugged it off and started down the hallway toward her bedroom, when Beth made her appearance into the hall. She let out a frightened gasp.

"Oh, Marilyn, baby girl, I'm sorry. I didn't mean to scare you." Maverick pulled her to him, wrapping her in an embrace. "I called out to tell you lunch was ready. When you didn't answer, I was worried you might have climbed on something in your closet and fallen and hurt yourself. I couldn't forgive myself if something happened to you." Maverick peered into her eyes. "I would never try to scare or hurt you on purpose, I hope you know that."

BETH NODDED BLINDLY. All she knew was Maverick

was holding her, and it felt good. It felt right. This was what she wanted, to be secure with her Maverick.

She shyly laid her head on his crisp shirt and breathed in his cologne. He made her feel like he had back then, safe and protected.

It wasn't the same, however. All those years ago, he'd assured her everything would be okay, and that's when everything had gone wrong. She would keep her resolve this time. It wouldn't melt and then disappear like it had done those many years past. She couldn't let that happen again. She knew her weaknesses. She was older and wiser now.

At least she hoped she was.

— 7 —

EMOTIONS WERE CALMER by the time Maverick guided Beth back to the kitchen, where he offered up his fabulous avocado and turkey pocket sandwiches, with coleslaw and whipped cream-covered fresh strawberries for dessert.

Beth took a bite, then smiled and said, "So, how did you become such an excellent sandwich chef? This is the second sandwich creation I'm enjoying of yours."

"Years of living on the road. I wasn't home much, Marilyn. And I got tired of eating out all the time, so I decided I'd learn to cook well enough to make myself comfortable wherever I was stationed."

"How did your wife feel about you being gone all the time? I know I wouldn't have liked it."

The off-hand comment made Maverick smile. He was pleased to know Beth would have wanted him home with her, because that's where he wanted to be more than anything, home with Beth.

"Do you really want to know about my life, Marilyn?" Maverick asked seriously.

"Sure, unless it's too personal. I'm not trying to pry." Beth toyed with the remains of her coleslaw, finally pushing it to the side with her spoon. Their dessert still sat on the counter, with a can of whipped cream to the side.

"My life and everything about me is an open book to you, Marilyn. The problem lies in you perhaps not liking what you read. But here it goes." Maverick started to talk in a slow, determined voice. "Well, our marriage was a little different than most. Things started off pretty good. I met her at the university where I was going on the G.I. Bill. We dated for a couple of semesters and decided it would be cheaper if we married. She was all about a big showy wedding, even though she was already pregnant. I was so excited to be a father. So, we did the whole nine yards. We even honeymooned at Niagara Falls. After our son was born, my wife lost interest in me, more or less. She made it pretty clear that she didn't want anything to do with me physically.

"That's why we adopted Mary Catherine. My wife was already drinking by then, a habit she had before I met her. I thought it would stop after college and marriage. I was wrong. She really didn't raise little Cathy very well. So, my parents had her for a while. Then ten years ago, Cathy went to confront her mother about some issues she had from her childhood, and Donna accidentally ran over and killed her. Donna was drunk, of course. Cathy had just turned twenty-one. It almost killed me. For days I couldn't talk to anyone, and I blamed myself, mostly. That's when I reached out to Maggie.

"Every time I've needed her, she's been there for me. She was such a blessing. She came and helped me through some of the darkest days of my life. Donna didn't go to prison, and that just made our situation worse. Then she started having health problems. It went on for several months before she finally went to the doctor and found out she had cirrhosis of the liver. It was too late to really do anything about it. But I tried. My son Colt and I had her cremated and put her ashes in her parent's crypt. That was seven years ago. So, not everyone can live happily ever after, but it's something to wish for."

BETH WATCHED MAVERICK, who had told his tale with his elbows on the table, in a very casual fashion, as if telling a story that had happened to someone else. Now, he leaned back, raised his eyebrows, and smiled at her. She could see the sadness in his eyes, but she was too stunned to speak. Maverick hadn't had a happy marriage; she couldn't believe that any woman wouldn't be satisfied with him.

Maggie had never told her where she went that time; she'd been gone two-and-a-half weeks. She said it was a family emergency, and she would tell her about it later. When Maggie finally did return, she had been sick with the flu and in the hospital for almost a week.

Beth never did question Maggie about the emergency. She was just grateful her friend had gotten well, and she'd let it go as of no consequence.

Oh, she wished she'd known. She didn't know what she could have done, but she did wish she'd known.

MAVERICK COULD TELL by Beth's expression this was all new information. He got up and carried his plate and glass to the sink. He set it down and turned to look at her.

"Before you get upset at Maggie, she and I have been friends for lots of years, too. She's helped me keep abreast of what's been happening in our growing little town. In fact, I wouldn't be here today if it wasn't for her. She's the one who insisted I come to this reunion."

Maverick could still see the bewildered expression on Beth's face. She seemed troubled by this new revelation about her best friend. He thought maybe a change of conversation might brighten the mood.

He busied himself at the counter, creating one dessert

with whipped cream and one without. He handed her the one with the whipped cream.

Beth looked at the two desserts, compared them, and then commented, "I remember you were lactose intolerant, weren't you?"

"Good memory. But I still enjoy the strawberries. Now, tell me about your family."

Beth took in a deep breath; she knew it would come up sooner or later. At least it wasn't as sad as Maverick's life.

"Well, there's really not that much to tell. My oldest daughter is an underwater photographer who works off the coast of Greenland, presently. She never stays in one place too long. My other daughter and her husband live about two hours away, and he's a pharmacist, as well as she . . ."

"Names, please. I'd like to know them more than as oldest daughter and youngest daughter," Maverick teased.

Beth managed to get out their names, Candy and Alexandra, and quickly took another bite of dessert.

"Did you actually name her Candy? That doesn't sound like something you'd do. Alexandra, I can see from your husband, but where did you get a name like Candy?"

"It's from her father's side, as well." She paused for a long moment, toying with her strawberries.

"What, baby girl?" Maverick wanted to place his hand on hers to ease her story, yet he knew he had to refrain himself. This wasn't the time or the place.

"My husband had heart trouble. It runs in Robert's family, but I had no idea I'd lose my husband so soon. Maverick, he was a good man." Beth finished and looked away as if thinking about something else. Her eyes were red, and he saw the emotional turmoil she endured.

"He'd have to have been a good man to deserve someone like you."

"Thank you, Maverick. I appreciate the compliment." Beth seemed to relax, and she broke into a big smile.

"Is that what it takes to get a smile out of you, just a compliment? How about your hair looks great, Marilyn, or

I like your eyes, Marilyn, or maybe even, you sure look more desirable today, Marilyn. Would you smile for those compliments?"

"Don't be ridiculous. I only smile at true compliments, not false flattery."

"They were sincere, trust me. I don't give my baby girl false words; never have, never will." Maverick moved in closer. "You do believe me, don't you?"

HIS NEARNESS MADE Beth a little uncomfortable. The conversation had turned to a more serious, personal vein, and she wasn't ready for that with Maverick. Not now, not ever, and because of him.

"Well, it's hard for me to believe you when you tell every female you meet they're the most beautiful woman in the world. You flirt too much for my taste, Maverick."

"I've never told Maggie she was the most beautiful girl in the world." He chuckled. "She'd know I was lying. Nor did I tell your pretty little secretary, what was her name, Chloe? I didn't tell her that, either. Who is it that I'm flirting with that you don't like?"

"It's like this Marilyn you keep saying. Everyone knows to whom you're referring when you say it. It's embarrassing." She was aggravated at being put on the spot.

"But, it's true, baby girl, you remind me of her. You have no idea how many thousands of times on my tour of duty I'd look at your picture and pray to God I'd make it back home alive to see you again. I showed your picture to the guys in my unit; they all understood why I didn't need a pin-up girl. I had you with me. When times were really hard, and we were cut off for a few days behind enemy lines, the guys would ask me to show them your picture. Just seeing an honest-to-goodness all-American girl would boost morale. Most of them were jealous, even my commanding officer."

Maverick finished by reaching for her hand and squeezing it gently. "Even now, I sometimes think I'm dreaming when I look at you and see how beautiful you are. And finally, I'm having a real conversation with you, and I'm awake."

Maverick's unexpected revelation made Beth wish the weekend was over more than ever, so she could go back to her safe, normal, and sometimes mundane life. If Maverick was around, nothing would be normal, and it certainly wouldn't be boring.

She smiled to herself thinking that Maverick and boring definitely weren't two words that went together.

MAVERICK STARED AT HER as he slowly released her hand. He saw her playful expression. He knew there was hope for them yet.

— 8 —

THE AFTERNOON WAS speeding by, bringing the 4Decades Reunion at Wellington Oaks Country Club closer and closer.

Fully aware of the time and wanting to put some space between herself and Maverick, Beth suggested he drive to his hotel, so he could ready himself for the evening and have time to visit his mother before picking up Beth and Maggie for the evening's festivities. The evening's itinerary had arrived in the mail days before, announcing Happy Hour from five-thirty until seven, followed by dinner, and afterward, a Walk Down Memory Lane, featuring a PowerPoint presentation covering the last forty years.

Nominations were planned, and ballot boxes would be available, with different categories just like in high school. The votes would be totaled after the PowerPoint presentation, with the winners announced immediately afterward.

The festivities would resume with Dancing Under the Stars on the country club's outdoor veranda, ending at midnight. Those who could make it were invited to a brunch the following day at eleven to close out the reunion's activities.

It would be a full and busy evening. Beth was grateful she wouldn't have to talk much to Maverick alone. Maggie was meeting some old friends there, and they would all sit together at the same table. Each table seated twelve people, so that should keep Maverick busy and away from her.

Beth wished Maverick a good afternoon and began getting dressed. She rolled her hair in a style reminiscent of high school, like in her senior picture. Everyone was supposed to dress up like they had then. She'd bought a new ballerina-length, beaded-and-sequined dark emerald green dress. Of course, it had been Maggie's idea. It had a sweetheart bodice with capped sleeves, with a scooped zipper in back. All her accessories were silver and diamonds. She dressed carefully, making sure not to miss a button or zipper that Maverick might notice.

She was just finishing her cologne when the doorbell rang.

She heard a giggle from outside and knew Maverick had already picked up Maggie. When she opened the door, she was amazed by her friend's appearance. She was dressed in a dark-pink-and-black dress with black fishnet stockings, so reminiscent of the 70s. She looked flashy and cute all at the same time.

"Where in the world did you get your outfit?" Beth asked, as Maggie and Maverick stepped through the door.

"Maverick picked it out. Isn't it great?" Maggie twirled around to show the matching pink garter under the skirt.

"It's definitely you," laughed Beth, a little perturbed that Maggie would let Maverick pick out her clothes.

MAVERICK, HOWEVER, was oblivious to everything but Beth. He put his hands on her slim shoulders and slowly turned her around. Beth's pale, creamy skin under his tanned hands felt like a satin shirt to him.

"You take my breath away, Marilyn, you truly do,"

Maverick said softly, as he released her. The rich green of the dress matched her eyes. The tiara made her look as if she had a halo on, a real angel. He'd have to watch her tonight. Every man, single or attached, would be after her, he thought darkly.

"Does the tiara look okay? I really couldn't tell if it's messing up my hair in the back. I think it's silly that all the sweethearts have to wear one," Beth said to Maggie.

"It looks great on you. The reunion committee thought it would help identify people. The homecoming queens will be wearing mums."

Maverick went to the refrigerator and got out the corsages and boutonniere. Beth's was plain white roses with baby's breath that matched Maverick's boutonniere, while Maggie's was hot pink roses with black satin ribbons around it.

"Ooh, I love it, Cadence. Thank you so much." Maggie reached up and kissed Maverick on the cheek.

"Yes, the flowers are lovely. Thank you, Maverick," Beth's response was stilted, as she glanced to Maggie, still touching and admiring her flowers.

"You're welcome, ladies. My favorite flowers for two of my two favorite girls." Maverick held his chin high as Maggie pinned his boutonniere on him. Beth smiled weakly as she watched the interaction and bantering.

The tension in the room was taut as a drum.

"WELL, HOW ABOUT IT? Will you, for old time's sake?"

Beth knew she was being questioned but wasn't sure what about.

"I'm sorry, Maverick. I didn't hear the question. What did you want for old time's sake?"

"Well, if you really want to know," and he winked at Maggie, and like always, she giggled. Beth thought about what she'd just asked and felt her face warm. "What I meant was—" She stumbled over her words and was glad to hear Maverick fill in the silence.

"I asked if you'd wear my senior ring, like you did in high school, remember? I'd give it to you in first period homeroom, and you'd return it with Maggie last period. That way your parents wouldn't know we were going steady at school."

"Yes, I remember wearing your ring. I almost got in deep trouble over it, too. One day, Maggie was absent, I forgot about it and wore it home. Thank goodness our dog jumped up, and I played with him until Daddy went into the house. I might have been killed, if my parents had known." Beth gave a reminiscent smile. "Do you want me to wear it on my finger, or can I put it on a chain around my neck?"

"I don't care, baby girl, as long as you wear my ring." Maverick's had his eyes only on her. "I'm hoping my ring will send a message to everyone else to keep off."

"Oh, that *is* like high school. You're really going for realism." Beth smiled, went into her bedroom, and got out one of the large rope chains she'd given Robert. She returned and put Maverick's ring on it.

Maverick fastened it as he kissed her on the back of the neck, causing her heart to catch in her throat and sending chills down her body.

Maverick and Maggie winked at one another.

"Well, I believe we're ready to go," Maverick announced dramatically, as he ushered the ladies out the door to a waiting limousine.

"Oh, I thought you were going to drive." Beth stopped on the porch, impressed and somewhat taken aback. This was too much.

"Not tonight, my princess. I want to enjoy the company I'm with." Maverick's took her hand and helped her into the luxurious car. Next, he helped Maggie inside, and finally, he folded himself into the interior, finding his place between the ladies.

LESS THAN FIVE minutes later, they were pulling into the country club's parking lot. It was only a quarter to six, but already people were arriving. Maverick escorted both ladies to the sign-in desk, where everyone put on a name-tag with the year they graduated. He then graciously escorted them to their table, where two of their classmates were already seated.

A gorgeous redhead named Susan Hollingsworth, better known as Suzy Q/Suzy Homemaker, was seated next to William Kindle, a.k.a. Billy the Kid. Susan was divorced, and Billy's wife, Wanda, was recovering from knee surgery. However, she'd insisted he go on without her. They'd been married for over thirty-five years. She knew it would do him good to see their old friends. She'd try to make it to the brunch tomorrow. As soon as Suzy saw Maverick, she licked her lips and called out, "Hello, stranger. Long time, no see."

She stood up, walked over, and promptly gave Maverick a kiss on the mouth. Maverick looked at her in stunned surprise, while Maggie giggled, and Beth fumed.

"That's for not doing that to me in high school," Suzy said, pouting.

"Let's go get a beverage, Maggie," Beth demanded, and headed toward a large punch bowl.

"I didn't even know you liked me then," Maverick retorted, while trying to wipe her lipstick off with his napkin.

"Of course, you didn't. Just about every girl in school had a crush on you. But you wouldn't even give us the time of day, because of Marilyn." She pointed in Beth's general direction.

"We were an item—"

"Little Miss Goodie-Two-Shoes was the only one you were interested in, and from the looks of things, I'd say you still feel that way," Suzy finished with a bitter laugh. "But you can't blame a girl for trying." She turned to go to another table, putting her hands on her hips, but not yet moving away.

She looked back at him with a gleam of hope in her eyes.

MAVERICK WAS TAKEN aback by Suzy's attitude. He didn't realize he'd been so transparent either in high school or now.

"I apologize for not kissing you in high school, Suzy Q. I'll try to do better in the future." He winked.

"Oh, you. You're hopeless." Suzy did smile, and she walked away, working her hips as she moved across the floor.

Maverick chuckled and searched for Beth, who had been cornered by Walter Grooms near the punch bowl. But Maverick was intercepted by several more classmates, and it was a good ten minutes before he finally reached Beth.

Walter had been in the band and was one of Beth's neighbors growing up. Maverick remembered the man had always liked Beth, but she'd thought him so obnoxious, she could hardly stand to talk to him in school or at home. Now he owned a chain of laundromats and car washes, and he touted a Vietnamese wife.

Maverick approached and greeted Walter, and then he turned and spoke to his wife in Vietnamese. She smiled and replied, also in Vietnamese.

They both laughed afterwards.

"I never could get the hang of that language, Cadence, not like you, anyway. How are you doing?" Walter extended his hand, and Maverick shook it.

"Pretty good these days. How about yourself? How many kids you got now?" Maverick made sure he asked specific questions so that Walter wouldn't get sidetracked.

"Phoun and I have four, three boys and a girl, along with nine grandchildren and counting."

"Well, that sounds like you're doing okay. It's good to see you."

Maverick put his hand on Beth's shoulder and escorted

her toward their table. Beth paused, stopping a few feet away, surprising Maverick.

"Well, I hope you enjoyed your little escapade with Suzy Q. Everyone saw you kiss her." She spoke through clenched teeth.

"Whoa, Marilyn. She kissed me. I had nothing to do with that."

"You certainly didn't resist or pull away," Beth insisted, as she took another drink of her punch.

"I was taken by surprise; you know that, baby girl. I had no idea she was going to kiss me." Maverick wondered what could have caused this sudden jealousy. He'd never seen Beth act this way before.

"How would you have liked it if Michael had walked over and kissed me?" Beth drained her punch cup.

Maverick just stared at her. "Why, I'd make sure he got a check every month . . . a disability check, get it? No other man *here* is gonna kiss your lips, especially not Michael."

Now Maverick was fuming. Why did she have to bring up Michael Dankirk? The man had been his archrival in high school. His family had owned several funeral homes and were from among the well-to-do people of the community. Beth's father and Michael's father had been friends and had golfed together. They got the notion their two children should date. As soon as Beth had heard the news, she'd told Maverick. He'd gone crazy. He had worked out every day, and during football practice one afternoon, he hit Michael with everything he had, fracturing his right arm.

Michael had been out for the rest of the season. But better yet, he couldn't drive with only his left arm, keeping Beth and Michael apart for the rest of the year.

Michael wasn't on Maverick's best friend list.

Beth had pulled away from Maverick and was headed back to the punch bowl, when he saw Maggie approaching him.

"You better stop Beth; she doesn't know the punch is spiked. I just found out, myself. She's had three, maybe four glasses already, and you know she doesn't drink. Who knows what she'll do this time. One bottle of wine all those years ago, and you know what happened. You're the one who brought the wine."

— 9 —

AT LEAST THAT explained it, Maverick thought, as he headed toward the punch bowl. Maybe the alcohol had relaxed her enough to let her true feelings for him show through. Maybe she was a little jealous of him. He smiled as he advanced toward Beth and the bottomless punch bowl.

"Baby girl, I hate to interrupt the party you're having, but I think you should come back to the table with me." Maverick had leaned down, and he whispered his words in her ear.

"Why? So I can watch other women kiss you?" Beth hissed her words. "No, thank you. I've seen enough of you and other women to last me a lifetime." She took another long drink of the punch.

"Baby girl, Suzy isn't even sitting at our table. She just did that to upset you. She knows how sensitive you are. You know I'd never try to upset you on purpose."

Beth took another long drink of the punch and retorted, "No." She turned and glared at him. "I don't think you really want to be here with me. You're too preoccupied with everyone else."

"Baby girl, you're the only reason I'm here tonight. Understand, there's no other person I want to talk to or be with but you."

"Really?" Beth took another drink of the punch. Her tone said she didn't believe him.

Maverick tried another approach. "Maggie said she needed to talk to you in private, so if you'll come with me, I'll take you to her."

"My best friend is your best friend, too. You even pick out her clothes. Then Maggie helps pick out mine. If she wants to talk to me, tell her I'm right here." Beth drained the punch cup and reached for the ladle for a refill, pouring the liquid into hers until it was full.

Maverick decided he had to tell her the truth. "Marilyn, the punch is spiked with alcohol."

"What did you say, Cadence?" A look of panic crossed her face. Maverick gently repeated what he said. He paused to let the information soak in.

"You mean I've had five glasses, no, six glasses of alcohol?" Beth's eyes brimmed with tears.

Maverick nodded the affirmative.

"The last time I drank any kind of alcohol was with you back in high school, and you know what . . ." Her voice trailed off as her eyes reddened, and they began to shine with the beginnings of tears.

Maverick put his arms around her and reassured her the same thing wouldn't happen again. He laid her head against him as he guided her back to her chair. He glanced around, dismissing the stares and whispers of others directed toward them. When they reached their table, he immediately ordered coffee and asked for crackers. The waiter returned with an ample supply of both.

"Baby girl, eat some crackers, and you'll feel better. Trust Maverick on this." He pushed the crackers and coffee toward Beth, and she lifted one and bit off the corner.

She looked at him, rubbing moisture from under one

eye, and whispered, "Thank you."

"No problem. That's what friends are for."

THEIR TABLE HAD almost filled up, and dinner was about to be served. Beth was starting to feel like her old self again. Thankfully, Maverick had stopped her.

She knew he would take care of her, now.

Once the dinner started, Beth ate a little and soon felt like nothing had happened. The meal was delicious, but it was almost impossible to eat two bites in a row, due to people constantly stopping at their table to speak to them.

She was aware most of their visitors wanted to speak with Maverick. They greeted her and Maggie, but they had stories to tell Maverick and wanted to catch up on his life. She'd forgotten how popular he was, and how shy she'd been. Many of her classmates had thought she was a snob or stuck-up. She was neither, just painfully shy. She'd matured early, making her self-conscious about her appearance, adding to her already shy personality.

Only Maverick had taken the time to get to know her in eighth grade. He was already in high school, but he'd wait to walk with her and talk to her. When her Daddy found out, she'd been forbidden to be seen with him anymore, but she would still walk with Maverick for the first block and meet up with Maggie to finish her walk home.

Although she'd never dated Maverick, she'd never been without him, either. This evening with all the familiar faces seemed to be a retreat to that earlier feeling of security, and she hated to see it come to an end.

The meal wound down, and the plates and glasses were collected. People sat waiting expectantly in their seats. Finally, they dimmed the lights, and the Walk Down Memory Lane started. It was fun to see old classmates the way they'd been then compared to the way they were now.

Maverick had put his arm on the back of Beth's chair and was gently rubbing her neck, and she began to relax. She'd been uptight because of the alcohol, making it difficult to really enjoy the evening. Now, in the darkness, with Maverick gently massaging her neck, she was beginning to feel comfortable.

The PowerPoint presentation revealed the classmates in alphabetical order. It came to the C's and showed Maverick playing football, basketball, and lifting weights. Then it showed him being crowned homecoming king. Then the next picture was of Maverick on a tour of duty smoking a cigarette and holding up a picture. He leaned over and whispered, "That's you, baby girl." Beth felt herself blush.

The next picture was of Maverick with his wife and son, and he was holding his baby daughter in his arms. Beth felt Maverick tense up, and she put her hand on his knee, gently rubbing it, as she whispered, "It's okay, Cadence. It's a beautiful memory." She patted his knee as she removed her hand, and she returned her attention to the presentation.

MAVERICK LET OUT his breath slowly. Beth had never done that before, touched him like that. There was a large photo of his son in uniform, and under it was written, "Like father, like son." Beth reached over and touched his leg again as she commented, "I'm sure you're very proud of him." In the darkness she wasn't as shy, and she left her hand resting lightly on his leg. Maverick smiled.

The crowd of revelers continued to laugh and giggle, as well as fall silent in memory of classmates who had died untimely deaths. Then came Beth's pictures.

Beth moved her hands to her lap, making Maverick aware of how anxious she was. She twisted her hands as a picture of her as the class sweetheart, the glee club captain with the caption "Baby Girl" beside it, and then her senior picture with Marilyn scribbled under it were shown.

Then there came the pictures of her family. One was her holding Candy's hand and almost eight months pregnant with Alexandra. There was another picture of her,

Robert, Candy, and Alexandra at Disneyworld. Then there was a picture of Candy graduating from college. There was one more of her in Russia taking photos at the Black Sea. There were two more of Alexandra; everyone could tell she favored Beth with her mother's blonde hair and good looks.

When they went on to the next classmate, Maverick leaned over and whispered, "Your oldest daughter doesn't favor you much."

"No, she takes after her father, and as you could see, he was very handsome." She kept her eyes down and didn't look at him.

"I noticed that."

Then the presentation moved on, bringing a round of laughter from the tables around them, distracting Maverick and Beth from their conversation.

Finally, the PowerPoint presentation was finished. Then the lights went on, and it was time to vote on the King and Queen of the reunion, the most changed, and the least changed. Everyone had a ballot, and there were several pencils at each table.

While the votes were being tallied, the dancing began. Maverick excused himself, went to Maggie, and said, "A promise is a promise."

"Why, thank you, Maverick. Beth, isn't he such a gentleman?" Maggie smiled brightly, clearly charmed, took Maverick's hand, and let him help her stand. He escorted her onto the dance floor to a slow melody made for romance.

BETH WATCHED AS Maverick and Maggie moved and swayed together. They made a nice couple, she thought unhappily. Beth was always nervous when she danced. Her husband would tell her to slow down or speed up, so she constantly had to watch her pace, and she'd never enjoyed it. In high school, it had been different. Of course, the only guy she danced with then was Maverick. He had made her feel wonderful. Naturally, everything about Maverick had made her feel good back then, before he had left for combat duty on the other side of the world.

The slow song was over, and another fast-paced one from their high school era began. Maverick escorted Maggie back to the table, and she sat down, laughing and flushed with excitement.

"Thank you, Maverick. I've not had so much fun in months. Woo-woo! You should try it, Beth."

Beth glared at her.

"How about some refreshment, ladies?" Maverick asked, as he left for the bar area, without waiting on a reply.

Maggie giggled after he left. "He's such a good dancer, Beth. You really should dance with him."

"He hasn't asked me, and besides, why would he dance with me when you're so much better at it?" Beth felt her irritation, and she hated herself for it.

"Because he doesn't love me, silly." Maggie froze and looked horrified, as though she'd take the words back if she could.

"Oh, and what does that mean?" The words were just sinking in, and Beth tried to place who Maverick might love. Not her, certainly. That might have been true decades before, but not now.

"Oh, Beth, promise me you won't tell him I said that, okay? Please, Beth, promise me, right now before he comes back."

"And if I don't?" Beth teased, not yet understanding Maggie's repentant act. Then it began to hit her, Maggie did mean her, that Maverick would rather ask Beth to dance. She felt a chill run down her back, and her face grew cold as she searched for Maverick on the floor.

Maggie started to tear up. "You wouldn't tell him, would you really?"

"Don't worry, Mags, your secret is safe with me." Beth was glad to see Maggie repentant. It took some of the edge off seeing her dance with Maverick, although it didn't mean all that much. It couldn't. Their love had died long before, and there was no way to bring it back to life again. She felt bad for her friend's distress, however, and she motioned like a lock at her lips and threw away the key. She'd seen the gravity on her friend's face and would never want Maggie to cry or suffer on her account.

"Thanks, Beth. I owe you one."

"One what?" Maverick asked, as he sat down with a ginger ale for Beth and a fruity concoction for Maggie.

"Thanks, Cadence," Beth smiled shyly at him like she was seeing him for the first time. She was thinking of what it would be like to love Maverick and him love her back.

Maverick glanced over at Maggie, but she was intently staring at her drink. He wore a puzzled expression on his face, but he didn't ask what was going on.

— 10 —

THE DANCING CONTINUED with another slow song, and again Maverick escorted Maggie out onto the dance floor.

Once more Beth sat and watched as the dancing started, until she felt a light tap on her shoulder and a deep voice said, "Care to join the fun? How about a dance, baby girl?"

Beth looked up into the face of Michael Dunkirk. He wasn't as tall as Maverick and was a little thicker through the middle, but he still had that winning smile, and his hair was completely silver, making his ruddy complexion a little softer in tone. But overall, he still had his good looks.

"Why, hello, Michael. I haven't seen you this evening. How are you?" Beth extended her hand to shake.

Instead, Michael made a sweeping gesture, as he brought her hand to his lips and kissed it. Beth remembered this had been one of the moves he'd made in high school to get the girls' attention

"Now, are you planning to tell everyone you've kissed me?" That's how it had worked in high school. Michael might have only kissed their hand, but he had kissed them. She laughed and glanced to the dance floor to see if Maverick had been watching.

Michael laughed, too, as he said, "Well, I guess my reputation precedes me."

"Only by about forty years." Beth pulled her hand free. "But I don't think I'll dance on this song. I believe I'll sit this one out."

"I shall make the sacrifice myself and sit with you then," came his teasing answer, and he turned a chair around and straddled it like he used to do in their school days. "What have you been up to lately?"

"Not much, really. I stay occupied with my job; it was such a godsend to have something to do after Robert died." Beth's voice died away. She remembered how lonely she'd been after her husband's death.

"You must have done something right to get Maverick to come to a class reunion. This is the first one he's been to since we graduated. We've sent him an invitation every ten years." Michael continued to smile, as he talked about being on the out-of-town planning committee for the reunion. "Maggie and I communicated almost daily over the last month to be sure all the details were in place. It seems like everything came together pretty well, don't you think?"

"It's a fabulous reunion, but I didn't get Maverick to come. It was Maggie. She's the one who keeps up with him, not me," Beth explained.

"Ah," Michael said, with a puzzled look. "I must have misunderstood Maggie. This sheds a new light on things."

"How's that?" Beth thought the situation pretty obvious. This was Maggie and Maverick's second dance.

Beth knew from Maggie that Michael was widowed as well as divorced. He had married shortly after high school, because his girlfriend was pregnant. They had stayed together almost eight years, long enough to have two more children, and then she divorced him and moved to the East

Coast. Michael very seldom saw his children after that. After his parents retired, he sold their funeral home business and married a very pretty, much younger woman he'd met on a cruise. She died about three years ago from cancer. He still had a roving eye, according to Maggie, and she wouldn't trust him as far as she could throw a rusted horseshoe.

"So, you're fair game, then?" Michael questioned.

"No game is fair if you're involved," came a voice behind Beth, causing her to jump. Maverick rested his hand on her shoulder, "I'm sorry, Marilyn. I didn't mean to frighten you," he said in a much more subdued tone.

"Cadence, how long have you been standing there?" Beth tried to recall what she'd said, if anything, regarding him.

"Long enough to know I can't leave you alone without some wolf trying to grab you up."

At that everyone relaxed and laughed, remembering that Michael had played the wolf in their high school's rendition of Little Red Riding Hood. Of course, Beth had been Little Red Riding Hood, and Maverick had played the Woodsman who had rescued Beth from Michael.

Michael looked between them, first at Maverick, then at Beth, and he smiled politely, as if giving ground to a more able competitor.

"So, how've you been these last forty years or so?" Michael asked politely.

"Busy, and yourself?" Maverick kept his hand on Beth, as if to let Michael and anyone else who was interested know he had staked his claim.

"Can't complain. Did your mother sell the ranch? I saw some oil wells being put in a couple of years back." Michael's question was directed toward Maverick, but his eyes were on Beth's reaction to Maverick.

"She sold some of the land, but we kept all the mineral rights; so every oil well you see on the old Crazy C is ours," Maverick announced.

"That makes you a very rich man, according to my calculations." Michael grinned. "I could be envious of that sort of money."

"I get by," Maverick remarked dryly.

"Get by! Why, Maverick Cadence, it's a sin to lie like that. You're stinking, filthy rich," piped in Maggie.

"Well, the stinking and filthy part might describe me sometimes." He winked at Maggie as he gently rubbed Beth's shoulders, directing his eyes back to Michael. The deejay began playing *Unchained Melody,* and Maverick stepped around and took Beth's hand.

"They're playing our song. Sorry, Maggie. I'm promised to Marilyn on this one."

Before Beth could say no, he was dragging her toward the dance floor and away from Michael.

"Cadence, I don't dance well. I—" Beth started.

"Shush, Marilyn, let me be the judge of that," he whispered, as he pulled her to him and began slow, measured steps around the dance floor. Beth didn't even feel her feet, she was so close to him. She seemed to be able to anticipate his every move as they swayed across the floor.

"Is what Maggie said true? Have your oil wells done that well?" She grimaced. She'd hoped to stay on a subject that didn't involve them, but discussing Maverick's money probably seemed nosey.

Maverick didn't seem put out by it in the least.

"Marilyn, I'm probably the wealthiest person in this room tonight. But you know what they say. Money doesn't buy you happiness; it just keeps you comfortable in your misery. But let's not talk about that right now; let's enjoy the dance."

"I'd like that."

Beth laid her head on his shoulder, and Maverick drew in an uneven breath. Neither spoke for a time but simply soaked up the presence of the other. Maverick finally broke the silence.

"You know, baby girl, this is the best I've felt in a

long time. I hope you feel the same way. I'm glad they're playing the long version of the song. I'd be fine if it went on forever." Maverick paused and then stared deeply into Beth's eyes. "Does this night feel good to you, too, Marilyn?" Maverick whispered the words in her ear.

"Yes." Her answer was shaky.

Maverick pulled away and peered into her soft, glistening green eyes. "Are you okay, baby girl? Am I doing something wrong?"

Beth blinked back the tears and said, "No, everything's perfect. I just don't understand it. I could never slow dance with Robert, and believe me, I tried. I haven't danced with you in almost forty years, but it's like it was before. I can do it with no problem."

Maverick smiled as he pulled her close to him again. "You're fine at this. You couldn't anticipate his next step, that's all, Marilyn. You're a great dancer. Don't let anyone tell you otherwise. Okay?"

WHEN THE SONG ended, Maverick thanked Beth for the dance and then had to help her to her seat, because she was a little unsteady on her feet. He felt a little off-balance himself, and he remembered the last time he'd felt this way. It was with the same woman he'd just danced with, only it was forty years and a bottle of wine ago.

Tonight, he didn't need any alcohol to feel this way. It was all Marilyn this time, and from the expression on her face, she'd felt something, too.

FROM ACROSS THE room, Michael Dunkirk had noticed them, as well.

— 11 —

BETH SAT, COMPLETELY out of breath.

Her exhaustion wasn't from the dancing, but from the myriad emotions she was experiencing. How could she still respond to Maverick like it was only yesterday that he'd been leaving to go across the world to parts unknown?

What was it about him that filled such a void in her life and made her so secure?

She couldn't get the thoughts out of her mind, as the dancing stopped in order to announce various awards, including the king and queen of the reunion. Jimmy Dane, dressed as James Dean, was the Master of Ceremonies. Jimmy started with the most changed.

"Our most changed award goes to 'Buzz' Buford Sweeny." Jimmy's voice rang over the loudspeaker, with only one annoying pop of feedback. An employee stepped up, adjusted something on the microphone, and that seemed to fix the problem.

Buzz truly did look different. He was bald, wore glasses, and had gained about fifty pounds. He won a trip to Las Vegas for two for three nights and four days at the Palms; everyone clapped and laughed, especially because he was a minister now.

"Our next award goes to the least changed. Would 'Maggie' Margret Della Jackson come on up." Jimmy held one hand over his brow, as if shading from the bright lights, and when he spotted Maggie, he pointed and motioned her forward.

Maggie let out a giggle as she claimed her award of a three-day spa treatment in Sedona, Arizona. It had a ninety-day expiration date. Maggie laughed and said she was ready to go tonight, bringing a laugh from the rest of the attendees.

More prizes were awarded. The person who had traveled the longest distance was Stella Thompson. She and her husband lived in Thailand. They were awarded frequent flyer miles.

Dennis Milton and his wife won a prize for having the most children. They had eight of their own and had adopted two. They were given passes to Sea World.

The king and queen of the reunion were the last ones of the evening. The names rang out in everyone's ears, "Maverick Dillinger Cadence and our own 'Marilyn Monroe' Mary Elizabeth Monroe Taylor. They're being awarded a one-week hotel and spa package to San Antonio to stay at the historic St. Anthony, along with a horse and buggy ride to La Margarita with dinner for two, and two tickets to a choice of various musical performances."

Classmates stood up and cheered, and several men hooted, calling for the couple to get up to receive their awards.

Maverick put his hand in the small of Beth's back and guided her to the stage to collect the prize. Jimmy handed Beth a plaque with the event and date, and he handed Maverick the San Antonio gift package. Maverick took the microphone from Jimmy and held it to his mouth.

"I want to thank everyone. I'm sure we'll put it to

good use." He winked, causing the crowd to break into fits of laughter, before he handed the microphone back to Jimmy.

Beth was appalled, and she was certain she'd turned a deep red in front of her classmates. Afterward, photos were taken of all the winners, both together and separately.

As they headed back to their chairs, Beth turned to Maverick and said, "Don't ever embarrass me like that again, Maverick. This is a small town, and people around here talk." She sat down silently with her head starting to hurt. She reached for her purse to get out some muscle re- laxers. Maverick saw her movements and put his hand over hers.

"Marilyn, I'm sorry. You know I was just joking around, and so did this crowd. Half of them are so intoxi- cated they won't remember most of this tomorrow."

"That's not the point. I don't like for anyone to think that I would go to a hotel with someone I'm not married to . . ." Her voice trailed off as she thought about the only man she had ever done that with. That was Maverick, and it had only been that one time.

Maverick turned her face to his. "I'm sorry if I made you feel bad or cheap just now, because the sweetest memory of my life is the time I was in a hotel room," he paused and whispered, "with you. It was what made com- ing home from my tour worth all the time I spent there, only to find you wanted nothing to do with me when I did. You'd started another life that didn't include me. I couldn't stay here knowing you were with someone else."

Beth could see the tortured expression on his face and felt a small twinge of guilt. Maybe she'd overreacted. It was late, and she wasn't used to being up. Being with Maverick had her jittery and nervous.

"We're both adults, and I guess there was no real damage done just now." Beth paused. "I'm still shy, that's all, Cadence. I'm shy and tired. I'm ready to go home when you are."

"Let me tell Maggie. I see she's dancing with Buzz. Look at Buzz's wife. If looks could kill, poor Maggie would be a dead woman." They both laughed as Maverick walked over to tell Maggie she could ride with them now, or he would send the driver back when she called.

She opted to stay.

Maverick said good-bye to several classmates as he headed Beth toward the door and the waiting limousine. Beth just smiled and spoke very little, content to have Maverick take care of the social scene on their way out of the country club. Robert would have insisted she speak and carry on a conversation with any potential investment clients. Robert had taken investment banking very seriously and had made a good living for her in the process. She'd never had to work, but instead had been a "trophy wife," as he'd called her. Beth hadn't liked the term but had kept her thoughts to herself.

Tonight, it was nice not to have to worry about anything. Maverick would handle it all. The driver opened the door, and she got in. Then Maverick slid in beside her. He put his arm around her and said, "Just relax, baby girl. Your Maverick will take care of you. That's what he's here for, to take care of only you."

Beth smiled, thinking of him being "her Maverick," like she'd called him in high school. She did what Maverick suggested. She let him rub her shoulders on the way home, and then she let him open the door and come into the house with her. He said he'd stay until Maggie called for the limo to take her home, and he'd leave then. That was fine with Beth. She was tired and wanted to rest. The night had been a big strain on her.

Maverick offered to make her a midnight snack while she got ready for bed. She was agreeable to that, and she headed off to change.

MAVERICK WENT INTO the kitchen to pour himself a bowl of cereal and possibly prepare an omelet later for

Beth. She returned in a long, soft pink robe covering a pink nightgown. Her hair was a little messed up, making her look even more attractive to him. He handed her a tall glass of milk with crackers to crush in it.

"Here you are, Marilyn. You didn't eat much tonight, and I don't want you to get sick." He opened the package of crackers for her.

"Thanks, sweetie," she said, without realizing what she'd let slip, as she let him put the crackers into her glass. Maverick heard the slip and smiled to himself. Someday she'd say it to him and mean it. For now, he was content to be feeding her crackers and milk at midnight like he used to do after the football games.

When she finished, they made their way to the family room. She sat on the small settee, and he squeezed in beside her.

"Do you mind if I take my jacket off? Wearing this tux keeps me from relaxing."

"I'm sorry, Maverick. Certainly." She leaned to the side as he worked it off, and he tossed in on the coffee table.

They reminisced about the evening, and Maverick began to run his hand up and down her arm, enjoying the feel of her skin underneath the silky fabric.

"That feels good," Beth whispered, with her eyes going soft.

"Of course, anything my baby girl wants, I'll do it." Maverick kept massaging her arm slowly, trying to keep his sanity, as he thought about how much he wanted to be with her forever.

BETH WAS TOTALLY relaxed with the feel of Maverick's hand on her arm, and with resting against him. This was what she had missed about him, his ability to take over and let her just enjoy the moment. Robert had always pushed her to do more than she wanted.

She vaguely heard a cell phone ring. Then she heard

Maverick's voice, "I'll be right there. Love you." She wondered for a moment who he was talking to.

MAVERICK SLIPPED OFF the settee and nestled a pillow under Beth's head. He got an afghan off the family room sofa, gently pulled it around her, and said, "Good night, princess," as he kissed her on the forehead.

Beth sleepily whispered back, "Love you, too."

"Baby girl, what did you just say?" Maverick froze at what he'd thought he heard.

Silence was his only reply. Beth was asleep.

— 12 —

MAVERICK WOKE UP at dawn on the sofa in his hotel suite. Maggie had lost her keys the previous night and didn't have a spare. At one-thirty in the morning, he'd given up and insisted on taking her back to his room, where he offered her his bed.

Now he needed a shower and coffee before he woke her up. He gathered up his clothing and shaving kit and headed into the bathroom.

A few minutes later, he stepped out of his hotel room revitalized. Maggie was still piled under the bedding and out like a light. He took the elevator and rode it down to the lobby, along with several other well-heeled guests, and ordered a cup of coffee in the dining room. Each table had a small rack with a folded newspaper inside. Sipping the steaming brew, he opened the paper and glanced at the pictures.

His cell phone rang. He looked to see that it was his son, Colt. He called Maverick every weekend unless he was out in the field or on an operation that wouldn't allow him to use any sort of electronic device.

"Hey, Colt. How are you?" Maverick asked.

"Fine, Dad, and you? How was your class reunion?"

"Great. Got reacquainted with a lot of old friends." Maverick swirled his coffee in his cup, thinking of Beth.

"The one Aunt Maggie set you up with, how's that going?" Colt inquired.

"Really well. I'll just have to wait and see."

"Wait and see, huh? Doesn't sound like you, Dad." Colt chuckled.

"This one's worth waiting for. Trust me."

"Sounds like the real thing. When do I get to meet her?"

"When I see you in Seattle next month."

"Does she plan to go on the Alaskan cruise with us? We've had the trip reserved for six months, and it's getting close. We can hardly change it now."

"She's going to be there, I can assure you, along with Candy, your new sister, and her husband."

"Right," Colt chuckled. "I recall. They married in a civil ceremony and want to have a formal wedding aboard the ship. There was something about me being a best man, I think. I suppose I need to order a tux."

"Already taken care of, Son. I've got to get back to my room and get your Aunt Maggie out of bed. She couldn't get into her place last night, and she took my bed." Maverick took a long drink of his coffee.

"Has Candy told her mother, yet?"

"You don't know my old girlfriend, my boy. She's got to ease her into it slowly. She'll tell her in good time, hopefully before they have their big ceremony on the cruise."

"That works. The sofa sleep okay?" Colt chuckled.

"I guess you know me pretty well. It slept fair. Won't mind getting my bed back when your aunt's gone." Maverick had used an extra pillow under his legs and only tossed and turned for the first thirty minutes.

"I bet. I was on the sofa for a month in college, when

my roommate bailed from our apartment, and I had to move in with Bubba. Remember, Dad?"

"Bubba with the goatee?" Maverick recalled his son desperately begging his father to rent him a new apartment, and Maverick had let him work it out on his own.

"I know you haven't forgotten Bubba. He came home with me for Spring Break."

"And nearly got you in trouble for hot-rodding down the street. No, I haven't forgotten Bubba." Maverick laughed. "I've just finished breakfast, and I need to take care of the bill. I'll see you later. Love you, Son."

"Love you, Dad. Bye."

Maverick hung up and checked his Rolex watch. It was nearly half past eight. He decided to give Maggie a little longer before going back to the room and waking her. He could fill the time reading the paper and enjoying another cup of coffee at the same time.

Half an hour later, Maverick folded the paper and returned it to the rack. He ordered a cup of coffee to go, called for the check, and signed for it on his room's bill. He visited with a charming couple on the elevator, before exiting and unlocking the door to his room. He quietly opened the door to find Maggie still in his king size bed sleeping peacefully and childlike.

Maverick admitted it would be so much easier if he loved Maggie. She loved him, and he knew it. It wasn't that she was "in love" with him, but she loved him.

His heart, however, had belonged to Beth since he was fifteen. She was thirteen, and he saw her walking across the football practice field with some girlfriends on the way to school. He'd been in love with her ever since.

At times he'd been able to slip his memory of Beth on a shelf in his mind and leave her there. He'd had to, or he wouldn't have been able to get on with his life; but the last few months, he'd been thinking about her more than ever. The reunion had been his excuse to reconnect with the only woman he'd ever really loved.

He stepped into the bedroom to stand at the bed and look at Maggie as she slept. He set the cup of coffee on the bedside table. The previous evening, she was slightly intoxicated by the time he picked her up, much to the disappointment of a couple of "gentlemen" who offered her rides home. But it wasn't her first rodeo. Maggie had told Maverick she knew he would take care of her and would expect nothing in return, and that's just what he had done.

"Hey, sleepy head. Are you going to get up today, or do I need to cancel your brunch reservation?" Maverick stepped to the window and opened the curtains to let in the sun.

"Hmm, let me sleep five more minutes, Mom, okay?" Maggie mumbled, as she rolled over in the bed.

"Take a closer look, Mags. I don't believe I'm your mother."

A slightly confused Maggie turned over to see Maverick smiling at her. Her hair was tumbled about her face, and there were smears of makeup on the pillowcase. She moaned and closed her eyes.

"Did we have a little too much fun last night?" he asked, as he helped her sit up in bed.

"You can never have too much fun, you know that. Where's my coffee? I can smell it." She held out a hand, waiting, only opening her eyes when she felt it in in her hand. "Cream and sugar?"

"Exactly the way I ordered it." Maverick smiled.

Maggie began to recount the events of the evening as she sipped on the coffee, apparently not so inebriated that she hadn't memorized every dance and award throughout the evening.

"Whoa, Mags. Remember, I was there, too. I only missed the last two hours. Now, about your keys—"

"My keys! Right, Maverick! I forgot where I left them. I remember I had them when . . ." She thought for a few seconds before she snapped her fingers.

"It's come to you?" Maverick laughed.

"Now, I remember, Beth's got them! Since I wasn't carrying a purse, I put them in Beth's so I wouldn't lose them. Will you call her and see if she'll bring them to me?" Maggie looked down at herself. "I can't go traipsing all over town in one of your shirts today." Maggie giggled at the thought of it.

"No, that wouldn't do. Anyway, that shirt would be the envy of my wardrobe, and none of my others would want to be seen with me." Maverick winked at Maggie as he punched in Beth's number. It rang three times before she picked it up.

"Good morning, princess. How did you sleep last night?" Maverick looked at Maggie and grinned, glad she was in on his game to win Beth back to his side.

"I SLEPT, UM . . ." Beth could hear giggling in the background. She could recognize Maggie's laugh anywhere. Maverick was already with Maggie. This was a little early for them to be gallivanting around.

"Princess, you there?"

"What? I'm sorry. I couldn't hear you. I was distracted by Maggie's giggling." Beth knew she sounded sour. However, to justify her attitude, she reminded herself she'd only been up about thirty minutes herself, and she'd awakened to find herself on the sofa, of all places. She'd only just carried her coffee into the bathroom to see if she could start her day.

Maverick asked, "Will you check and see if you have Maggie's keys in the purse you carried last night?"

"Just a minute, I think I left it in the . . ." Beth glanced around her bedroom.

"It's on your nightstand, unless you've moved it. That's where I put it last night," Maverick interjected.

"Oh," she said in a small voice, wondering what he'd been doing in her bedroom. She walked over and opened it to see. "Yes. Cadence, they're right here. I haven't had my bath, yet, or I'd bring them to you. Do you think you can pick them up later?"

"I'd like to come and get them right now, if that's okay with you. Maggie's holding one of my shirts hostage until I find her keys."

"Sure. I'll unlock the back door and put them on the dining table for you," Beth replied.

"Thanks, Marilyn. You're a life saver." Maverick hung up the phone, leaving Beth agitated and trying sort things out.

She faintly remembered Maverick telling her good night. She'd been so comfortable next to him that she'd almost fallen asleep before he left. She remembered he had to pick up Maggie from the reunion and then take her home.

Maggie must have forgotten Beth had her keys, and so did Beth, or she'd have told Maggie to get them. Maverick must have taken her to his hotel room, and they'd spent the night together there.

Now Maggie was wearing one of Maverick's shirts as a nightshirt, and Beth frowned. She didn't like Maggie being with her Maverick so much, especially sharing a hotel room. It was all she could think about as she got into the tub.

Beth was finishing up her bath when she heard the doorbell ring. "Who? Oh, no!" She'd forgotten all about unlocking the back door and the keys. As she stepped out of the tub, she heard her cell phone ring. She hastily picked up.

"Marilyn, your house is all locked up. I checked both doors including the garage. I even rang the bell. I'm glad I carried my cell phone."

"Oh, Cadence. I'm sorry. I'll be right there." Beth hung up, wrapped her towel around her, and grabbed her robe as she headed toward the front door. She hurriedly put on her robe, tying the waist tight, and tossing the towel to the side. She was kicking the towel as she opened the door, and she stumbled and nearly fell.

Maverick offered her a hand and helped her up, and neither of them said anything for a second. They just stared at one another as Beth gripped the collar of her robe to keep it tight around her neck. Then Maverick stepped through the door, shutting it behind him, as he picked up her towel and offered it to her.

Beth felt her face already burning and was on the verge of tears by the time Maverick pulled her to him and softly whispered, "It's okay. It's only me."

The flood of tears came anyway. Beth stood there while Maverick held her and tried to comfort her.

"This wouldn't have happened," Beth sniffed, "if Maggie hadn't spent the night with you."

Maverick corrected her. "No, Marilyn, this wouldn't have happened if you'd left the door unlocked."

"Well, I was thinking about what you said, and about Maggie, and . . ." Beth stopped before she went any further. She didn't want Maverick to know that she was aggravated over Maggie being with him overnight.

"What were you thinking concerning Maggie and me?"

"Nothing. It's just that it isn't . . . well, you know . . . the proper thing to do," Beth finished lamely, and she knew it. Her excuse for not leaving the door unlocked and the keys out didn't have anything to do with proper. She knew Maggie had probably been in hotels with other gentlemen before. But she didn't like the idea of Maggie being with her Maverick where people could think the worst, not so much about Maggie, but about Maverick.

It would break her heart.

MAVERICK SMILED TO himself, pleased that Beth had some feelings for him. Even though she knew Maggie and he were only friends, she was a teeny bit jealous.

"You know there's no need for you to worry about Maggie. Who do you think wrote me while I was deployed? It sure as . . . well, it wasn't you." Beth colored a little at the remark, while Maverick continued. "I got Maggie's address from my folks and wrote her to find how why you hadn't answered any of my letters. She's the one who broke the news of your marriage only six weeks after I had shipped out, but she didn't tell me until I had been there almost a year."

"I'm so sorry. I didn't know." Beth wiped a tear from underneath her eye.

"I cried like a two-year-old, Marilyn. You were my world. But she wrote me faithfully once a week. It was Maggie who kept me from going crazy over there, giving me hope. And when I came back and saw you, it was Maggie who told me how things would work out for me, if I'd give it time. Part of what she said came true. And when my daughter was killed, it was Maggie who helped me figure out how to keep on living by helping me find something to live for. It was Maggie who insisted I come to this reunion and see you one more time. Then I'd know if I could finally let you go, and I think we both know the answer to that."

MAVERICK WRAPPED HIS arms around her, and that was what Beth needed. She wanted to be reassured that he belonged to her and only her. She responded by laying her head on his chest and shyly resting her hands on his upper arms.

"Baby girl, you've never voluntarily reached for me since I've shown up for the reunion, except in the dark during the Walk Down Memory Lane. Even on the dance floor last night, I had to make you put your arms around me. And it was after we'd been around the room a couple of times that you finally relaxed enough to enjoy the dance."

"I'm sorry, Maverick. I've had a hard time with this." She had, but she couldn't tell him why. It was something she couldn't tell anyone.

Maverick kissed her on the forehead. "I know you

have. However, here you're letting your true feelings show, just like you did before I shipped out almost forty years ago. It makes me crazy for you." He took in a deep breath.

They stood silently holding one another until her tears stopped and Beth was calm. In the quiet of the tastefully appointed room, they let the stress of their lives outside the four walls slowly fade away.

"Are you okay now, baby girl?" Maverick rested his cheek against her hair.

"Yes, I think so," she said with a shaky voice, and Maverick released her and looked into her eyes.

"Is something still wrong, Marilyn? It's me, your Maverick. You can tell me anything. You know that, don't you?" He paused. "Is it what I just said? I can take it all back."

"No, it was very sweet, and I appreciate it. I don't know what's happening to me. I feel mixed up, just like in high school. So many things happened back then that I wish I could change."

"We both feel that way." Maverick motioned to the sofa, and Beth took one end, and he sat down, leaving open space between them. She looked at him questioningly, and he smiled, almost in apology. "The space is important right now, baby girl. I feel God telling me pull back on the reins, so I guess I'd better listen to Him."

"I feel Him telling me the same thing. He's smarter than we are, isn't He?" She smiled and pushed her hair behind her ear, bashful now that they were more in control of the situation. "Everything was new in high school, wasn't it, Maverick, and everyone was just discovering what real love and emotions were like. I shouldn't feel this nervous and scared, not at my age."

"It's not a matter of age. It's a matter of the heart. Our emotional hearts don't understand age. That's why love is timeless."

Beth started to say that she felt the same way, but

Maverick's cell phone rang. He pulled it out and saw Maggie's name on the screen. He held it out for Beth to hear as well.

"Hey, Mags. What can I do for you?"

"Where are you? I've had my shower and need to get dressed. Mav, are you at my house, yet?"

"No, not exactly." He chuckled.

"Are you still at Beth's?" Maggie let out a giggle.

"Affirmative."

"Oh, I'm sorry. I didn't mean to disturb you guys."

More giggling came across the line, and Beth smiled. She couldn't be jealous. Of course, Maggie was her best friend and only wanted Beth to be happy. It was as much her fault as it was Maggie's about forgetting her keys.

"He'll be right there, Mags," Beth called out, making Maggie giggle even louder. Maverick told Maggie he'd wait on Beth, and they'd come together.

Beth smiled as she headed down the hall to get dressed. It felt good to have Maverick around again, just as it had years before.

— 13 —

BETH, MAVERICK, AND MAGGIE arrived at the brunch right on time. They pulled up in Maverick's vintage Camaro and were one of the last ones to arrive. They were seated at a long, connecting table directly across from Suzy Q and Michael Dunkirk.

As they sat down, Suzy looked across the table and said, "I'd like to apologize for my behavior last night. I'd already had a couple of drinks before you two arrived. And naturally, Beth, you being the most beautiful woman in the room made me jealous." Beth blushed. "Maverick, you always took my breath away. Now I'll need an oxygen tank just to sit across from you. Please forgive my rude behavior, okay?" Suzy smiled at the two of them.

Maverick nodded. "No hard feelings." He noticed that Michael was sitting closer than usual to Suzy and wondered if the two were up to something. All those years of military training hadn't been wasted. He'd keep his eyes on them.

Maverick ordered black coffee for him and Marilyn. Maggie ordered orange juice. Conversation hummed as people exchanged e-mail addresses and cell phone numbers. When the waitress returned for food orders, Maverick chose the Cattleman's Breakfast, which consisted of bacon, sausage, country ham, eggs, hash browns and pancakes.

Beth softly asked him if he should have that much cholesterol. Maverick smiled and changed his order to what he had the last time, the three-egg-white-and-vegetable omelet, turkey sausage, and pancakes. He ordered Beth the silver dollar pancakes. She didn't say anything. She just smiled, happy that her Maverick was taking care of her.

Maggie ordered a slice of spinach quiche and yogurt. She announced she was back on her diet. She wanted to look good when she went to her spa treatment in Arizona. Everyone laughed, because Maggie had always been on a diet, even in high school, and she was always trying to lose that ten extra pounds.

Down the table, Jimmy Dane asked Maverick if he planned to stay long after the reunion. Maverick commented that he was thinking about relocating here due to his mother's health. He glanced at Beth, saying, "And for a few other reasons."

Maverick grinned.

THAT TOOK BETH by surprise. She was just thinking how life would be back at its normal pace after Maverick was gone. She knew she couldn't handle him being around without something happening. She couldn't afford to have him live here. An extended week was one thing. She'd lived through it, but barely, and she wasn't prepared for him to stay. That just wouldn't do. Even as much as she loved him, it would be too risky.

"Did I say something wrong, Marilyn?" Maverick took her hand in his.

"N-n-no, it's just that I wasn't planning on you staying here. I mean, our town is so boring, you wouldn't enjoy it for very long." Beth managed to get at least something out, before letting out a nervous sigh. What would she do if he did move here? What would she have done if he'd never left? At that thought, her heart skipped a beat. She closed her eyes for a minute and tried to think of Maverick in her life, now that she had it organized without him.

She knew that wasn't true. She'd never organized her life without Maverick. She'd never been without him. That was the one thing that had brought her peace all these years; Maverick had always been a part of her, whether he knew it or not.

Maverick chuckled. "This town had better get used to me being around. I'm here to stay." He turned to Jimmy. "I'm planning on building a new house out at the ranch and letting Lupe and Maria stay on in the old place and continue managing the property. I probably won't start building until the fall, after I take care of a few unattended details."

Suzy's face lit up. "Oh, that's fabulous, Cadence. You'll be close to all of us. I still live in the area, too, only thirty minutes away."

Michael didn't seem as enthusiastic.

"I haven't moved back home yet, but I've been considering it. Since Suzy and I've gotten reacquainted, it might be nice to live in the area, again."

The whole time he was speaking, he was ignoring Suzy and staring at Beth. Beth checked to see if something was amiss. She felt the necklace she'd put on this morning.

"Oh, Maverick, here's your senior ring. I forgot to return to you."

"Keep it. I know where it is if I want it." Maverick winked at her, making her face warm, and then she elbowed him in the ribs. "What?" Maverick asked innocently. "I know you have my ring, if I need it back. It only fits my pinkie now, Marilyn."

"Oh, uh, never mind," Beth said weakly, glad their food was arriving.

"What did you think I meant?" Maverick questioned her mischievously. "We ordered last. It'll take a few minutes before ours arrives,"

Beth felt her face warm again. She never knew how to take Maverick. When she expected the worst, he always behaved his best.

MICHAEL WAS WATCHING, not quite catching all the conversation, but he could tell that Beth was nervous about Maverick returning to town. Maybe he had a chance at her after all.

He knew she was loaded with money. Her parents had left her well off when they died several years ago, and her husband had been an investment banker, as well. Michael would enjoy having his cake and eating it, too. He'd live on her money this time. She was still attractive and had a great figure, so he wouldn't mind being seen with her, anytime, anywhere.

THEIR FOOD ARRIVED and Maverick handed Beth the butter and the syrup.

"Do you want me to butter them for you, baby girl?" he asked.

"No. If you do, I'll gain ten more pounds," she replied, barely applying any butter. She only put a tablespoon of syrup on them as well.

Maverick looked at her pancakes and said, "What? You'll want more butter, of course. I'll help you out." With that, he put a big slab of butter on Beth's pancakes and smeared it across. Then he covered them with syrup. He looked at the pancakes and said, "You're welcome."

It was Beth's turn to giggle. Maverick could be so funny when he wanted to. She took a bite of her pancake, looked over at him, and said, "My taste buds thank you, as well. However, my scales at home may have just declared war."

"I'm willing to take that risk," Maverick said as he

took another bite of his own pancake drenched in butter and syrup, and then he smiled with his eyes fixed on Beth.

MICHAEL LOOKED AT Maverick. He knew he had a fight on his hands, but it'd be worth it if he could get Beth and her money. Nothing ventured, nothing gained, he thought. Besides, he knew Suzy wanted Maverick. He could set that up and then convince Beth that Maverick had gone after Suzy. Beth would need someone to console her, and good old Michael would be right there.

ANOTHER QUESTION CAME, directed at Beth this time.

"Didn't I read in the paper where your eldest daughter announced her engagement and upcoming marriage?" The question came from Billy's wife, Wanda, who had been able to come to the brunch after all.

Beth almost choked and dropped her fork. Maverick handed her a glass of water to help her swallow. Beth cleared her throat before answering. "Y-y-yes, you did read that. But her wedding isn't until next month. It's out of town."

"I don't remember her fiancé's name, or where it was going to be." Wanda smiled encouragingly.

This time it was Maggie who spoke up. "Seattle. That's where Candy's fiancé, Drew Keegan, is from. They plan to marry aboard a cruise ship and honeymoon at the same time. They don't have much time off, so they decided to do it all at once. He has some government job that keeps him busy, and her photography keeps her occupied. So, they seem to be perfectly matched."

Beth was glad Maggie left out the part that Candy was trying to get pregnant as soon as possible so they could start their family life immediately. Beth didn't want that spread around. Candy knew Beth didn't approve, as it didn't fit with God's plan for marriage, but she loved her daughter, despite her strong-willed ways.

"How did they meet?" was the next question.

Maggie continued, "I believe it was a dating service over the Internet. They've been seeing each other for over a year, now."

Wanda nodded, satisfied with the answer, while Beth had quit eating. She didn't even want to look at Maverick. She was afraid of what her eyes would reveal.

MAVERICK HAD SOME interesting thoughts of his own.

— 14 —

AFTER THEIR GOODBYES were finished, Beth, Maverick, and Maggie got back into Maverick's car. As they drove Maggie to her townhouse, she asked Maverick about his future plans.

"Are you planning to live at the hotel the entire time while you decide what your new house will be like?"

"Well, I don't really see a choice. I don't want to rent a house and be tied up with a rental agreement, nor the upkeep. I don't like apartments; they remind me too much of military life. I might end up at an extended stay residence. At least there I can do my own cooking and still have maid service. My concern right now is my vehicles. This car is one I gave Colt. He's crazy about anything from the sixties and early seventies. I also have my Benz that I usually garage as well. There's no covered parking area at the hotel I'm considering."

"Well, I've got two covered parking places where I live. It's not a garage, but you can certainly use one, if you need it," Maggie offered.

Beth felt uncomfortable. She had plenty of space in

her garage, but she didn't want Maverick to use it. She couldn't handle him coming over every day to pick up his car. That would be too much with the wedding plans and all she had to do to prepare for her trip to the Northwest over the next two weeks. Besides, who knew what hours Maverick kept, anyway? He might bring the car home late, and she'd think it was an intruder.

Maggie sweetened her offer. "For that matter, you can stay at my house. I've got a spare room. I only have it filled with my clothes and junk I need to get rid of anyway. You don't have to stay by yourself. Not when you have friends like us around, right Beth?"

Beth was really uncomfortable. She didn't want Maverick in her home, but she also didn't want him staying with Maggie.

"I'm certain Maverick will want his privacy, Maggie. He wouldn't want to stay with either of us. He'd rather have his own place, I'm sure. But he's welcome to park the vehicle he doesn't drive in my garage. As long as it stays parked, I see no problem with it being there." Beth was quite pleased with the compromise she'd made regarding Maverick.

Maverick chuckled. "Well, ladies, I appreciate your offers, but I'm still not sure of my plans. So for now, I'll keep the Camaro over at Maggie's and drive the Benz, like I had originally planned. Colt's coming out sometime in July, I believe, and I want to be sure he has his car."

"Oh, I can't wait to see him. It's been almost two years since I saw him in Hawaii," Maggie blurted, then stopped and put her hand over her mouth.

Beth sat in shocked silence while she digested Maggie's revelation. No one said a word while the tension built. Beth gained her voice first.

"So, what's this about?" Beth turned around and looked at Maggie in the back seat. "I thought you told me you were going to see family in California."

"I did. I was there overnight coming and going. I

stayed with my Aunt Ruby," Maggie insisted, defending herself.

"So, you were gone for ten days and only saw your aunt for two of them?" Beth was more agitated by the minute.

"Yes," came a teeny voice from the backseat.

"But Hawaii was beautiful, wasn't it, Mags?" Maverick added, making Beth even more upset.

Beth didn't know what to do. Her best friend was vacationing with, with . . . well her best friend wasn't supposed to do that with her Maverick.

Beth looked at Maggie darkly and asked, "What else have you done with Maverick?"

Maverick broke in on the conversation. "Do you really want to know? You know want they say, ignorance is bliss."

He winked at Beth, making her even more angry.

Maggie spoke up, "Don't talk like that, Maverick. You know that will upset her. Beth, we've never done anything, honest. You're my best friend, and I'd never let anyone or anything mess that up."

Beth had her arms crossed and was staring out the window by the time they arrived at Maggie's house. She was no longer interested in Maggie's "truth." She ignored Maverick as he helped Maggie get out of the car and gave her a hug. Beth didn't even speak to her friend as they drove away.

Maverick headed the car toward Beth's house, and he spoke softly to Beth, "Marilyn, it was a no-win situation. If Maggie had told you, you'd have been angry. Now that you've found out anyway, you're still angry with her."

"Don't even talk to me, Maverick Cadence. This is entirely your fault, and you know it. She'd have never gone if you hadn't invited her. She didn't have the money to go to Hawaii, and I know that for a fact."

"Why does it matter so much to you, anyway? Would you have gone if I'd invited you? No way. You wouldn't even write me, so I know you wouldn't have spoken to me. A trip with me? Impossible. Maggie was my only connection to you and the life I was deprived of."

There was a sharpness in his voice that made Beth defensive. "Things were different then. There were complications I couldn't work out, not alone. You were gone. Your military posting was on the other side of the world, and I was stuck here. You know how my father was. He would have killed me if he'd known I ever had anything to do with you."

"Yeah, I never could figure that out." Maverick rubbed his forehead and looked at Beth. "I sometimes thought he just didn't like teenage boys."

"I think he never liked your father because he was a rancher and needed a loan from the bank from time to time. He said as much once by saying ranchers were the same as gamblers. But I couldn't help myself back then. I was a very shy teenager. You were popular, and you didn't make me feel shy or embarrassed. You really tried to know me. You never made a pass at me, like a lot of the other guys at school. I could trust you. You made me feel safe."

"What happened? Why did you feel you couldn't trust me anymore?"

Maverick had stopped his car in Beth's driveway, and he killed the engine. With the windows up, the silence of the moment, contrasted with the earlier rumbling of the vehicle's massive powerplant, made the moment feel intimate.

"You know what happened," Beth slowly replied.

"The night before I shipped out?" Maverick raised one eyebrow.

Beth nodded yes and felt her skin warm at the memory.

"Marilyn, I admit I brought that one bottle of wine. But that was to help you loosen up. I knew how high strung you were, and sensitive, too. You worried about everything. I didn't try to get you drunk. How did I know you hadn't eaten that day? That wine went to your head, and you were like a siren no man could have resisted. I just wanted to be alone with you, relaxed, for once. I didn't plan for us to ever go that far. But you made me crazy for you. I couldn't help myself. I was so in love with you." Maverick stopped for a moment, and he tenderly brushed a tear from under one of Beth's eyes.

The memories had come flooding back, memories Beth had carefully put away and never discussed with anyone, not even Maggie. No one knew what went on that night but she and Maverick. And now, here they were, forty years later, with the same memories, as real as the night they had happened. Maverick started to continue, but Beth stopped him. It was time to get this over with. Beth wanted to clear her conscience, or at least part of it.

"I've tried to blame you all these years for that night, Cadence, but I know I'm the one to blame." Beth took a deep breath and continued. "I'm the one who begged you to come home before you shipped out from basic training. I'm the one who told you to find us a place where we could be alone." She drew in a haggard breath and paused before going on. "And, I'm the one who wanted to do what we did. It wasn't you."

"Wait, Marilyn. You can't just blame yourself," Maverick began.

"Enough." Beth stopped him from going on. She needed out of the car, and she opened the door, pushing it wide. She stood, put her hand on the door, and wanted to close it.

She also wanted to get back inside. Being in the car with Maverick was what she'd dreamed of, and now, she didn't want to be around him. The past and all its memories were too painful.

"Marilyn?" Maverick called to her from his seat. "May I come in?"

"I think not. Good bye, Cadence." She closed the door and started for the house.

As she stepped past the front of the Camaro, Beth glanced at Maverick to see his window down, and she stopped to get out what had to be said to clear the air. "By the way, I wasn't drunk that night. I poured most of my wine down the sink in the hotel bathroom. I wanted you to want me . . . and now you know the real me."

With that, Beth hurried into the house and refused to answer the doorbell when it rang five seconds later. She also ignored her cell phone when it rang ten seconds after that. She unplugged the house phone, took a couple of muscle relaxers, and laid down for an afternoon nap, leaving Maverick to deal with her news.

She woke up a few hours later feeling somewhat better, glad to get some of the guilt of her youth off her chest. She'd needed to tell Maverick that for a long time. Now that she had, she felt a release of some of the remorse she had experienced. She'd wanted to be with him that night. She'd wanted to be with him for a long time. Her whole senior year she'd thought of nothing but being with him when he was home on the weekends from college. And when he was gone to boot camp, she realized how much she truly loved and missed him. She didn't want him to leave ever, and she'd begged him to come home one last time.

Then he was gone again. She was already enrolled at the university, and that's where she met Robert. He was a nice young man who seemed to enjoy her company. Robert had been faithful in his performance of his husbandly duties, but never had her heart stopped when Robert walked into the room, and he'd never made her feel the way she felt about Maverick right then.

She stopped and let out a deep sigh. What was she thinking? She whispered, "I still love him after all these years, and I still want him."

It was too late. If he knew the truth, he would despise her for sure. She couldn't let that happen.

No, Maverick would have to return to being a

memory, no matter how hard that might be. It was a decision she'd made years ago. She had done it before. She could do it again. There was no choice in the matter. She couldn't expose what she had so carefully concealed.

— 15 —

LATE THAT AFTERNOON, Beth's cell phone rang, and she checked the caller I.D. to find Candy on the line. She answered, surprised her daughter would call her on a Sunday evening.

"Hello, honey. How are you?" Beth asked.

"I'm fine, Mom. Are you okay?" Candy's voice was filled with concern.

"Yes, darling. Why do you ask?" Beth had no idea what Candy's call was about.

"Well, I tried calling your cell and got no answer. Next, I called the house phone and no one answered. Then I called Aunt Maggie's, and she said you were angry at her. So I finally tried again on your cell. What's up? You've never been angry at Maggie in your life." Candy sounded worried.

Beth ran her fingers through her hair and thought a minute.

"Mom, are you there?"

"Yes, baby. I'm here." Beth let out a deep sigh.

Candy asked again, "Mom, what's wrong? Is Aunt

Maggie still coming to my wedding? You know I want her to help with the reception."

"Yes, dear, I know. We just had a little misunderstanding, that's all. I found out something that got me upset. I didn't feel like talking, so I unplugged the house phone."

"Everything gets you upset, Mom. You need to loosen up," Candy shot back a bit bluntly.

"Cadence Margret Taylor, that's no way to speak to your mother."

"Mom? I don't think I've heard you use my full name in nearly thirty years." Candy laughed. She continued in a calmer, more placating manner. "I wasn't trying to upset you. But it's true. You come unglued over the least little item. You and Alexandra both need to chill. But she's not as bad as you. Mom, there are things I want to tell you right now, but I'm not sure you can handle them without getting distressed. Or getting a headache or overreacting. I can never be totally open with you."

"What is it, Candy? You can tell me, and I promise I can take it. Go ahead and talk to me. Is it about your wedding?"

"No, Mom. Are you sure you want to hear this? You know what they say, ignorance is bliss."

Beth let out a surprised gasp at her daughter's remark, thinking about who else had said it earlier in the day.

"Mom, are you sure you're okay?"

"Y-y-yes, honey, I'm fine. Tell me what's on your mind." Beth was nervous, worried if something was wrong.

"I'm six weeks pregnant! Isn't that great? By the wedding, I'll be a little over nine weeks along." Candy sounded ecstatic.

Beth was silent, thinking how lost and alone she'd felt when she was pregnant with Candy. Her morning's devotional from *Following in the Footprints of Jesus* was in her mind. "We love him, because he first loved us." She'd loved her daughter so much, just because she was hers.

She wished she'd been able to share the news with her own mother, the way Candy was sharing with her. She never wanted her daughter to feel the way she had all those years ago. She slowly said, "I'm so happy, because this is what you wanted. I knew you were ready six months ago when you told me you wanted to get married so you could start a family. What does Drew say about it?"

"He's thrilled, Mom, and so are his folks. He couldn't wait to tell them. He phoned them earlier today. I told Aunt Maggie already. I hope that was okay with you."

"Honey, I'm glad you told Maggie. You two always seem to get along so well together. You were like the daughter she never had. She's loved you since the day you were born."

"Of course, Mom. She's your best friend. Or should I say, of course, Grandma, she's your best friend."

Candy laughed a deep laugh, reminding Beth of another person who shared that same laugh.

"I'm so excited for the two of you," Beth said with true sincerity.

"Mom, I'd better let you go. Plug in the house phone, okay? Now, you'll be here with Maggie in two weeks, and you're staying for two weeks after that, right?"

"Yes, honey, I've already made plans and can't wait to see you. Give my love to Drew, and take care of yourself. No silly life-threatening adventures, okay?"

"Right, Mom. I'm calling Alexa and telling her next. Love you."

"Love you more, always have, always will," Beth responded as they hung up.

Beth sat down and cried, thinking how she'd felt all those years ago when she was expecting Candy, and how much she loved her. Candy had filled a void in her life. This was the next step. Candy was going to be a mother, and that would make her, Mary Elizabeth Monroe Taylor, a grandmother. She wondered what Maggie had thought when she heard the news. Her friend had stood by her during the hardest time of her life. She was a good friend despite everything. She hoped Maggie wouldn't tell the whole world, namely Maverick. That was the last person she wanted to know.

MAVERICK picked up his phone.

"Cadence, here."

"Oh, Mav, I've got the best news. I just got a call from Candy. You'll never believe this. Guess." Maggie's excitement carried over the line like she was in person.

"Okay, you tell me."

"She's having a baby. She's six weeks along!"

Maverick broke out into a big smile, certain Maggie could see it over the phone. He talked excitedly as he opened a drawer and pulled out a freshly pressed pair of jeans and a comfortable shirt.

"I'm going over to Beth's, and either she's talking to me, or she's calling the police on me for disturbing the peace. I'm not letting her get away, not after what she told me this afternoon."

"What did Beth tell you that you didn't already know?"

Maverick chuckled. "Well, Mags, let me just say we were both fooled by her. Now that I know this, I won't be fooled again. She's mine for good!"

He said good-bye and hung up the phone. Fifteen minutes later he pulled up to Beth's house only to see a black Lincoln quickly pulling away from the curb. He thought he'd seen that car at the reunion as well as at the brunch. Maverick walked toward the door and rang the bell. No answer. Had Beth left with someone? He called the house phone to make sure. An unsteady hello came over the line. He could hear in her voice that something wasn't right.

"Marilyn, is that you? It's your Maverick. What's wrong?"

The line went dead. He started to dial the phone again

when he heard the door unlock. There stood a petrified Beth, with her body visibly shaking. Her face was ashen except for a slightly red mark on one cheek that looked like a bruise might soon appear.

"Oh, Maverick," was all she could say. He pulled her close as he shut the door behind him. She wasn't crying, which was unusual for Beth. She was so sensitive that Maverick knew she would normally be in a torrent of tears. Something was terribly wrong with the whole situation.

"What happened? Baby girl, who did this to you?" Maverick's voice had an edge to it, yet he was strangely calm. Beth just lay against him not saying a word. He could tell she was scared and had probably never been this frightened in her life.

He wished she felt she could tell him the truth.

"I answered the door without checking to see who it was, because I thought it was you." Beth's voice continued to shake. "He came in and tried to kiss me. He'd been drinking, and then he, he . . ." Beth stopped and pressed herself closer to Maverick.

Maverick knew she was avoiding his question.

"Who did this to you, Marilyn?" he insisted in a steely voice. He peered into her soft green orbs, trying to discern any hint of what had taken place. The ugly red mark on her face made his blood pressure skyrocket. Somebody was going to pay for this.

Beth took a deep breath and whispered in his ear, "I can't tell you. He threatened me, and he meant it, Maverick."

Maverick separated from Beth. He stared at her furiously and spoke between clenched teeth. "I mean it, too. You'd better tell me. No one is going to ever hurt my Marilyn without living to regret it. I'm calling the police."

"He told me if I called the police, he'd would hurt me even worse. Neither you nor the police can protect me all the time. He'll do something to destroy you, and you'll hate me for it. He said he'd do it." Beth was starting to cry softly with large tears dripping down her red-stained cheeks.

"How can he make me hate you, Marilyn? No one could ever do that." Maverick put his hand under her chin. "Just give me a name, baby girl. That's all I ask, just a name."

— 16 —

MAVERICK COULD HEAR the hopelessness in Beth's voice and see the misery in her face. He couldn't understand how she could be so afraid. Nothing anyone could say would change his heart. He'd tried to block out Beth for the last forty years. He'd married, raised a family, worked a sixty-hour-a-week job, and stayed as far away from her as he possibly could.

But Beth would be there, haunting his dreams two or three times a week, reliving that last night before shipping out, or in the backseat of his car, making out. Or, he would hear a song that reminded him of her. He would smell another woman wearing Beth's cologne. Finally, when he couldn't take it any longer, he would call Maggie and listen to her giggle. Only then could he calm down and keep going, knowing that the person he was talking to would also be talking to Beth. And now that he had finally decided to give love one more try, someone was threatening to destroy them. He couldn't, no, he wouldn't let that happen. He had come too far with Beth over the past few days to let someone stop him now. He would go Rambo on them before he let that happen.

Maverick looked at Beth and calmly said, "I'm moving in. If you don't like it, call the police. That's the only way you'll get me to leave. No one, and I mean no one is ever going to make my Marilyn afraid."

BETH STARED BACK at Maverick and knew it was useless to argue. She gave out a defeated sigh. Besides, she could feel a headache coming on, and she didn't want to take any more muscle relaxers; she'd already had two today. And an argument with Maverick would put a headache into full swing.

Maverick gave her a hug and whispered in her ear, "I can tell you're stressed. You probably haven't eaten since the brunch. Do you think you could eat something, baby girl? I think that might help you." His voice was gentle, and he reached and rubbed the back of her neck, causing her to almost melt.

Maverick's hands felt so good.

Beth shook herself. What was she doing? She should be upset and yelling at the thought of Maverick trying to move in instead of thinking how nice it would be to have Maverick massage her daily and how secure she would feel knowing that he'd be here to take care of her and protect her.

"Yes, maybe I should eat something. Just crackers and milk, okay, Cadence?" Beth replied, as she forced herself away from Maverick's powerful touch. She headed toward the kitchen.

"Whatever you say, Marilyn." Maverick followed her. He got out the things for her snack, pouring himself some cereal with soymilk.

"Park your car in the garage. I don't want the neighbors to know you're here," Beth said, as she started eating.

"Sure, baby girl. I planned on doing that. I don't want anyone to know I'm here, not even Maggie, alright?"

Beth breathed a sigh of relief. She didn't want Maggie

to know Maverick was living here, either.

Beth didn't look at Maverick until she finished her crackers and milk. She could feel his eyes on her, and she couldn't face him knowing she didn't intend to give him the information he wanted. When she finally did glance his way, she could see the hurt and disappointment in his eyes. She knew she was responsible for it.

She had only seen this expression one other time, and that was when he returned from his tour of duty. He had begged her to let him see her. She made sure Candy was taking her afternoon nap and Robert was at work. She had been about six months pregnant with Alexandra. Beth had talked Maggie into leaving work early to be with her, too. Maverick had come by the house and stayed for about fifteen minutes.

He told her then how much she'd hurt him, but he would always care about her. However, he wouldn't treat Robert the way he'd been treated. He knew Beth must love Robert to marry so soon and start a family so quickly. Maverick left that day after saying he was determined not to undermine Beth's marriage or the life she had without him.

Beth never forgot the look in his eyes that day, and here it was again. She was putting Maverick through suffering he didn't deserve.

"Maverick—" Beth started softly.

"DON'T EVEN START, Marilyn. Saying you're sorry doesn't help now, just like it didn't help then."

Maverick spoke in a heated voice. He'd been thinking during the silence as well, and he had to let some things go. Beth would need to understand him better.

"All I've ever wanted since I was fifteen years old was to make you happy and to make you mine. But you don't trust me to do the right thing. How can I fix what I don't know is broken? Marilyn, you're the reason I signed up in the first place. I knew I was a poor cattle rancher's son, and you were the rich banker's daughter. I didn't have enough money to finish my college education without going into debt. I thought if I chose the military that your family would respect me, and I could finish my education on the G.I. Bill and make a decent living for you. Then maybe your father would esteem me worthy enough to marry you. That's why I went to war, so I could marry you.

"But you didn't trust me enough to wait on me. You got scared, married someone else and had a life without me. Now here I am again, wanting to help, and you still won't let me in your life." Maverick broke away angrily and strode from the kitchen. He called back, "You want a life without me, then you've got it. I can't try anymore. Keep your life and your secrets. I hope they keep you warm at night." With a frustrated sigh, he opened the front door and left.

Maverick was angry, but not as angry as he let Beth believe. He'd already decided to take care of the dark Lincoln himself, without involving her. If he stayed at her house, it might be a little too risky. He got into his car and started making phone calls. Let Marilyn play her own hand. He had to know if she loved him the way he loved her.

INSIDE HER LARGE, luxurious home, a devastated Beth sat in her family room feeling completely devoid of life. She felt a cold chill through her entire body. She had finally done it. She had finally gotten Maverick to not love her anymore. It was the loneliest feeling she had ever experienced, leaving her empty, like part of her had died.

She hadn't felt this way, even after Robert passed away. She missed Robert's companionship, certainly, but little else. That's all she'd thought of him as, a husband and companion.

Maverick had been her lover, someone she ached for during the nights, longing for the taste of his mouth and hungry for his kisses. She had been restless with the thought of him, craving him at times so badly she had reached out to Robert, only to be disappointed.

Now Maverick was gone, and it was her fault. She began to panic. She was truly scared.

What would life be without her Maverick?

— 17 —

MAGGIE ANSWERED HER phone, shocked to hear Beth's voice on the other end. She thought Beth was angry with her.

"You've got to come over here, now!" That was the most desperate Beth had sounded in years.

"I'm on my way." Maggie couldn't imagine what could have Beth so upset without it involving Maverick. She made a phone call while en route to Beth's. Maverick picked up his cell phone.

"Cadence here," came his usual greeting.

"Is there something I should know before I arrive at Beth's in five minutes?" Maggie asked.

"Why, what makes you think something is wrong?" Maverick drawled, checking his watch. "By the way, I've been gone from Beth's fifteen minutes."

"Maverick, what did you do to make Beth call me and beg me to come immediately? She sounded desperate. What was worse, she wasn't crying, she was that upset. She totally ignored the fact that she's been angry with me."

Maverick briefly told her what was going on and about the dark Lincoln. He made Maggie promise not to say a word. They finished talking just as Maggie pulled into Beth's drive.

Beth was waiting for Maggie at the door when she got there. One look at Beth's tortured expression told Maggie this was serious.

"Promise me you won't say a word to Maverick. I mean it, if you want to stay my friend. You have to promise, not a word, peep or mutter," was the first thing out of Beth's mouth.

"Of course, I won't tell Maverick, if you don't want me to," Maggie said sincerely, while thinking to herself, *Unless it's for your own good.*

Beth dropped into a chair like a lead weight. "I probably shouldn't tell you, but I have to tell someone, and the only other person I've ever confided in is Candy, and I certainly can't tell her."

"And?" Maggie saw the tears coming, and she handed her friend a box of tissues.

Beth just sat silently staring at nothing, just taking in a deep sigh and dabbing at her eyes. Finally, Maggie spoke up.

"Well, what is it, and what happened to your face? Did Maverick do that?" Maggie tried to sound suspicious and accusing.

Beth immediately defended him. "Don't be ridiculous! Of course not. You know my Maverick would never do anything to hurt me."

Maggie smiled to herself, knowing it was true. Maverick would never hurt a woman, especially not Beth. Maggie was reassured by Beth's reaction.

"Then what did happen, and why did you call me to rush straight over, if nothing's wrong?" Maggie took Beth's mangled tissue and offered her another one.

"You promise you won't say a word?" Beth pleaded with Maggie.

"I've already said I wouldn't. What is it?" Now she was starting to worry. This was sounding more serious than she first thought.

Beth took a deep breath and barely made an audible whisper, "It was Michael."

"Michael Dunkirk?"

"Yes. He knows everything, and I mean everything," Beth blurted in a rush of words. "And he's going to tell Maverick if I don't do what he wants. If my Maverick finds out, he'll hate me for eternity. Oh Maggie, I think he already does. I think I've lost Maverick forever."

A torrent of tears that had no intention of stopping started down Beth's face.

"No matter what happened in my life, I was always comforted by what Maverick said that last time we spoke. Remember when he came home and said good-bye to me?" Beth asked through the tears.

Maggie nodded yes.

"He said he'd always care about me. But I made him change his mind today. And it's all my fault."

Maggie wasn't troubled about Maverick. She knew how he felt about Beth, so she tried to focus her.

"How does Michael know?" This was what had Maggie concerned and nervous.

Beth slowly dried her tears for a moment and tried to regain her composure. "Remember his first wife was a nurse's aide at the County Hospital? She was getting her training to be a nurse. Well, apparently she was in the room attending while I was delivering Candy. When the labor got intense, I started yelling for Maverick," Beth stated quietly.

"There's no way. I was the only one in that room besides the doctor. And yes, you did yell for Maverick, but no one heard you but me and the doctor. That's why I never mentioned it. The doctor asked if he was the baby's father, and I said yes. I was thankful he didn't ask if he was your husband. He commented that it was an unusual name and then let the nurse in to clean up." Maggie felt like an idiot as she suddenly remembered. "The nurse was standing in the corner observing. She never did anything until the baby was delivered. I didn't think about her being there. But it couldn't have been her. This was a nurse, not an aide."

Beth just stared at Maggie, as if unsure why she didn't understand. "It was decades ago, Maggie. Things were different then. Maybe she was doing it for part of her training. All I know is that Michael knows the truth. His comment to me was, 'Well, at least my ex was good for something.' He's going to tell Maverick the truth, and now it probably won't matter because he doesn't love me anymore, anyway."

Beth started to cry again as Maggie sat and thought about what she'd just heard. This made things more complicated, but it was time.

Maggie took her friend's hand. "Well, Beth, have you thought about the truth? Have you ever once thought about just sitting down with Maverick and telling him the honest-to-goodness truth? I believe he can take it, and I don't think he'll hate you. And you said you have nothing to lose anymore."

Beth replied while still trying to stop the tears, and her words came out in a muffled sob. "Of course, he'll hate me. I wasn't honest with him. I couldn't take a chance on losing everything. Even now it would still hurt people I love. I don't think I can ever do that."

Maggie was getting aggravated. Beth needed to be reasonable, and Maggie sniped, "So, it would be easier to let some jerk threaten you with doing whatever he says when he says it rather than to just tell Maverick the truth? When did Maverick ever let you down or turn his back on you? Never. You did it to him forty years ago, and you're doing it to him again because of Michael. Think about what you're doing, Beth, and for once in your life, follow your heart!"

Maggie put her arms around Beth. She loved her, but Beth needed to hear the truth.

Beth whispered, "I can't tell Maverick that I let him believe a lie. You don't do that to people you love."

Maggie heard what she suspected all along. She had just listened to the confession with her own two ears.

Beth had never stopped loving Maverick.

— 18 —

MAVERICK PARKED AND locked his car in a well-lighted area of the hotel parking lot. As he stepped into the lobby, the concierge motioned for him to approach.

"Yes, what can I do for you?" Maverick had his key already out and a bag of dry cleaning over his shoulder.

"Sir," the concierge shared, "a woman was asking to be let into your room. She said it was supposed to be a surprise. I told her we couldn't do that without your permission. She seemed angry and said she'd wait for you at the bar. I hope I didn't do the wrong thing."

"No, never let anyone into my room unless I'm with them or tell you otherwise. Thank you for following my requests." Maverick handed the gentleman a fifty-dollar tip.

The concierge thanked him profusely.

"By the way," Maverick asked, "she wouldn't by any chance be a redhead?" The concierge nodded yes. "Perfect," Maverick said and walked in the direction of the bar.

Suzy Q sat in a dimly lit corner of the bar. She was dressed in a very flimsy, revealing blouse and low-rise shorts revealing a sliver of a very tanned tummy. She'd been drinking but didn't appear to be drunk. As soon as she saw Maverick, she yelled out, "Over here, handsome."

Maverick walked across the room evaluating the situation. He wasn't sure, but he suspected what she wanted. He might have wanted it years ago, but he now had a relationship with God, and there was only one woman he desired. He sat across from her, gently placing his dry cleaning on the seat at his side.

"I've been waiting for you forever," Suzy said to him, "or at least for forty years. I was afraid you'd bring Miss Goodie-Two-Shoes with you, but then she wouldn't be Miss Goodie-Two-Shoes if she'd done that." Suzy laughed at her witty quip.

Maverick shook his head, and he wrapped his fingers into a double fist and rested them on the table. "Suzy, Suzy, I hate to hear you say that. It's mean of you, and you're better than that."

"Come now, Mav, how do you know I'm better than that?" She lifted the tumbler before her and downed a swig.

He quizzed her in a very somber tone, "So, you were trying to get into my room? What could you possibly want in my room?"

She colored and wiped her hand on her shorts, to remove the dampness from the glass. "It was just old times, Mav. I wanted to surprise you. I've been waiting for a long time for a man like you." She reached forward, wrapped her hands around his, pressed her ankle against his leg under the table, and twisted her foot slightly to ensure he could feel it.

Maverick had no trouble understanding her intentions. He pulled his hands away, dismissing the overture. "Well, thank you for the compliment, but I believe I'll pass. There's a better way, Suzy, God's way. He lives here, and I couldn't do what you want." Maverick tapped his chest as he spoke. "And you're right; Marilyn would never have accompanied me here. She has upstanding, Christian morals, something a lot of people have forgotten about. Be sure and tell that to Michael when you see him."

"Why, how can you say that? You think Michael could convince me to come here? Maverick, I'm hurt."

She reached for his arm with her fingertips, only to have him move his elbows out of her way, to rest them on the back of the bench seat.

"He did, didn't he?"

Suzy puckered her mouth into a petulant sulk, and when Maverick didn't yield, she laughed and turned her head to look at the people in the rest of the bar.

"Well, it seemed like a good idea at the time. I'm sorry, Maverick, and embarrassed that Michael talked me into this."

"What did he promise you? Suzy, you're beautiful and better than this. Go home. Wake up in the morning glad you didn't follow through on this nonsense."

"You've said it twice, so it must be true." She looked really embarrassed, like she'd sink into the floor, if she could.

"What's that?" Maverick smiled.

"I'm better than this, and you know, I am. Riding in Michael's Lincoln does things to a girl, and now I feel foolish, with you being all gentleman. I have a bitter bill to swallow, and if you don't mind, I'll walk away while I still have a little pride left."

"You do that, darlin'. Here, for a taxi to get you home." Maverick offered her a fifty and stepped aside as she got up and left the bar.

He'd had just reached his room when his phone rang. He glanced at the display and answered it.

"Hey, Mags. What's up?"

"I know you just got back to the hotel, but you'd better do something quick. Beth thinks you hate her, and it's all her fault. I've never seen her this depressed, ever. She thinks she's lost you forever. She looks so despondent.

You need to make nice and fix this up. Let her know things are okay between you two. I'm afraid she'll take too many of those muscle relaxers of hers and that will be the end."

Maverick asked, "Did she say she might do anything like that?"

"No, but you know how she is. She's not thinking clearly right now."

"All I want is for Marilyn to finally decide how she feels about me. If it's the same as it was then, I'm hers. If not, I need to know. I can't go on hoping she'll love me someday." Maverick hung his clothes, tossed his key on the bed, and sat beside it. "And did she say who the jerk was that threatened her and did that to her?"

"I want to tell you, Maverick, but Beth wouldn't forgive me." She paused, saying nothing else into the phone.

"I don't care what you told Marilyn. Tell me who it is," Maverick demanded.

"I promised her I wouldn't tell, and I won't break the promise. But you know who it is."

"That's all I need to know. He's a dead man."

"And one other thing Beth said, something I thought you might, maybe, perhaps be interested in," Maggie said in a more playful voice.

"It can wait. I have something, rather *someone* I need to attend to."

"Even if Beth said she loved you?" Maggie questioned.

"What?" Maverick nearly shouted. This added a whole new dimension to the situation. "She said it, you're sure?" He was excited beyond belief.

"Yes, she said that she loved you, and that she'd deceived you, and you would never love her or trust her because of this one thing." Maggie giggled, fueling even more of Maverick's enthusiasm.

"All the more reason to take care of business. No one is ever going to threaten or hurt Marilyn as long as I'm alive."

Maggie cautioned him, "But don't do something that'll get you into trouble or that you'll regret. I couldn't handle knowing something happened to you because of what I said. You've got a lot to live for now."

"Don't you think I know it? I won't blow this. I'll just make a certain someone sorry he ever came to the reunion."

Maverick then continued to tell Maggie about Suzy Q as well. Maggie was shocked that Suzy Q would try such a thing.

"Well, I'm glad the concierge didn't let her in. No telling what she would have tried to blame on you."

"Exactly, and with the state Marilyn's in, that's all she would have needed to decide I didn't love her. Maggie, take care of my girl. I'll be gone a couple of days. When I return, everything'll be okay. I promise. Don't worry about me. Just take care of my baby girl, okay, best-friend-a-Maverick-could-ever-have?"

MAGGIE LAUGHED AND agreed. Poor lovesick Maverick sounded silly, pleading on the phone. Of course, she would take care of Beth, she assured him. Beth was her best friend. She didn't need Maverick to remind her to do that. She'd been taking care of Beth since grade school, when she found out she could talk; she'd been just too shy to. Maggie had been Beth's voice for the last fifty years or so. She wouldn't stop taking care of her just because Maverick was back in the picture. That would just make it more exciting.

And if there was one thing Beth needed more in her life, according to Maggie, it was excitement. With Maverick around, Maggie was sure they would have plenty of it.

— 19 —

BETH NUZZLED HER pillow, enjoying Maverick's strong hands as they massaged her bare shoulders. Then he whispered that he loved her and gently kissed her neck.

The alarm went off, and she woke up from another nightmare.

Any dream Maverick was in was now a nightmare to Beth. She couldn't seem to get him out of her thoughts, day or night. It was Tuesday morning, and she hadn't heard from or seen him since Sunday evening, when he had said he was leaving her for good.

She had half hoped for, half dreaded Maverick's appearance at Shadetree Assisted Living Center to visit his mother. But he hadn't shown up, according to Chloe, who had kept an eye out for him.

"Oh, Beth," Chloe said, when Beth had asked her about Maverick the previous day. "I noticed how good you two looked together, and with your sad face this week, I knew he must be the reason. He's such a handsome man. Not many older gentlemen carry themselves so well. You two would be perfect together. I'll notify you right away if he shows."

"Stop that, Chloe. I just have a few forms for him to go over." She dismissed her assistant's assumptions, but her description of Maverick made her ache for him.

Beth was applying her makeup when her house phone rang. She checked the caller I.D. to find a number from an unknown area code, and she let it go to voice mail.

A few seconds later her cell phone rang with the same unknown area code. Irritated, she didn't answer it either, as she was running late to work. She could check the message on the way to the office, and if they didn't leave one, it wasn't important, anyway.

She got in the car with her cup of coffee and put her phone on speaker. The message was from Michael. He said that he had tried her at home but couldn't get her, so he was calling her cell. He wanted to make sure she understood that if she said anything, he would tell Maverick the truth about Candy. And for a little insurance, he thought Beth should start thinking about marriage, to him.

He made it clear he was smart enough to know that people would question her if she suddenly changed her behaviors and they moved in together. But he was willing to let the reunion be the reason they got together, and that they didn't want to waste any more time being apart.

He announced that this coming weekend would be the perfect time for them to elope. He once again threatened her if she told anyone, and the message abruptly went dead.

Beth felt sick. She couldn't believe she was being blackmailed. And if she wanted to keep Maverick a friend, she had to do what Michael wanted.

But who knew if Maverick would even talk to her now. She hadn't heard from him since that awful argument. Even Maggie said she hadn't heard from him. Now Beth was being forced to do something against her will, again, and for the same reason: her love for Maverick and his daughter, Candy.

Finally, she said it out loud to herself, "Maverick's daughter." She'd never called her that, not to herself, and not to Maggie. Candy was the only reason she'd been able to live without him all these years. She had a part of Maverick with her. It was the best part, their love child. And Candy had his eyes, his beautiful, penetrating blue eyes.

Beth had never been overly strict on Candy, because she knew it would have done no good. She'd been like her father from the day she was born. She had been adventurous, inquisitive and curious about everything.

Alexandra had been the quiet, conservative blessing to raise. She'd inherited Robert's practical side and Beth's good looks. She and her husband had their lives all planned out. They were having their first child sometime this coming year and another one in two years. They'd traveled and bought expensive cars and boats and owned a beautiful home. Now they were ready to have children.

Candy on the other hand had traveled with the Peace Corps, had worked for UNICEF and lived in Paris, France for a couple of years studying art. She had secrets she would share with no one. Beth knew this from her childhood. She would ask odd science related questions about DNA and genes. Beth would encourage her to go ask Robert. Sometimes Candy would, and other times, she would just stare at her with her father's eyes, haunting Beth.

Maggie had once told Beth that Candy asked why her mother had named her Cadence, which meant a short military dance. Maggie had told her that her mother had been so happy to find out she was pregnant, that she'd done a little dance, but she didn't think Dance would be a nice name for a girl.

Maggie had rescued her, and Beth was grateful.

Beth had put away her freshman and sophomore yearbooks so Candy would never see that name in print. Beth had also talked Robert into attending church in another town when Candy was starting junior high so he could "network" more clients than just the ones in their small community. All of this was for Candy's protection and Beth's own sanity.

But high school had been another thing, and Beth had taken no chances. She'd sent Candy to a private Christian School, where very few people knew Beth or her family. She'd worked hard to make sure Candy was happy and content.

She didn't invest the time, nor did she need to with Alexa. Her father gravitated to her more, becoming very involved with her, and parenting her with an intensity Candy never knew.

Beth supposed it was understandable. He'd been busy finishing school when Candy was born one month "premature." She'd always added a month to whatever due date the doctor gave her, so when she did give birth, it would appear to be a premature delivery. Since Candy was small, weighing barely five pounds, unlike Alexa who tipped the scales at seven-and-a half pounds, it had seemed reasonable. With five years difference between the girls, she and Robert had been more settled by the time Alexa had arrived. By then Robert had been making good money, and they'd been able to afford more.

Beth pulled into the drive at work and pushed her thoughts aside. She'd let her life slip by living in fear of someone finding out about her and Maverick. And now her worst fears were coming true. They'd only been together that one time, wildly and passionately, and then again the next morning right before he'd left. But that was all it took. She was living proof of that. Beth had begged God to forgive her, but she realized she'd never forgiven herself. Only by admitting part of it to Maverick had she truly felt better.

Now someone was trying to force her to live the lie to even a greater degree. She couldn't do it. Not anymore. Maverick or no Maverick, she refused to marry Michael Dunkirk or share his bed. She would call Maggie and tell her that she was right. Maybe it was time to tell the truth, the whole truth.

Better late than never, she would tell Maverick the truth.

Once in her parking spot, she dialed Maggie's number. When her friend answered, she said, "Maggie, I have some news to tell you. You'd better sit down for this."

MAGGIE HUNG UP the phone and dialed Maverick's cell. He should be coming back today, anyway, but he would flip out when he heard this.

"Cadence here."

"Maggie here."

"Hey, what's up? Anything wrong?"

"Beth asked if I would try and get hold of you." Maggie let out a long breath, and at the end, she gave a short whistle, just to pique his curiosity.

"Regarding what?"

"The truth!" Maggie couldn't hold it in. "Can you believe it? Beth said she wants to tell you the whole truth. I nearly fell out of my chair. I had to ask her to repeat it, just to make sure I wasn't hearing things."

"Well, we'll see if she does. I'm not calling or seeing her until this weekend. This will let me know if she's really in love with me or just trying to protect Candy. I called my daughter yesterday and told her that all the plans were coming along as expected. She's so excited."

"Wonderful!" Maggie could hardly wait.

"So, you can tell Marilyn you talked to me and that I'll talk to her on Sunday. Let me know how she takes the news. I may have to change my plans. Oh, we're boarding. I'll call you when we land. Love you, Mags."

"Same here." Maggie hung up the phone, wondering what kind of game Maverick was playing.

Three hours later Maggie's phone rang. It was Maverick. "I'm back, and I've rented a car so Beth won't see mine around town. I have it parked out at the ranch. So, look for a silver BMW. That'll be me. You're going to have to trust me, Maggie, that everything will work out the way it's supposed to. I can't tell you what's going to happen, because I don't know myself. It's up to Marilyn. She's going to have to let me know how to play my hand. Just make sure that she doesn't do anything crazy between now and Saturday."

"I thought you said Sunday."

"I did. Come Sunday it will all make sense one way or another."

Maverick ended the phone conversation.

Maggie wasn't sure what to think. But she knew Beth would be upset that she couldn't talk to Maverick until Sunday. It would be difficult keeping her calmed down, especially if Michael called.

Now that Beth wanted to tell Maverick the truth, Maggie would be hard pressed to keep her away from him. The man had something more than his arm up his sleeve, and he wasn't letting anyone know what it was.

Then, of course, that was Maverick for you.

— 20 —

IT SEEMED LIKE an eternity before Saturday finally arrived. Beth had tried to contact Maverick through Maggie without success. She'd even tried to reach him once herself but wouldn't leave a message, only, "This is Marilyn."

She was growing more anxious as the weekend approached. She was determined not to let Michael or anyone else stand in the way of her living her life on her own terms.

Now that she'd decided this, a new emerging courage manifested itself in Beth, giving her hope. She wanted to be with Maverick for the rest of her life. She'd always loved him. No one else had ever claimed her heart, because he'd had it since she was thirteen.

Maverick was her soul mate. He was the man she dreamed of and yearned for in the late night and early morning hours when sleep wouldn't come. Maverick was the name she had screamed when the pangs of birth were more than she could stand.

Not once had she asked for her husband at either birth, but she had screamed and begged for Maverick when both of her daughters had come into the world.

And when things were going badly, she'd look in Candy's eyes and know that a part of Maverick was with her.

She wanted to enjoy hers and Maverick's grandchildren together. She was tired of looking over her shoulder and worrying about what someone might say or do that would expose her secret.

She didn't want to live a lie anymore.

Michael had sent instructions to Beth via courier regarding the plans. Beth had directions on where to meet the scoundrel. It was a small wedding chapel about an hour away. The minister would perform the ceremony, and they would stop and get the license afterward.

The ceremony was just a formality, so questions wouldn't be raised. They'd have photographs taken, so everything would appear that this was what Beth had wanted to do. They'd then honeymoon for a week before Beth left to go to her daughter's wedding.

Michael had said she should continue with the plans she had made so as not to arouse suspicion. But he made it very clear that he would destroy her, Maverick, and her daughter if he was in any way endangered or exposed.

For insurance, he sent a picture of her daughter with her fiancé smiling from her post in Greenland.

Beth knew Michael had to have connections to be able to obtain a photograph she didn't have, and she was confident he wasn't making an idle or hollow promise.

So it was with extreme caution that she drove toward her destination. Her heart pounded almost out of her chest. Her mouth was dry. She tried her best to think of exactly how she was going to tell him: No matter what, she would never marry Michael Dunkirk. Whatever the outcome between her and Maverick, she wouldn't be bullied and blackmailed. She'd told Maggie to wait for her call, and if she didn't receive it, for Maggie to contact the police.

When Beth arrived, she was surprised at how cute the

wedding chapel looked. It was like a page from a fairy tale. It was a church with old-fashioned shutters and stained-glass windows, with a small bridge in the front over a narrow creek. The outside of the building was lined with beautiful pink roses and white lilies set in pots at the front door.

A lattice archway covered with greenery and roses stood near the entrance.

Beth's nervousness didn't let her enjoy any of the charm. She had to be strong enough to get this over with. After stopping the car, she got out, locked the door, and straightened her clothing. With newfound inner resolve, she walked with a straight back over the bridge and onto the porch. She put her hand on the antique doorknob and prayed she would be brave enough to follow through with her plans.

Once inside, the chapel was filled with fresh flowers, twinkling lights, and iridescent gossamer covering everything. It was breathtaking. She couldn't believe Michael would have taken so much care in planning this farce of a wedding.

A gentleman approached who identified himself as the minister. Then she heard a cough, and coming out of a side room was Michael. He was dressed wearing a white suit. He walked toward Beth, and her knees began to shake. Michael reached out and took her hand.

"Beth, honey, why didn't you wear a wedding dress?" he asked sweetly.

Beth glanced at her simple summer dress and sandals and into his face. "Because I don't plan on getting married," she said in an unsteady voice.

"What? I don't believe I heard you correctly." He sounded angry.

"You heard me." Beth spoke in a flat, defeated tone. She took a deep breath and continued. "I made a mistake when I was young. I was pregnant with Maverick's baby, the only man I've ever loved. I should have waited for him. But I was afraid of my father. He'd already threatened me about Maverick when I was younger, saying he would send me away to a boarding school. If he knew I was pregnant by Maverick, he'd have made me give up the baby for adoption. I could've never given up our child. Maverick's baby was all I had to live for.

"So I did the best I could and slept with Robert one time so I could tell him I was pregnant. That was my crime, loving my baby and her father. But I won't be threatened by you. My father almost ruined my life; I won't let you, Michael Dunkirk, ruin the rest of it. So, if you think telling Maverick will bring you some sadistic satisfaction, then go ahead. He doesn't love me, anyway. But you won't hurt his daughter or destroy her happiness. I'll kill you myself before she has to live what I've been through. I won't marry you. That's final!"

Beth let out a sigh and dropped, exhausted, on the pew next to where they'd been standing at the back of the chapel. *God,* she sent up in a desperate cry, *why have you let me come to this?* She was shaking, but she refused to cry.

"Was that what you wanted?" Michael asked, looking behind Beth. Beth turned, and there stood Maverick, her Maverick. All the breath went out of her body, and a chill ran over her.

"Yes, that's exactly what I wanted to hear," Maverick said hoarsely, with tears coming to his eyes. "That's all I've ever wanted to hear." He stood staring at Beth, who was still in a state of shock at knowing what Maverick had just overheard. No one spoke for several minutes. Maverick continued to stare at Beth, with a smile on his face and happiness in his eyes.

Finally, Michael spoke up. "We had a deal, remember?"

"Yes, I remember. You get to live another day. But if you ever come near her or make her feel uncomfortable in any way, you'll wish you'd gone to prison instead, got it?

God has tied my hands, telling me I can't punch you in the face, but if you come around again, I'll see if God will give me permission to do more. Do I make myself clear?"

"Crystal," Michael's replied.

It was then Beth noticed the make-up Michael was wearing to cover the shiner he had under his left eye. She'd been so nervous she hadn't noticed anything but his white suit. Maverick nodded affirmatively in Michael's direction and waited as he headed toward the exit. He muttered as he left that he was leaving the state and would never return.

Beth wiped her frustration from her eyes and turned to Maverick. "You knew about this and didn't try to help me? You were going to let me go through with this?"

Maverick carefully pulled Beth up and stood facing her with his hand under her chin. He lifted her face gently so she could see only him. He spoke in a soft, low tone so only she heard him.

"Why do you think I'm here, Marilyn? I trusted God to work out the problems between us, and this is the way he showed me. I had to know the truth once and for all. I had to know that you loved me back then as much as I love you right now. I had to know there was hope for a future with you. As soon as I figured out who it was that had hurt you, I went after him. Michael was more than happy to cooperate rather than spend time in prison. He told me everything he knew. But I'm the one who sent you the courier package." He paused, and then said, "And yes, I'm the one who sent you the picture of our daughter."

"I've prayed for the same thing. I've so wanted to be with you again." Beth felt lightheaded, and that was all she remembered until she heard Maverick questioning her.

"Marilyn, honey, are you okay? Maggie, give her some more water to drink."

Beth slowly opened her eyes. She was still in the wedding chapel, and only Maggie was with them. She didn't remember fainting.

"What's Maggie doing here?" she asked, puzzled, unaware she was lying in Maverick's arms on the floor.

"I've come to be the witness." Maggie giggled softly. "I'm thankful you're coming around from your fainting spell."

"Witness to what?" Beth became aware of Maverick's arms around her.

"Marilyn, you fainted when I told you about the photograph I had of Candy and Drew. I caught you in my arms as you went down. Maggie was just coming in the chapel when it happened. She brought you a cup of water from the fountain. And here you are," Maverick whispered tenderly, as he looked into the emerald eyes of the woman he had waited a lifetime for.

Beth was still alarmed by the events that had just occurred. How did Maverick know about Candy, and how long had he known? Beth started to speak, but Maverick interrupted her.

"Did you mean what you said about loving me? Do you want to spend the rest of your life with your Maverick, Mary Elizabeth Monroe Taylor?"

It was the first time he'd ever called her by her true name. She smiled just thinking about it. She'd fantasized about how wonderful it would be to be with Maverick forever, without any secrets. She felt calm and serene, more at peace than she could ever remember.

"Well, baby girl." Maverick sounded slightly anxious. "Do you?"

Beth felt her face warm that she hadn't answered him. "Yes, I want to marry you, Maverick Dillinger Cadence. I want to be with you every minute of every day for the rest of my life."

"Well then, Maggie, help her get dressed. We've got a wedding to attend to," Maverick said excitedly.

Again, Beth was confused by everything. "Whose wedding and what dress?" Beth looked to Maverick for answers.

"Our wedding!" Maverick grinned from ear to ear. "In case you didn't notice, the entire wedding chapel was done to your taste and with you in mind. All the flowers, decorations, everything was chosen by Maggie for our wedding. She just didn't know when it would be. I hinted it might be when we went on the Alaskan cruise next week. So, she innocently helped me out. But the wedding dress was all me. All I needed was your size and a few alterations from a borrowed dress I took from your closet the first night you fell asleep." Maverick grinned, seeing Beth's eyes widen at his disclosure.

"You mean you planned to marry me all along?" Beth wasn't sure she understood him correctly.

"Yes, Marilyn. I was hoping we could start our lives where we left off, still crazy for each other, but this time with God in control. I know my heart hasn't changed. I just wanted to know that you in some small way felt the same, too. After talking with Maggie and Candy, I dared to hope that we could have a chance. I hoped I had the possibility of being one of the luckiest guys on the face of the earth."

She nearly cried when she saw Maggie approaching with the most beautiful mermaid-style sequined wedding dress she'd ever seen. "You mean right now? I don't have my makeup, or shoes, or my hair done." Beth felt panicked as Maverick helped her to her feet.

Maggie piped in, "I brought everything you need, and it's in the bridal chamber."

Maverick said reverently, "I don't plan to ever lose you again, baby girl." He pulled her to him and gave her a long, passionate kiss, taking her breath away, as she melted right into his arms. "And I can't wait another week to make you mine," Maverick almost growled. "Hurry!" he yelled out as Maggie led her away.

When Beth opened the bridal chamber door, Lily, Maverick's mother, was sitting there.

"I wondered how long you would make him wait this

time. I knew you loved him when I heard how you wanted to keep his baby. But I already had my suspicions years ago when you married so quickly after he shipped out.

"Then, I saw your little girl when she was about three or so, and I knew she was Maverick's. She looked just like him. I saw her again when she was about ten. I had tears in my eyes when I wrote him about her. And when they put her picture in the paper as the valedictorian of her private school, I mailed the paper to Maverick. He's known for years. But when his little Cathy died, he finally had the gumption to do something about it. He finally contacted her." Lily paused for a moment, watching Beth's startled expression about the revelation of the news.

It was Maggie's turn to come clean with Beth, once Lily started it. "Candy told me she was relieved to find out Robert wasn't her father. She told me she'd always known something wasn't quite right. Since she was a little girl, she'd been allergic to milk products, and no one else in her family was. Also, Robert's eyes were brown, and yours were green. Candy knew there was no way she could have blue eyes. She never questioned you, but along with her biology professors, she sure did ask me a lot of questions. When she finally met Maverick, it answered a lot of inquiries she had about herself."

Then Lily continued, "When she and Colt met, they immediately knew they were brother and sister. We all had a wonderful time in Hawaii getting better acquainted. The only one missing was you. You've been a stubborn one. But now that you're getting married, we can finally be one big happy family on our Alaskan cruise."

Beth froze. "You mean everyone's going?" She thought she'd heard Maverick mention it earlier to Maggie.

Lily replied, smiling slyly, "Yes, Candy and her daddy planned this six months ago. They had to so Colt could put in for his time off. Candy said she especially wanted her brother to meet her mom. He doesn't know everything yet, because we weren't sure about you. But you know what they say, all's well that ends well."

Beth was totally astonished by this new information coming from the oldest member of the of the Cadence family. Everyone had known about her well-guarded secret, but no one had said anything to upset her. No wonder her daughter had wanted her to loosen up. She'd known Maverick for the past ten years, and they'd schemed together the past few months to get Maverick back into Beth's life without too much stress on her. They did all this out of love for her.

It brought tears to Beth's eyes. She would be thankful to marry a man who loved her that much and to be a complete family with a daughter and a son.

Maggie helped Beth put on the lace-and-sequin-covered form-fitting dress. Maverick whistled, describing her as a vision of loveliness as she walked down the aisle and repeated her vows, holding a beautiful bouquet of soft pink roses and white lilies with Lily softly crying to see her son finally happy. And when the rings were exchanged, a five-carat diamond was placed on Beth's slender finger, while a plain gold band was given to Maverick. The minister ended the ceremony with a prayer for guidance that God would keep his hand on every aspect of the couple's new life together. Maggie smiled with tears in her eyes to finally see what should have happened forty years ago.

After the pictures were taken, the marriage license was obtained, and it was officially signed, Maverick said, "I have a confession to make."

"What?" Beth wondered what secrets he could possibly have.

"Let's wait until we get to the hotel. I want to make up for some lost time." He winked, and this time Beth didn't blush. Instead, she nodded yes and snuggled close to him, giving Maverick even more reason to get to the hotel immediately.

— Epilogue —

SEVERAL HOURS LATER, Beth and Maverick lay together on the first night of their honeymoon, totally relaxed and complete in one another's arms.

Beth shyly said, "It was worth the wait. After almost forty years, it was better than I remembered."

Maverick totally agreed, as he kissed her hair and held her close.

Beth whispered, "I haven't forgotten you had something to confess." She rested her hand on his chest, as she nestled against him. "What's the confession you have to make?"

Maverick looked a little sheepish, with his boyish appearance piquing Beth's curiosity.

"Candy had wanted us to get married aboard the ship along with her and Drew. But I knew I couldn't wait another day, much less a week to make you mine. Marilyn, do you think a week would be too soon to renew our vows?" Maverick grinned.

"Not if we can have a second honeymoon." Beth smiled seductively.

"The first one's not over yet," Maverick said, as he pulled Beth to him again.

TRUE HEART REUNION

— 1 —

"GREAT," ROSEMARY BRUTON sighed to no one in particular when she checked the airport's app on her phone and read the notice that her friend Jenny Carleton's plane had encountered bouts of heavy rain. Overhead, the flight number rolled across the display, with the dreaded word: *Delayed.*

She brushed her shoulder-length chestnut hair with her fingers and tucked it behind her, as she glanced warily around the airport at the travelers moving past. She caught sight of herself in a silvered metal panel, and she looked away. Her friends told her she was as attractive as the day she graduated high school, but she saw the lines around her eyes and her mouth that revealed her age.

With her fortieth reunion celebration gearing up, she was nervous about the people she might see walking through that gate. Her stomach was in knots. At least Jenny was staying with her, and they'd have the chance to catch up on the past year.

She worked her phone into her tailored handbag, with its bronze metal trim and contrasting stitching. Her hand brushed her pocket Bible, and she was reminded of her decision for Christ a little over a year before. She knew her past transgressions were forgiven, but standing in the middle of Pflugerville's Austin Executive Airport, her upcoming reunion kept reminding her of mistakes from four decades earlier. She tried to brush them off and considered heading home for something to eat. Her phone would send her flight updates if the plane made it in before the airport closed.

An exterior door opened as a couple exited, letting the brittle sound of rain inside, and she shivered, recalling the bright days filled with sunshine only the week before. The pelting showers gave the October air a newfound chill. She glanced out the rain-spattered glass to the gloom just beyond, where two planes taxied across the runway. Last week, the temperatures around Pflugerville and her hometown of Round Rock had hovered in the eighties. Today's gloomy weather was forecast to blow out by morning, and she was ready for it to be gone and for the warmth to return.

With optimism, she noted a fresh set of passengers arriving, some in bright, flowered summer wear, possibly from a holiday on the Mexican coast. Two men sported business attire, and one little girl wore a party dress. Rose caught sight of a woman who seemed familiar, one she thought might be arriving for the reunion. Pflugerville was one of the easiest airports to access from Round Rock, and it was likely many attendees would arrive here. The lady was arm-in-arm with a tall man and in an involved conversation, so she didn't call to her.

After about ten minutes, Rosemary headed toward the lone service counter to inquire if her friend's plane might arrive at all that evening. She wasn't sure what her next step should be. She'd tried to reach Jenny on her cell phone, but she hadn't expected to get through if she was onboard. She'd left a message, but it hadn't helped her darkening mood. Other people around her appeared equally irritated and aggravated. From behind her, a loud voice startled her, abruptly bellowing out her name.

"Rose Petal, is that you?"

No! It couldn't be, not that voice, with its deep, unforgettable, resonating sound coming across the airport terminal. She would recognize that man's reverberating, bone-jarring tone anywhere. Thornton Jebulon Wilder. It must be! Despite her astonishment, Rosemary was hardly surprised to be recognized. After having her son Gill, Jr. at twenty-four, she'd maintained her trim figure, and her hair was the same color as in high school, thanks to her awesome stylist. Rose Petal, however, was also from high school, a name that should have stayed in high school, not shouted across the Pflugerville airport. She'd been Rosemary Penndel, and many of her friends had teased her by dropping the Mary and changing her last name ever so slightly. Rose Petal had stuck.

Her eyes skipped across the strangers around her until the man she recognized caught her eye. She let out a sharp breath when her eyes fixed on his broad shoulders and thick head of hair. There was no mistaking Thorn Wilder, a head above the crowd just as she remembered.

How she wished Jenny's plane had arrived on time! Then she'd be gone, and she wouldn't be standing here facing this disaster from her past, one she knew only too well. His dark, penetrating eyes had always been able to see right into her soul. They were the sort of eyes that made others feel as if he was drilling a hole through them and didn't care who knew it.

He was the last person she wanted to see.

Rosemary closed her eyes for a moment, breathed a quick prayer, and then opened them again, hoping beyond hope the moment would magically go away and Thorn would disappear. Yet, his voice was real, and so was his dominating presence.

What was worse, bigger than life itself, Thorn bore down on her, with his eyes locked on her.

"W-why yes, it's me, Thornton. Nice to see you," Rose stuttered, the reality of the moment jerking her roughly back to the present. Indeed, he'd been a literal thorn in her side, and seeing this man wasn't nice at all. A flush of anxiety wrapped warm fingers of dread around her heart. She forced her arm outward and anxiously presented a clammy hand to shake.

As he continued staring, she felt herself grow more apprehensive. Clearly, he was seeing a Rosemary from forty years ago, and it wasn't a look she appreciated. Judging from this brief encounter, Thorn hadn't changed one bit in the past four decades, not in the way he carried himself or his behavior.

After a lengthy pause, he reached his hand as if to shake hers, but just as they touched, he pulled her up close. His warm breath and the faint smell of his cologne took Rose by surprise, and she found his lips on hers before she could push him away. It was all the emotions from high school once again rushing over her in a torrent. As she rose to her tiptoes to meet him, it was as if she had no control of her own.

After the kiss, he gently set her feet back on the terminal floor. Unsettled, her knees weakened with the intensity of the moment, she had trouble getting her balance for the first few seconds. Without thinking, she grabbed his arm. Then, aware of how that small intimacy might seem to others, she placed her hand on his chest and pushed him roughly away. She wouldn't allow her sudden display of emotions to get in the way of keeping her distance from this man.

"Good to see you too, Rose Petal. I can see you're still as sweet as I remember. What was it you said to me the last time we saw each other?" Thorn's deep laugh resonated.

"What do you mean?" Rosemary tried to recall the events of a day she'd worked desperately hard to forget over the past forty years.

"I believe you said come hail or high water, you'd never kiss me again. Well, darlin', there's fixin' to be a flood. You better build you an ark, 'cause you're coming on high water and about to drown!"

With that, Thorn gave a crooked grin, turned heel on his cowboy boots, and strode off, leaving a very bewildered Rosemary standing alone in the airport terminal, as several rows of lights dimmed, and the announcement rang out that the airport was closing in thirty minutes.

— 2 —

"I WAS HOPING I'd get here first to tell you Thorn was coming to the reunion."

Jenny Carleton, a make-up artist with numerous Hollywood films on her resume, patted her face, flushed from her scramble to exit the airplane after a full night of delays. She luxuriated in the cool air inside the terminal as the words tumbled from her mouth, and there was anticipation on her face as she glanced at Rosemary to gauge her reaction. Outside the building's windows, the morning sun dusted the Hill Country with autumn's glory.

"That would have been nice." Rose gave a shallow smile, one that barely broke the fire-engine perfection of her lips.

"Since we haven't been talking much, I really didn't want to call and give you such upsetting news over the phone. I thought you might think I was doing it out of spite. He made two reservations on the very first invitation we sent out almost ten months ago. You remember, the *Save the Date* flyer. He paid for his weekend activities then, too." Jenny pursed her lips to cover a smile. Rose unexpectedly meeting Thorn at the airport the night before was a boon she couldn't have anticipated.

They worked toward the baggage pickup section, and it seemed as if every delayed flight had arrived at once. The two women were jostled repeatedly, and it was as if there wasn't a square foot of airport terminal to spare. Part of it was exhaustion. Both women were tired from the chase of resolving yesterday's bad weather issues.

"Two reservations . . . mmm . . . That's more than one, Jenny. Does that mean he's bringing someone with him? Uh . . . he definitely appeared to be alone last night." Rosemary's words stumbled as she recalled the previous evening. "He made such a spectacle of us. I was so embarrassed I almost died right there on the spot."

"Embarrassed?" Jenny reached into her pocketbook and pulled out a mirror, holding it to one eye. She groaned at her smeared mascara.

"You heard me. Maybe more than embarrassed. Humiliated, even." Rosemary began to recount the events of the prior evening to her friend. Her voice was calmer as she reached her hand to tuck a loose strand of hair behind her ear. The small motion, unthinking and careless, showed her continued tension as she recalled the unexpected meeting and the emotions that had stirred up potent feelings from the past.

"You poor thing." Jenny's eyes caught what Rose's hands were doing. She wished she could have been a fly on the wall to see the encounter. She smiled to herself and quickly stifled it, putting a serious look on her face. She placed her hand on Rose's arm in what she was sure would come across as sincere empathy. "I wish I'd been here to run interference for the two of you. I hate that you had to face him alone. Just to be clear, he definitely made reservations for two for the banquet."

Jenny tried to sound consoling while she thought of the rugged good looks Thorn had once exhibited. At the same time, she wondered if he'd changed much. Every girl in their high school had wanted to be noticed by the "Wild Thorn." His athletic build had dominated all the other boys on the football field, and Jenny couldn't imagine him any other way.

"Were you able to recognize him? Has he changed a whole lot?" Jenny felt certain that Rose hadn't revealed everything from the accidental meeting the previous day.

ROSEMARY BREATHED IN deeply as they slipped Jenny's luggage in her car. She was glad she had something to keep her hands occupied.

"Actually, it's been so long since I've seen him. He was, I guess, well, if I had to say, he looked even taller and broader than I remembered. He seemed as fit as ever." She paused, closing her eyes. The thoughts running through her head were more than just a memory. This was a reconnection she didn't want to make.

She opened her eyes when Jenny cleared her throat. She shrugged, fighting to keep her voice calm, and whispered, "His hair was definitely different. It was showing silver all around the edges. I saw that up close when he picked me up."

"And? What does that mean?" Jenny smirked.

"He still has those same rough features so many women find attractive, if that's what you're asking." Rose reached for a final valet bag she recognized, understanding the importance of the make-up inside. She carefully worked it in, and she pushed the button on her key fob. She stepped back as the whine of the trunk's motor pulled it gently closed.

"You used to like those features, too, if I remember correctly." Jenny laughed her friend's direction.

Rose jerked her eyes to her friend, her irritation sudden and strong. A few choice words came to her mind, and for a moment, she wished this reunion weren't taking place at all. She didn't need these jabs. Perhaps meeting Jenny hadn't been such a good idea.

Then, biting her lip and looking away, she took a deep breath, and she sensed her new-found faith in God reminding her of the pastor's sermon the previous week. Control of her tongue was vital to her Christian witness. Anyway, what Jenny said was true. That was what pained her. She knew every word was exactly the way she remembered it. That didn't mean she wanted to be reminded of it.

"That was a long time ago, and a lot of muddy water's disappeared under that bridge. More than I care to remember. Let's not bring all that up. I want to enjoy this reunion despite Thorn."

JENNY KNEW WHEN to stop. Rose's agitated sigh sent her a very clear message. As kids, they'd tormented each other unmercifully. However, since high school, Rose hadn't been able to take being pushed. She would just balk and do nothing at all, distancing herself from the situation, even cutting off her friends. Jenny had long ago learned that when Rose became too irritated, only a sincere apology—as well as the offer of a facial or makeover—would get through her shell.

That was what had happened last year when Jenny had asked Rose an innocent question about several events from their high school years. Rose had found the questions nosy, and she had cut Jenny off, refusing to answer her entreaties for reconciliation. Jenny had waited for her to calm down, hoping for a response, but after a year, with the reunion looming, Jenny had been forced to break the ice without Rose's help.

"I'm with you all the way, Rose," Jenny began, hoping to smooth her friend's newly ruffled feathers. Before she could offer more than the barest support, Rose interrupted her.

"I don't even want to go to the reunion, now that I know the 'Wild Thorn' will be there." She glanced at Jenny, her eyes red with emotion. "But if I don't go, I'll miss seeing all the old friends I do care about. I feel like he's trying to cause trouble for me. You know that if I go, I'll have to deal with him. But if I don't, I'll feel like he ran me off just like he did after high school." Rose reached for a tissue to blow her nose.

"Of course you're going to the reunion. Don't let Thorn scare you away." Jenny was very determined, and while she intended to be supportive, she intended to convince Rose to attend this reunion, no matter what, especially since Thorn would be there. She would side with Rose, because their friendship needed repairing, even skipping some of the reunion's scheduled events, if necessary, but that wasn't her plan, and it was entirely too early to give up now, even though she was certain Rose would weaken and try to back out later. That just meant Jenny had to put more effort into it.

Besides, she was interested in how Thorn had turned out after all these years. If he was anything like Rose had described him from their brief encounter at the airport, he couldn't have changed much and must be as attractive as ever.

"Oh, I won't," Rose assured her. "I just wish Gill was here with me. He was always so supportive." She drooped in her seat, her emptiness at the loss of her husband draining her for a moment. "I really miss him at times like this."

Jenny nodded that she understood. Rose's husband had died from a stroke only three years before. However, despite Rose's wish for her husband at her side, Jenny knew she had been dominated by him. Gill had been an extremely possessive man. It had taken every effort for her to become as independent as she was now.

The unspoken truth was that if Gill were still alive, Rose might not be allowed to attend the reunion. He had maintained a tight rein over her, and he was always looking for an excuse to be jealous. Jenny had realized that after the first time she met him. He hadn't been comfortable with the two women talking about their high school years. He hadn't wanted his wife mentioning anything about her life from before their marriage. Jenny was certain he'd felt threatened by any man from Rose's past, but especially Thornton Wilder.

Rose and Jenny arrived about ten minutes later at Rose's picturesque Austin stone home just outside of town, hers since shortly after Gill died. The rugged terrain made the homes in the area blend into the environment, and being outside town, deer roamed the yard. Her old house had too many memories tied to it, and she'd let it go as quickly as possible.

Jenny put her things in the main guest room, glad to see that it had a private bath. She loved the antique furniture, and especially the elegant brass bed that accompanied this room. The bed and furnishings had belonged to Rose's great-grandmother, Doris. Being here made her feel like she was at a very stylish bed and breakfast.

"Do your son and his wife stay here when they visit?" Jenny walked into the family room to find Rose drinking a glass of water. On the table were her vitamins and supplements. She stepped to her friend and picked up her vitamin bottle to see just what she was taking now. She looked at her with raised eyebrows and laughed. "Silver vitamins? Honey, you need the titanium bottle."

Rose chuckled and took the bottle from her, moving it and all the rest to the back of the table. "And you keep your hands off my supplements. To answer your question about my son and his wife, sometimes they stay with me, and other times they insist on a hotel. I think it's more for their privacy than mine. I have plenty of room for them and the two grandbabies, well, they're not grandbabies, any longer. However, even when I insist otherwise, Junior and Evelyn always feel like they're intruding in my life."

Jenny plopped into a comfortable chair. "Do you prefer for them to stay here?" She smiled at the softness of the cushions, running one hand down the arm.

"I ENJOY HAVING them near me. It was Gill who wanted his privacy. He was always so possessive, even when it came to his own son. He was jealous of anyone taking my time away from him." Rose smiled, remembering the times her children and grandchildren had spent with her both before and after Gill's death. Before he had died, they'd been a breath of fresh air. Afterwards, she'd welcomed the company.

"Then you should always insist on them staying with you. This is such a wonderful place that I wouldn't stay anywhere else, if I were invited." Jenny crossed her legs and bounced one foot in the air contentedly, certain her friend would get the hint.

Rose sighed and picked up one of her vitamin bottles to peruse the label absently. "It should be that easy, Jenny. Looking back, I realize Gill could be an extremely selfish man at times. But I didn't have many men to judge him by, since my father was in the military and always gone. I liked the fact that Gill was around and wanted me near him. It wasn't until later in our marriage that I realized how controlling he was." Rose paused, then continued with a brighter tone. "The kids all stayed with me the last time they were down, so perhaps they'll be here more in the future. Gill, Jr. knows I want him here, but old insecurities and habits are hard to break."

"I'm glad you've made them feel welcome. With any luck, this will be where they come from now on." Jenny glanced at her watch, frowning.

"What, Jenny?" Rose saw the look at the watch. "Surely you can't have an appointment for a facial so soon after arriving in town." She winked, teasing her friend. It really was good to have her staying in her home with her.

Jenny smiled at Rose, and she held out one arm, patting the inside crook of her elbow. "I've been on the plane since early this morning and haven't eaten. I must keep my insulin levels in mind, because my sugar level could drop at any time. Diabetes. Type two. At least I don't have to stick my arm, just maintain my illness by regular food intake. My waist line doesn't like it, but my taste buds sure do." She stood, reaching for her purse. "Are you hungry? How about us grabbing a bite for breakfast? It'll be my treat."

"Breakfast, huh? Is that how you do it?" Rose looked at her friend for a minute, amazed that this friend of hers could eat a regular breakfast and still manage to hang on to her beautiful looks four decades out of high school, diabetes or not. Maybe there was a trick she could pick up there.

"Do what, Sweetie?" Jenny dangled her purse, missing the point altogether. "Ready?"

Rose laughed, standing to gather her things. Jenny was a guest. Of course, she would go. "Breakfast, it is. I completely forgot about your blood sugar. Where do you want to eat? The Big Griddle serves a great breakfast, if that's what you're thinking, or there's a buffet in the hotel downtown."

Rose grabbed her purse and moved toward the door, her fingers working the house alarm. She held the door for Jenny as they headed out to the car, their conversation already on which restaurant they would choose.

— 3 —

THORN IDLED HIS truck into the parking space and peered at the cars in the lot. The first thing he'd done upon taking possession of his rental was put Rose's address in the navigation system. Her address on the destination bar called to him, and he forced himself to look away. He killed the engine and let his eyes rest on the car next to him. At the airport last night, there'd been one just like it parked next to him. Rose's? He thought it looked like one she'd drive.

He wondered if he'd see her inside.

The reputation of the establishment was the best in town, and if she was eating breakfast in Round Rock, this is where she'd be. Taking a deep breath, he unlatched his door, climbed down, and headed inside.

The hostess offered him a choice of a secluded table or a booth that was more open. He asked her to give him a moment, letting his eyes roam the seated clientele. He smiled to himself when he saw Rose, the source of his night of insomnia. Across from her sat Jenny Carleton. A waitress was just leaving the table. Things were falling into place quicker than he'd anticipated.

THE WOMEN HAD chosen a booth with large, sweeping views of the dining room. Rose had ordered orange juice and black coffee, while Jenny requested coffee with French vanilla-flavored creamer, along with a large glass of milk. Asking for a minute to select from the menu, they were engrossed in the choices when a deep voice interrupted them.

Rose's head immediately shot up to see Thorn's football-player frame looming over them. Her heart began to pound, and irritation—or something she could later claim as irritation—surged through her.

Thorn was intruding on her space once again.

"Mornin'." Thorn's eyes were bloodshot as if he'd been up all night, but at least he was clean-shaven and faintly smelled of soap and cologne. Without asking her permission, he announced, "Move over, Rose Petal."

Rose was taken aback. How dare he! Even as she raged inside, she felt his kiss from the airport as the same unwelcome emotions swept back over her. It was happening again; she felt herself enveloped by this man who had loved and left her.

"I don't guess I own the restaurant, do I?" Her hand involuntarily squeezed the menu, crushing one corner. She quickly put it aside. In disbelief, she found herself scooting down to allow Thorn to sit.

She cringed inside, furious at the control he still exerted over her. All he had to do was walk back into her life, and she caved. She should be strong around this man, and that was something she hadn't done well so far.

Thorn filled the booth with his considerable six-foot-four height and broad shoulders. Then he leaned his elbows on the table and looked at Jenny.

"Well, hello, I-Dream-of-Jeanie."

"NICE TO SEE you, too," Jenny shot back, finishing with,

"Thorn Bird!" She was surprised by his bold actions, just waltzing up and making himself at home with the two of them. And to think, she'd even looked forward to seeing him again.

Now she wasn't so sure.

She wondered if he'd even considered they might not want his company. It was clear he still had his daring good looks, and it didn't seem like he'd changed all that much in the last forty years. There were a few laugh lines crinkling around his eyes and mouth, and his skin was deeply tanned. That probably meant he still worked outside as he'd done as a teenager. She did notice one discrepancy in Rose's description of him. His hair that was "silver at the edges" was rich and sleek, burnished with a metallic sheen, and showing only traces of a well-remembered auburn sprinkled through it.

Before Thorn had time to remark about Jenny's less-than-enthusiastic greeting, the waitress returned with the women's drinks. In his rumbling voice, Thorn ordered black coffee as well and told the waitress to return in a minute for his breakfast selection.

ROSE WISHED SHE'D just gotten up and left the restaurant. Yet, it was as if Thorn could read her mind.

"This is quite a surprise running into you twice in less than twenty-four hours, when I haven't seen you in almost forty years. I certainly wasn't prepared for this rendezvous." He nodded at both Jenny and Rose. Then, with a quick motion, he reached and tapped Rose's nose with the tip of one finger.

She felt a current go through her like a lightning bolt. It was a motion she remembered well, and she'd enjoyed it as a teen. Now, however, he needed to keep his hands off. He simply looked at her and winked, making her even more uncomfortable. She was determined to run at the slightest provocation—or open space at the table. Oh, if she wasn't trapped between the wall and this man!

Rose took a deep breath when the waitress returned to take their order, placing a cup of black coffee in front of Thorn. It gave her a distraction from what he'd done. With abandon, she pointed to the French toast on the menu, unable to force herself to say what she wanted. Her brain was crazy with the man next to her, remembering old sentiments and wanting him gone at the same time. In her heart, she didn't care if she had French toast, or if the waitress brought her nothing at all. With Thorn next to her, she didn't think she could keep anything down.

"I THINK MY friend wants the French toast." Jenny took Rose's menu and handed it to the waitress. She brightly ordered the Garden Omelet Breakfast, winking at Rose. Anyone could see that the poor woman was uncomfortable, and it had all started with Thorn's sudden presence at their table. She covered her giggle with her hand, hoping Rose didn't notice.

THORN ORDERED THE Simple Breakfast, which included two eggs, bacon, toast and hash browns. He hadn't slept the previous night, and the pounding in his temples had only gotten worse with the rising of the sun. He needed fuel, and he needed it quickly. He even found it hard to respond with good humor when the waitress flirted shamelessly with him. After she stepped away, he raised the coffee to his lips, closing his eyes and drawing in the aroma. It was what he needed to perk up his morning.

"WELL, I CAN definitely tell you haven't changed that much." Jenny laughed, chiding Thorn, thinking how many girls had liked him in high school and hadn't minded letting him know. He'd garnered quite a reputation for being the man to chase.

"Hey, I had nothing to do with what happened all those years ago." Thorn grinned, finally brightening with a sip of his coffee. He pushed a package of sugar around the table with his finger. "Women are just cinnamon mocha to me. They show up, and the aroma draws me in. I can't help it if I still have that animal magnetism so many women crave." He rolled his eyes as he said it, letting Jenny know he was teasing. Taking another sip from his cup, he turned his eyes to Rose, "You weren't jealous there for a moment, were you?"

ROSE'S EYES FLASHED. This was too much!

"Jealous? Should I be? Is there a reason for me to be jealous of that woman?" Her words snapped at Thorn like a rattlesnake.

Thorn smiled even broader.

"Still the same Rose Petal, never letting anyone know how she feels until it's too late." Despite his smile, his voice had a bitter edge to it. He drummed his fingers on the table, and the bantering fell quiet.

Now, what was that supposed to mean? Rose thought to herself. She could feel Thorn watching her intently, but she sat in stony silence. She wouldn't try to engage him in polite conversation. She wanted breakfast to be over and Thorn to be gone.

JENNY, HOWEVER, WAS of a different persuasion. She had begun enjoying Thorn's company, even if she knew Rose was piqued. She laughed brightly, reaching to tap the man's arm, as she chatted about her life over the last forty years. Her words paused from time to time for the appropriate oohs and aahs from Thorn when describing various parts of her relationships with her family.

Then, Jenny changed directions, asking about some of the wild antics Thorn was accused of pulling in high school. Hanging his head at some, and smiling gleefully at others, he admitted to most of them. Jenny even questioned Rose about an incident or two, but her friend was less than forthcoming. At each prompt, she simply gave a little cough and tried to keep the conversation centered on

Jenny. It was obvious she didn't want her past mentioned, especially not with Thorn sitting at her side.

THEN, THANKFULLY, THEIR food arrived, and for a time, Rose could relax. There was no additional discussion about Rose's past or Thorn's rapscallion behavior.

Thorn dug into his Simple Breakfast, and Jenny had no trouble attacking her omelets. The same wasn't true for Rose, who did no more than nibble her French toast. It was too much of a struggle to eat with Thorn sitting so close.

Finally, Rose dropped her toast onto her plate and sighed, certain that Thorn was gradually moving her direction. By this time, she felt he was practically in her lap.

"DOES THE FRENCH toast taste bad?" Thorn pointed at Rose's plate. He noticed she'd only eaten one of the four slices.

She turned her eyes to him, pushing the plate his direction. "I'm really not much of an eater in the morning. Coffee and juice usually are enough for me until lunch."

"Oh, they are, are they? So that's how you've kept your trim waist." He grinned, then he reached his fork across her plate and cut off a piece of the toast for himself. He dipped it in her syrup and bit off one end, chewing it slowly and thoughtfully.

"Hmm, not bad," he said and extended his arm for another bite.

JENNY WATCHED IN astonishment. This was just like in high school. Thorn had always sat with Rose and eaten off her tray. Well, and everyone else's, too, but that was beside the point. He was still doing it, and from the look on Rose's face, she didn't like it one bit. She just wanted this ordeal to be over.

Jenny fought a smile. It was too cute for words.

"How'd you sleep last night, Rose Petal?" After his third bite of French toast, Thorn looked at Rose with a wink. Then he chuckled. "Did you rest well?"

"I . . . I slept fine, except for worrying about Jenny's flight being delayed until this morning," she replied.

"Well, I thought maybe that little good night kiss you gave me might have kept you awake," Thorn shot back at her, and he turned so only Jenny could see his face. A grin appeared, and it was clear the jab had been intentional.

"THORNTON JEBULON WILDER, I in no way initiated that kiss!" Rose raised her voice at him, as her skin turned hot with anger. He wasn't going to blame that incident on her. "I had nothing to do with that, and you know it. I didn't even notice you in the terminal. You recognized me first."

Thorn chuckled. "Well, I guess there was that chance I might have been mistaken, I admit. I wasn't sure it was you, you looked so trim. I'd have expected your long ponytail and bobby socks, you know. Now your hair hangs barely below your neck and your legs look—"

HE DIDN'T GET a chance to finish before he was interrupted by a warm-sounding hello from a former classmate and friend, Roxanne. The warmth covered an ulterior motive, though. She'd seen Thorn from across the room and had waited to be sure it was him. She'd carried a crush on him in high school, along with every other available female. Even so, he'd always been with Rose Petal.

"Hey, Jenny and Thorn. When did you arrive?" Thorn's massive bulk had blocked Rose from view, and now Roxanne was surprised to see a third person at the table, and even more stunned to find that it was Rosemary.

It was too bad things had never worked out for them after high school, she thought to herself. They should have had each other.

"HEY, BEAUTIFUL!" Thorn stood up to give Roxanne a big hug, and then he pointed across the table, telling her to sit down by Jenny. With a chuckle, he returned to his spot by Rose, gruffly apologizing for the lack of space. It didn't stop him from sliding right up against her, though. All Rose could do was sit there and pretend it didn't affect her, but she could feel her pulse race. She wanted to think it was anger, but it felt too much like emotions she'd expunged decades before, back when she and Thorn were together.

She didn't like this at all. She vowed to find a way to exit as soon as she saw a chance.

"How are you doing, Rose?" Roxanne stretched her arm across the table and offered it to her. "I didn't see you there next to your old beau." A wink to Thorn accompanied her words.

"I ARRIVED LAST night, and Jenny just got here this morning." Thorn pretended to take no notice of Rose's reaction to him. However, he could read her like a book. She wasn't hiding anything from him.

"When Jack and I spoke to Rosemary at church last Sunday, she didn't tell me you were coming to the reunion," Roxanne continued. "Did you, Rose?"

"She didn't know, because I wanted to surprise her," Thorn revealed smoothly. "She and I have a lot of catching up to do." With that comment he reached over and patted Rose's hand, smiling.

ROSE KNEW IT wasn't a real smile. Thorn was up to something. She just didn't know what. Her gut instinct told her one thing for certain:

She was going to find out, whether she wanted to or not.

— 4 —

WHILE THEY WERE enjoying breakfast, Thorn didn't
bother to mention to Rose he'd been up all night after their
chance meeting in the airport terminal. He hadn't expected
to see his Rose Petal there, and he'd been shaken to his
core by her appearance. That night after reaching his hotel
room, he hadn't been able to sleep no matter how hard he
tried.

He'd planned to see her and confront her at the reunion that weekend, so he could finally have closure. Afterward, it would be over between them forever. The airport
terminal changed all that. Rose Petal had been searching
the faces around her. Seeing her had brought back all the
old memories, and impulsively, he'd swept her up and
kissed her.

He hadn't been able to help himself. It was as natural
as breathing to him. All the years of anguish and torment
had seemed to wash away in that one instant when he finally saw Rose and called out her name. After forty years,
he'd been caught up in the aroma of her perfume, and it
had taken him to a time he'd thought forgotten.

She hadn't pulled away—or at least she hadn't rejected him out of hand. That had been a surprise. He'd expected her to lash out at him, to berate him verbally when he grabbed her.

If he could believe what his parents had told him about their last meeting with her, he had expected her to call security. He clung desperately to the knowledge she hadn't turned him away, instead giving in to his embrace.

Even so, he'd come for the reunion this weekend to erase her memory from his life forever, not to rekindle an old romance. He'd been certain that his youth and lack of experience had made that long-ago Rose appear more desirable than she really was. He'd hoped to find a woman who was just someone he'd known back in high school, someone he wouldn't look at twice if he saw her walking down the street.

He was so wrong. In that short five minutes in the airport, he'd been reminded just how beautiful she really was to him.

Now, at the restaurant, just to be sitting beside her in the same booth. This wasn't some high school boy's crush. This was an all-out addiction, and the only way to cure it was to get more of Rose.

Yet, the reality of his life pulled at him. He couldn't turn loose of the last forty years so easily. He'd been a mess since high school, and all because of Rose. No matter how much he felt the old attraction, he wouldn't give in to it. She'd been the cause of all his years of unrest and unhappiness.

As he gazed at her, doubts clouded his thoughts. He'd done his best to forget her. Alcohol, other women, and even a military tour of duty across the farthest parts of the globe hadn't erased her from his mind. He reminded himself that she'd betrayed their love and ultimately destroyed their brief marriage. Thorn's father was a two-star general at the time. His parents had warned him about Rose, but he'd been stubborn. They said she was just using him to get her father, a sergeant, a promotion, but that didn't matter to Thorn. He'd loved Rose, no matter her father's rank. Then she'd turned out to be just what Thorn's parents had claimed her to be.

Still, sitting next to her was magic.

Thorn finished eating and sat morosely, staring at an empty plate. Next to him, equally miserable, Rose did her best to ignore him. Roxanne rambled on about her husband Jack, her hand flitting through the air, emphasizing her every word, telling about how he was planning to attend the reunion as well. It was when she reached to touch Thorn on the wrist with the tips of her fingers that he could take no more. Without warning, he stood and said his good-byes. Rose breathed an audible sigh of relief when she realized he intended to leave her friends and her in peace.

Thorn frowned. He knew his presence had made an impact on her. He couldn't be certain whether it was a positive or a negative one, not unless he based it on her response at the airport. That brought a smile to his face; maybe she'd had a difficult time forgetting him, too. It was a comforting but fleeting thought. If she'd really missed him, she would have done something about it long before now.

He set his jaw in a stubborn line, irritation eating at his heart. It was the remains of an old love, one that had yet to be extinguished. It had burned low over the years, sometimes pushed out of mind, but never cold. No, never cold. He realized it wasn't cold now, as much as he hoped it would be.

"I guess you'll have to wait until later to see me again." As he said his teasing words, Thorn reached for Rose's hand and kissed it. He lifted his eyes to see her cringe and look away.

Refusing to be goaded, he picked up the tab for the three women and left a too-generous tip.

IN ROSE'S MIND, Thorn's tip was excessive for a waitress who had flirted way too much, and she made it known with narrowed eyes and pursed lips. Thorn snorted in amusement, and even that irritated her.

As for the kiss, she knew he was just showing off to Jenny and Roxanne. He didn't care for her, and she knew it. She didn't know what he was trying to prove by giving her so much attention.

She intended to find out, though, before Thorn pulled some stunt that really embarrassed her.

— 5 —

"GIRL, I THINK he has it as bad for you as he ever had."
Jenny put her hand on Rose's. Her eyes crinkled, and there
was laughter in her voice.

"Amen to that, sister!" piped in Roxanne. "I know
every rose has its thorn, but this is ridiculous. He couldn't
keep his hands off you. It was like he'd never touched a
woman before. He was behaving just like he did in high
school, and maybe worse." Both women giggled at Rose.
She shifted in her seat, uncomfortable with their comments, and her irritation showing in her dark looks.

"No, girls. You must be mistaken. Thorn can't stand
me. He's just doing this as some kind of test or show."
Rose tightened her mouth in memory of what had happened at the airport. "Last night he even told me, 'There's
fixing to be a flood,' so I don't think this is about love at
all."

She cringed at the other things that had happened at
the airport, but she couldn't share that with the women
across from her. Nothing made sense to her. She hadn't
understood what had happened between Thorn and her all

those decades ago, but now she was more confused than ever. What kind of trick was he trying to pull? He'd made it abundantly clear years before that he wanted nothing to do with her. So why the big show of affection now? This wasn't what Rose had expected on her fortieth class reunion. She'd been looking forward to visiting with old classmates, not being mauled, manhandled, and insulted by Thorn.

She'd always felt an emptiness and void after her break-up with Thorn. She'd been praying for a change in her life. Then along had come Gill. She'd tried to fill the void inside with her new husband, and later with Gill, Jr., among other things. Vacations, a new house, and later a series of expensive cars had all given her momentary fulfillment. It had seemed to work for a while. A few times she thought she was over Thorn.

Now that she was alone, she felt the emptiness more than ever.

As the appeal of each new thing in her life faded, she'd often asked God what her purpose was. She would tell him that she needed something more, hope she could wrap her days around, an interest that could fulfill her. Her answer hadn't come, not in forty years, and she was certain Thorn wasn't it now.

This must be a test to see if she really did trust God to be in control of her life. Either that or it was a test to see if she believed in true love. Either way, Rose wasn't happy that Thorn was back in town, even if it was only for a few days. She could have lived another four decades without seeing him. Driving Jenny back to her house, Rose was confident that any attraction for Thorn she might have felt at the airport wouldn't return.

She would see to that.

JENNY WAS TOTALLY shocked by Thorn's behavior as well. There had been rumors after high school, but Rose never spoke about it, and Jenny never asked. Rose would come unglued at the mention of Thorn. One rumor said that he and Rose had gotten married. Another said she had his love child. Some people suggested Rose dumped Thorn for reasons unknown.

What little Jenny knew had come from a hysterical Rose a long time ago. It seemed the bad blood between the couple had happened after both their parents were transferred to different military bases. Rosemary's family ended up in Germany, while Thorn's family was stationed in Japan.

Jenny knew this much: That was when Thorn had signed up. His parents tried to stop him. His father pulled rank to garner stateside postings, but he went abroad anyway, volunteering for the most dangerous missions. He made it back all in one piece, never to return to their old hometown.

Jenny shrugged Thorn off. Other people's lives had changed, just like his. She'd lived away for a while now, too. Her two brothers had both moved away, as well. Andy and his wife Pauline lived in the next town, about thirty minutes away, and when she told Rose she planned to see him after the reunion was over, Rose said she thought it would be nice to see them again, if Jenny didn't mind her tagging along. Jenny was pleased. After seeing Thorn over the reunion weekend, Rose would definitely need a distraction.

Andy was a couple of years older and had three children. Only his youngest child, a nineteen-year-old daughter, still lived at home with him and his wife. Her brother had liked Rosemary when she first started high school. When she and Jenny had become friends, he had been even more enthusiastic about going out with her. He was already a junior, and their relationship didn't last more than a few dates. Despite that, they had remained friends.

They made plans for Sunday afternoon to drive over and visit for a few hours before Jenny had to catch her plane.

AT LEAST THEY thought that was the plan. Their only problem was they hadn't run it by Thorn, who had made a few plans of his own.

All his plans included Rose, whether she was prepared or not, and all her plans would have to be put aside.

Thornton Jebulon Wilder was back in town.

— 6 —

ROSE FOUGHT TO wake as she lay in her bed.

It was early Friday morning, and a recurring dream had haunted her night. She was still a teenager in the dream, and it was always the same. She heard a baby crying, and the doctor said it was a girl.

Then everything was silent.

It wasn't a nightmare, but like someone was lost. She would wake in a hospital or in a room of solid white and be completely alone. She wasn't afraid, but she always knew something was missing. She never could put her finger on it, but she knew something wasn't right.

It always made her sad as she thought about her own losses.

Pushing the dream aside, she yawned. It was an old one, and she needed to get up, get a shower, and start her busy day. She had to get her hair and nails done before the barbeque. The pavilion had been reserved at the lake, and some of the local classmates were setting up grills and doing ribs and brisket at noon. The picnic, however, wasn't until five-thirty. She was responsible for potato salad for thirty and three lemon meringue pies.

Since Jenny was from out of town, she would be bringing chips and dip and ice for the tea. This would be the casual family gathering. Everyone was invited. Tomorrow night was the banquet, and only the reunion couples would be allowed to attend. Rose had already bought a cute overall short set to wear today. She pulled it out of the closet to show Jenny and get her opinion, certain her friend would approve.

"THAT MAKES YOU look too skinny and too old." Jenny held up the short set next to Rose. "It's at least two sizes too big. Don't you have some denim shorts and a tank top?"

Rose was shocked at the idea of wearing a tank top at her age. Gill had been so jealous that she never bought anything that was form fitting or revealing in any way.

"No, I really don't wear shorts much. Usually just capris."

"Well," Jenny quipped, grabbing the bag the clothing had come in, "before we do another thing, we're taking this back to the store and trading it for something a little fashionable, something that looks good on you."

Jenny sounded like she was making plans for Rose's clothes, and Rose wasn't sure she liked that. The first part of the morning was spent finding something they could both agree on. Jenny wanted Rose to look like a fashionista, while Rose was still selecting clothes too loose for her. Finally, they compromised on a turquoise tank top covered by a matching lace blouse. They paired that with fitted black denim shorts that came down to the top of her knees. Then Jenny talked Rose into buying a strappy black sandal with chunky turquoise stones on them. The overall look was fresh but not too flirty.

Jenny accompanied Rose to her hair appointment. She had Rose's hairstyle transformed to a wispy look from the staid uniform style to which she was accustomed. She had the nail girl apply acrylic nails on Rose's long fingers, and along with her toenails, paint them a creamy orange sherbet. By early afternoon, Rose felt as if she'd experienced a complete makeover.

On the way home, Jenny bought chips, dip and ice. Over the next few hours, they worked until they had the food ready, preparing the potato salad and the pies.

Then Jenny volunteered to do Rose's make-up. That felt like the last straw.

"I don't know what you're trying to do, but I don't like it. I'm me, Rosemary Josephine Bruton, not some runway model. I think I still know how to do my own make-up," Rose snapped harshly, immediately regretting her words. Her upsetting evening and her morning with Thorn had worn her nerves to a frazzle.

"I'm sorry, Rose. It's just that you look so incredible, I thought maybe some of my colors of lipstick and blush might bring out your skin tones better with your new clothes." Jenny sounded truly remorseful. Rose felt a little sheepish at her own dramatic display of annoyance. Jenny was just trying to help, like she always did, and since she did this professionally, it probably wouldn't hurt.

"Oh, I suppose so. Do what you can." Rose let out a defeated sigh. She never wore a lot of make-up, just a little mascara, lipstick, and a good moisturizer. Jenny always looked so well put together and stylish. It might even be fun.

"Great! Let's get to work," came Jenny's eager reply, as she began working on the contours of her friend's face. In just a matter of minutes, Rose could not believe the transformation. Her eyes seem to jump out and sparkle, while her new rich lip color seemed to invite an engaging response. She didn't look like the Rose everyone expected. This was a new improved version!

"Wow! Even I don't recognize myself." Rose smiled as she gazed into the mirror. She looked softer, and dare she think it? Even somewhat appealing. Just the right make-up with the perfect clothes to complete her look.

At least that was what Jenny told her. They packed their things in the car and headed for the picnic and a reunion neither of them would soon forget.

— 7 —

ROSE AND JENNY arrived at the barbeque picnic just as the food was being brought to the tables, and they were drawn in by the pungent aroma of the meat the local men had been smoking all day. Rose put her potato salad next to Roxanne's pasta salad. Then she carried her pies to the dessert area while Jenny took her ice to the beverage center.

Rose turned around at a low whistle and saw Jack and Roxanne both staring at her.

"Girl, when you clean up, you clean up good! Where was this Rose forty years ago?" Roxanne walked up to her, reaching a hand to touch her hair, and she took Rose's chin in her fingers and studied her face. She smiled to show how much she approved.

"Uhh, hmm," came approving sounds from Jack.

"Husband, watch it!" Roxanne poked him in the ribs.

"I was just agreeing with you, Roxie. That was all, honey," he said weakly. At the same time, he winked at Rose, causing her to laugh.

"Jack, you're such a character! I don't know how

Roxanne's put up with you all these years," Rose teased, in a mock-reproving tone.

"Unfortunately for me, it's true love," Roxanne admitted. She reached up and gave Jack a kiss on the cheek. "Maybe someday I'll get over him, but not today." They laughed as they strolled off arm in arm together.

For a moment Rose looked at them with envy. They had been married for over thirty years and were still in love. Roxanne hadn't been an angel in high school, but when she went off to college and met Jack, she had come back and seemed to have been happy ever since.

Rose knew what had made the difference. The transformation in Roxanne had occurred when Jack introduced her to his personal savior, Jesus Christ. They'd married, and she'd taught school while Jack coached. Together they raised their two sons. They were involved in church, and their boys were respectful young adults. Rose was still staring wistfully in their direction, when she heard a voice from behind her, startling her ever so slightly.

"Would'a, could'a, should'a."

She could tell it was Thorn before she ever turned around. She knew he'd seen her watching Roxanne and Jack, and she wondered how long he'd been standing behind her. As she turned around to make eye contact, she heard the air in his lungs escape in a hollow gasp.

THORN COULDN'T BELIEVE his eyes. Rose had never looked more beautiful in all the time he'd known her. She'd been a naturally attractive girl in high school. But seeing her dressed like this was overwhelming. Her trim outfit set off her hair, and her flawless make-up made her face come alive. He could smell just a hint of perfume, and suddenly, he couldn't even remember that girl from high school. In front of him stood a woman who knew how to use the beauty God had given her. He breathed in deeply trying to soak in her loveliness.

Then, just as suddenly, a nagging thought slipped in.

Why was she dressed like this today? She was either with someone, or she was waiting for someone to arrive. She'd never dress like this for herself.

He didn't want to see Rose with anyone but him, he admitted to himself, as if trying to face some awful truth. He tried to push away the seed of jealousy he felt deep within his heart and tried to reassure himself. He had a purpose this weekend, and it was one that was forty years in the making. What could he be thinking? Old feelings didn't matter. He didn't want Rose. He didn't care about her. She could do whatever she pleased. It wouldn't matter one bit to him.

He fought to hold on to that, even as he felt it slipping away. He took a deep breath, accepting that reality was reality. His determination to be strong wasn't working. He was jealous that Rose might be with any other man than him at the reunion.

"Thorn, are you listening?" Rose interrupted his thoughts.

"What, Rose Petal?" Thorn fought to remember what he'd been saying.

"I ASKED WHAT you just said to me, but never mind. If you don't remember, I certainly don't care." Rose turned to leave the dessert area. She had no time for this man. Sleepless nights and a kiss in the airport were certainly no cause for her to change her opinion of him after all these years.

Thorn glanced at the baked confections, his eyes stopping on the pies. "Did you make the lemon meringue pies?"

"Yes," Rose replied, in a curt, indifferent tone. She had no need for his questions, but it was an innocent one that she would answer for anyone who asked.

"I remember the time you made one just for me. It was right after—" He was interrupted by a loud voice yelling at him from across the park.

"Thorn, is that you?"

Thorn looked with irritation to see who was calling to him. It was one of his old high school buddies, Bobby Edwards. Bobby hurried over to shake Thorn's hand, and then he noticed Rose.

"Well, I see it's still true. Every Rose has its Thorn, even if it's a wild one." He caught up Rose in a hug and planted a kiss on her forehead. Rose smiled and patted his arm. Thorn frowned at the display of affection, but Bobby didn't seem to notice.

"I read about your husband in the paper a few years back. I'm sorry for your loss, Rose. Even though I live in Austin now, I still take the *Leader* to keep up with events around here. It makes me feel like I'm still connected."

IT WAS MORE than that. Bobby was into politics, and he liked to keep his hand on the pulse of the people he represented. He worked hard to be the sort of representative his people needed. Besides that, a photo or two taken with him and the people, to be seen with his constituents, was always good for politics. The *Round Rock Leader*, the local paper, would be happy to publish an article about their elected representative being back for a homecoming reunion.

He had to be careful, though. Rose was entirely too appealing today, and he wouldn't want to be photographed with her at the picnic. The rumors might start flying in Austin. He and his wife lived a very upscale lifestyle, and they needed to keep a low profile.

Bobby smiled broader, entranced by Rose, and beside him, a frown creased Thorn's brow.

"Is your wife with you?" Rose asked, breaking the silence and easing Thorn's mounting tension.

"No, Liz couldn't make it this time. She had a speaking engagement at the local women's shelter." Bobby looked around, taking Rose's hand in his for a moment. "I'd love to stay and chat some more, but I promised

Chuck I'd look him up as soon as I got here. It's great seeing you two again. Later, Thorny Rose."

BOBBY SMILED AND walked off, not realizing the impact he had made on the couple by calling them by their old high school nicknames. However, when Thorn reached to take the hand Bobby had let go of, they both felt a sizzle, and it had nothing to do with the barbeque on the grill.

— 8 —

ROSE DELIBERATELY TURNED away from Thorn, pulling her hand from his. She didn't want to be anywhere near him nor paired with him for any reason. Her days of being his Rose Petal were long gone, as well as the relationship they'd shared. He had dumped her at one of the most critical moments in her life. When she'd needed him most, he'd deserted her, leaving her to feel the loneliest she'd ever experienced.

It had taken years to get over it. The pain had gone away in time, along with the aching desire for him. Gill had made sure she never had time to think of anyone but him. After a while Rose thought she had actually forgotten about Thorn and the heartbreak of her youth. He'd been like a distant memory faded and maybe not quite real, until yesterday when it all came back at a startling, breakneck speed

Rose realized she had forgotten very little.

Her memories were once again haunting her, with those of Thorn leading the entourage. However, she wasn't that person from high school any longer. She was a changed person. She was stronger and indifferent to Thorn's charm. She wouldn't let the reunion serve as a scenario to reunite them in any way.

Rose searched for Jenny. She finally found her by a grove of trees talking with some other classmates. She didn't know who might have seen her talking with Thorn, and she had no desire to listen to questions from any of them concerning that nightmare that had returned to haunt her. When Jenny waved to her, she gathered her courage and joined her.

"Rose, did you know Helen and her husband are grandparents to triplets? Their daughter, Karen, gave birth four weeks prematurely just two-and-a-half months ago. Their pictures are too cute." Jenny motioned Rose over, holding up the photos.

"Two boys and a girl at one time. What a challenge," Rose murmured. The smiling threesome were in little matching outfits. She'd always wanted a daughter, but the doctor said she was lucky to have the one child she did. She'd endured a difficult delivery, and she couldn't have any more children after that. Too much scar tissue, the doctor had told her. She was grateful for Gill, Jr., but she had always regretted not having a houseful of children.

A car honk was the signal it was time to eat. There were between fifty and sixty people laughing and having a good time as they approached the buffet line. As Jenny and Rose were stepping up to reach for their utensils, Thorn cut directly in front of them. He grabbed three of the extra-sturdy paper plates. Rose and Jenny made no comment but rolled their eyes and followed behind, watching as he filled all three of them.

He smiled as he generously loaded his first plate with potato salad, slaw, macaroni and cheese, and garlic bread. The next plate he piled high with smoked sausage and ribs, along with several slices of brisket. He went to a table and put them down. Then he strolled over to the dessert table and took almost one-fourth of one of the lemon meringue pies Rose had made. He didn't bother even looking at any of the other desserts. Then he went back and sat down.

Rose and Jenny went to a table at the other end of the pavilion and put down their plates. Rose made sure her back was to Thorn. She didn't want to know he was there. She tried to focus on her food, but she kept feeling as if she was being watched. Knowing Thorn was under the same roof was keeping her from enjoying her meal and enjoying time with her friends. It was as if he was there to torture her.

Rose wished she knew why he was doing this. He'd left her, not the other way around. It had taken years to get over being abandoned by him. Now here he was trying to edge himself back into her life.

She was determined, however, to have a good time despite him. After a few more minutes of nibbling at her plate, she accepted she could eat no more of what was before her. Pushing it aside, she stood to go to the dessert table. She had brought a pie, and she wasn't leaving without at least tasting it. As she approached, she heard a deep voice behind her.

"Will you cut me one more piece of pie, Rose Petal?"

Of course, it was Thorn. She recognized his voice as soon as he finished the first word. But before she could comment, Spunky Mulligan, another classmate, suddenly appeared and called, "Smile."

Thorn grabbed Rose around the waist and flashed a big smile. Rose stood in astonishment as the camera clicked. Spunky thanked them and walked off, still taking pictures of the crowd.

"Now about that pie," Thorn repeated.

"Which one did you want?" she shot back, pretending not to know exactly which one he meant.

"Why, yours, of course. The lemon one. You know that's my favorite."

Thorn's honeyed tone took her by surprise. Was he being nice, or was he being sarcastic? In any case, his request was innocent enough. Rose would serve a slice of pie to anyone who asked her.

"S-sure, Thorn. Here you are." Rose served him a large slice, avoiding eye contact. It was difficult enough handing him the slice of pie with his hand brushing against hers. She felt sparks fly at the momentary contact.

Thorn held onto her fingers under the plate until she finally looked up at him. His eyes like black ice peered at her as if he were reading her mind and examining her deepest, most intimate thoughts. The thoughts were the ones she kept trying to push away. They were thoughts about him and her and their tumultuous past. They were the thoughts that she had guarded and kept suppressed all these years that were now trying to surface.

She inhaled a deep breath.

"So, you feel it, too," he said, as he slowly let go of her hand. Thorn then turned and walked back to his table with his slice of lemon meringue pie, leaving a much-shaken Rose.

She paused for a few minutes trying to digest what had just happened. Was he trying to send her a message? She was more bewildered than ever.

With her hands shaking, Rose turned to the dessert table to survey the pies and cakes. She couldn't face anywhere else for the moment. She knew she would look silly just standing there, so she reached to the closest pie she could find. Cutting a fresh slice, she put it on a plate and turned to face the throng of her ex-classmates.

What was Thorn trying to pull by sounding so nice? She knew she couldn't trust him as far as she could throw him. His behavior over the last twenty-four hours had been extremely bizarre, to say the least, not to mention what he just said to her.

Thorn was up to something, but what, Rose didn't have a clue. She was determined to find out before something else happened that she might both dread and regret.

— 9 —

ROSE LEFT SHORTLY after the barbeque dinner. The rest of the evening was geared more toward families and their activities. They had set up horseshoes, a volleyball net, and someone had mentioned softball. There were large photo albums of different families being passed around. Some ladies had even brought scrapbooking materials to work on a fortieth reunion scrapbook. Everyone seemed to be taking pictures. Every time someone turned around, someone else said to smile.

Rose hoped none of the pictures had put her and Thorn together other than the one at the dessert table. Jenny stayed and said she would catch a ride. She wasn't through visiting with all her old friends.

The weather was humid for October. The recent rain at the airport had only increased the already soaring humidity. Rose's clothes clung to her in an uncomfortable way. She had seen a couple of men looking her direction in a way that annoyed her. She didn't want to be stared at or presumed to be a person who enjoyed that kind of attention. She tried to be a good Christian example for others.

As soon as she arrived home, she immediately prepared for a shower. She couldn't wait to get comfortable. Afterward, she slipped on her coolest cotton gown. Then she settled in front of the family room television. The stress of the day had worn on her, and besides, she hadn't gotten enough sleep the previous two nights due to the scene at the airport. With the soft sound of the TV in the background, it was only a few minutes before Rose was sleeping restfully on the large, overstuffed, cream-colored leather sofa.

She felt like she had just fallen asleep when she heard the doorbell. Jenny had said she would catch a ride with someone, and it was about time for her to return. She pulled on a robe, made her way to the foyer, and slowly opened the door.

"Come in," Rose began, before she noticed her friend wasn't alone. She pulled back to hide behind the door. "I wasn't expecting company, Jenny. I'm not presentable."

JENNY COULD HEAR Thorn whistle softly as he caught sight of Rose. Her hair was disheveled, and the flush of sleep colored her face. She was wearing a cotton gown under her fur-fringed robe. To Thorn, she must be the loveliest creature he'd ever seen. All he could do was stare.

It made Jenny laugh to see how much like high school students they were behaving. They clearly belonged together, even if Rose couldn't see it. The giggle must have finally awakened Rose. As she focused, she realized Jenny's visitor was Thorn, and she gasped and immediately shut the door.

Jenny stood shocked, staring at the exterior side of the closed door.

"Are we welcome or not?" Thorn chuckled.

"I don't know." Jenny looked at him with a smile. "Either way, I'm staying here, and my things are inside. I guess that means I have an invitation, and you're my invited guest. Welcome, Thorn. You may come inside."

Jenny grasped the handle and twisted, relieved Rose had left it unlocked. She pushed it wide and motioned for Thorn to enter.

ROSE RAN TO the sofa and wrapped up in the afghan that had been lying across her. She looked up as Jenny opened the door and motioned Thorn in. Jenny followed on his heels.

"What are you doing here?" Rose questioned grumpily. She could feel his presence in the room. His aura took up all the space.

"Why, darlin', I was just escorting Jenny home. I thought it was only proper to see her to the door. I had no idea you'd already be ready to turn in for the night." Thorn grinned as he spoke.

"What are you talking about? First of all, it's very late; second, I was asleep; and most of all, this is my home, and I can go to bed whenever I want. I didn't invite you in, nor would I have invited you here, regardless, and I would never spend an evening with you." Rose spoke in a huff, still slightly groggy, and irritated at the man's welcome intrusion.

"Now, wait a minute, Rose Petal. I believe you're mistaken." Thorn's good mood clearly wasn't dampened by Rose's boisterous protests. "I distinctly remember spending an evening with you after the Junior-Senior Prom. Don't tell me you don't remember that night—"

Rose interrupted him before he could finish his walk down memory lane. Her voice whipped out in acid-laced rivulets. "Oooh, Thorn. You make me so mad. I don't ever want to think about you and high school or what happened afterward. I've tried my hardest to forget any part of my past that involved you. I'm not the naïve person I was then. I think you need to leave right now!" She was finally wide-awake and growing angrier by the second. She felt her face grow hot.

Thorn just smiled. "Well, all I was doing was trying to set the record straight. Have a good evening, Jenny. You too, Rose Petal."

"You've said enough. You need to leave, Thorn." Rose sat straighter, as she held her afghan around her.

With that, he tipped his hat and walked toward the front door. "Have pleasant dreams, girls. I know I will." He looked at Rose and winked.

She grabbed a throw pillow, aimed it at him, and let it fly. Thorn picked it up, and with an easy motion, he placed it on a nearby chair.

"Now, Rose Petal, don't do something you'll regret tomorrow, like the time you threw the pitcher of tea at me and broke the beautiful cut-glass heirloom your grandmother gave you, not to mention staining the wall." His eyes twinkled with the story. "I helped you clean up the mess you made. If you make a mess tonight, you're on your own."

With a wave, he turned and opened the door. He laughed as he shut it behind him. Rose growled, grabbed a second pillow, and threw it just where he'd been standing.

JENNY TRIED HER best not to laugh. It was truly like a lover's quarrel, except that Rose had emphasized to her several times over the past day that she didn't care about Thorn one iota.

"Oh, that man makes me so mad sometimes. I can hardly stand to be in the same room with him. What gets me is just when he starts acting nice, that's when you know to watch out, because he's about to pull something. I'm glad I have his number. He's not going to pull one over on me. I'll be careful around him, you can rest assured of that. Jenny, you can't trust a Wild Thorn."

As Rose finished, Jenny was relieved her friend's anger appeared to be spent. In Rose's final words, she was certain she heard remorse.

That could mean only one thing: There was still room

for hope. Jenny was encouraged, but she couldn't let it show.

— 10 —

THAT NIGHT WAS even worse. Rose tried to return to the peaceful slumber she'd enjoyed prior to the doorbell ringing. Sleep, however, wasn't her friend. It avoided her at every turn and twist in her bed. For a time, she was too hot. She threw the sheet off, to find she was too cold, and she would reach for it again fifteen minutes later.

Finally, she got up and took a sleeping aid. It was the only way she would get rest that night. Then the dreams manifested themselves: dreams of Thorn and her in high school; and visions of them now, still in love. She could almost feel his warm breath as he kissed her, making her want him even more.

Slowly, she heard something like a faint bell in the distance separating her from her nocturnal lover. She reached for Thorn as he disappeared, to hear the ringing became louder and louder. Rose wrestled with waking, realizing it was her alarm. She hated those dreams, yet she knew she couldn't control what her mind brought to her at night. She was grateful this night, however, was over, along with the fantasies it had brought with it.

Still, even with the rising sun, Rose didn't feel rested. Her dreams had left her empty and alone. What was worse, her dreams had her longing for Thorn again. That was the part that upset her most, having feelings for someone she knew would only hurt her once more. She had no desire to be with a man who had been so cruel to her in her youth.

"Why must I be tormented and troubled by Thorn?" she mumbled to herself, as she sluggishly climbed from her bed. She didn't want to be a target for his emotional and self-esteem-driven assassinations. She'd barely lived through it once. She didn't think she could survive it again, no matter how much others thought he had changed. Thorn was still Thorn, and she was Rose. He might be the same person from high school, but she'd undergone a transformation. She wasn't the innocent teenage girl to be so easily fooled a second time.

She had become a stronger woman in the past year by being more dependent on God than on people. She could pour her heart out to Him, and He wouldn't judge her or turn her away. She'd discovered He was a God of love and forgiveness. She found great consolation in reading the Psalms and Proverbs from the Bible. It comforted her like no other book had.

She sat at her bedside and read a few passages from God's Word. She drew renewed strength from it. She could face the day and what lay ahead, even if it did involve Thorn.

She felt better as she dressed for the day. Tonight would be her classmates' fortieth reunion banquet held on the top floor of the bank building downtown. It would be an extremely formal event. She'd bought a long dress for the occasion, a soft pearlescent peach affair that was fitted all the way to her hips where it flared ever so slightly. The muted hue blended well with the new color of her nails.

She set out her pearls and her pearl-colored heels on the bed. Everything matched perfectly. She'd get Jenny to help with her make-up. Her friend had done a remarkable job yesterday, from all the compliments she'd received at the barbeque.

Feeling better about the festivities ahead, she headed toward the kitchen, intending to check whether Jenny needed anything. To her surprise, Jenny was already up when she passed by her room. She found her on one of the kitchen barstools with toast and coffee and reading the paper. Rose got the orange juice from the refrigerator.

"Well, good morning, Rose." Jenny looked up with a smile. "I didn't hear you come in."

"I'm sorry. I didn't mean to surprise you. I didn't know you were already up. It's nice to have some help in the kitchen." Rose noticed extra toast and a full pot of coffee.

"It isn't much, but with the day ahead of us, I thought we needed a little something to get us started." Jenny stood. "I haven't gotten out plates. Just you have a seat, and I'll get the table set. I still remember my way around your kitchen, you know." She rifled through a few cabinets, and soon plates and utensils were on the table. She pulled out a couple of glasses and cups, and the drinks were ready.

The two women sat down to the toast, juice, and coffee. Rose always drank hers black, but Jenny had rummaged around and found the cream and sweetener for hers. They were both lost in their thoughts as they began to consume their meal. They turned on the news just in time to catch the daily weather report.

It wasn't good news. The meteorologist predicted microburst showers in the area, off and on until sometime tomorrow afternoon.

Jenny frowned. "I really didn't want to have to worry about my evening being marred by rain. Oh, my." She picked up a slice of toast and bit off the corner, as she looked out the window at the building clouds.

The last thing Rose needed was an impending storm added to the already volatile situation between her and

Thorn coming up this evening. They could produce sparks in the wettest of seasons. It didn't matter what was in the atmosphere, them coming together could produce a blazing inferno.

With the dark, ominous clouds brewing, who knew what would happen before the reunion was over?

— 11 —

THORN WOKE UP on the wrong side of the bed, just like he did almost every day. He never seemed to wake to the thought that the day would be a great one. His life was a rut and he knew what a rut was.

"A rut's nothing but a grave with the ends kicked out," he groaned to himself, as he crawled out of bed to make himself some coffee.

He'd never been the same after the break-up with Rose. Even though it was forty years ago, he still felt the loss. Sure, he went through the motions of being alive. He got up, showered, and went to work. He came home, watched a little TV, ate some dinner, and then usually slept.

One of the things he was grateful for was his job. It was hard and demanding outside work. It kept him tired and often exhausted. Even though he was a supervisor, he didn't stay in the office. He went out in the field and checked on his workers every day. He often had to help make sure the job was done right. Too many kids these days didn't seem to care or take pride in their work. Thorn felt he had to be there to watch for careless but costly mistakes.

Today would be different. He was going to his high school's fortieth reunion. The love of his life would be there.

He smiled as he thought about her, but just as quickly, his smiled paled as he considered his plan. What if it didn't work? What would he do then? Could he walk out on Rose, knowing they might've had a go at a second chance? Would he be able to cut her out of his life forever?

His thoughts plagued him as he drank his morning coffee and worried about the evening ahead. It was so easy to plan with Rose at a distance, nothing more than a memory or slight distraction in his day. But now that he'd seen her and kissed her, he didn't know if he could go through with the plan he'd so carefully devised.

He'd thought he wanted to hurt Rose, crush her spirit, and leave her the way she'd left him. Now he had different feelings about her. Seeing how vulnerable she was made him feel like he needed to protect her, but from whom?

With slow, insightful trepidation, he came to the realization that he needed to protect her from himself. All he was ever going to do was hurt her. Yet now, at this moment, that was the last thing he wanted to do to his Rose Petal.

A part of him still loved her. He thought he'd finally killed out any tender feelings he had for her. He thought the ache in his heart had finally stopped. Somewhere, deep in the recesses of his soul, there was a part of him that had never stopped loving her, and that was the part tormenting him. That was the part that had made him grab her with reckless abandon in the airport terminal and kiss her.

That one tiny part of his heart had never let go of her. Now here it was bigger and stronger than ever, and it still wanted Rose. It was more than a want. It was a need. He needed Rose, despite what she had done to him; he still needed her, and now maybe more than ever. He was filled with desire for her; he wanted to know her every thought, feeling, and sentiment about every little thing.

That was a dangerous place for his heart to be.

It wasn't the plan he'd so carefully mapped out. He'd have to see his original plan through or end up in a bigger mess than he was already in. His one true love would learn to understand the old saying that all's fair in love and war. He was ready for the war, because he knew he couldn't handle the love. He had already tried that route. Rose would probably just rip him apart like she did the last time. If she did, there was no distant battlefield to escape to.

He also had someone else to think about now, someone he could never hurt no matter what happened to him. He would have to keep on his preplanned path, even if it meant losing all hope of being with Rose forever. He didn't have a choice.

Sometimes life was cruel like that. People didn't get to pick the choices they would like. They were stuck with the hand fate dealt them, or at least that was what Thorn thought. And he was tired of trying and getting nowhere. Yes, it was all about to change, and it had nothing to do with the hand of fate.

— 12 —

ROSE HAD DONE some thinking of her own.

Nothing Thorn was doing was what she'd expected, based on their last meeting and the lecture she'd received from his parents. She'd never forgotten that horrible day nearly forty years ago. It was a day she'd tried hard to erase from her mind, but it came back occasionally to haunt her in her dreams, asleep or awake.

When he'd walked out on her, and his parents had told her he didn't love her and never had, the truth had consumed her with its finality: He'd only married her out of duty's sake. They said he didn't even want to tell her good-bye.

Then when he came into the room where she was and tried to kiss her, she'd said she would see him in his grave first. Those had been bitter words from a young girl with a broken heart, a girl who had just watched her life's dreams evaporate before her eyes. Her hopes had been cruelly vanquished, with no hope of restoration. Thorn's parents had assured her of that.

She'd been so hurt by what they told her that she

didn't want to speak with him ever again. However, that had been youth and rash behavior speaking. She knew she wouldn't respond that way now. She'd changed a lot over the years. She'd been married to Gill for nearly four decades, and she'd raised a wonderful son. Then, there was her newfound faith in Christ. Rose knew she'd matured and would have handled the situation very differently, if she'd felt then what she did now. At times like this, she wished she could have been born old. Then, her choices from so long ago would have been the better ones she now knew how to make.

"Penny for your thoughts."

The words jarred Rose back to reality. "What? Oh, I'm sorry. Jenny, were you saying something?" Rose realized she'd been distracted, and the silence in the room must have been obvious.

"You were so deep in thought, and it seemed so serious, that I didn't want to interrupt you, but I thought we might need to map out our plan for the day." Jenny smiled. "You didn't even hear your name the first time I spoke it. Where were you?"

Rose didn't answer her question, instead pausing until Jenny reached and touched her arm. Then, with a smile, she forced herself to go on. "A plan. We do need to map one out, don't we? I'll need to get ready. I want you to do my make-up again, if you have the time. Everyone loved the way I looked yesterday afternoon, so maybe a repeat performance would be nice."

Rose had been very brusque the day before, and she wanted to make it up to Jenny. Besides, she really thought her friend had outdone herself, at least if Rose judged by the compliments she'd received.

"Repeat performance, nothing." Jenny winked at her. "We'll go for an even more exciting look." She stood and pulled Rose from her seat. "It's the evening, and everyone will look more glamorous. We'll show them what you've really got. Let's start by putting a few curlers in your hair in random directions, so your hair will stand out when it falls in wisps down your neck." She giggled and began lifting Rose's hair just to see what the effect might look like.

Jenny sounded truly excited about giving Rose a makeover again. Rose was relieved her friend didn't hold a grudge. Jenny had always been that way, forgiving and letting anger and disappointments go. She always seemed focused on the future and the next adventure coming her way.

Rose sighed. She wished she could be more like that. However, she always took things seriously and never backed down once her mind was made up. She had a difficult time apologizing, and she wanted to blame most of her faults on others. Even now that she was truly a Christian, it was a laborious effort to admit she was wrong.

Seeing the excitement in Jenny's eyes as she planned her makeover, Rose felt guilty. Jenny had asked her a question last year that had made Rose angry, and she hadn't spoken to her in the intervening months. If Jenny hadn't reached out to her, she might have lost her friend forever. It embarrassed and saddened Rose to think she had treated her friend that way.

"Hm, Jenny?" Rose felt her words stumble. She wanted to apologize, and she was finding it very challenging.

"Yes?" Jenny was gathering her hair supplies, and she paused to give Rose her attention.

"I just, well, I just wanted to say I'm sorry about the misunderstanding we had back at Thanksgiving last year. I've always thought of you as a true friend and still do. Can, can you forgive me?" Rose finished in a halting tone, and she looked away, not sure of Jenny's response.

"But, of course, I forgive you," Jenny replied warmly, as she gave Rose a hug to reassure her there were no hard feelings.

As Rose felt relief course through her, she hugged Jenny back, and she felt a few tears at the corners of her eyes, revealing even more of her emotions.

"I'm not letting a little confusion wreck our forty-five-year relationship. It'll take more than that to make me stay angry at you," Jenny continued.

Rose smiled. At least she had one friend she could trust and count on. Maybe she'd be able to get through this last part of the reunion after all. Thorn didn't have to ruin it for her. She could stay close to her valued companion and trusted friend. She looked up to see Jenny motioning her to a kitchen chair.

"Let's see. I have a spray bottle here somewhere. We must wet each strand of hair as it gets rolled. That'll make it hold its shape."

Rose smiled as Jenny busied herself making her beautiful. It was good to be fussed over, no matter the results this makeover incurred, and Rose was content to let Jenny be the one to do it.

— 13 —

BITTERNESS LIKE GALL ate at Anna Wilder-McQueen. She had thought this would be a good idea, but now that she was here to confront her birth mother, she wasn't so sure.

She gazed at herself critically in the mirror. Tonight, she wore a soft peach dress with pearl sequins on the bodice. The top was fitted with a scooped neck. The dress tumbled in loose folds from the waist down. She was tall like her father, standing nearly six feet, but that was where the similarities stopped. She didn't favor her father or her grandparents. She'd never seen a picture of her mother, but she knew she must favor her by the remarks her father occasionally made about her eyes or complexion, though his comments were usually whispered under his breath and not meant for her to hear.

Memories of things her grandparents had told her had started to surface since arriving in town, causing the hurt and angry emotions of her childhood to resonate in overwhelming feelings of rejection and abandonment; and the idea of facing someone who had never wanted her to begin with was a hard pill to swallow.

Yet, she needed to show the world she'd overcome those emotions, and she needed people to see how well she'd done, despite not being loved or wanted by that woman. She had graduated valedictorian of her senior class and had finished her bachelor's and master's degrees in physical therapy before going on and pursuing her doctorate. She now worked for a very prestigious sports therapy company. The love and concern she'd been raised with had been enough. Her *grandparents* had been enough. She'd demonstrated to the world she hadn't needed what everyone said she must have to survive: a mother's love.

Now she intended to prove to the woman who'd cast her aside that she'd never needed her to begin with. Tonight, once and for all, she intended to prove to herself and the world, but most importantly to the woman who gave her birth, that she had succeeded. The woman who had given her away and never looked back would know. The woman who had never given her a chance, but who had simply turned her head and walked out on her while she was only seconds old, would see a successful Anna.

She'd been told the story repeatedly as a child when she questioned her grandparents or her father about her mother. Her father usually didn't say much, telling her, "She didn't love either of us, Anna." Then a somber expression would edge across his face, and he would be lost in thought.

Her grandparents, however, were always quick to explain just how much her mother didn't love her and how fortunate she was to have loving grandparents who did. She'd been raised by them in the early years of her life, interspersed with brief stints spent alone with her father. He was usually off somewhere on some job, out of the state or out of the country.

It wasn't until she was fourteen and her grandparents were both tragically killed in a car accident that her father was forced to care for her full time. Anna had been in the car with them, but thankfully she'd been protected in the back seat of the large luxury vehicle, when a moving van suffered a blowout and swerved into oncoming traffic, hitting their car head on. Both of her grandparents died instantly.

Anna underwent physical therapy for several months while her broken legs and fractured hip healed. It was a slow and painful process. Despite that, she made a full recovery with no permanent damage to either her legs or hip, doing well enough to play basketball her junior and senior years of high school. Her experience from the wreck was what prompted her to become a physical therapist.

Her father turned out to be a very loving and patient man. He quit his military career, and he took a civilian job, so he could be home with her. Anna realized he'd made a sacrifice in his lifestyle to do that, but she never heard him complain about it. He always made her feel special, like she was the most important person in his world. That was why she'd agreed to come to this activity with him. She wanted in some small way to show him the gratitude she felt because he had been so selfless and altruistic.

Her thoughts continued to ramble as she began to get dressed for the evening, and she dressed and redressed, adjusting her outfit's tasteful accoutrements over and over to occupy her time. She had purchased some pearl-hued sandals and a matching handbag. Her father had given her a long, beautiful strand of pearls he brought back from Thailand. She had packed them carefully and wanted to wear them, so her father would know how much she treasured the personal gifts he lavished on her.

— 14 —

JENNY WAS FINISHING Rose's make-up, telling her friend that her hair had turned out adorable. It made her look ten years younger. With the darker make-up for the evening, she looked even more attractive than she had the day before at the picnic.

Jenny laughed and held up a mirror. "No one will be able to take their eyes off you. Your hair and make-up look fabulous on you. Let's see how the dress does."

Jenny was doing her best to encourage Rose. She had to. Rose had been hesitant about her hair and make-up, saying it was too heavy. In the mirror, though, Jenny was sure Rose could see her smoky gray eyes as they twinkled, bringing out depths of color that were normally not visible with the make-up she usually wore.

Jenny also pointed out how Rose's dress complement-ed her soft complexion, contrasting with the rich shade of her hair, with its soft chestnut brown color set off with a few darker auburn red highlights scattered throughout. Her hair made the dress look even more muted and subdued.

When Rose stood, her dress cascaded to the floor, revealing only the toes of her shoes. The fitted peach gossamer gown made Rose look ethereal. She had a fairy-like quality, being so petite, with a fluttering layer of the sheer, sequined gown hanging loosely over the satin underneath.

Jenny was very pleased with the final product she'd brought out in Rose. Now she had to work on herself. She'd bought a stretchy, black, slinky dress whose fabric had a satin-like sheen. It hung to the middle of her calf. She added a hairpiece and pulled her own hair up and under it, letting a few tendrils hang loose in the back and around the edges. She clipped on oversized black faux-diamond-accented jewelry. Her heels were black with large, chunky faux diamonds across the toes over black pantyhose. When she finished her make-up, she'd transformed herself, as well.

Both women would stand out in the crowd this evening, despite the efforts of others who might try to outdo them.

Jenny finished her final layer of lipstick just as the doorbell rang.

"I've got it, Jenny!" Rose called to her friend.

"It's probably Roxanne and Jack. Tell them I'm about ready."

Jenny smiled, certain Roxanne and Jack would be caught off-guard. She entered the living room just in time to see them walking around Rose, unable to get enough of how beautiful she looked. Then, Jenny stepped into the room, making her entrance, and taking the two visitors aback once again.

"Girl, you've turned up the heat in your all-black style." Roxanne giggled and prodded Jack with her elbow.

After the first glance, Jack had the good sense to not even look, and with a deep breath, he asked if they were ready to go. Even though they were a few minutes early, everyone seemed anxious to get the night started. Rose grabbed her purse, set the alarm, locked the door, and walked outside with everyone else in tow. She told Jack and Roxanne how pleased she was to have the opportunity to ride in the new Lincoln they'd bought only a few weeks before.

Jenny walked up to the car, reaching out to touch a piece of chrome. "I feel like a rock star tonight." She raised her arms in the air as if waving to adoring fans. The other three laughed, and Rose reached to pull her arms down.

Rose turned to Jack, "Seriously, this will make for a great time this evening. It's nice being chauffeured, even if Jenny does feel more like a rock star than someone attending her forty-year reunion. Thank you again for offering to drive. It takes a lot of stress off me."

"Happy to do so. Besides," Jack laughed lightly, "I enjoy escorting beautiful women into the city."

"Oh, you do, do you?" Roxanne popped out, causing everyone to laugh. She gave him a playful pinch before she crossed her arms and glared at him.

DURING THE RIDE to the reunion, the three women laughed and regaled each other with stories they'd learned about their ex-classmates at the barbeque the day before. Jack just listened, grabbing an occasional glance in the rear-view mirror of the two women he and Roxanne had picked up. Roxanne only pinched him one more time, though, as he was very careful to glance when she wasn't watching, and the trip ended without incident.

When they arrived, the line of cars to be parked moved quickly. At the door, the three beautiful women and their escort stepped from the interior of the car and into the soft glow of the bank tower's lighted parking garage's porte-cochere. The valet smiled at his chance to take the keys to Jack's new Lincoln, and the four walked inside the bank's glass elevator.

Jack escorted Roxanne while Jenny and Rose walked together to the elevator. Once they stepped inside, Jack pushed the twenty-first floor button. With a soft surge, the elevator made its way to the top floor of the bank tower, with the numbers on the readout clicking swiftly through their proscribed pattern.

As the group stepped from the door, they were bathed in soft candlelight. The overall view was breathtaking. The room had an elegance reminiscent of a bygone era with large chandeliers, lots of crystal, silver, china, and huge palms and ferns.

THE GROUP SIGNED in, put on nametags, and looked for their table number. They were sitting together, along with four more people from their class. Fortunately, Jenny had been on the planning committee and had put Thorn and his guest as far as they could be at the other end of the ballroom. There were only a few people at their end, so Rose was able to relax and focus on the events ahead and not on Thorn. At least that was what she hoped to do.

Everyone ordered drinks, and several appetizers were served, while guests mingled and waited for the dinner to be brought out. Rose quietly sipped her beverage, and then Jenny whispered, "I see Thorn, and I think he's headed this way."

"I believe I'll go powder my nose." Rose got up and headed to the ladies' room. Once in the safety of the private space, she let out a deep breath. She'd been holding it, afraid she would hear her name being yelled from across the banquet room like at the airport. She glanced around and noticed a couple of other classmates touching up their make-up and talking on their cellphones. She spoke and visited with them for a minute or two before they left to go back to their tables.

Finally, after about ten minutes, Rose decided she would head back to her table as well. She wouldn't let Thorn ruin her night. She had a right to be here as much as he did. Things would be fine if he kept his distance.

With new resolve, Rose started for her table and the shock of her life.

— 15 —

AS SOON AS Rose arrived back at her table, she knew something was amiss. The expression on Jenny's face was one of total bewilderment. Roxanne's was more akin to confusion, bordering on horror.

"What's the matter? What happened while I was gone?" Rose questioned, looking curiously from Jenny to Roxanne.

Jenny spoke up with hesitation in her voice, "Is there anything you want to tell us about you and Thorn, anything, perhaps, that you've never revealed?" She spoke slowly, making sure Rose got her question.

Rose frowned. She was already aware Thorn was present, and that was bad enough. Now her friends were acting strangely, and they were asking questions on a topic she wanted to put as far from her as possible. She brushed off the question with a pert reply, "Not really. He's in the past, and that's where I want to keep him."

Roxanne leaned in closely, staring intently at her friend. "You mean nothing happened between him and you that you want to share with us? Maybe, like, you know, something important? It seems there were a few months just after graduation that were unaccounted for. In fact, if I remember correctly, there was almost a year you and Thorn were out of touch with everyone."

Rose took a deep breath and replied as civilly as possible, "No, nothing I can think of that would matter now. That was a long time ago, and it was just a year better forgotten."

She had no intention of discussing it with them. It didn't matter now, anyway.

"Even if you don't think it's important now, can you think of something in your past that Thorn might bring up, something that might surprise us?"

Jenny's question dug a little closer to home, and Rose began to squirm. It was as though her friend had to ferret out some truth from Rose, when she didn't know what they expected her to say.

Rose looked at their faces, realizing they were almost ashen in color. What could Thorn have said or done that would make them react like this?

Rose thought for a minute and then sighed, "Well, for about seven months, right after high school, Thorn and I were married. But—"

"And then what happened?" blurted Roxanne, before Rose had a chance to finish.

"Nothing," Rose replied. "He dumped me and went off to find himself a war. I've not seen him since, not until this weekend. That's why I never mentioned it before. We were together for such a short time, and then he and his family moved away. We never spoke again until the other night in the airport, when he welcomed me to a weekend of torture."

Rose could tell by the expressions on her friends' faces she hadn't answered their questions. In fact, they looked more puzzled than ever.

"You mean you were married, and nothing else happened during that time that you want to share with us, something that we believe could be important?"

Roxanne kept questioning her, and Rose wondered where this could all be leading. By this time, she was a little aggravated at the questioning. She had just shared the most secret part of her life. Even Gill, Jr. didn't know she had been married before. Now her friends were acting like she had some big secret to share. She didn't appreciate being interrogated by them about something Thorn had obviously contrived to make her look bad. She was determined not to let him ruin her evening.

"Where's Thorn?" she questioned Jenny. "I'm getting to the bottom of whatever it is he's accused me of." Rose stood and looked out over the ballroom. About a hundred people were scattered throughout the space.

Jenny jumped up, too.

"I'll help you find him, Rose." She took Rose's arm and began aiming her toward the other end of the banquet hall. They had only taken about twenty steps or so when Jenny whispered, "Rose, I see him. He's straight ahead."

As Rose stepped forward, it was as if the crowd parted and let her and Jenny through. People were staring and whispering, some in shocked surprise, others almost laughing.

Rose was becoming more upset by the minute, and she intended to set the record straight.

THORN HAD BEEN visiting with some of his classmates when he noticed the pair approaching out of the corner of his eye. He slowly turned toward Rose, gaping at her, speechless.

The most beautiful vision of loveliness he could imagine was standing only a few feet from him, and it was his Rose Petal. She was coming toward him; the most stunning creature in the world was walking up to him.

He flashed a huge smile. It was then he realized she wasn't smiling.

In fact, she looked irate or worse.

Rose glanced at those standing around Thorn, and she motioned for him to bend down so she could whisper in his ear. Just as he started to lean toward her, a woman approached him. Thorn turned his head to her, and Rose's eyes followed.

It was then Rose's legs buckled, and Jenny grabbed her just before she went to her knees.

— 16 —

ROSE DIDN'T FAINT, but she felt very close. In front of her stood a near replica of her, all the way down to the peach-colored dress Rose wore. The woman sported a similar color gown, merely a shade darker, which brought out the deep highlights in her hair. Around her neck, she boasted a long strand of pearls to match those sewn on Rose's dress. The only noticeable difference was Thorn's wavy auburn hair and his height.

Her face, however, was Rose's.

She had Rose's creamy complexion and high cheekbones. The shape of her cloudy blue eyes and delicate mouth could be from no one other than Rose. Her slim neckline mirrored Rose's as well.

Rose stared at her in shocked surprise, stunned into complete silence. The woman also seemed to be taken aback by Rose's appearance, seeing a diminutive mirror of her own face. She simply gawked at Rose, as Thorn looked from one to the other. He seemed pleased at how they favored.

"Well, at last they meet. Rose Petal, I'd like to introduce you to our daughter, Anna. Anna, this is your mother, Rosemary, better known as Rose Petal." Thorn spoke just loudly enough for the two women to hear.

All the air went out of Rose. She couldn't breathe, and she felt herself starting to fall. She was helpless to control it. The next thing she knew, strong hands were lifting her and reassuring her everything was going to be okay. It was as if she were having one of her unexplainable dreams. Only now it was real.

A few seconds later, Rose was reclining on a gold brocade couch with a glass of water being pressed to her lips. Then she heard voices.

"Come on, Rose Petal. Drink this."

Another asked, "Should we call a doctor?"

Rose opened her eyes. It wasn't a dream. There was Thorn sitting beside her and offering her sips of water, while Jenny patted her hand. Things were slowly coming into focus. But where was the other woman? Then she looked beyond Thorn and saw her with eyes blazing. The creature who looked so much like Rose lashed out at her.

"Is this the little act you put on to get my Daddy's attention? Well, it might work for him, but it certainly doesn't work for me," Anna spat venomously.

"Wait, I'm confused." Rose tried to pull herself up, and she paused as she thought about what Thorn had said to her before she blacked out. The memory of his words crystalized in her mind, and she rasped out her words. "What do you mean, our daughter? We never had any children, Thorn. Not any that lived. The only baby I gave birth to that lived was Gill, Jr."

Wrapped in the overwhelming revelation washing over her, Rose could see only Thorn and the unknown woman he'd claimed to be her daughter. She was blinded to the people around her by this sudden turn of events, and she threw harsh words at him.

"The child you and I had was stillborn. Your mother told me that when she came into the hospital room. She said it was born dead. She didn't even tell me if it was a boy or a girl."

Rose glared as she realized everyone in the room now knew their shared history, all the while moving her eyes between Thorn and the strange woman that looked so much like her.

"Well, I'm very much alive, with little thanks to you, mommy dearest." Anna stepped forward, her voice a biting tirade against Rose's angry defense. "You don't have to continue to put on this dramatic scene, when you very well knew I lived. My grandmother told me how you wouldn't even look at me when I was born, and you said you wanted nothing to do with my father or me. She said you were sorry you'd ever met my father. So, don't go and try to change the story now!"

Anna was almost shouting in Rose's face. Other guests were starting to gather around, and Rose could only watch the face that was so much like hers.

JENNY, WHO KNEW Rose well, could tell by her expression this was all new information to her. Rose seemed almost in a state of shock. Thorn was watching her, and from his expression, he was beginning to have growing doubts himself.

She stepped to her friend, and she took her hand to comfort her.

THORN HAD NEVER actually questioned Rose back then. He'd taken his parents' word that she'd said all those hurtful things. In fact, they had insisted that he not even go in to say good-bye. They said she didn't want to speak with him, and he needed to let her have her way.

They had repeated themselves more than once and forbade it explicitly.

Thorn couldn't let her go that easily, not his wife, not the woman he loved. He was distraught at the idea she wouldn't want to see him. There had been no suggestion before the baby's birth that she felt this way.

When his parents went to sign the papers, he snuck in Rose's hospital room. That was when she said she'd see him burn before she ever kissed him again.

She was angry that day; he'd had no trouble telling that. Rose had never been much of an actor. She wore her feelings on her face, and her body language was usually easy to read.

Right now, Rose was stiff, and her pallor revealed that she was alarmed and even fearful. After a few minutes, she spoke in a labored tone.

"Thorn, this is the cruelest joke I've ever known anyone to pull. To find some woman who resembles me to help you carry this out is even more malicious and spiteful. That you would use our precious baby, something I'd wanted more than anything in this world, and turn it into some kind of twisted, hurtful comedy is even beyond what I ever thought you were capable of."

As soon as she finished speaking, Rose turned to Jenny. "Please help me to my feet. I believe I've had all of this reunion and all of Thorn I can stand."

Anna spat at her, "Oh, make a big scene and then exit. How very theatrical of you."

She was quickly interrupted by Thorn.

"Anna, leave Rose Petal alone. She doesn't need this right now."

Anna pressed her lips together and crossed her arms, not happy about this situation at all.

Thorn could see the pain and suffering on Rose's face. Something was wrong. This scenario wasn't going as planned. Rose hadn't been embarrassed by his divulging her secret. She was hurt and angry, and more than anything, she appeared surprised.

Rose turned to him and spoke through gritted teeth. "Don't ever speak to me again, Thorn Wilder. As long as you live, I never want to hear from you or see you again. You've hurt me for the very last time. I never want any dealings to do with you, ever! If you were trying to embarrass me, you've succeeded. If you were trying to make me despise you, well, you've accomplished that goal, as well."

WITH HER LAST remark, Rose stood and walked to her table to retrieve her purse and leave. She told Jack and Roxanne she would catch a taxi home. Jenny offered to accompany her, but she said she needed to be alone. She never looked back. She didn't stop to see the expression of utter and complete devastation creeping across Thorn's broken features.

— 17 —

THE REUNION CROWD was abuzz after Rose left. Not everyone knew what had happened, but everybody had watched Rose leave, and most of them saw Thorn's face afterward. They could tell his daughter seemed to be a big part of this puzzling night as well.

Only minutes after Rose left, Thorn and Anna made their departure as well, leaving onlookers more perplexed than ever. Jenny, however, went back to her assigned table. She sat down stoically and just stared at the food placed in front of her. What had been revealed tonight would change lives forever.

Jenny just couldn't figure this out. Rumors were all she'd known of Thorn and Rose and that missing year. None of them had ever been substantiated, though. Apparently, from her face tonight, poor Rose didn't seem to have a clue what was going on.

Thorn had started out the evening so smugly, but he had seemed tormented in the end. Then there was his daughter, rather, their daughter, who had been a secret all these years. How could Rose not know the baby had lived?

His parents couldn't have kept that from her no matter how much they wanted to. The doctor would have told her at delivery.

Yet, Rose had never mentioned a doctor. Surely there had to have been a doctor who delivered the baby. He would have told Rose the truth.

Roxanne interrupted her thoughts.

"What happened back there, Jenny? It was like World War Three was about to start. And the woman Thorn introduced as his daughter, how is she involved? I thought Rose only has the one son."

"So did Rose, until now," explained Jenny. She told everyone at the table about the incident and Rose's reaction. No one could believe it. The story sounded like something you'd see on television, not reality played out right before their eyes.

"Poor Rose. So she never knew she had a child by him? How can someone not know something like that?" Barker Sampley, a guest seated at the table, asked the question. Jenny recounted Rose's conversation and Thorn's earlier comments about how big Anna had been when she was born.

"Rose was put to sleep for a caesarian section because the baby was so big; you know how small Rose is compared to Thorn. But it was too late. The baby was already coming, and it delivered the normal way.

"When she awakened, only Thorn's mother was in the room. She told Rose the baby was born dead. At least that's what I understand, from what Rose just told Thorn."

Jenny put her hand over her mouth, still dazed by it all. After that, she just picked at her food. She had no appetite and couldn't enjoy herself knowing her best friend had just received such shocking news.

She excused herself and went to the ladies' room to call Rose on her cell. When Rose didn't pick up, Jenny became alarmed. Back at the table, she shared her concerns with Roxanne and excused herself for the evening, explaining that she was going to Rose's. She would help Rose uncover the truth once and for all about Thorn.

Jenny phoned for a taxi and headed down the elevator for the ground floor. What a night this fortieth reunion had turned out to be!

Her ride was waiting when she reached the lower level. She gave directions and thought about the evening's events, while he drove into the night. The vehicle had only reached the outskirts of the city when her phone rang. She breathed a sigh of relief, certain Rose was returning her call. She tapped the answer icon and spoke with emotion into the device.

"Rose, I was so worried when you didn't answer your phone a few minutes ago. Are you okay? I should have gone with you, but you said you didn't want company right then, and you'd see me later. But then when you didn't answer, I got worried. I'm on my way over."

There was silence, and then a low, guttural, broken voice spoke, "This isn't Rose. It's Thorn."

Now it was Jenny's turn for all the breath to leave her body. Why was Thorn calling her?

— 18 —

"WE NEED TO talk before you get to Rose's. I'm really messed up right now. I've got to unload all this on someone. Can you meet me somewhere?"

Thorn's voice came out in ragged bits edged with panic, not his usual liquid, smooth tone. Jenny thought for just a second before responding. He sounded desperate, and that frightened her. In her mind, Thorn wasn't afraid of anything or anybody.

"Yes, sure. I'll meet you. Where?"

"How about that all-night truck stop on the Interstate? The restaurant is open, and I'll buy us both a cup of coffee."

"Okay. I'll see you there in about ten minutes," Jenny replied, and the phone went dead in her hand. She looked at it, certain of how devastated Thorn must be to not even say good-bye.

Jenny's taxi pulled to the front door of the Double Clover Twenty-Four Hour Restaurant. Thorn was waiting and paid her cab fare. He also gave the driver a substantial tip. Jenny thanked him as he escorted her in and led her toward a back booth where it was quieter and less crowded.

The waitress came by and took their order for some coffee and toast. She tried to flirt with Thorn, and she was disappointed when he ignored her completely. Thorn just stared ahead glassy-eyed, like Jenny wasn't even there. He seemed to be in his own world.

Finally, he spoke.

"Jenny, I have a bad feeling about tonight, like I really blew it," he started. "I have a sense that Rose didn't even know she had a daughter."

He paused for a moment, glancing Jenny's way for an instant, then as quickly looking away. His face twisted as he tried to regain his self-control.

"Hmm," Jenny murmured, not sure what to say.

"But I know that's impossible. What do you know about Rose and me after high school? What's she told you?"

Jenny waited for a minute while the waitress poured their coffee and set down their toast.

"Well, I do know the rumors that you two were married for a short while during that year after high school, although Rose never talks about it and has sworn me to secrecy with what little she's told me; I don't think even Gill, Jr. knows his mom might have been married before. She called me right after you broke up with her and left. She was so distraught I'm certain she doesn't even remember doing that. By the time I could get home from college to console her, her parents had been relocated to Germany. They were stationed there for the next several years."

ALL THORN HEARD was that he had broken up with Rose. The words twisted in him: *She called me right after you broke up with her and left.*

"Wait, hold on a second." Thorn's eyes pleaded with Jenny, hoping for her to correct her story. He didn't even hear the last of the conversation. His brain was locked on *you broke up with her*. "Did you just say that I was the one that broke up with her?"

"Yes, Rose has always said you broke up with her when she needed you most." Jenny's eyes let him know it was the truth.

Thorn felt like he'd been sucker-punched. He stared into his coffee cup for what seemed like eons. Slowly, he raised his head.

"Jenny, I want you to hear the truth from me, exactly as I remember it. Don't interrupt me, just listen. We can talk about discrepancies afterward. Right now, I just want to talk."

Just as he began, his cell phone rang. He glanced at the number as he answered it.

"Hi, Sugar. No, I'm fine, really. I just needed a cup of coffee, that's all. I've run into a friend here, so I may visit for a while. Head on to bed. I've got my room key. Don't wait up. We've both got a plane to catch tomorrow. Love you, too, Anna. Bye."

He looked at Jenny sheepishly. "Daughters can be so over-protective, sometimes."

"So can wives and girlfriends," Jenny nodded, as she replied with a dry twist to her words.

— 19 —

THORN BEGAN, "MY folks never did approve of Rose Petal. They considered her family poor white trash, because during the time they were both stationed in Killeen, her father was only a sergeant and my father was a general. They accused my sweet Rose Petal of trying to get her dad a promotion by using my father's influence. Not once in our entire relationship did she even mention her father's rank to me. But my parents brought it up every time I turned around.

"Rose Petal and I had been going out since our junior year. Her parents were strict on her, and we dated very little. We'd only shared a few innocent kisses. Finally, the senior prom came around, and her parents agreed she could stay out until 1:00 a.m. We ditched the prom about 11:00 and took my parents' big new Cadillac and went parking out at the lake.

"We'd never made out like that. She was like a drug to me. I couldn't resist her. The more I had of her, the more I wanted. I couldn't stop once we got started. It was only that one night, but that's all it took.

"She didn't tell me until she knew for sure, a month or so later. Her father came over to my parents' house ready to kill me. Of course, my parents accused her of seducing me, which wasn't true.

"In the end, we married and moved into an efficiency apartment. It didn't seem to matter to Rose. She was always happy and kept the place spotless.

"I was so in love with her, I didn't see any faults in her, but my parents sure did. They were constantly saying things like she wasn't a very good cook, or she slept a lot. She was pregnant; of course, she slept a lot. She didn't cook because the smell of food made her nauseous. But the few times she did cook, her food was always fabulous. I didn't care. I loved Rose, and she seemed to love me.

"Then my parents came by one time while I wasn't home, and some guy was at our house. That's when they began to accuse her of cheating on me. Then I became divided between believing her or my parents.

"Later, I found out it was your brother bringing a letter from you at college. But by then, seeds of jealousy were rooted in my heart. I'd call her during the day, or check to see if she'd really gone to the laundromat, anything, just to keep tabs on her. My parents were making me crazy.

"Finally, when Rose was so big she could hardly move, they started telling me she was lazy. Rose was having a difficult time even walking. Anna was born almost three weeks premature, due to her size; she weighed ten pounds and four ounces. She was to be delivered caesarian at the last minute, but the baby had already started down the birth canal.

"It was a very scary time. Rose Petal almost died. Of course, my folks were right there to accuse her of being pregnant by someone else, and that was why the baby was early. The doctors had put Rose to sleep because of the pain she was in. Her parents weren't there because my folks refused to call them and let them know until after the baby was born and we'd left the hospital.

"After the doctor delivered Anna, my parents came out of the hospital room and said Rose didn't love me. They said she was angry because the baby had ruined her figure. They said she never wanted to see me again, and she didn't want the baby, either.

"I was so crushed I didn't know what to think. The happiest day of my life had just exploded in my face. I knew we had a few problems, but I loved Rose Petal with all my heart.

"My parents assured me they would adopt the baby and raise it. They also said Rose's last wish was that she never see me again. My parents then went in another room to sign some paperwork.

"I couldn't help myself. I had to see her just one last time to try to convince her to stay with me and not leave. I thought if I could just talk to her or kiss her, I could per-suade her to stay. But when I went into the room, it was already too late. She looked at me with such disgust and hatred that I knew it was over.

"But I was still determined to try. I wanted to kiss her good-bye, but she made it clear I was one match away from a bonfire if I touched her. That was the last time I saw her. She completed all the divorce proceedings through my parents. I was already scheduled to ship out by then, and I didn't care if I lived or died.

"My heart was so broken by Rose Petal's rejection of me and our daughter, I had no will to live. It was only the mercy of God that kept me alive and brought me home. He knew my little Rose would need me later in life."

Thorn stopped and took a sip of coffee.

JENNY SAT TOTALLY blindsided. This wasn't the story she'd heard from Rose. She had only uncovered Thorn and Rose's turbulent break-up in bits and pieces over the years, and it didn't match what Thorn had just relayed to her.

Now Jenny didn't know what to believe.

— 20 —

"WELL, DO YOU have anything to say?" Thorn finally asked Jenny after several minutes of quiet.

"What? Oh, sorry, I was just trying to digest everything. Your version of the break-up doesn't match what Rose has told me, which isn't all that much, but I'm sure this isn't what she believes happened."

Jenny looked at her hands and fiddled with a ring she was wearing, and then she reached for her coffee. She was at a loss what to say, and she needed time to come to grips with Thorn's version of events. Just then Thorn's hand reached for hers.

"Jenny, you've got to convince her to talk to me. Please, if not for my sake, for our daughter's sake. Little Anna has grown up with the belief that her mother never wanted her or loved her. She's filled with bitterness and resentment toward her like you wouldn't believe. Most of the time, I thought it was deserved, but the scene I witnessed tonight told me it can't be true." Thorn peered deeply into Jenny's eyes, with tears forming in his. "Please, you've got to help me. I can't stand this torment any longer. I must know the truth, so I can be free, and my daughter will be liberated as well. Please say you'll help me."

Jenny saw a man who was desperate to right a wrong. He loved Rose Petal. That had been evident over the past two days, as he had soaked up her presence like a man drinking his last drop of moisture in the desert. He was constantly looking for her, wanting to be around her, and even now trying to gain her approval. Jenny nodded her head yes, letting this desperate man know she would help him.

Thorn squeezed her hand and said, "You've given me hope. I won't forget this. But please, don't let Rose Petal know we've talked, or she may not trust you. Just call me and let me know how things are progressing. Try to find out exactly what she remembers on the day she gave birth to Roseanna. I'm sure there was some sort of mix-up or perhaps even sabotage, looking back and knowing my parents. Do what you can, and call me tomorrow before I fly out. My flight is at 7:00 p.m." Thorn loosened his grip on Jenny's hand.

"Anything I can do, I will, without letting Rose know." Jenny patted Thorn's hand. When she pulled out her phone to call for a ride, Thorn offered her his services. She finished her coffee and stood to leave, as Thorn paid the check. He escorted her to the burgundy-colored pickup truck he'd rented for the weekend. When Jenny started to offer him the address, he reminded her he'd taken her to Rose's already, and the address was in the navigation system.

Once they arrived, he smiled as he opened the door for her. "I really appreciate this, Jenny; I'll make it up to you someday. I want to know everything I can, so I can decide what to do next."

Jenny said good night and walked up the sidewalk to the door. She rang the bell and waited for Rose to answer. A few seconds later, the foyer light came on, and she heard

Rose on the other side.

"It's Jenny, Rose. Open the door."

"Are you alone?" Rose's voice quivered.

"Of course, I'm alone. Now let me in. I'm getting cold." She heard the deadbolt move, and the door squeaked open, barely letting her through.

"I-I thought maybe Thorn was out there, trying to get in. He's been calling me all night, so I muted the phone. I never thought about you coming home. I'm sorry. I just noticed you called only a few minutes ago." Rose's face revealed she'd been crying, with her swollen eyelids and reddened nose.

Jenny put her arm around her friend and spoke soothingly, "That's okay. After everything you've been through tonight, I surprised you can even think at all."

It was then Jenny noticed the living room's disheveled appearance. When they left earlier, the house had been spotless, the way Rose always kept it. Now, it appeared like a small tornado had happened. Boxes were strewn around the living room.

Rose followed her friend's eyes and began to explain. "I was looking for it. I knew I had a copy of it somewhere," she started, as she moved to a box and closed the lid.

"Looking for what?" Jenny didn't understand.

"Why Gill, Jr.'s birth certificate, of course. I found it. Naturally, it was in the last box from the garage. Come sit down and look at it. It plainly supports what I said tonight."

Rose was beginning to sound more like herself, but now Jenny was confused. How could Gill, Jr.'s birth certificate solve anything between Rose and Thorn?

It didn't make sense.

— 21 —

ROSE SHOWED JENNY the birth certificate. As Jenny scanned the document, she came to the section regarding other births. In a square plainly marked by the hospital was the proof that there had been no recorded live births before Gill, Jr. There was one stillborn birth clearly stated on the birth record.

"See? I told him I never gave birth to a live baby other than Gill, Jr. I don't care how he tries to accuse me. Thorn's a liar now just like he was then." Rose seemed to be trying to convince herself as much as she was Jenny.

Jenny sat for a moment staring at the document. Then she calmly asked, "Who supplied the hospital your previous birth history? How did they know about your other birth to begin with?"

That was all it took for Rose to crumple. She sat down like a balloon that had just had all the air let out. She spoke in an almost inaudible voice.

"I told them. They asked a lot of questions before they delivered little Gill. I had a hard delivery with him as well, but nothing compared to the first one. With Thorn's baby,

I thought I was going to die. Gill, Jr. had to be taken by caesarean." Rose paused for a moment, growing more and more distressed.

"So, how does this birth certificate solve everything?" Jenny continued to study it, as if Rose's answer might make a difference.

"Oooh! Finding this didn't solve anything, did it? It's still Thorn's word against mine. But I would never lie to my doctor or to anyone else about something as important as this. My baby didn't live." By now, Rose was starting to shake, and tears were streaming down her face. "I would have never given up my baby. They said it was dead, still-born."

Jenny interjected, "Did the doctor say that? Do you have a record of that baby's death certificate?"

Rose sniffled for a minute and thought. "I don't remember the doctor coming in after that, but I was still groggy from the anesthetic. All I remember is Thorn's parents came in and said the baby had died, and Thorn held me responsible for it. Even though it was stillborn, he never wanted to see or speak to me again. They said he was sorry he'd ever married me. It had been a mistake, and he never wanted to lay eyes on me again. Then they walked out of the hospital room and left me alone.

"I was still dazed from the medicine, and then I was reeling from the news they blurted out to me. They couldn't even wait until I could process the loss of our baby before they let me know Thorn's true feelings. It was by far the worst day of my life. I didn't hurt that bad after the loss of my parents or Gill. I prayed to die right then and there.

"Then, of all the nerve, several minutes later, Thorn came into the room to kiss me good-bye. After everything he had said, I lost it. My temper was out of control from the pain he'd caused me. I never wanted to forgive him. He left the room after a few choice words from me.

"It was about forty-five minutes later when my parents

showed up. By then, the Wilder family had left. My folks stayed with me the remainder of the evening."

"The doctor? Surely he came in and spoke with your parents." Jenny couldn't see how the doctor would ignore someone who'd just lost their baby.

"We never saw the doctor again. My parents asked repeatedly to see him. A nurse came and checked on me over the next four days. Finally, on the fourth day after my delivery, the nurse said I was well enough to go home, if someone was there to look after me.

"My parents were glad to get me away from the hospital and back in their care. My mother was very nurturing, and I recovered rather quickly. She did her best to keep me calm and relaxed. After about two-and-a-half weeks at home, I was able to pretty much do what I had done before my pregnancy.

"It was the heartbreak of losing my baby, 'my little wild thorn,' as well as my husband that took forever to heal. I was depressed for months. But it really didn't matter, because my daddy got new orders. Three-and-a-half weeks later, my parents and I were on a plane headed to Germany where we stayed the next three years. I didn't come back to the States until I was twenty-one. By then I had my degree, and I had hardened my heart so it would be almost impossible for me to be hurt again." Rose finished with a deep sigh. "But I never forgot my little Wild Thorn. We'd called the baby that from the time we were married until I went into the delivery room."

— 22 —

THORN AWAKENED IN his bed in a cold sweat. His dream had been so real. He and Rose Petal were together, and they looked the same as they had at the reunion. They were taking turns holding a little baby girl. But just as he was about to hand the tiny infant to Rose, she smiled at him and walked away. He called out for her to stay, but she kept walking.

That was when he woke up.

Even though he hadn't smoked in over ten years, he wished he had a cigarette. Just one puff would help him relax and forget about life for the moment. That's all he wanted to do right now, forget about life.

This was one of the worst weekends he'd ever faced. He had thought this would be the opportunity that would finally set him free. Instead, he felt more bound up and imprisoned than before. At least before tonight, he had entertained fantasies about how he would confront Rose, and how she would beg for his forgiveness as he walked away the victor. Now, he didn't feel victorious. He felt traumatized. He didn't trust his feelings anymore, because they were telling him one thing, and it conflicted with what he'd been told for years.

He'd believed how bad his Rose Petal was and been devastated by what she'd said to him in that hospital room. But if her version was different than what he'd been told, he needed to know.

Right now, he couldn't discern the truth. Things had gotten too mixed up to know what had really happened. His daughter was full of bitterness from a past that might never have existed. He was still hurting from Rose's cruel words all those years ago, words that taunted him even now in his dreams.

Thorn glanced over at the clock on the hotel nightstand. It was only a few minutes after four. He knew he couldn't sleep anymore, so he got up and headed to the shower. He felt revived as ice cold water washed down his body. Afterwards, he dressed and decided a cup of coffee might finish waking him up.

The Big Griddle closed at 1:00 a.m. and reopened at 4:00 a.m. to allow time for the building to be cleaned and fresh bread and pancake dough to be made for the next day. Thorn left a voicemail with room service to tell his daughter where he was, in the event she woke up and was worried. He got into his truck and headed toward the restaurant.

At least that's where he'd planned to go. But first he made a detour by Rose's. He drove slowly and stared at the darkened house. Only a light at the corner of the garage was on. Thorn let out a deep sigh and headed to the restaurant.

As he pulled in the parking lot, he noticed only a handful of cars were there. Parking his rented truck in the semi-darkness, he headed to the door. Stepping inside, the hostess immediately seated him. As he passed the first booth, he heard a squeak and immediately turned his attention in the direction of the sound.

There sat Jenny and Rose Petal.

The air went out of Thorn's lungs. He just stared at the couple sitting in the booth. Rose's hair was damp, as if she'd showered recently. Jenny's eyes looked like she was doing all she could to keep them forced open.

The waitress noticed the group had an obvious connection, and she asked. "Would you care to sit here, sir?" She pointed to the open space by Rose.

Thorn couldn't believe his luck, and he mutely nodded his head.

ROSE HAD SEEN Thorn walk in, and she saw the waitress question him, looking their way. She muttered to herself, "He wouldn't dare try to do this!"

Jenny stared at the floor, not wanting to get caught in the crossfire between these two.

Thorn's face had a tormented look. His eyes dared Rose to deny him access to her booth.

Rose was curt, her words aimed at the waitress, Jenny, and Thorn. "It's a free country. I guess he can sit wherever he chooses."

She couldn't believe he had the gall to speak to her after everything that had just happened only a few hours ago. She thought she'd made it clear that she never wanted to be near him again.

Right now, she didn't want to face Thornton Jebulon Wilder or listen to anything he might have to say.

THORN WASN'T ABOUT to be intimidated, especially after the dream he'd had of them. There was no way Rose was getting the upper hand in this situation. He could goad her right back, and he did.

"Well, Rose Darlin'." Thorn took a deep breath. "Since you put it that way, I believe I will sit here."

At that, he dropped into the seat, almost dislodging Rose, as the cushion shifted under his weight. He glanced at her and smiled, his eyebrows lifting in mirth. Jenny covered her mouth and tried her best not to laugh, as did the waitress.

ROSE GREW HOT and clenched her teeth. She was furious, but she wouldn't let Thorn break her. He'd done so once, but she was stronger than he was now.

AS THE WAITRESS left to get Thorn's cup of coffee, tension swirled inside the booth. Why of all places, and at this premature hour, did Thorn have to show up here? What reason did Rose Petal have to be up so early? These questions plagued both Rose and Thorn as they sat beside each other in the crowded booth. However, their shoulders were touching, and part of the tension came from the fire shooting from that electric physical contact.

JENNY WATCHED THE scene. As tired as she was, she could tell. A storm was brewing, and the lightning was about to fly.

— 23 —

ANNA AWAKENED MUCH earlier than usual.

She blamed it on the chain of events from the previous evening. Seeing her mother for the first time was a shock. Then her blatant denial of Anna's existence had infuriated Anna even more. Finally, to watch her dad almost take that woman's side was even more exasperating.

She would be relieved when this town was nothing more than a bad memory, and she could put all this behind her. She just wanted to get on with her life. At the thought of life, Anna rubbed her still-flat belly. Deep within, she could feel the new life beginning inside her.

That had been part of the reason she'd been anxious these past two weeks to meet her birth mother. Now that she was finally pregnant with her own child, she wanted to see who her baby might resemble. Anna had never seen a picture of her birth mother, so she didn't know just which traits had come to her from her father and which from her mother.

After seeing the woman her father claimed was her mother, she had no doubts. Anna knew she was the spitting image of her except for her height and hair. Her mother was beautiful even now, and it was understandable why her father had fallen in love with her so long ago. She could only imagine how gorgeous she'd been in her youth. It was no wonder he had married so young. It was also obvious that beauty didn't always go with outstanding character.

Anna was only six weeks pregnant, but she already felt a bond to the small being sharing her body. She'd be thirty-nine in January, and her baby was due in June. She felt the excitement of becoming a mother. At the same time, she felt a deep resentment toward her own biological mother. How could she have not wanted Anna, her own child, her flesh and blood, after all the months of carrying her in her body? Anna couldn't comprehend the thought of not wanting her baby after only six weeks. Her grandmother had said her mother didn't even want to look at her and didn't ask if she was a boy or a girl. At the same time, her grandmother repeatedly reminded her of how much she was loved by her grandparents and her father.

She knew her dad had come to this reunion for closure. He had never been what she would call happy, not in his personal life. He'd tried, having been married a couple of times she knew of, besides his first. Not living with him, it had been hard for her to keep track. The marriages always ended in divorce. But he never seemed overly sad or disappointed about it. He appeared numb to any emotion toward anyone except his daughter.

Then, last night, for the first time, Anna saw her father reacting differently to a woman. Something had caused his emotions to kindle. Even Anna could see that. When Rose's knees had buckled under her, he had been worried, and it had showed. Without even thinking, he had grabbed her and carried her to the sofa. He barked orders for someone to get water for him. He'd sat there and given her sips from the cup, nursing her until she opened her eyes.

It was when Anna saw the sigh of relief on her father's

face that she knew the emotional attachment he still felt to his first love. It was like no other expression she'd ever seen. He was totally euphoric as Rose's eyes fluttered open. It was obvious he still had deeply rooted feelings her.

That was what worried Anna now. Would he be able to walk away from her once and for all with her denial about Anna? It would be trying over the next few hours to see how her father fared after all the excitement died down. Her father alone with his feelings of betrayal and abandonment wasn't a good thing. That was what this weekend was supposed to help heal, but from what she saw last night, all it did was ignite a bonfire from smoldering ashes. And now it was her job to try to put that fire back out and kill it for good. She couldn't let her father continue to long for something that would never be. If his old love had hurt him before, she'd do it again. Anna had to prevent that.

She hoped she was up to the task.

She also knew she'd have to tell her father soon about her own pregnancy, despite her separation from Sam a little over a month ago. That was something else she wasn't looking forward to. Now, she needed to see if she could catch her dad at The Big Griddle for breakfast. His message indicated he'd been there about forty-five minutes. If she was lucky, she could catch him before he left for the hotel.

— 24 —

THORN JUST STARED at Rosemary, and he refused to budge an inch. Rose could feel his eyes boring a hole through her, but she still refused to look his direction. She was praying for strength and for God to give her wisdom. Every time she'd opened her mouth all weekend, she'd let her old emotions and lack of self-control lash out. She always felt guilty later. After her sarcastic comment earlier, she thought it would be best if she kept her mouth shut, no matter how Thorn baited her. Then and only then would he know she'd changed.

She wanted him to see she wasn't the same emotional teenager she'd been when he walked out on her all those years ago. God had truly helped her become a better mother, grandmother, and overall person. Of course, when it came to Thorn, she seemed to immediately become reactionary, and all thoughts of self-control seemed to fly out the window.

What was it the Apostle Paul said? What I don't want to do, I find myself doing, and what I want to do, I don't. Did he know humanity or what? That was exactly how

Rosemary felt while Thorn's bulky frame filled the booth.

The waitress arrived with two black coffees and one water. Jenny groaned, accepting a cup of coffee. She muttered that it didn't matter if she couldn't get back to sleep. Everyone could survive on three hours a night, right?

JENNY DECIDED ROSE had good instincts, because they weren't there five minutes, and Thorn showed up. She could tell he'd freshly showered by his damp hair. It was obvious they were both wide awake by the way they tapped the table, all the while ignoring one another.

The waitress delivered their drinks and asked them if they were ready to order. Jenny requested a bagel with cream cheese. With the coffee, she would never get back to sleep if she ate any more than that.

THORN ORDERED BISCUITS and gravy. Rose ordered a single toast. Thorn looked at the waitress and back to Rose. He wasn't satisfied with Rose's meager selection, but she could order whatever she wanted. He couldn't control that.

"What else do you want?" he demanded gruffly, not meaning food. Rose shot him a sideways glance. She had ignored him as much as she could. However, this was a direct question, and Thorn intended to force her hand.

"I already told the waitress what I want."

Rose referred to the toast. Thorn was thinking of the vicious words she'd said at the reunion. They still preyed on his mind and heart.

"Do you really mean it, Rose Petal?" he questioned, in a much more subdued tone.

"Are you deaf? All I want is toast. I'm still too nervous from everything that's happened to eat anything else."

ROSE FINALLY LOOKED at him. She saw a myriad of emotions on his face. She could tell he was in torment, but what did that have to do with toast?

What did he think she meant?

THORN SAW HER trying to read his facial expressions, and in his relief at realizing he'd misunderstood her answer, he broke into a huge smile. Rose blushed, turned her head away, and looked at the other side of the booth at Jenny.

Maybe she hadn't been trying to hurt him intentionally just then.

The waitress finally broke in, "So, is there anything else?"

"No," Thorn said almost cheerily. "We're good here." He continued to tap on the table, but it was a much lighter sound, matching the lighter mood in his heart.

JENNY NEEDED TO get Thorn's attention without Rose noticing. However, like always, he was caught up with Rose and only Rose.

Jenny wondered how this couple had ever managed to break up with the way they acted around each other. It was as if someone had sabotaged their relationship. They had been so much in love back then. There was no way either of them would have given up the other without a fight.

Even now they were like lovestruck teenagers. They were always aware of each other's presence, even if it wasn't acknowledged.

THORN PUT HIS arm across the back of the booth. He wasn't exactly touching Rose, but he wasn't exactly not touching her, either. Rose could feel his arm on the back of the booth, but she tried to ignore it. If she moved, he'd know it bothered her, and then he'd know he was having an effect on her.

She tried not to respond as his arm slowly slipped down until it was touching her shoulders. Then she felt his hand ever so softly stroking her hair. That was the last straw. She knew she'd overreacted at the reunion. Honestly, the joke was the worst thing anyone could ever pull, but Thorn had always been crass like that. Still, he'd insulted her, called her a liar, and now he thought it was okay to touch her hair.

This wouldn't do.

"Excuse me, Thorn. I believe I need to go wash my hands." Rose spoke to him in an even-keeled tone. She would keep her voice under control, even if he was infuriating her.

THORN GLANCED AT Rose, gave a crooked grin, and climbed out of the booth. He turned and helped her out, holding her hand a little too long. She simply stared at him until he released it. Rose then headed to the ladies' restroom. The timing could not have been better, creating a perfect opportunity for Jenny. She quickly drew open her purse and spoke in a hushed tone.

"Thorn, quick. Get a load of this. It's Gill, Jr's birth certificate. I think you're in for a big surprise. It may answer some questions about the past and start you thinking about new ones."

— 25 —

A DARK LOOK swept across Thorn's face as he read the document.

"Where did you get this?" he demanded.

"Rose had it when I got to her house. She'd been looking for it ever since she returned from the banquet. She immediately showed it to me to prove her story was true. The only problem is, she admitted she was the one who supplied the hospital with the information about your daughter's birth. However, she truly believes this is the truth. She insists that you left her."

Jenny had barely finished speaking when she saw Rose returning from the restroom. Jenny reached for the paper, but Thorn pleaded, "Let me keep this for a few days. I promise I'll return it in mint condition." He slipped it into his jeans pocket as Rose approached their table.

"WHAT, DID I hear Thorn Wilder say please? Surely my ears are playing tricks on me. I didn't even know that word was in his vocabulary." Rose dripped acid with her words.

"You'd be surprised by a lot I'd say, if you were

around me more," Thorn replied in a soft, deep voice, as he stepped from the table to let her be seated.

Rose looked at him. She didn't want to be cornered by him in that booth again. She turned to Jenny, who was preoccupied with not watching either of them. Rose sighed. At least she wasn't alone with him.

Thorn waited, giving Rose that look again, the one that made her think she was about to be his breakfast, he was so hungry for her. All she could do was scoot in next to him in silence. She was afraid to utter anything regarding his last remark.

Thorn carefully sat back down. This time Rose didn't come bouncing off the seat. Jenny glanced up and cracked a smile, saying nothing.

THEIR FOOD ARRIVED, and no one said anything while they ate. Jenny was so sleepy she could barely spread her cream cheese on her bagel. Thorn and Rose seemed not to notice. Thorn was busy looking sideways at Rose nibbling on her toast, looking totally content. He consumed his biscuits and gravy in only a few bites, and he flagged the waitress down to order more coffee.

Rose on the other hand was taking very measured breaths. She wasn't letting Thorn bother her in any way. She would maintain control of her emotions around him regardless of how he behaved.

Jenny finally finished her breakfast and was ready to go. She was too tired to really pay attention to the sparring couple. She needed to get back to Rose's and get some much-needed rest before she went to see her brother that afternoon, and she no longer thought Rose would want to accompany her.

She spoke up, "I don't know about you two, but I'm sleepy and would like to take a nap before I go to see my brother this afternoon. So, Rose, if you don't mind, do you think you could take me home?"

ROSE BREATHED A sigh of relief. This was just the out she'd been waiting for. "Sure, I'm ready right now. Let's go." Rose shot a glance at Thorn as she asked, "If you'll excuse me, I need to get Jenny home, and then I want to get ready for church."

Thorn cut his dark eyes at Rose, responding, "Sure, Rose Petal. Anything you want." He slowly stood and helped Rose from the booth, his massive frame towering over her. Thorn got out his wallet to pay the check. Rose stopped him and said, "We were here first, so we'll pay this time."

"Then I'll get the tip," he replied, as he pulled out a twenty.

Jenny turned, smiled at him, and said it was good to see him. She said she hoped it wasn't another forty years before they got together again. Thorn repeated almost the same thing to her and laughed as he gave her a hug good-bye.

Rose tried to slip by Thorn undetected, but her purse got caught between his knee and Jenny as Thorn hugged her good-bye. Rose had no choice but to wait until they had finished their salutations.

Then Thorn turned to her. But instead of saying or doing anything, he took her hand and pulled her toward the door, leaving Jenny at the counter paying the check. Once outside in the shadows of the early morning, Thorn again lifted Rose off her feet and held her in his arms.

"Oh, Rose Petal. You're like a bad habit for me. I can't seem to break it no matter how hard I try." Then Thorn kissed her very gently on the forehead and set her down. "But I'm trying. Honestly, I am."

Rose was speechless as she regained her poise. Thorn looked at her, waiting silently, as Jenny came out to Rose's car, and they got in and left. Once they disappeared, Thorn walked toward his truck.

TWO ROWS DOWN, a very shocked Anna had witnessed

the entire scene from her rental car. She knew, now. Her daddy was in deep, maybe too deep for anyone's help this time. Grandpa and Grandma weren't here to save him this go round. But from the looks of things, it didn't appear he wanted anyone's help at all.

— 26 —

"THANKS, JENNY. YOU were a real lifesaver getting us out of The Big Griddle so quickly." Rose patted her friend on the arm, profuse in her gratitude.

Jenny mumbled, "You're welcome," as she tried to stay awake on the way back to her friend's home. There was no traffic at that early hour, and they arrived at Rose's house in less than twenty minutes.

By the time Rose opened the door and turned off the alarm, Jenny was already headed to the guest bedroom. She quickly changed into her sleeping shorts and was off to bed. Being in the middle of Rose and Thorn's tumultuous relationship had taken a toll on her. She couldn't keep pace with their emotional roller coaster connection. As soon as her head hit the pillow, she was asleep.

Rose, on the other hand, was completely awake, with adrenalin coursing through her veins. Thorn had surprised her by not being his usual aggressive self. He'd seemed to consider her feelings. It was as if he had changed from an ogre to a human in just a few short hours.

She snuggled into her favorite chair in the family room

and thanked God for the change He'd brought about, not only in her, but also in Thorn. She knew it took someone greater than them to help keep their emotions in check. She picked up her Bible from the coffee table where she left it each day after reading her devotionals and opened it to the verse that said, "All things work together for good to them who love the Lord and are called according to his purpose." She thought about what God was saying to her in that verse. It meant that in every situation, God would use the events for good in her life. That meant even this weekend with Thorn. According to God's Word, it would, in some way, bring something positive into her life. Rose closed her eyes and smiled. God would truly have to do a miracle for that to happen.

HER RINGING PHONE woke her. Roxanne was on the line.

"Are you going to church this morning? If so, do you want us to pick you up?"

"Well, um . . ." Rose tried to focus on the time but couldn't think where she'd put her watch.

Roxanne asked Jack a question Rose couldn't hear, and then she continued, "I still haven't got my make-up on or my hair done. It would be at least half an hour before we could come by. Would you like that?"

"That will be perfect. I'll leave the car for Jenny, if she wakes up and decides to go early to see her brother. I'll see you in about thirty minutes." Rose hung up the phone and found her watch on the chairside table. She was relieved to see she'd been asleep for almost three hours.

She hurried to her bedroom, trying to decide what to wear. She considered one of her more casual outfits, because she was short on time and wouldn't need to put on hose. She had a couple of almost floor length cotton print dresses. She selected one with turquoise accents, to go with her new sandals and matching purse.

She quickly applied her make-up, using what Jenny

had left in her bathroom last night. She was spraying cologne when she heard her cell phone ring. She answered to Roxanne on the line.

"Honey, we're right outside. Are you still planning on riding with us? If you're short on time, we can go on, if you want."

Rose asked them to wait just a minute, and she scribbled a note to Jenny and attached it to her door. Rose closed the front door after her, making sure it was locked, and she hurried outside to Jack and Roxanne's waiting car.

They arrived at church with only minutes to spare before the morning service. They usually made it to Sunday school as well, but after the debacle yesterday, they couldn't feel too guilty. The threesome found their way inside and were pleased to see their usual spot unoccupied as they slid into their seats.

Different ones waved and smiled across the congregation as they sat down. They noticed some were continuing to smile and wave, and when they turned to see, they discovered Thorn coming down their aisle. It seemed he was heading right for their pew.

As he stepped next to Rose, he asked, "Mind if I join you?"

Rose was too bewildered to answer the question.

Roxanne's jaw dropped, and Jack scratched his head, as he leaned around and answered, "Of course not. We're glad you could be here."

Thoughts swirled in Rose's head. What was Thorn doing at her church? Didn't he know this was a house of God?

The senior pastor opened with prayer. Rose was so taken back by Thorn's appearance she hardly heard the poignant words resonating through the hushed sanctuary until the loud "Amen" was repeated by the worshippers. Thorn's deep voice vibrated in her ears as he affirmed the prayer with the rest of the congregation. Rose was more surprised than ever, first that Thorn would even be in church, but more so that he would give a confirming word at the end of the prayer.

The praise and worship service began with several new choruses interspersed with traditional hymns. Surprisingly, Thorn kept up with most of the music. Rose did her best to concentrate on the service, but it was next to impossible with Thorn at her side. She could feel him glancing at her from time to time, and his breath brushed her forehead as he sang some of the songs.

She was acutely uncomfortable.

Roxanne reached over and squeezed her hand for support. That helped some. But for the most part, she felt like it was just Thorn and her standing alone in the vast building.

Finally, the congregation was seated, and the offertory prayer was given. A beautiful hymn was played. Thorn bumped Rose getting out his billfold, and she did her best to ignore the simple brush of his leg against hers.

Even here in church, she felt a current of electricity rush through her.

— 27 —

AS THE SERVICE continued, Thorn became more relaxed. His parents were Christians, but he had been raised in a more formal faith. They had attended every Sunday morning. His mother had served on the local church board. No matter where they were stationed in the U.S., his parents had always located a church they felt comfortable with and transferred their membership to that congregation.

In contrast, Rose's church with its more relaxed atmosphere and feeling of family made Thorn wish this was how he'd been brought up. The pastor gave a simple message of faith, hope, and peace. He didn't use a lot of flowery words or disconnected stories. His straightforward approach touched Thorn's heart. He then gave an invitation to anyone who would like to have the peace he spoke about to join him at the front.

Thorn thought about all the years of unhappiness he'd experienced. He remembered all the hurts and disappointments he'd survived. He was tired of carrying the burdens himself. If what this pastor said was true, he could rid himself of all his cumbersome emotional weights once and for all. He wouldn't have to use Rose to have closure in his life. God would take care of that for him.

Without another thought, he stood and made his way to the front of the church where a few others had already gathered. The pastor and several members collected around each individual and prayed with them. The senior pastor came and stood with Thorn. He questioned him about his salvation. The minister offered him a new relationship with God and the world around him.

Thorn accepted Christ as his personal savior and released his past to him. He felt like he was a newborn baby. All the cares of the world seemed to float away. Never in his life had he felt like he was finally free of all the entanglements life had bound him up with. Tears of joy streamed down his face. He was exactly what the pastor had described, a new creature in Christ.

Everyone at the front of the church hugged him, while the congregation cheered for the new converts. It felt to Thorn as though he was the only one there. Then he looked where he'd been sitting. Jack and Roxanne were still there, but Rose was gone.

ROSE HAD QUIETLY disappeared as soon as Thorn went forward. She was in the ladies' lounge trying to process the series of events taking place in the auditorium.

Did Thorn really intend to accept Christ as his savior, or was he doing this as a show to impress her? What made Thorn pick this day and this time to make a decision for Christ? She had so many doubts about herself, how could she trust anyone else?

When she emerged from the lounge, the first person she saw was Roxanne. Her friend stepped up to her and put her arm around her shoulder.

"There you are. We were beginning to think you had walked home. Are you okay? We were getting worried about you, especially Thorn. Isn't this wonderful, that he got saved today? After everything that happened at the reunion, Thorn's changed his life around." Roxanne seemed to bubble with joy and enthusiasm.

Rose fought her emotions as she pulled her friend back into the lounge. She wanted to speak her mind, but not in front of the entire church. Once inside, she let her anger erupt.

"Oh, yeah. That's great for him. He can just walk away guilt-free and not be responsible for anything in his past." Rose spat the words with an edge. She hardly believed Thorn would change, and she was sure her face told her feelings.

Her attitude took Roxanne by surprise. "Why, Rose. I thought you'd be pleased with anyone who found Christ as his savior. I'm really disappointed by your reaction."

Rose felt her eyes burn with emotion. She knew she should be overjoyed about anyone who entered the kingdom, but this was Thorn. He couldn't be trusted.

She turned to Roxanne, "I am. It's just that, well, I'm not sure I believe Thorn's confession is real. He's done so many things to hurt me, I wouldn't put anything past him." She paused to run her fingers around her eyes, and then she continued, "I truly hope his decision for Christ is genuine."

"All we can do his pray for him. He'll need it, judging by his daughter's behavior last night," Roxanne added, as they exited the ladies' lounge. Rose said nothing, but in her mind, there was no daughter, just a cruel hoax.

They headed to the parking lot and found Jack waiting for them. Thorn was nowhere to be seen. Rose breathed a sigh of relief. At least she wouldn't have to face him right now. If she was lucky, she might be able to avoid him altogether. She hadn't seen him for forty years, so why not make it another forty before they made contact again?

— 28 —

THORN PULLED INTO the hotel parking lot. The sign towered over the building, and it caught the sun, reflecting it onto the cars in the lot. Several high clouds danced across the sky, caught in wind currents that had yet to make it to ground level. He drove past several vehicles until he came to an empty spot just down from the entrance. He had a lot on his mind he wanted to share with his daughter. He used the key fob to lock the truck and headed inside through the glass entrance doors. Waiting on the elevator, he whistled a light-hearted tune, and he greeted the couple exiting before stepping inside and pressing the button for his floor. He whistled a new tune as he approached Anna's door. After a quick knock, he identified himself, and his daughter let him in.

"How's Sam doing these days?" Thorn smiled as he inquired politely. "I know he's been working out of town, and I'm sorry he couldn't come with you."

"I suppose he's fine. I haven't spoken with him today. Don't you look all bright and shining? Daddy, where have you been? I hope it's not out with her. She broke your heart before, and she'll do it again. I know her kind, and so did Grandmother."

Thorn listened patiently, and he continued to smile and wait for his daughter to finish her tirade. He knew she didn't like her mother, but that was based on the information she'd been fed by her grandmother. He was here to set the record straight, as well as to tell her about his newfound faith. One had everything to do with Rose, and the other had nothing to do with his Rose Petal.

Finally, Anna stopped and stared at him. "You haven't heard a word I just said, have you?"

"Well, most of it," her father admitted, with a sheepish grin. "But what I want to know is if you're going to listen to me." Thorn searched his daughter's face for an answer.

"I always listen to you; I just don't always follow your advice," Anna replied honestly, looking intently into her father's eyes.

"This is one time I really want you to pay close attention to what I'm about to say." Thorn knew it was vital to have her focused on his words and not on her feelings about Rose.

ANNA COULD TELL by the somber expression he wore that her dad had something of importance he wanted to share. She sat on the bed across from him, pulling one leg under her. "Okay, Dad. I'm ready."

Thorn leaned forward, resting his elbows on his knees. "This morning, for the first time in a long time, I went to church. It wasn't for the right reason. I went to see Rose Petal.

"I knew she attended that particular church, because Jack had told me the three of them went together. Jack and Roxanne have been members there for years. Rose just started attending this past year. While I was there, something wonderful happened." Thorn reached across and took his daughter's hand as he spoke.

"Anna, I accepted Christ as my personal savior and

have been born again." He stopped and wiped a lone tear from one eye. "It's the greatest feeling I've ever experienced in my life. Just knowing I don't have to fight my battles alone, and that my past is forgiven forever is almost unbelievable." Thorn took time to pull a tissue from the bedside table and pat his eyes. "This has nothing to do with your mother and me; this has to do with a new relationship between God and me. I'm a true Christian now, honey."

Anna couldn't believe what she was hearing. Her father had gotten religion and was now calling himself a Christian? He'd abandoned that years ago.

"Did she coerce you to do this? What feminine wiles did she pull to get you into this position?" Anna didn't believe this at all, and she pressed her father for answers. "I've seen her in action, and she's pretty slick. She had to have said or done something that would make you want to become a Christian."

Anna's laced her tirade with sarcasm, and she stood and faced the window. The shears were drawn, but the light-blocking shades were open, and she could see hazy activity on the streets.

"Actually, sweetie, she had nothing to do with it. She won't talk to me, and she certainly didn't want me to sit by her during the service. It was just knowing how tired I am of everything in my life. I've wanted a change for a long time. I just didn't know how to go about it. When the pastor spoke this morning with such conviction and assurance, I knew what I wanted. So, I went to the front and gave my heart and life to God. When I went back to my seat, Rose Petal wasn't there, and I haven't seen her since." Thorn peered into his daughter's face, as if trying to read her thoughts.

Anna just stared back, astonished by what she'd heard. Her father's ex-wife had nothing to do with his decision; he'd done it all on his own. Wasn't that a hoot? Maybe it was just leftover desire from the parking lot this morning.

Anna knew her dad must be trying to impress his first wife, even if he wasn't aware of it. She hoped he wasn't desperate enough to do something even more rash just to make an impact on her.

"Dad, let me clarify, you're sure you're not doing this to get, hmm, my *mother's* attention?" She had a difficult time saying the word.

"Anna, it's like I told you. My decision for Christ has nothing to do with my relationship with your mother, who by the way really thought you were stillborn."

The change of subject immediately stirred Anna's emotions. "Just because she says something doesn't make it true. I don't care how hard you try to convince me, Dad. It just won't work." She lashed out at him. "You've never denied what Grandma and Grandpa said. Why now are you suddenly having second thoughts?" She flipped her hair as she glared at him.

"One reason is the expression she wore when she saw you and tried to put the pieces of the puzzle together. The other reason is this." Thorn reached into his pocket and pulled out the birth certificate that Jenny had given him. He carefully unfolded it. "Read this," he said, as he pushed it into his daughter's hand.

Anna glanced at it. "Who is Gilland James Bruton, Jr, and why do you have his birth certificate?"

"He's Rose Petal's son, your half-brother." Thorn spoke quietly.

Anna was silent as she studied the document for several seconds. "So, what am I supposed to be looking for?"

Thorn reached to point out the part where it showed a previous stillborn birth.

Anna handed it back to him and laughed. "This doesn't prove anything. Anyone can forge these."

Her father replied, "I know. That's why I'm going to the county tomorrow and get another one issued. This one is notarized, so I believe it's real. But I intend to make sure."

"You can do anything you want, Dad, but it still won't convince me. Maybe she didn't want a girl, and that's why she kept her other baby. After all, it was a boy. All I know is she didn't want me, period."

"OH, HONEY, YOU can't know that." Thorn wanted to give his daughter a hug, but before he could stand, she turned to him with pain on her face.

"You can betray my love for you and try to get back with her, but I'll never be a part of her life. She didn't want me then, and I don't want her now." Anna's voice was ragged, and her eyes were on the edge of tears. She finished in a torrent of emotion, finally releasing tears to gush down her cheeks.

Thorn leaped to his feet and hugged his daughter close. He loved her more than anything. He didn't want to do anything to hurt her, but he had to find answers of his own. He had to know the truth, and the more he thought about it, the more he realized how naïve he'd been. He'd never tried to talk to Rose after that one time, taking everything his parents had said as truth.

Now, looking back, he'd never do that as an adult. He would have questioned her himself and made her say she didn't love him or want him ever again. Holding his daughter and feeling her pain made him more determined than ever to get to the bottom of this unresolved issue that had eaten forty years of their lives.

He would start tomorrow. He wasn't leaving town until the truth was known, no matter how ugly or sordid it was.

— 29 —

"BY THE WAY, I saw you this morning at The Big Griddle." Anna said the words as an accusation, and also to make her father aware she wasn't clueless.

Thorn smiled as he patted Anna's arm. "I saw you, too, sitting in your car. If you hadn't been there staring, a whole lot more might have happened between your mother and me."

"But Daddy, you had her in your arms. She wasn't even touching the ground."

"I know. That way, Rose Petal couldn't get away. I've always had to do that to keep her captive. She's never been the type to come after me."

"Daddy!"

"It's not something I was even aware of before I came to the reunion, but the truth is, Anna, I still love Rose Petal. I think I have all these years. I think that's the reason I've never been happy with anyone else, no matter how hard they tried to love me. I just didn't love them the way I love your mother. She does something to me no other woman can."

"How can you love someone who's mean and hurtful and just uses people to get her way?" Anna's bitterness pierced her words.

Thorn thought for a moment before answering. "I think it must be the way God loves us. Unconditionally. He sees our true heart, the one He created for loving Him. That's why I was so relieved to become a part of His love today. According to the pastor, He never gives up on us. God is always there waiting to accept us as we are. Sure, your mother and I had problems in our marriage. We were so young and inexperienced, but I always loved her, and I believe she loved me."

"You can't mean that, after what she did." Anna was incredulous.

Thorn paused for a second and gave the only answer he had to give. "I'm the one who loved her. Your grandparents always disliked her immensely."

"It's because they saw her for what she was, a user," Anna spat.

"How was she a user, Anna? Was it her idea to get pregnant? No, she's the one who begged me to wait and tried to get me to slow down. She never attempted anything to persuade me to be intimate with her. Her parents were very strict. She had to dress very modestly and be in by ten on a date night.

"We only stayed out late because of the prom, and it was only that one time. Then it was her parents that came and confronted mine about doing the right thing. Your grandparents didn't want us to marry. They just wanted her family stationed elsewhere, content for her to have the baby by herself, illegitimate or not. But I loved her, Anna. I loved your mother. We got married, despite my parents. And those next seven months were the happiest in my life. No, your mother didn't use me. If anything, I used her."

Anna dropped on the bed. This wasn't what she'd expected. Her father wasn't just in love with her mother, but he was deeply in love with her. He defended her on every turn. He was telling stories that were totally contrary to her grandparents' tales. Surely her Dad didn't expect her to think everything he was saying was true.

"So, how long are you going to stay here?" Anna needed to know how bad this could get.

"Until I get the whole truth and the answers to every question I have about my marriage, your birth, and my divorce from your mother." Thorn spoke with such conviction it startled his daughter. "So, however long that is, that's how long I'll be here. It might be a week or maybe a month, I don't know. But when I do leave, it'll be because my heart and mind are both satisfied."

Anna sighed. He was grown up, after all. She knew she didn't have enough power over him to change this, and she did have a flight to catch.

"I guess your mind is made up. Will you at least take me to the airport, so I can catch my plane back home?" She was no longer sure how her father would answer.

"Of course, sweetie. I'll be happy to see you off. Will Sam be there to pick you up? You know I wouldn't leave you stranded. You may not understand this right now, but I'm doing this for the both of us. When I get back, I'll be a better person. I want us to be able to enjoy the rest of our lives without any regrets. It's because I love you so much that I have to do this."

"Don't you worry about Sam." She laughed sourly. "Thanks, Daddy. I know you love me, and I appreciate it. I love you, too."

THORN SMILED AT Anna as he spoke. He loved his daughter and wanted her to know the truth, so they could both find peace and contentment in their future.

— 30 —

ROSE WAS UP and dressed when she heard Jenny pull into the driveway. Her friend had left to see her brother before Rose returned from church, and Rose was grateful. She had needed a nap, and her exhaustion had taken over. Not only was she physically tired, but also drained emotionally from her confrontation with Thorn during the service. She had barely gotten in the door and eaten a sandwich, before she found herself dozing off in the living room. She'd given up, undressed, and crawled into her bed.

Now she felt much better. She glanced at the clock, realizing she'd slept nearly four hours. Jenny rang the doorbell, and when Rose unlocked the door, she came through with a smile on her face.

"Thanks for loaning me your car. It was so good to see my brother again. I hardly recognized my own niece, she looks so much like an adult now. It's amazing how time passes so quickly. And speaking of time, I've got to get my things together and get to the airport pretty soon."

"Yes, we need to leave in the next forty-five minutes

to be there to catch your flight. Praise God, there are no showers predicted for your flight home. That's the last thing you need after a weekend like this."

Jenny nodded her head and went straight to the guest room to gather her things. Minutes later she reappeared, ready to depart. "Do you mind if we stop and grab a few snacks for the flight? I don't want my blood sugar to get out of whack."

"Of course, not. I'll be happy to stop on the way," Rose replied with a smile.

Minutes later, they were headed for the terminal and Jenny's flight home. Rose insisted on helping Jenny check her bags with the skycap. As they approached the check-in booth, they both stopped short.

Directly in front of them were Thorn and his daughter. Even from a distance, there was no mistaking her resemblance to Rose. Without all the heavy make-up from the banquet, it was easy to see her defined cheekbones and large eyes. Her slightly turned-up nose was an exact copy of Rose's.

Rose swallowed hard, as Jenny squeezed her hand and said, "Don't worry, they'll be gone in just a few minutes, and your life will get back to normal. Just hang on a little longer, and this whole ordeal will be over."

Rose nodded and drew in another sharp breath. They watched as Thorn hugged his daughter good-bye, and she headed through airport security. Jenny and Rose checked Jenny's bags, and Jenny gave Rose a quick hug and reassured her Thorn would be gone soon, as well. Then she stepped through security and toward her flight.

No sooner had Jenny disappeared out of sight than Rose heard Thorn, or felt him, or perhaps it was a little of both. He was there beside her walking in step with her toward her car.

"Did you stay to see Jenny off?" he questioned her, in a conversational and pleasant tone.

"Yes," she replied brusquely, hoping he'd tell her he

would be checking his bags and heading through security soon. Rose continued toward her car and her life without him. Thorn kept up the easy pace next to her. Finally, exasperated, she turned and questioned him, "What time is your plane departure?"

"Oh, Rose Petal, I'm not going anywhere for a while. There's too many memories here I want to explore. I plan to stay in our little town until I get all the answers I want." With that, he smiled and put his arm around her waist, stopping her in her tracks.

"Thorn, this isn't appropriate." She glanced around to see who might be watching.

"Rose, hear me out. Something happened in your church that's never happened in my life before. I feel different. I tried to explain it to Anna, but she refused to accept it. She thinks it's some plot you're using against me, or that I'm trying to win you with this so-called religion. But it's neither." He gave Rose one of his piercing gazes. "I've accepted Christ as my savior, Rose, and now I need to know that you've forgiven me as well. I think we need to have a long and serious talk about what happened forty years ago."

Rose just stared at him. Why would he want to have a talk now? There was nothing left to say. She just wanted him to go away. She was glad he'd found Jesus, but he needed to share his newfound joy somewhere else.

"Well, what do you say? Is there?" Thorn probed her, as if she hadn't been listening.

"Oh, uh, Thorn. I didn't hear you. What did you ask?" Rose was infuriated that this man could make her lose focus like that.

Thorn repeated, "I asked you if there was a place where we could be in private, undisturbed by anyone or anything. I would offer my hotel room, but I think it might be a little uncomfortable with just a king size bed. I didn't order the suite like our daughter did."

"There's no daughter, Thorn, and I can't believe you

expect me to want to discuss anything with you after this weekend." Rose took in a deep breath and turned from him, wincing at the word "our." Why was he playing these mind games with her? What was he trying to accomplish?

"All I want to do is talk, Rose; honestly, I need to know the truth from your lips, not what someone told me you said. I made that mistake before, and I won't let it happen again."

Rose turned to look at him. His jaw was set, and his face was determined. She'd seen that expression enough in their brief marriage to realize he was through talking about it. Only action would do now. She wouldn't have any peace from him unless she talked with him, even though there was nothing to say. He would keep bugging her, and she really wanted this to be over. She couldn't take much more of Thorn without something happening.

She also wanted to get home, so she agreed to have him meet her at her house in an hour.

— 31 —

THE FIRST THING on Rose's list once she got home was to freshen up. Afterward, she made a pitcher of iced tea and cut a slice of lemon meringue pie from the one she'd kept at home. With that in front of Thorn, maybe he'd have something to do besides think of ways to lie to her. When the doorbell rang nearly an hour later, she said a prayer, took a deep breath, and opened the door.

Thorn took up the whole opening with his broad shoulders.

"Come into the kitchen. I thought we'd be more comfortable there," Rose offered.

THORN FOLLOWED HER to the breakfast nook and to the waiting piece of pie and iced tea. He sat down slowly and let his whole body relax.

This was what he'd always wanted, to be with Rose, together and alone. It felt like home to him. No man could ever ask for more than the love of a sweet woman. That's what Rose had always been, sweet. Even when she was angry, he thought she was cute, and he'd told her so.

That, of course, only made her angrier, and she'd often start a fight that would end up with them falling asleep in each other's arms. That antique brass bed was only a double. He'd slept at an angle with Rose in his arms, so she wouldn't tumble off.

The memory of them together made him smile.

ROSE ON THE other hand was uncomfortable in the silence of her kitchen. She'd wanted this to be as quick and painless as possible. She'd tried to anticipate his every move to stall this conversation. He'd want a drink, or he'd be hungry. Would she have a snack? She had his tea and pie sitting on the table waiting for him.

Now maybe they could get down to business.

"Well, what do we need to talk about?" Rose asked anxiously.

Thorn looked at her and replied, "Do you still have that antique brass bed your grandmother gave us?"

Rose was stunned. What did that have to do with forty years ago? "Yes, I still do. It's set up in the guest room."

"I was just thinking of how difficult it was to get comfortable until—"

Rose immediately interrupted him. "Thorn, we didn't come here to discuss our sleeping habits from our brief marriage."

"I don't remember getting much sleep back then." He bored into her with his obsidian eyes, and he smiled until Rose turned her head away.

"I didn't invite you here for a walk down memory lane. I thought you said you had some questions you wanted answered. But if this is what you came to discuss, you need to finish your pie and leave."

"Whenever I see a lemon pie, I always think of you, sweet and luscious with a bite to it." Thorn took a bite of the pie and slowly brought it to his lips. He grinned as he swallowed it, followed by a gulp of tea.

Rose crossed her arms. She would have to wait him

out. No one ever rushed Thorn or pushed him into anything he didn't want. Finally, he took his last swallow of tea.

"THANKS, ROSE PETAL. That was good."

Thorn stared at her a moment, thinking a thousand thoughts about how he wished life had been different, but cold reality had brought him here. He needed answers; he needed closure.

But would it be possible, if he still loved and wanted that person as much as ever? He'd reached that conclusion about his own feelings only hours after seeing her again. The desires and aches that had driven him then were still there.

He knew his heart had to have answers, no matter the outcome. He braced himself for what she might say, and he let his biggest question roll off his tongue.

"Rose Petal, did you want to marry me, or did you do it only because you were pregnant and felt a responsibility for the baby to have a last name?"

Thorn finally had his cards out on the table.

ROSE STARED AT him, and she was totally shocked. She couldn't imagine he'd even ask that. She chose her words carefully. There could be no mistake in her reply.

Softly, she let her words escape, "It was because of my love for you that I wanted to marry you and have your baby. Thorn, you were my world back then. That was why I was so devastated when you left me. I knew then you'd only married me out of obligation and not love. Then, when the baby was stillborn, you'd found your opportunity, and you used it as an excuse to leave."

Rose finished almost inaudibly, but she didn't cry. She wouldn't cry. She'd done all that forty years ago. These were just fragile memories dragged out of her past.

She waited in the silence for a response, and when she looked up, she noticed the appalled expression on Thorn's face.

"Rose, stop and repeat what you just said about me leaving you. Say it again real slow. I want to make sure I heard you right. Don't leave out any details. Start at the hospital."

"Your parents came in the hospital room and told me the baby was stillborn, and the only reason you married me was because I was having your baby. Since the baby didn't survive, you wanted nothing to do with me. The biggest favor I could do their son was to honor his wishes and leave him alone.

"They said they'd take care of any incidentals regarding the death, and they hoped they never saw me again. Your mother insisted how much better off everyone would be this way.

"Then a nurse walked in and asked her to leave, so I could get some rest, explaining that I'd been through a hard ordeal. The nurse checked my vital signs and went to get me some water. You suddenly appeared and acted like everything was fine. You just wanted to give me a little good-bye kiss.

"I was almost hysterical at that point. I was distraught over the loss of our baby, then your mother being so cold and dismissive about it made me hurt all the more. At that moment, I never wanted to see your face again. I'd just lost our baby, and instead of you being supportive and caring, you walked away like nothing had happened. All you wanted was a good-bye kiss from me.

"In my heart, that was the last thing I would ever give you."

— 32 —

THORN COULDN'T HAVE appeared more alarmed if someone had just hit him in the head with a baseball bat. He looked glassy-eyed and almost like he was about to pass out. Rose could immediately see something was terribly wrong.

"Thorn, are you okay? What's wrong? Do you want me to call 9-1-1?"

He made no response, just kept staring ahead. After a couple of seconds, Rose became anxious. She tried to talk to him again.

"Thorn, answer me. Are you okay?"

He collapsed against her, almost pushing her off her chair. He made a deep, heaving, moaning sound. He remained motionless, but Rose could feel his warm breath against her neck. Finally, he spoke in a slow and labored way, as if suffering from great pain.

"Oh, Rose Petal, my sweet, precious Rose Petal. Never did I want to be divorced or away from you, never!" He growled intensely as he kept his head buried against her shoulder.

Rose listened in complete surprise. That wasn't what his parents had told her.

Thorn slowly raised his head to gaze into Rose's eyes. "Rose, our baby wasn't stillborn. Roseanna is your daughter. My parents came out of the hospital room and told me you didn't want to see the baby, and you hated me for ruining your figure and your life. They also said you never wanted to see me again. That was why I was so desperate to get in to see you. But when I was finally able to go to you, the damage was done. You hated me; I could see it in your eyes. But I hoped that if I could get close enough to kiss you, it would be okay. I just wanted to touch you and make everything the way it was before. I wanted us to be a couple. I wanted us to raise our baby together.

"Instead, my parents raised her until their deaths when she was fourteen. By then, they had poisoned her against you forever. That's become my greatest fear. I was so lost and hurt without you, I signed up for military service. I didn't care what happened to me at that point. It was only when I got back and saw your sweet face reflected in our child that I could feel anything at all."

Thorn took Rose's hand and pressed it to his face. It was only after several minutes that he went on.

"Oh, baby. If I'd only known, I promise I'd have never left you. I didn't realize how mean and vindictive my parents were until it was too late. Even with Roseanna, they tried to poison her against me. They wouldn't let her come and live with my second wife and me. Roseanna was eight, then. But it was just as well. The marriage only lasted a couple of years. I couldn't seem to get you out of my head. At night I'd wake up saying your name. My second wife didn't appreciate that. She wanted more than I had to give."

By then, Rose was in shock. "Don't lie to me, Thornton Jebulon Wilder, not about this. Please don't lie to me," she pleaded, tears flooding her eyes, as she searched his face for some kind of revelation. Even without his words, she could tell from his haggard expression he was telling the truth as he knew it.

This changed everything and, even so, it changed nothing. The damage was done forty years ago. How could anyone have been so cruel? Why would anyone want to hurt a young girl who was in love with the only man she'd ever desired? Now all she could do was regret what might have been. Her shoulders drooped as large, salty tears slipped down her face and chin.

Thorn pulled her hand to his lips, and as he kissed it, she clung to his hand. She began to sob with the pain of all the years gone so wrong.

"Oh, Rose Petal, baby. Please don't cry, baby. Please don't. I didn't know, honest. I would have never left you, no matter what my parents tried to do." Thorn brushed the moisture from her warm, tear-stained cheeks. Rose couldn't resist him. She needed him. She leaned in to him, in an action brought on by desperation and hope.

Thorn brushed his lips against hers, before pulling away. "Rose, this isn't what I want. I want a real relationship with you. Not the one we had when we were kids, but a mature takes-whatever-life-brings-us kind of relationship. And as hard and difficult as this is, I should leave now. But I want you for now and forever. I realized it when I kissed you at the airport; I've never truly stopped loving you. I'm as impassioned by you now as I ever was. I'm not prepared to lose you, and I want our relationship to be right this time. I also want to have God's blessing and guidance in our lives. We still have a lot of obstacles to conquer. You and I have several questions about us to resolve. In addition, there's our daughter as well as our future together."

Rose knew he was right. He made her feel like no other man had ever made her feel. All the years of dealing with his rejection had made her insecure and lonely. She didn't even believe in true love anymore. She had thought that was what she and Thorn had shared when they were young. Then, it had been cruelly shredded before her eyes in the hospital, in as cold and calculating a way as possible. Now she was afraid to consider loving again, but she wanted to.

She struggled with the idea they could have a daughter, as the doctor had said the baby was stillborn. As she held Thorn's hand, she tried to recall everything she could about that fateful day. She only vaguely remembered the doctor. She'd been in so much pain, and then she'd been put to sleep.

Now that she thought about it, she only remembered Thorn's parents telling her about the baby being stillborn. She didn't remember the doctor saying that. She didn't even remember seeing the doctor after the delivery. Was Thorn's version of what happened the truth? Had his parents lied?

Surely there was proof of this somewhere. There had to be an answer to all these questions.

"The birth certificate, Thorn. I have to see the birth certificate." Rose spoke softly, as she moved away from him, giving her bruised emotions a chance to recover.

"What, Rose Petal? What about the birth certificate?" Thorn released her as she moved.

Rose looked him directly in the eyes and insisted, "I need to see our baby's original birth certificate. I never got a copy. I requested one several times. It was always the same response, that no such record had been documented. Now I want to see exactly what happened that cold January day. I want real answers from you, Thorn, before I'll ever believe Anna is my child. I want to believe it. I really do. But I must see the proof and then figure out how a doctor could pull off such a thing in a hospital. Before we get any further along, I need some answers, for my peace of mind. I must have them! Better yet, I want a DNA test run. I can't live with this uncertainty in my heart. I have to reach a conclusion about all this, one that I can accept."

Thorn replied, "So do I, Rose Petal. So do I."

— 33 —

THORN LEFT ROSE'S house more confused than when he arrived. He had solved no problems. He'd only created more for himself. He was certain Anna wouldn't consent to a DNA test, not as angry as she was at Rose. Then, he'd practically told Rose he was still in love with her, but she hadn't returned his feelings, not verbally.

He wanted her to love him. He knew he couldn't be in the same room without wanting her. He also realized that if he was ever going to have a chance with her, it would take time and effort to prove his love and win her trust.

He was certain there was still a spark between them. He wanted to be with her, and she must want to be with him, at least in some small way. Where there was a spark, a flame could be fanned. At the picnic, just touching hands had energized them both.

But it would take more than sparks to set their love ablaze. Thorn would need to find cold hard evidence, facts that would possibly change how he felt about his parents, and possibly alter Anna's life forever.

His daughter might not find it in herself to forgive

him, but like Rose, Thorn had to know the truth, and Anna needed to know as well.

IN THE SECURITY of her Austin stone home outside Round Rock, Rose sat in the deepening shadows of the late evening recounting the day's events. This hadn't been a typical Sunday by any means. Thorn had become a Christian, which alone was a wonderful, miraculous occurrence. But then to hear Thorn say their baby hadn't died was more than Rose could fathom. How many times had she thought that if only their child had lived, then maybe she and Thorn would have stood a chance, no matter how rocky their marriage had started?

Later, when she gave birth to Gill, Jr., she couldn't even answer the doctor's questions about her previous delivery. She'd explained to him how large the baby had been, and due to her own small size, she had been put under a strong anesthetic. She'd been in agony for days before she finally delivered.

Now to be told that her baby had survived and was alive was almost too much for Rose's heart and brain to absorb. She'd seen Anna, and yes, she did look like her, but her mind was unable to accept Anna as her child. Too many years of suffering with the pain and loss of her baby interfered. Rose knew she had to find the truth.

The sun was shining outside, and the dappling shadows sprinkled the last of the evening light across Rose's living room. She had no lights on yet, and the gathering gloom was a perfect muse to Rose's meandering thoughts. As she sat in her suede side chair, the phone rang.

"Yes, this is Rose."

"I made it safely. I'm home"

"Jenny?" Rose glanced at her phone to see her friend's name on the Caller ID window.

"Of course, it's me. What's wrong, Rose?"

Rose shared with her the information Thorn had told her earlier in the day. "Jenny, I gave him up for forty years. I was devastated by a man I loved with all my heart. Now I find he felt the same way about me. We never knew."

Rose wiped the tears from her face, as silence filled the phone.

Jenny whispered, "Rose, what are you going to do?"

"I can't trust him, Jenny. I can't throw away forty years of distrust in one weekend. I hate it that I still feel attracted to him, but I must admit I do. Yet, I have this snake of hate in my stomach tearing at me each time I'm around him. You know, like yin and yang."

"Yin and yang, Rose?"

Rose laughed, but it was one of near hysteria, not humor. "I'm sorry, Jenny. An old college term. Opposites. That's me. My heart wants Thorn, and I have four decades of distrust inside. No, I have four decades of hate that I've boxed up and pushed into the back corners of my mind. Now that man is trying to rip those boxes open, and I'm afraid of what might come out."

As the shadows in Rose's living room deepened, a light in the tree outside her window clicked on. Moments later, a small table lamp in the front hall came on as a timer attached to the plug shifted position.

Muted light filtered around Rose, creating a cocoon of light to cradle her distress.

"I need proof, Jenny. Not just Thorn's assurances. I told him I wanted a DNA test. Oh, Jenny. Forty years wasted. What if they didn't have to be thrown away? I loved Gill, Jenny, and I won't take that away from him. However, I should have been with Thorn all those years."

"Have you spoken to God about it? You've told me how much you trust His protection on your life."

Jenny listened as Rose did just that.

"God, please give me guidance. I've been without direction for two-thirds of my life. If Thorn's parents did this, I have no recourse against them. I only have you. I love this man, and I also know love cuts like a knife. Right now, he's slicing out my heart."

"Rose, honey," Jenny cautioned. "What if Thorn's telling the truth?"

"Jenny, I don't know. I told him I needed proof before we took our relationship anywhere." Rose sniffled as she gathered her emotions underneath her fragile shell of self-control and security.

Jenny was silent for a moment. Then she pressed Rose, "How does Thorn plan to prove all this, if it's really true? His parents are dead, and that military hospital has been closed for years. What does Thorn have to even start on?"

Rose replied in a hushed tone, "He's got her original birth certificate signed by the attending physician. Thorn said he would start from there and see if he can locate the doctor, if he's still living. From what I remember, he was fairly young at the time."

"When, Rose?" Jenny asked with bated breath. "I can barely stand the idea of waiting. I've seen you and Thorn together, and this weekend, you two needed each other like ice cream needs chocolate."

"Thorn plans to get this started first thing tomorrow. Oh, Jenny, I could have had a daughter and a son. This really boggles my mind to think about it. And if it's true, it also makes me angry and hurt to know this was kept from me. Back then all I ever wanted was for Thorn to love me and for us to be a family. Perhaps because of his parents, all that was taken from me."

Rose paused, crushed by the thought, and she had nothing more to say.

Jenny broke the silence. "I'm astounded by all the information you just shared. If all this is true, it could change yours and Thorn's future course in life. Rose, this is something you've got to find out as soon as possible. But I feel like Thorn is telling you the truth about your daughter. All of us at the reunion could see the resemblance she bore to you. She's a carbon copy, only in a larger size, Thorn-style. I don't think there's a way to duplicate that much of you without being related. I'm pretty sure she's yours."

Rose couldn't agree totally, being barely able to allow the possibility it might be true. "Maybe time will tell," was all she could say.

"Honey. Rose. This will work itself out. I'll call you next week and the next. I promise it won't be nearly a year like last time."

Rose laughed at their promise to call each other weekly. She agreed and whispered good night.

Rose got ready for bed, read her Bible, and said another prayer to God asking him for his guidance and direction. She asked for wisdom on how to handle the coming days ahead. She then laid down in her king size bed and attempted to sleep.

ON THE OTHER side of town, Thorn was trying to do the same. His prayer had been a little more desperate in nature. However, his spirit was sincere. Yet, as he lay in the darkness, sleep didn't come.

Both hearts were longing for the other, neither of them satisfied to be alone again.

— 34 —

THE NEXT FEW days passed in a blur. Thorn was online contacting various websites for more information about verifying his daughter's birth, including information on DNA tests. His number one method, he discovered, sh ould be to visit the county seat.

He also reviewed local birth announcements from nearly forty years before, as well as hospital records that had been digitized. The records clerk at the courthouse was his best ally, and he ordered and received a certified copy of Anna's birth certificate.

He called Rose and asked her to meet him.

He studied the document as he made the drive to Rose's house. *Roseanna Joy Wilder, born January 10.* It was stamped and notarized by Bell County and the state of Texas. It had been filed at the courthouse almost two months after the birth, which seemed very odd. But since she'd been born on the military base and not in the local hospital, there could have been a delay in transferring the records, according to the records clerk.

Thorn stood nervously at Rose's door, as he rang the

bell and waiting for her to answer. He was unsure how she would react. She'd doubted what he knew was true, that Anna was her daughter, and he hoped the birth certificate settled things in her mind.

"Thorn? Come in." Rose swung the door back, and she stepped aside to give him plenty of room.

"Thanks, Rose Petal." Thorn nodded his head respectfully and stepped past gingerly, hoping to keep on her good side, at least until she read what he had in his pocket.

He held his breath as Rose read the document placed in front of her. The mother was listed as Rosemary Josephine Penndel Wilder, age 18, a housewife. The father was Thornton Jebulon Wilder, age 18, a welder. The baby's weight was 10 pounds and 4 ounces, all there in black and white. The doctor's signature was difficult to read, but it appeared to be a Dr. James Allen.

It was a validation of everything Thorn had said.

ROSE STARED AT the paper as if it were invisible, and she shook her head. She kept repeating the words, "I never knew. I never knew." Tears formed in her eyes. All this time she'd lived with a loss that never existed. Yet, for her it was still a loss, because she never had the joy of experiencing her daughter's life. How could a doctor allow such a thing to happen, to let someone believe her baby had died?

She smiled a bitter smile. "At least you gave her the name I picked out for her. I thought she would be such a joy in our lives, sealing our love forever. Never did I think she would tear us apart." Rose sniffled and patted her eyes with a tissue.

"She didn't tear us apart. It was my parents," Thorn responded vehemently. "They threatened to roast me for naming her Roseanna. They wanted her to have no part of your name. But she was my child, and I insisted. So the name she has is from us, not them."

Rose gave a wan smile, the best she could do in the catastrophe that had enveloped her. At least Anna had grown up with her father's love. She'd always hoped Thorn would be a good father. But when he rejected her because of the death of their baby, she'd doubted him. Then he was deployed across the ocean, and Rose was sure he'd come back a mess if he came back at all. He certainly wouldn't be father material after fighting in battle. Now she was glad she'd been wrong. He told her his military service made him appreciate the life he had back home. He'd loved his daughter and been a good provider for her.

With the truth from the birth certificate in her hands, Rose could finally let the truth soak in, and she found it empowering. She was ready for the truth to be revealed. She, as Rosemary Wilder, had given birth to a healthy baby girl. In addition, her daughter was alive. She wanted to call Jenny, Gill, Jr., Roxanne, and the whole world just to let them know she had a daughter and a son.

Rather than rejoicing, Thorn cautioned her.

"Rose Petal, I'm not sure Anna is ready for this. From our conversation the other day, she still doesn't believe me, and for good reason. She did live with my parents all those years. She thinks you abandoned her and wanted nothing to do with her. It'll be a lot of hard work before we can convince her otherwise.

"She's always known about you. You're the one that's the victim here. We didn't know it, but you were innocent. I should have seen it ages ago, but I was so blinded by the hurt and agony over losing you that I never considered my parents being at the bottom of it.

"I had no idea they were that malicious. I knew they didn't like you, but it never crossed my mind they would go to the extreme they did. However, we can't pull those years forward and relive them. The damage is done, and now all I can do is pray that God will help Anna understand and believe the truth."

Rose slowly nodded her head in agreement. She agreed with everything Thorn had said, and she only hoped she could learn to trust him again.

She had started, but it would be a long road for Rose, as well as for their daughter.

— 35 —

ANNA HUNG UP her cell phone. Her dad had gone nuts. He was telling her that Rose had never known about her, and he was trying to convince her that her grandparents had lied to her.

Now he wanted her to submit a sample for a DNA test to prove she was who she said she was. It was crazy! How could anyone not know about her own baby and whether she'd lived or died?

After forty-five minutes on the phone with him, Anna simply disconnected the call. She'd had enough. That he was still in love with her mother was obvious, but to try to make up a lie just so they could all be one big happy family? Well, that was over the top, and Anna wouldn't hear of it.

She had never known him to be like this, so irrational. But that was what Grandmother had said when Anna was twelve, that Rose had some kind of power over her father that no one could conquer.

Anna had innocently asked what her mother was like and why they didn't like her. She could still see the reddening of her grandmother's face as she spoke.

"We got you out of there just in time. She didn't want you, and she certainly didn't know anything about raising a baby. Why your father had anything to do with her, I'll never know. It's like she was a drug. He couldn't stay away from her no matter how we tried to keep them apart. We knew she wasn't good for him, but he wouldn't listen to us until it was too late. By then, she'd trapped him by getting pregnant with you. He wouldn't leave her then, not when she was in a family way. So we let him marry her, knowing it was the biggest mistake of his life. Her parents put on a little show of trying to blame your daddy, but we knew the kind of girl she was."

"Couldn't Grandfather have requested a different posting?" Even a twelve, Anna knew how the military machine worked.

"We thought of that. The problem, however, was she was pregnant with your father's baby, and there wasn't one thing we could do about it."

Ann remembered how, from that time on, her grandmother had reinforced how awful her mother was and how she'd used her dad. But from the conversation she had with him on the phone, it didn't sound like her dad believed it had been that way at all. It sounded more like her dad was trying to push this whole family thing on her.

He must really want her to like her birth mom to go to the extremes he was talking about.

Despite this newfound change in her father's attitude toward her mother, Anna knew the truth. It was her grandparents who'd sacrificed and suffered for her well-being. They had even remained stateside when offered a better position in the Philippines.

Anna had only been about eight at the time. Her father had been newly married for a few months when her grandfather was posted to Manila. At the last minute, changes were made, and her grandparents decided to stay stateside. According to her father many years later, it was because he intended to keep her with him, and they didn't want that.

They didn't like his second wife, Julia, any better than his first. Her grandparents were constantly finding fault with her. She'd been a bit of a socialite, and that had been interesting to her grandmother at first. But when she realized that she was only interested in what made her happy and not in the Wilder family values, her grandmother's taste changed. She refused permission for Anna to go over, unless her father was there. She wouldn't let Julia take her shopping or to the zoo or any other activities unless her father was present as well.

Her grandparents seemed to resent anything Julia did for her.

After their divorce, her grandparents seemed more dominant than ever. When Anna's dad married the third time, they had nothing to do with that wife. She was a short, bossy woman, they said. But whatever the reason, Anna didn't see her father much during the brief, nine-month marriage. Anna was almost twelve at the time. After that, her father didn't marry again. It wasn't until her grandparents' death that Anna spent extended time with her father. The longest time she'd been with him before that was overnight, and that on rare occasions, maybe twice a year.

It would take more than her daddy saying her mother had wanted her. It would take cold hard facts, which she was pretty sure he wouldn't be able to supply, especially since her grandparents were the only ones at the hospital when she was born. Her daddy had dug himself into a hole he wouldn't be able to get out of, and all because of her mother, that Rosemary woman. She seemed to hold some elusive power over her father, just like her grandmother had said, and it hadn't diminished over the last forty years.

Anna rubbed her belly as she dressed for bed. She felt a great satisfaction knowing she had a new life growing inside her. It wouldn't be too much longer, and she'd have to tell her father. Her baby-belly was beginning to swell.

But one thing she did vow to herself: She'd make sure her baby felt loved and wanted, no matter what it cost. She'd see to that. Whether the baby's father was involved in its life or not, she would make sure it never lacked for love and acceptance.

Feeling more resolved than ever, Anna climbed into her bed and rubbed her nicely protruding belly as she whispered, "Goodnight my little wild thorn. Your mommy loves you."

— 36 —

"AND THAT'S WHY I did it. I'm not proud of myself, and I've had to live with the shame of my youth and fear these forty years now. It's truly been a cross to bear, but I've no one to blame but myself." Dr. James Allen looked Thorn in the eyes as his hands worked the pencil in his hand, revealing his anxiety at admitting what he'd done.

Thorn sat completely dumbfounded.

It had taken almost a month, but he had finally located a Dr. James Allen in the Bethesda, Maryland, area. After several inquiries, it was confirmed he'd practiced in Texas forty years before. Further investigation revealed he'd been the base doctor at the time of Rose's delivery.

Eventually, he'd spent several years as one of the doctors posted to the White House Medical Unit, responsible for the health of the White House staff and visitors.

That was all Thorn needed to pursue the truth. When he found the gentleman's address, he made plans to meet him, giving his name as Jebulon Thornton. He didn't want the doctor to be suspicious, in case he remembered the last name Wilder, because if Thorn's father was involved, which he strongly suspected, he didn't want the doctor to be put off from the beginning.

He scheduled their meeting on the pretext of interviewing him about his illustrious career and arranged to meet him in a local coffee house.

"How did you end up in Maryland when you started in Texas?" Thorn asked, after they were introduced.

Dr. Allen replied, "Well, I put in for a transfer, and it was granted. Texas was so desolate, and I was from the Chicago area. I had no desire to be there. So I transferred as soon as I could."

"You were awfully young to get such a transfer, weren't you? With America's military commitments across the globe, I thought all the young doctors were posting overseas. At least that's what I saw when I did my tour of duty." Thorn noticed how the doctor winced at the mention of military commitments and overseas postings.

The doctor paused, and he clasped and unclasped his hands. He took a deep breath before he replied.

"Yes, that's true, but I had a friend in the big brass section. He helped me out. You know how that is." He took a sip of water and gave a faint smile that quickly faded. He glanced down and traced the small circle of moisture from under his water glass with a bare fingertip.

Thorn questioned again, "So this friend in the military did you a favor. Did you have to do one in return? How did you pay him back?"

Thorn could read body language and knew the old man was uncomfortable with this line of questioning. He moved slightly as if getting ready to cut the interview short. Thorn decided to ask about Anna, regardless of the circumstances. He told the doctor his real name and watched him flinch at the name Wilder. He knew the old gentleman remembered his father.

He confronted him with the bizarre story of his daughter's birth. He pulled out her birth certificate to show him the evidence she'd been a live birth. The old doctor seemed to draw up even more and become wizened as Thorn spoke. He pulled a crisp white handkerchief out of his pocket and dabbed his watery, faded blue eyes.

"I knew it was wrong, and I told the general I couldn't do it. I couldn't go back in and tell that young girl her baby had died. But he assured me I didn't have to. All I had to do was disappear for a few days. He'd see I got my transfer. He knew I was afraid of an overseas posting. So many of us went over there and never came back. Those rice paddies were our cemeteries. No one was returning. I was a scared kid, and the general used it to his advantage."

The old man wiped his face. It was hard for Thorn to watch him relieve those moments. Yet, Thorn also knew this was the only way he and Rosemary, along with Anna, could ever have closure to their past and a fresh start on a new beginning.

Dr. Allen continued, "I never spoke to the girl having the baby. All I said after the delivery was, 'It's a girl,' and I left the room. I doubt the poor child even heard me, with the anesthetic she was under. I was afraid she wasn't going to make it, as large as her baby was. We had to break both of the baby's shoulders in order to deliver her. It was one of the most difficult deliveries I ever did."

The old doctor looked around, letting his eyes trace the ceiling tiles, as he recounted the harshness of his memories.

"I paid a price for what I did. I'm sure it was nothing compared to what the baby's mother endured. For years, that young mother haunted me in my dreams. I'd read or hear about a lawsuit brought on by an angry patient, and I'd panic that I could be next. I finally made peace with myself.

"After that, I never let politics or power rule my decisions. I learned a very hard lesson at a very young age.

"I'm sorry for the heartbreak it must have brought the baby's mother. But the general assured me that she was unfit to raise a child and would probably abandon it. He said he was doing the mother and the baby a favor. I had no idea what the result would be."

The old doctor sounded exhausted. He wiped his face once again, and he slipped the handkerchief into his pocket.

Indeed, there was a new peace in the doctor's appearance that Thorn hadn't noticed before. Maybe this was what he'd needed, to tell someone about the horrendous mistake of his youth and get it off his chest. He'd carried that burden far too long.

Thorn thanked him for his time, and assured him there were no ramifications from his past coming to haunt him, if he'd do one thing for him. Thorn pulled out an envelope with hair from his daughter's brush back at the hotel in Austin. He just needed to get it tested for DNA and get home and tell Rose Petal the truth.

Then he'd have to tackle Anna. That would be the challenge, getting Anna to accept the truth and realize her grandparents had lied.

— 37 —

ROSE WAS SURPRISED by the information Thorn had obtained. She knew she should have expected it; since he'd made this his mission, she knew he'd eventually uncover the truth. He had the sworn affidavit by the attending physician that her daughter, Roseanna Joy Wilder, had been a successful live birth, as well as a promise of a DNA test for further proof. In addition, he'd implicated his parents of lying and fraud to take the baby.

Rose knew now in her heart that Anna was indeed her daughter. She also realized from everything Thorn had told her that it would be a daunting task to convince Anna that Rose hadn't known about her existence. Despite that, Thorn said he was determined to make her understand, no matter what.

He also said some other things that had Rose's heart in a flutter.

"Rose Petal, now that you know the truth, how do you feel towards me?" He asked her that as soon as he finished telling her everything the doctor had said.

"I feel relieved to know you didn't leave me and join

the military because I made you angry," Rose answered him softly.

"Baby, I went to the other side of the world to forget about you abandoning me and our daughter. I couldn't stand the thought of living without you in my life." Thorn reached for Rose. She laid down the official documents from the doctor, and she placed her head on his shoulder as he put his arms around her.

"Rose, I never want anything to come between us again, and I mean anything, including our daughter. It will take some convincing, I'm sure. I believe that eventually she'll have to accept the truth. But whether she does or not, I can't lose you again." He searched out the depths of her eyes, and she fell into his in pursuit of the happiness that should have been theirs.

ROSE FELT THE temperature rise, and she listened and understood exactly what Thorn was saying. He wanted to be with her, not because of guilt or a pregnancy, but because he truly cared about her. She buried her head in his shoulder and whispered, "I feel the same way, too, and I don't want to ever go through this feeling of loss again. Now that I know the truth, I'm open to loving you. It's what I needed all along. If I'd only known, I'd have never let them take our baby. I'd have stayed married to you regardless of what your parents said or did. I just didn't know. My parents thought it was odd they got sent to Germany so soon after coming home from South Korea. Dad had only been in the states eighteen months when we shipped out again. Now I wonder if it was your parents trying to separate us even more. With me in Germany and them in Japan, there was no way for me to know anything about the baby. I wrote for a death certificate before we left but never received one. Now, the entire blur is beginning to make sense."

Rose once again felt the agony of the loss swell up inside. This time, however, she had Thorn to help her through it.

"I believe you're right, Rose Petal, and my parents were behind all of the trauma during our break-up and separation. They couldn't stand for me to make my own choices. They were convinced you wanted a promotion for your father, even when I told them you'd never mentioned it." His voice shook with emotion. "Oh, Rose Petal. If only I'd known how you really felt back then, none of this would have happened. My parents had me so jealous and anxious, I couldn't think straight. I constantly worried about losing you. And then my worst fear came true. When that happened, I lost all hope.

"It wasn't until I returned from my last posting and saw how beautiful our daughter was that I even wanted to live. She looked so much like you, I had to love her. Of course, my parents caused problems with her in every way they could. But upon their deaths, Anna had no choice but to live with me. Sadly, a lot of emotional damage had already been done.

"It took a couple of years before she completely trusted me, and I was her father. My parents made me out to be a near-mental case. They told her not to believe anything I said unless she confirmed it with them first. Only now do I see how vindictive they were."

Thorn pulled Rose closer. She didn't resist but instead reached to put her arms around him as she said, "We have to be a family, Thorn. I want that for us and Anna."

Thorn replied, "I do, too, Baby Rose Petal. I do, too."

THAT NIGHT, AS Rose thought about the day and her future, she thanked God for all He had brought about in her life because of her class reunion. As she climbed into bed, she said a prayer for her daughter, as well. During her sleep, the dream she'd had so often returned. She was in the hospital, the doctor said it was a girl, and then he seemed to disappear.

The next morning when Rose awakened, it was as if a

fog had been lifted. She remembered hearing the doctor and even saw his face in her memory. She realized her subconscious had tried to tell her all these years that she did indeed have a daughter.

Now she had to convince Anna of the truth. Before that could happen, though, it was time to tell Gill, Jr.

She reached for the phone and began to punch in his number.

— 38 —

ANNA WASN'T HAPPY about the situation, about her father coming to see her, or his insistence that he visit with Anna and bring along his first love.

She couldn't bring herself to say *her mother.* No, that woman wasn't her mother. She'd never had a mother. Her only mother had been her grandmother, and she'd died when Anna was fourteen. Since that time, there'd been no mothering influence in Anna's life. She was certainly able to do without one now.

She had to resign herself to accepting that her dad had never gotten over his first wife, even during those years they'd been apart. He'd dated during her growing up years and even married, appearing to genuinely care about each of the women he'd been involved with.

Yet, nothing compared to how he'd reacted that weekend around his first wife. In just the short time Anna observed them together, it was like her father had become a changed man. He seemed to hang on her every word and treat her as if she were some precious, fragile, priceless piece that could break at any moment if not given constant attention.

He'd never come close to treating any of the other women in his life that way.

The two of them seemed to understand what the other one wanted and how to influence each other to get it. It was like they'd never been apart. They could effortlessly read each other.

As much as she disliked the relationship, Anna could easily tell it wasn't one-sided, either. Her "mother" seemed as enamored with her father as he was with her. Now they were trying to force their rekindled romance on her.

She wanted nothing to do with it.

Her grandmother had told her the truth over the years, and she didn't need some simpering woman to try to convince her otherwise. She'd set them straight as soon as they arrived. Her father might not like what she had to say, but he'd have to deal with it. She wasn't being taken in by this woman's lies or deception. She wasn't a sentimental fool, and she'd let them know it as soon as they arrived, which would be any moment.

The doorbell rang, pulling her from her downward spiral in her bitterness towards Rose. As she opened the door, she was surprised to see her estranged husband standing at the door with roses in one hand.

"What brings you here?" She questioned him, harsher than he deserved, and she instantly regretted it. "I'm sorry, Sam. I was expecting someone else. We've been having family trauma, and you caught the edge of the storm. What are the flowers for?"

"Roses for my favorite Rose," he smiled, as he handed her the beautiful Tropicana-colored bouquet.

"Why, thank you!" Anna's face brightened. "You know how much I love this color. Let me get a vase." She was surprised to see Sam, although she was pleased. She went toward the kitchen for a vase in which to put her flowers, glancing back at him to smile, before stepping through the door.

"Other than the flowers, what made you stop by?" Anna called. She was curious why he would just show up at random, especially since they'd separated weeks before. They planned counseling in hopes of saving their relationship once Sam's out-of-town job was settled, but that hadn't come about yet. In the meantime, she felt it was better this way, as she couldn't deal with the long-term relationship side of his working situation. At least they'd split on friendly terms. If he loved his job more than her, that would become apparent very soon, and they could move on with their separate lives.

As she filled the vase with water, she thought of the baby. Until she was sure of why he'd come by, she needed to be cautious what she said around him. Before he had time to answer, the doorbell rang again.

"Excuse me for a just a minute, okay?" Anna made her was back to the front hallway, handing him the flowers and the half-filled vase.

This time it was her parents and an older gentleman standing outside her door. She had no idea who he was, but she welcomed all three of them into her home.

"Dad, welcome in. Your two guests, too. I've got someone here for you to meet." It was turning out to be quite a party. Her father wouldn't be expecting Sam, who was in the dining room settling the flowers into the vase.

"Thank you, Anna." Thorn took her hand, at first hesitantly, then tighter when she didn't push him away. He leaned in and kissed her on the cheek, whispering, "I have someone for you to meet, also."

Anna made the introductions on her side. "Daddy, you know Sam, and Sam, this is my father's first wife, Rose Pet . . . I mean Rosemary." She faltered on the name. She had heard her dad call her that too often.

Sam looked at Rosemary and then back at Anna, and he gave a short laugh. "I can see the resemblance. This must be your mother, Anna. You look almost exactly alike. It's nice to meet you," he said, as he shook water off his hand and reached to shake.

"The pleasure is all mine," Rose replied, smiling at the tall, handsome young man, and taking his hand.

Anna looked at the older man, wondering why he was there, but certain it probably had to do with her in some way.

"Daddy, I don't believe I've met your friend," Anna said politely, turning to the distinguished older gentleman.

"Oh, honey. Let me reintroduce you to the first person who ever saw you. Dr. James Allen, please meet my daughter, Roseanna Wilder." Thorn made the introduction, while watching the expression on his daughter's face.

Anna said, "Oh! Well, it's nice to meet you, and I'm sure they've brought you here for a reason. Won't you all come in and sit down?" She turned abruptly as she led them toward the living room.

Dr. Allen began to explain as he followed her, "Yes, at my insistence, I convinced your father to let me tag along. I'm here to set the record straight once and for all. I was the attending physician at your birth almost forty years ago."

Anna stopped, looked at Sam and asked, "Do you think we can talk some other time, Sam? This is a family meeting, and I'm afraid it's an awkwardly private matter."

Thorn interrupted his daughter, "Anna, I'm the one who invited him. He is family, after all."

"Oh." She turned to face her father and gave him a sharp look. This seemed to be getting more complicated by the moment. "I didn't know. Then, let's be seated. Why did you invite Sam?"

"I just thought he should be here when the truth came out."

"The truth about what?" Anna asked, afraid she knew. Why else would a doctor from her childhood be sitting in her living room? She was the only one still standing, and she positioned herself on the edge of the sofa, ready to leap up if the answer wasn't what she wanted to hear.

"Your birth, of course," Thorn replied.

That was more than Anna could stand. It didn't matter who was in the room, and she stood and let her frustration fly.

"I already know the truth! Grandmother told it to me years ago. My mother abandoned me, period. That's the end of the story." She spat out the information like venom. She glared at Rose as if to dare her to dispute it.

It wasn't Rose who spoke. It was the old doctor.

"My dear, there was a terrible injustice done to this woman sitting right here." He pointed at Rose. "I delivered a ten-pound, four-ounce live baby girl. However, through a series of circumstances of which I'm not proud, this woman was led to believe the baby died."

Before he could go on, Anna blurted out, "How much is she paying you to say this? I know this isn't true. My grandparents were there and saw the whole thing." She glared smugly at the doctor.

"I know your grandparents were there. It was General Wilder who convinced me to do the horrible deed. He was my commanding officer at the time. He said he would keep me from being deployed to Cambodia or South Vietnam. Remember, we were still there until the late seventies. That was where I was afraid they were going to transfer me next. He told me he could use his rank to get me a position stateside. I accepted the bribe. It's something I'm not proud of. That's why I came all this way, to try to right a wrong that should have never happened. Your mother almost died delivering you. You were too large. We tried to stop the birth, but she wouldn't let us. She was willing to sacrifice her life so you could live. It was a miracle she survived."

Anna stared at the older man. How could he say this? Why was he trying to make her believe a lie?

Dr. Allen continued, "I know you may have some doubts, but here's my physician's card from my billfold.

Here's my driver's license. And you can check my military record to see I was stationed at Fort Hood where you were born. I've no reason to lie. What I want to do is to clear my conscience, so I can live out my days in peace." The doctor stopped talking, and he pulled out a report from his pocket. "If you still have doubts, this should clear them up. I have a DNA report I've had run, and there's no doubt you and your mother are a perfect match."

She took the paper and looked over it, before looking to Rose, then cutting a hard look to her father.

"I think I should sit. I don't feel well." Anna swayed on her feet, and she was relieved to feel Sam at her side. She let him help her to the sofa. Her face felt warm, and her stomach was nauseated.

"You don't look like you feel well; do you need a glass of water? Sugar, when's your baby due?" Dr. Allen asked.

Suddenly, all eyes were on Anna. She felt herself growing hot. She glanced around the room uncomfortably. "Well, I, well, uh, I'm due in June," came out in a whisper, as her voice faltered.

"What?" Rose, Thorn, and Sam all said at once.

"You're pregnant? When were you going to tell me?" Sam was the first to ask.

"Another Little Wild Thorn. How wonderful," Rose murmured.

Anna's head shot around to Rose, "What did you say?"

Rose started to turn red from embarrassment. "It was just something I always called you before you were born. I called you my Little Wild Thorn," she finished quietly.

Anna shook her head. That was the same thing she said to her baby when she rubbed her belly each night.

The doctor spoke up, "Well, I've seen thousands of pregnant women in my years of practice, and a June due date isn't likely. I'd say you're further along than you think, or you could possibly be expecting twins."

"Twins!"
Now, everyone was talking.

— 39 —

ANNA COULDN'T TAKE in everything the old doctor had told her. For the next hour, he quietly recounted the events that involved him and her birth. When faced with all the facts, along with the DNA proof, it added up. Her grandparents had lied to her, but why?

"They never wanted me in control of my life," her father answered. "They were afraid of losing me. My father controlled everything around him in the military; however, he didn't control me. By doing the things they did, they lost me anyway."

Anna was bewildered by the new information. The doorbell rang again.

"Who could it be now?" Anna muttered, as she opened it wide. She stared for a moment, unable to comprehend what she saw. Then she giggled. Standing in front of her was a man with her eyes and features; he even had her nose. He was about an inch shorter than she was and maybe five or so years younger. There was no mistaking him, though. He could only be her brother.

"You must be Anna," the man said with a smile, as he

put out his hand.

"And you must be Gill, Jr." Anna answered him, with humor in her voice, as she shook his hand. "Won't you come in?" she offered.

"Thank you. I believe I will." Gill stepped through the door in his ostrich cowboy boots to see his mother and the man who was obviously Anna's father standing arm-in-arm. His mother reached out to greet him.

"Gill, honey. I'd like for you to meet Thornton Wilder, better known as Thorn."

"Well, I feel like I know you already, your mother speaks so often of you." Thorn removed his cowboy hat, put out his hand, and squeezed Gill's tightly. "I hope this is the beginning of many happy times we spend together."

"If my mother's happy, then I know it will be," Gill replied, staring at the man whom his mother had said was her first love. "Mom called and told me all about her youthful past. I admit I was surprised and shocked at first, but after I thought about it, I was also pleased." Giving Thorn a meaningful glance, he continued. "Now I won't have to worry about her being alone. From the looks of things, it's obvious she won't stay single much longer, which of course is fine with me."

THORN CALLED TO the people in the house, "I've asked everyone to be here today to help put my past with Rose Petal to rest. There were lies, sabotage, and deceit in our youth. We both lost our way. Despite everything, with God's help, we found the answers we were looking for and have come to terms with it." He looked at Rose and reached for her hand. "Now I'd like to start a new future with her as my wife. I'm asking my first and only true love to marry me, with God's blessing, and make me the happiest man on the face of the earth."

Everyone began clapping and smiling. Rose started crying, which made Anna start crying as well. She tried to hide it, but everyone saw the large, transparent teardrops coursing down her cheeks. She couldn't seem to help it.

"What is it, honey?" Thorn put his arm around Anna's shoulder. "Why the tears, now?"

"My father's finally going to be happy, and it took my mother to make him so." Anna brushed at her cheeks, and she chuckled. "It's obvious you two truly love each other. I no longer have any doubts about either of you. Look, even Dr. Allen has a tear or two in his eyes."

As she spoke, the old doctor reached for his handkerchief and began to pat his eyes.

Sam spoke up, "I think Anna and I need to talk in private. I think this may need to be a double ceremony. We need to renew our vows."

Anna's eyes opened wider than they'd been all evening.

"Anna, what's this about?"

"I haven't told you, Daddy. Sam and I have been separated, but I think we've worked things out."

Cheers went up from everyone as Sam and Anna walked toward her bedroom.

THORN LOOKED AT Rose as her eyes stared up at her one true love. She couldn't believe what had happened, all because of their class reunion.

This indeed had become a true reunion of the heart.

www.ingramcontent.com/pod-product-compliance
Lightning Source LLC
Chambersburg PA
CBHW061506020726
47502CB00006B/1953